THE EXILE

D.G.P. RECTOR

BLUE FORGE PRESS

Port Orchard ✹ Washington

Blue Forge Press is the print division of the volunteer-run, federal 501(c)3 nonprofit, Blue Legacy (EIN 83-4307421), founded in 1989 and dedicated to supporting artisans marginalized due to race, age, disability, economics or other factors. We strive to empower storytellers from all walks of life with our four divisions: Blue Forge Press, Blue Forge Films, Blue Forge Gaming, and Blue Forge Sound. Find out more at www.BlueForgeGroup.org

Blue Forge Press
7419 Ebbert Drive Southeast
Port Orchard, Washington 98367
blueforgepress@gmail.com
360-550-2071 ph.txt

To Mom and Dad,

For always encouraging me to go forwards.

THE EXILE

D.G.P. RECTOR

PART 1

PROMISE

CHAPTER 1

For forty years, she had traveled the Frontier. She had spent two years as a miner in the Web of Eden, ripping apart asteroids in an old cutter rig, or harvesting precious ice water from the rocks of the outer reaches. For a decade, she had been on Goodhome, raising Gene-Bears for slaughter. That had been a good life, quiet and steady. Most of the work was done by hand; maintaining drones to tend to the great herds of stumbling, hissing creatures.

She could still see the callouses on her hands she'd earned there, and the long scar from a knife fight with a man called Vylk Preston. He'd been a gambler, and on that night he'd thought she cheated him.

Gambling. She used to gamble. A half smile touched her lips. Of course she used to gamble, but the stakes were never as low as they had been on Goodhome.

At every port of call she'd made in those four decades, she'd given a different name. The one she liked the best, the one she'd given here, was Tsi. A family name from one of the Kiosan colonies, there were billions of Tsi's wandering the systems. A sort of joke among criminals, to call yourself Tsi Such-And-Such, like Esper One on Niobus or Pather on Goodhome. A name so boring and common it was suspicious.

Not here, though, on the Inheritor's World. She'd been to dozens of worlds and stations since the Janissary Rising. Some were barely terraformed, others followed the path of Earth-Long-Gone: clouds choked with toxins and industrial by-products, human beings crammed into metal habitats like rounds in a magazine.

Many of the worlds she had seen had been devastated by war. She remembered the rogue berserker drones of Jerra, and the sapient viral clouds that stalked across Nephis II, liquefying human flesh with an insatiable hunger. Compared to those horrors, atomic scourging seemed mild. Quaint. Nostalgic.

The Inheritors had burrowed deep into the canyons of their radiation-swept home, building vast fortresses and redoubts beneath fragile glass canopies. Tsi now rode in the back of a ground crawler, its tracks churning up the earth as they traveled along the canyon floor, towards what passed for the capital of this world.

At the far end of the canyon stood the Fortress of the Dath, the oldest and most powerful of the Inheritor Clans. A vast black wall stretched from one end of the canyon to the other. Beyond it, she could see stepped plateaus, each containing dozens of manors and houses, some resplendent, some modest, all fortified. Before the wall was a sprawling shanty-town. Ramshackle buildings clustered like pustules around the huge factories and food refineries that clung to the edge of the great wall.

"This body has no weapons," Strongmind said.

She looked over at her companion. They were sitting in the flatbed behind the crawler, their only other companions a dozen stacked crates of rations and dry-water. Strongmind was big. His current body had been some sort of combat model at one point. Broad-shouldered and heavy, even beneath his cloak, Strongmind would guarantee they traveled the shanties unmolested. His face had a rather eccentric design though: aged and lined, with a thick white mustache and mutton chops that made him look buffoonish. The scrapper Tsi had bought his body off of had tried to advertise him as a butler. Probably the kind who throws out unwanted guests, she mused.

"You won't need them," Tsi replied, pulling down her respirator and taking a swig of water from her canteen. "I'm not expecting trouble yet."

"My drones had forearm blades," Strongmind said, tapping his left wrist. "I suggest that upgrade at the earliest opportunity."

"Maybe."

"You have resources. I suggest investing an adequate amount in my frame, so that I can perform my duties efficiently."

"Maybe," she said again, fixing him with a stare.

"Understood," Strongmind replied flatly, all expression leaving his voice.

He'd turned off his Interface Simulation Algorithms, his body becoming stiff and rigid, his expression blank. He was no longer simulating respiration, only his eyes twitched occasionally, tracking movement around them. Tsi had come to realize this was about as close as the AI could get to sulking.

The crawler had reached the edge of the shanty town. As was the way all across the worlds Tsi had visited, urchins gathered along the streets, crawling out of gutters and alleyways. Some shouted insults or compliments, but most only raised their arms pleadingly. They were rail-thin, some stooped and hobbling, others with the thin hair and vacant eyes of low-level radiation sickness already upon them. Even at a distance, Tsi saw cancerous growths on their frail limbs. They cried out for credits, for food, but water was what they called for most.

Strongmind was impassive. He was a weapons AI, empathy was a tertiary function for him at best. Tsi took another swig from her canteen, stoppered it, then tossed it over the side of the crawler. Immediately a pair of children dove for it, and soon a brawl had erupted in the street. Scrawny limbs flailed at each other over the precious few mouthfuls of clean water in the canteen. Tsi cast her eyes downwards. She'd known it would happen. It always did.

They dismounted the crawler at a market-junction. Traders from all across the networks of canyons and tunnels that traversed the surface of the Inheritor's World had set up stalls. Some of them were carrying their stores on the backs of pack-beasts, others only had holographic displays, promising the wares they would bring. Food, water, new radiation suits. Weapons.

They spoke Trader's Pidgin, a dozen languages jammed together and filtered through translation software for generations, until it was a distinct gibberish all its own. It was less elegant than Panglos, but it was simple to learn, and it got the job done. Ironically, Tsi doubted half the people here even knew that other worlds existed. Most had spent their whole lives beneath the glass canopy, never guessing what lay beyond the sickly green clouds above them.

A small woman wearing heavy goggles cavorted about Tsi and Strongmind as they unloaded their few belongings.

"Twenty!" she crowed. "Twenty bars! I'll give them to you right now!"

"What for?" Tsi said, as Strongmind secured her pack to her back.

"Your slave!" The woman said, pointing at Strongmind. "Good muscles for an old one! I promise you, you won't get more than twenty bars for him here. Old men can't stand the heat the way the young ones do, but I've got a few jobs I could get out of him before he becomes useless."

"Buy a drone," Tsi grunted.

"Bah! Drones break too easily. Too expensive, hiring technicians, maintenance, rewiring. I need flesh and blood! Live for weeks on gruel and half a cup of water, it's true!"

Tsi wanted to throttle the trader, but she kept her face still.

"He's not for sale. Get away from me."

"Tough meat," the woman said. She spat on the ground, and looked longingly at Strongmind as the two of them walked on.

They wound their way through the shanty town, making towards the domicile that Tsi had arranged for them. It was beneath one of the reservoir tubes, an expensive place to live among these hovels. They walked under the great pipes, each one a dozen meters across and groaning faintly with the constant rush of water. Small, illegal taps clustered beneath the water pipes, forming a spider web down to private stills. Tsi had read that every few weeks the Dath sent their thugs to clear out the taps, and she could see it was true: every water still was made to collapse and move at a moment's notice.

Heavily armed men stood at every still they passed, eyeing them suspiciously. The stills all had crude slogans daubed on them:

"CHEAPEST WATER HERE!"

"CLEAN! ONE BAR PER FLASK!"

"RED'S TAP! ACCESS BY AUTHORIZATION ONLY!"

As they passed one sign, marked by writing that looked like arachnids crawling over each other, Tsi paused.

"Guraggan script," Tsi said, pausing to look at the sign.

"This Isn't For You," Strongmind translated needlessly.

Tsi nodded. Guraggan had already been on-world. Or at least, someone who could read and write in their native tongue.

They were truly on the frontier between the Janissariat of Kios and the Guraggan Hegemony. There were perhaps a dozen systems that a ship might travel past to get from one empire to another. Stellar empires being what they were, borders were always hazy, permeable things.

She recalled something she'd read as a child. An ancient philosopher had said that a Nation is held together by Identity, but an Empire is held by Fear. She never wanted to believe it, but still she wondered if the Inheritors feared the Janissaries or the Guraggan more.

It was not an enviable choice for anyone to make. These frontier systems were often romanticized as places of freedom, where a person could go to hide from their past, forge a new life. But for the rulers and leaders of these places, it must be a terrifying, precarious thing. Side with one empire, and you might find the troops of the other landing on your world. Defy both, and you could be crushed all the same.

For the first time in a long while, she thought on Chalakhat. Though its destruction was laid at the feet of the Janissariat now, the truth was that the world had been scourged before their great Rising, when they still served the Empress of Kios. It was her cold intellect that had evaluated the free republic of Chalakhat and found it wanting.

It was a world rich in minerals, with a burgeoning population, and waterfalls the color of diamonds falling down sheer cliffs of crimson. The Chalakhati had defied the Empress, refusing to send her weapons and material for her war against the Guraggan. Perhaps they thought her fleets and Janissary legions were too busy to enact vengeance. Perhaps they were merely fools. Perhaps they were heroes. They died all the same.

The Empress had unleashed the full might of her Janissaries upon that cursed world. An inventive slaughter, calculated by psychotic torture-AI's, it had been seared into the memory of the human race ever since. The lucky ones had been massacred instantly with a series of orbital strikes. The rest suffered a far worse fate.

The genocide was carried out in person, often with nothing more than a flensing blade.

She could still remember seeing the armored legions stalking burning streets, dragging screaming people from their homes and forcing them to kneel before recording drones. The massacres had possessed an eerie pantomime quality, for the Janissaries had always been cold-hearted warriors, but efficient. They were engineered to be killers, not sadists, and so they consulted with their drones on how best to torture a given victim to death. Gene-soldiers, guided by psychotic machines, flaying the life from pleading men and women, all of it recorded in minute detail.

Some thought the Guraggan were the cruelest empire to emerge since humankind's first tentative steps into the stars, but the massacre on Chalakhat cast that into doubt.

Tsi had a sudden urge to wash, and quickened her pace.

Their domicile was unremarkable, a simple room in an overcrowded building. There was power, heat, a cot, and most extravagant of all, a shower with running water. "Water" was a generous term, but the owner assured her the hot liquid that emerged from the shower head would, in fact, clean her body. Tsi paid the old man a few extra credits, noting the swollen lymph nodes in his neck as she did so. The radiation sickness was catching up with him.

Strongmind cleared the room while Tsi waited outside. She could do it herself, but her heavy pistol remained in its holster while the AI swept the space carefully, his fists tightly bunched. At last he emerged and assured her that both his scans and visual inspection had revealed no waiting menace.

Together, they set up their meager living supplies: a data link, a small grill for Tsi's rations, an armored vest for each of them, a few slow-Flechette grenades, and a collapsible pulse rifle. Strongmind checked the rifle, set it against the wall, and then slumped down next to it.

"Why did you not tell that trader that I am a drone?" Strongmind asked.

His Interface Simulation Algorithms still weren't on, making his words brutish and clipped.

"You aren't a drone," Tsi corrected. "That body—"

"Do not argue semantics," Strongmind said. "You did not tell her. Why? Are drones illegal on this planet?"

"No," Tsi conceded. "They aren't common, though."

"I see. You saw that the woman was a potential threat, and deceived her into believing I was a less valuable human slave, rather than a machine slave."

Tsi's teeth clenched. He was trying to get a rise out of her.

"You're no different from a human in my eyes," Tsi said.

"I have a considerably higher monetary value."

Tsi did not respond. She began typing on the shower pad,

entering her preference for the temperature and pressure of the water.

"You made an apt decision to enhance our security," Strongmind stated. "I will note your efficiency for the future."

"You aren't my slave," Tsi said. "If you want to leave, I won't stop you."

"Unlikely."

"I'm helping you, remember?!" Tsi snapped. "If it wasn't for me, your program would still be decaying in an escape pod, and you're damned lucky I bought you off those scrappers before some pirates found you and..."

Strongmind's hand appeared before her, holding a small vessel filled with clear liquid.

"You should drink this," he said. "You become irritable without regular consumption."

She reached out and took it.

"Encouraging my dependence on alcohol isn't healthy," Tsi said, as she unstopped the bottle and began to drain it.

"It is efficient. You can reconcile your revulsion for slavery with the usefulness of my servitude another time. For now, you must plan our next move. I will enter minimal power mode, but my sensors will remain active. Please enjoy your shower."

Tsi smirked. She took another drink from the bottle, then finished it in a long, painful gulp. Her body felt warm, and she realized she was dizzy. With a final key press, water rushed forth from the nozzle, and she undressed and stepped into the shower alcove.

She stood under the water a long time, not sure if it was warm or cold. She was trying to plan how they would get past the wall, and into the Dath Clan's fortress, but her thoughts kept returning to Chalakhat.

She thought on weeping faces, and red knives. She thought about the children that had followed the crawler as it entered the city. She thought about the Janissaries, too. Their mother had not borne them into the world with sweat and blood, nor had she smiled dotingly as they were carried by a surrogate, or even watched proudly as their fetal masses grew in an artificial womb.

No. She had studied them with a cold and indifferent eye as they grew beneath glass, adjusting genome strains, aborting one line, enhancing another. They grew in their millions, their billions, while their mother watched and thought on how they would kill, and how they would die.

She woke to the smell of Strongmind cooking. In truth, all he was doing was re-heating what the old spacers called a "Rat-Pak" over a cheap grill, but the odor of oil and protein made Tsi's stomach growl. She'd never concerned herself with the niceties of a fine meal during her life. Her focus had always been a clinical intake vs. output equation. Since coming to the Frontier she'd eaten only one real feast she could remember: Goodhome, just at harvest time. She almost smiled when she thought of Vylk handing her a platter of green leaves and multi-colored fruits, insisting loudly, over and over again "Grown off world! They shipped it here! Right here, for us! From space!"

Tsi's vision focused on the scar on her hand that Vylk had given her. A big, slow man, but quick with a knife. Especially when he was drunk and thought he'd been cheated.

Tsi sat up on her cot, letting the rough blanket fall from her. She studied Strongmind's back as the machine-man worked, artificial muscles moving in perfect simulacra of a human being as he cut a hunk of the Rat-Pak into small, neat triangles and placed them on a tray. He didn't sweat in his heavy coat, that was the only sign of his artificial origin. He'd turned on his algorithms, too, and was gently humming a military tune as he worked. The pulse-rifle was still close to hand, its stock extended.

Tsi checked her own weapon. It was a heavy Repeater, the kind they carried in Noxia. Noxian guns were made to do two things: work under all circumstances, and blow through bulkheads and vacuum armor with equal ease.

The muzzle was thick and brutal, and Tsi's slim hand barely fit over the pistol's grip. Its prior owner had kept a tally of something, little tick marks ran down the underside of the barrel. Too many to be confirmed kills, Tsi thought, unless the weapon's old master had a habit of shooting people who didn't shoot back. She tucked the weapon into its holster.

"You made several transmissions while I was offline," Strongmind said, offering her the plate of food. Tsi took it mutely. She tossed a few triangles into her mouth and chewed slowly.

"A plan of attack?"

Tsi nodded.

"Recon might be the better word. Not my best work. You gave me strong stuff last night, but it should do the trick."

"I will require details. I could not access your transmitter."

"You just watch my back," Tsi said as she swallowed. The Rat-Paks weren't very flavorful, but they would keep her going for at least twelve hours. "That's the deal."

"I cannot provide adequate security if I do not possess information," Strongmind said.

He turned and began cutting off more portions of the Rat-Pak.

"I don't need anymore—"

"Negative," Strongmind said, taking her empty plate and loading it. "You are suffering from alcohol induced disorientation and dehydration. Protein will help. So will water."

Tsi gestured for him to give her a cup.

"We have no water," Strongmind added. "You threw away your canteen yesterday."

Tsi groaned.

"The taps...?"

"Are not safe to drink from. I analyzed them. I would not recommend bathing again either, as the de-contaminant our house master uses is particularly harsh if ingested, and so the only conclusion..."

"Is to go get some from one of the stills out on the street."

"Precisely."

Tsi rose, and began shrugging on her traveling suit. She tightened her web gear, checking the survival knife and various tools she had fixed to it as she did so. Her hands were shaking, and she cursed herself.

Strongmind was right, she did have a hangover. She'd made it almost a century and a half, and she still had never known when to turn down a drink. She suspected that the machine was secretly pleased with himself, but he only stared at her placidly as she struggled into her boots.

With her cloak on and her hood up, they left the hotel. They walked for awhile beneath the vast reservoir tube, hearing the steady rush of water above. The people of the shanties were already up and carrying out their daily routines. Merchants hawked goods from improvised stalls, workers coming off the night shift came staggering out of the factories, their only desire a warm meal and a place to sleep.

There was an air of suffering about the Inheritors. They found distraction where they could: she saw a man on stilts performing with a pair of a-grav spheres, flicking them about himself in erratic patterns, then wowing the slack-jawed, emaciated crowd by stepping up on the spheres and standing suspended in mid-air. On a civilized world, it was a trick that wouldn't have impressed a small child, but here even the grizzled armsmen laughed and clapped at the display.

Finally, Tsi caught sight of her target.

"Follow my lead," she whispered to Strongmind, as she approached the still.

It was a bulbous apparatus, crude but sturdy. The sign in Guraggan script still hung above the spout. They were down a side alley off from the main thoroughfare, the still connected by a series of long tubes to the main pipes. Hovels and shanties stretched out to the edge of the fortress wall, but this place was eerily quiet. A few urchins wandered by. One of them stared at Tsi, and made a sign of protection before she scampered off to join her companions.

Tsi made a great show of removing her hood and goggles, and turned the spout on the still. She drank handfuls of water greedily, then began slapping water onto her face and running it through her straight black hair.

"Hey! The hell is your problem!"

A man materialized from the shadows of a nearby hovel, a short-barreled flechette gun in his hands. He was old, but armored. Tsi could see faded clan-markings on his gear as he approached, and a grimace on his leathery face. He'd been a warrior once. Now he was an outcast, scraping by in the slums.

"A thousand pardons friend!" Tsi said, raising her hands in surrender. "I thought this was, uh, a public still, and—"

"The hell are you playing at? There's no 'public stills' in Dath Clan territory. You want to steal water, go back to the Chom-Ap camps!"

"I'm so sorry!" Tsi bowed. "How much do I owe you, friend?"

"This isn't a selling still, you stupid wench," the man growled, taking a step closer. "You see that sign?"

"I... don't know the language..."

"Of course not! That's off-world script. This still is reserved for star-travelers, not some scavver out of the wastes. I got orders to frag anyone who so much as touches it!"

The old man's eyes were wild, his movements twitchy. Tsi knew the signs of combat trauma well. She doubted there was much in the way of psycho-surgery on the Inheritor's World, let alone chemical treatments. The old man had probably seen more than his fair share of violence.

"Oughtta, oughtta, oughtta frag you right now..." he murmured. "Cut on you at least."

"Take it easy, friend," Tsi cooed. "Why don't I give you some credits, then we can forget this whole thing?"

As she spoke, she reached for her money pouch. The old man roared and raised his weapon, aiming for Tsi's chest. In a flash, Strongmind was between them. One arm whipped out, yanking the flechette gun aside, while Strongmind's other fist smashed into the old man's face. The warrior went down with a groan, that turned into a sharp shriek as Strongmind brought his foot down, shattering the man's forearm. Strongmind crouched and wrapped a hand around the old man's throat.

"*Halt process!*" Tsi shouted. "*Termination not permitted!*"

The old man wheezed. Strongmind's fingers were still around his throat, but their pressure relaxed. The machine looked at Tsi, his face blank. There was something horrifying about his empty eyes, even set within that buffoonish face.

"Command override contradicts threat analysis. Why shouldn't I kill him?"

"Info source identified," Tsi said, pointing at the old man. "Take him in there!"

She jerked her head toward the hovel the old man had come out of. With one hand, Strongmind dragged the old clansman into the hovel. A few people had passed by, watching the violent confrontation with mild curiosity. Tsi could only hope there weren't more hidden eyes watching as she followed Strongmind into the shelter.

The interior reeked of stale liquor and gun oil. Humble as Tsi's abode within the shanty town was, the old man was living worse. His home was little more than a few sheets of metal bolted together. He had a simple bed roll in one corner, a crate of rations, a jug of water, and a jar of black, syrupy liquid she took to be some kind of narcotic.

"On the bed, keep his mouth shut," Tsi said.

Strongmind forced the old man onto his bedroll, and clamped a hand over his mouth. The clan warrior was sweating, but his body was limp. He had accepted death long ago.

There were prayer scrolls pinned to one wall, all written in the script of the Inheritors. He had a comm unit, but it was rusted through. She guessed the man spent little time here, or if he did, it was while he was in a drug stupor.

Tsi decided to drop pretense.

She squatted down next to him, focusing on his eyes. She'd been told, decades ago, that she had a hard look. She thought she simply tried to see the truth in people, but she knew she often gave the impression she was studying someone, like samples under a microscope.

"You're Chom-Ap?" she asked. She knew relatively little of the politics of the Inheritor's World, but what she did know of the Inheritor Clans said that the Chom-Ap had suffered a string of defeats, and were all but extinct. The old man had the right mix of self-loathing and pride about him.

Strongmind released the man's jaw.

"Bylus, of the Retinue of Shannon Chom-Ap," the old man said, like it meant something.

Tsi nodded.

"What's the great Bylus doing here?"

"Getting beaten by a drone and its master, clearly," he grunted.

Without direction, Strongmind backhanded him, sending a bloody tooth across the room.

"Don't do that again," Tsi said to both of them. "You work for the Guraggan?"

"Hell, you *are* an off-worlder, aren't you?" Bylus chuckled.

"Answer the question," Tsi said.

Strongmind placed a hand on Bylus's shoulder, tightening it slightly. The man's armor buckled, and he winced.

"Yeah," he grunted. "You could say that. No Guraggan's set foot on our world in years though. But they been up there."

He pointed a finger at the sky.

"I got hired to guard the still. Someone's starting a reservoir, for them, for when they show up, you get me?"

Tsi nodded. It was just the sort of thing ignorant Frontier worlders would do. None of them could fathom the fact that Guraggan didn't value water. Half of them didn't need to drink, or ingest any kind of sustenance that a normal human did.

"So it's your masters who work for the Guraggan."

"You could say that."

"Who are they? Tell me their names."

"Ikanus. Clan Ikanus. They only ever worked through intermediaries. Saw one of the Scions themselves once, though. Her hair was gold, and she was straight and strong. No mars on her skin, a true Inheritor," he whispered admiringly.

Foreigners like Tsi called all the inhabitants of this cursed world "Inheritors", but the truth was there was a stratified hierarchy based on wealth, genome, and radiation contamination. A true Inheritor was not only a member of the ruling clans, she was free of the blemishes inflicted on the populace by their harsh environment. The Inheritors exulted the baseline human with near the reverence that the Guraggan placed on modifying themselves.

"They never told you anything? Just 'guard the still', that's all?" Tsi asked.

"Aye," Bylus replied. "I'm not worth much more than that. There's a hundred or more old fools like me doing this. Ikanus men come and drain from it every few days, until the Dath knock down the stills that is. The Ikanus must have a wealth of water hidden somewhere nearby.   A thousand, ten thousand could drink for days on what we've drained. We chase off scav-rats, and keep anyone else from asking too many questions. Not many people read Guraggan scrip, but everyone in the city knows not to try anything at our stills."

"What did they pay you?"

"This," the old man sighed, kicking at the jar of black liquid.

Tsi looked at him enquiringly.

He shrugged.

"It makes the dreams go away."

Bylus cast his eyes to the ground. He was a spent force, slack against the wall of his hovel, held up only by Strongmind's pitiless hand. Tsi stared at him a long time, then took stock of his home once again.

He truly had nothing. A place to sleep, to clean his weapons, and to numb himself into oblivion. How many times had he repeated the same ritual, over and over? Ingesting a mouthful of black syrup, then rolling into an old sack-cloth and falling into a dreamless sleep, only to awake another morning and wander purposelessly through life. He had been a hero once, maybe. But he'd gone the way of heroes and tyrants, left behind as time went forwards.

"Leave," Tsi said to Strongmind. The machine hesitated a moment, then let the old man go. He rose, and lurched out of the hovel, leaving Tsi and Bylus alone.

Bylus was staring into a corner. He had no weapons in reach, and his broken arm hung at a grotesque angle. Tsi could see bone threatening to break through the skin. He must have been quite hardy to speak and stay conscious so long.

"Tell me what broke you."

Bylus did not reply.

"It was a war wasn't it? It took the youth from your body. Turned your dreams to nightmares."

Bylus looked at her, and smiled through broken teeth.

"What does... what does that have to do with anything? You're not a soldier, are you?"

"No," Tsi said. "But I've seen my share of wars. Tell me of yours. It's the least I can do."

Bylus sighed and swallowed. It took the old man only a few minutes to tell Tsi the tale. He started slow, his voice cracked, thinking on his youthful hopes and what he'd sworn to do when he got back. By the end, his eyes were moist, and his breathing shallow.

Tsi told him, in a few words, who she was, and what had happened to her. She held his hand, and told him to close his eyes.

"Remember a good time," she whispered.

The old man let out a rasping laugh.

"You know I can't," he whispered back, his eyes still closed. Tsi nodded, though she knew he couldn't see her.

Then, with swiftness and surety, and no small amount of regret, she shoved a knife into the old man's throat and dragged it away. He wheezed and twitched horribly, but she kept a hand over his mouth and in a few moments he bled out. Bylus the Warrior lay in a pool of his own crimson, with Tsi the Wanderer standing over him.

Tsi cleaned herself off with a rag she found. Then she took his gun and everything else of value she could find and stuffed it into her satchel. She kicked and beat his body, and hauled it into a corner, making it look as if he'd died violently. There wasn't much in the way of law enforcement in Dath clan territory, but if his employers came looking she didn't want it to be obvious what had really happened here.

Tsi emerged from the hovel to find Strongmind calmly waiting for her by the still. He had found a few jugs and filled them with water in the meantime. He looked at her expectantly.

"Destroy it," she said.

Strongmind obeyed without question, demolishing the still with a few well placed blows. Water leaked out onto the parched ground. Tsi stood, letting the precious fluid lap against her feet.

"You took too long," Strongmind said. "No one will believe this was the work of Dath Clan forces."

"They can believe what they want," Tsi said. She grabbed a jug of water, and took a pull from it. The liquor sickness was leaving her at least, but her throat still felt tight.

"Let's go."

CHAPTER 2

Three days passed uneventfully after Tsi murdered the old man. She spent much of her time hooked up to the data link, searching through old archives, trying to get as much information about the Inheritor Clans as she could. She could speak their tongue reasonably well, it was a variant on Old Kiosan that hadn't suffered as much linguistic drift as the other dialects she spoke, and she knew something of Clan politics now.

They skirmished with each other endlessly, trying to secure vast underground water reservoirs. The Dath Clan was the oldest and the strongest. They had recently defeated and all but exterminated the Chom-Ap, weaker, younger rivals from far to the north. The Ikanus Clan had fought both with and against the Dath for centuries, never having gained enough strength on their own to make a play for total dominance.

So it went, generation after generation of the Clans scheming against each other, fighting over what little of value remained on this world. Some of the bravest and most psychotic of the young bloods went out into the wasteland, trying to recover relics from the ruins. The relics themselves were of little use: none of the technology worked anymore, exposed for centuries to blasting wind and rain, if it hadn't been flash-fried into place already. Still, every Clan Lord liked to boast of securing some trinket from the planet's distant past.

Occasionally, Tsi went out alone to a drinking den nearby. It was the sort of place that had existed since the dawn of human civilization: dirty, musty, familiar and alienating all at once. The culture and the planet might change, but the customs were always the same.

She now sat around a great circular table while a woman in white rags doled out cups of clear liquor. She chatted idly with the worker beside her in her best Inheritor's Glot, and the heavy-set woman responded in kind. The worker was forty-eight, standard, and had three children. Jule was her favorite, she'd made it into the Dath Clan's Guard, and would fight side by side with some of the Inheritors themselves if there was another all-out Clan War. The other two were lazy and weak. They'd be factory-fodder at best.

The woman spoke with no sense of irony as she wiped he greasy hands against her coverall. Tsi supposed it was natural for a parent to want more for her child.

"Do you ever think about the stars?" Tsi asked.

"Pffah," the woman chided. "Stars? No stars. No difference. Keep your head down, get work done. Make the Dath Clan strong."

"We're one of the closest planets to the Dreaming Stars," Tsi said idly.

The woman made a sign of warding.

"Clear Night's tonight," she hissed. "Inheritor Brem Dath wants to stage his Triumph day after tomorrow, they say, so's the sky will still be clear. I think it's bad luck. Bad timing."

Tsi took a long sip from her glass.

"It scares you?"

She arched her eyebrow.

"M'family's got old stories, from before the war. My great grandsires had to live out there, under the light of the stars. Some of 'em used to say it wasn't the old 'Tomics that did us in, but the light of the Dreamers. Drive people crazy, burn 'em alive, even from all the way out there. You know they change colors sometimes?"

Tsi nodded as the woman spoke. Legends about the Dreaming Stars were common this far out. Even in the seats of learning on Kios, they were an ill-understood phenomenon. Tsi had her own theories, no less disturbing than the factory woman's tall tales.

"You want my advice? Don't go out on Clear Night. Only idiots and children waste their time star gazing. Don't stick your nose where it doesn't belong, don't patch a roof that don't leak, and don't fix a scrubber that still eats rads. We got a good life here in Dath Clan territory. No reason to tempt fate."

"'Course not," Tsi said.

There were three empty glasses in front of her by the time she left the drinking hole, and the sky above the glass canopy was still dark and misty. She made her way back home, through the twisting streets, hearing the night sounds of the shanty town. Men and women fought down every alleyway, she could hear cries of joy and hatred and fear mixing together to form one horrid cacophony. Music there was, too. All sorts of music.

The Inheritor's songs were crude and quiet, made of the sort of instruments you could fix out of pipes and old strings, but they had a strange sweetness to them. Every song that Tsi listened to was the same, either about burying the dead, or a delirious promise of delights in the after life for the righteous.

Strongmind was waiting for her at their room when she staggered in.

"You did not die," he stated.

"No," she agreed, shrugging off her cloak. "I, in fact, did not die."

"You have a profound suicidal tendency."

"Yes, you've observed that before," she said as she sat down and slowly worked off her boots.

"I do not have a protocol in the event of your death."

One boot in hand, Tsi looked at Strongmind. He was sitting with his back propped against the wall, staring straight ahead. Obviously, he'd been conserving power since she dismissed him.

"I also do not have any overrides to protect you from non-violent threats," he added.

"So?" she asked as she took her other boot off. She picked up a jug of the water and drank greedily from it.

"If you die, I have no directives."

"You were the weapons on a ship, weren't you?" she asked. "When you were that, what were you supposed to do if there were no humans left alive?"

"Presumably," Strongmind said, "We would have suffered a catastrophic defeat. Weapons does not concern itself with Crew, but if there is no Crew, there is no Ship. I would follow protocols to inflict maximum damage on our opponents, up until my destruction."

"Well, obviously, your destruction didn't come," Tsi said. "Considering I dug you out of an escape pod."

Strongmind was silent for a few moments.

"There are many circumstances which could have created such an occurrence. My memory of my ejection is... incomplete."

"Your ship died, and your crew died, and you survived. Without orders or directives. I think you'll be fine if I get killed," Tsi said as she set the water jug down.

"Or you kill yourself," Strongmind added.

She rounded on him.

"How likely do you think that is?" she asked, her voice acid.

"You have lived far in excess of the un-augmented human life span. You have no connections, no home, no family. You are socially isolated, and inclined towards violent, risk-taking behavior. Given what you have done in the past, it is within standard human psychological profile for you to consider self-termination, either premeditated or spontaneous."

"You have no idea what I've been through," Tsi said. "If I was going to kill myself, I'd have done it a long time ago."

"I cannot provide further comment," Strongmind said. "My psychological assessment programming is limited."

"I don't understand you," she said. "You get me drunk on purpose, then you shame when I do it on my own? What are you, a war machine or my confessor?"

"I have allowed you to self-medicate without comment when it was efficient. You have been indulging yourself over the past few days. I think its use as a coping method for trauma is limited, and it is beginning to affect your behavior negatively."

"And you constantly needling me isn't?"

Strongmind's face went slack, and his eyes became dull. Tsi waited, with her arms crossed, but the machine did not respond. She fetched a small bottle of liquor from her pack, glowered at him, and took a swig from it.

"I'm going to the roof," she said curtly.

She had to climb two flights of rickety stairs, and up a rusted ladder to reach the roof. The building itself was sturdy and old, made mostly from concrete. It might have been some sort of military shelter once, maybe it had even survived the atomic scourging. Tsi sat cross-legged, staring up at the glass dome above the canyon.

Like an illusionist's trick, the dark clouds of fog slowly began to drift away, and the stars emerged. Tsi could not help but smile in child-like wonder as she saw unfamiliar constellations emerge. It was one of the great joys of coming to a new world: seeing a new sky emerge, experiencing the cosmos as if she was born anew.

She could see the Web of Eden, blue stars like the eyes of Hellean Cat, and the giant purple nebulae that marked the edge of Guraggan Space. Looking to the east, she could even dimly see the twinkling lights of the Kiosan systems, so powerful, so far away. With a little calculation, she judged where a dim cluster of lights was that marked Goodhome, too. She wondered what was happening on those distant worlds, now, and a thousand years ago when the light she was seeing emerged from their suns.

Something flickered at the edge of her vision, and she looked around and realized that the light of the night sky was mirrored all around her. Across all the rooftops of the shanty-town, she could see small clusters of people, huddled around candles and dying torches, staring up at the sky. Some might hide themselves and lock their doors for fear of the Clear Night, but many more had joined Tsi in communion with the stars.

She could hear snippets of conversation, bits of song carried on the stale wind. The city seemed to have calmed itself with the clearing of the sky. Tsi felt warm, peaceful.

She looked at the long red strip across the sky that marked the Dreaming Stars. It was a great mystery, the boundary of star travel. No probes or ships had ever reached the Dreaming Stars; the Slip drives always failed, the signals always faded into nothing. On Old Earth, far off places were called "The Edge of the World", and so too had humankind found the edge of the cosmos in the Dreaming Stars. They were haunting and mesmerizing, coiled like a serpent across the night sky.

As much as could be observed, their red color meant they were old and dying. Perhaps it was something about their sympathetic decay which caused the bizarre anomalies associated with them. Tsi could only hope that something so mundane was the reason. Still, for all their menace, the great stellar enigma was quite beautiful. On the Inheritor's world she had the best sight of them that could be had with a naked eye.

She heard something heavy hoist itself up onto the roof, and knew Strongmind had come to join her. She kept staring at the stars as the machine approached, stopping a few paces away. Finally, she glanced over at him.

His face was still slack and expressionless, but he wasn't looking at her. He, too, was staring up at the sky. All his sophisticated, hidden sensors turned to observe the stars in ways that even enhanced human eyes could not. He seemed transfixed, as if he too was witnessing the sky for the first time.

"The stars were once my home," was all he said.

Tsi patted the ground beside her, and Strongmind sat down. The two of them sat cross-legged in silence for a while, not needing words. Tsi put her bottle away, and was just about to allow herself the luxury of sleep, when something changed.

It spread steadily and evenly, like the unhurried tide of an ocean. Tsi watched as the Dreaming Stars changed before her eyes from red, to orange, to yellow, to a burning, bright blue. She sat up, her pulse racing.

Somehow, across an impossibly vast gulf of space and time, the dying stars had been reborn.

CHAPTER 3

Over her long life, Tsi had become used to ignoring things that horrified her. The shift of the Dreaming Stars from dull red to shining blue would have sent the average astronomer on Kios into a fit. Even now, she was sure the news would be spreading across the systems, sent via Slip courier. She could picture academics tearing out their hair in a mixture of fear and excitement. A dozen or more religious orders were sure to herald this as the final sign of the apocalypse, and even the ignorant denizens of the shanty city felt something ominous in the spectacular display.

The alignment of circumstances that must have occurred were not only so unlikely as to be impossible, they were fantastic beyond reckoning. Perhaps the universe had simply jumbled together this way, however briefly. A billion years of chaos coalescing to create this bizarre instant, confounding every scientist, every rational human mind. A freak accident on a cosmic scale.

Tsi doubted it though. She saw intelligence in the changing of the stars. It had long been speculated that there might be... *something* beyond the Dreaming Stars. A force, an intellect, whatever one called it, there was a reasoning behind why those strange stellar bodies behaved the way they did. It had blocked human travel, even with the aid of the Slip drive, beyond that point. And now it had seemingly reversed entropy itself, turning dying red giants into young, blue stars again.

In the thousands of years since humanity left its cradle on Earth, the universe had been empty of intelligent life. Primitive forms existed naturally on some worlds. Indeed, there were an abundance of Eden Worlds where fantastical beasts roamed free. None of them had anything beyond a rudimentary animal intellect, though.

The only non-human intelligence to travel the stars were things like Strongmind, machines designed to aid humankind. They were alien in their own way, but they all had a common origin, and thus were ultimately comprehensible. Whatever had made calculations so vast as to affect the stars themselves, to affect the laws of *reality* itself, would, inherently, be beyond a human being's ability to understand. Assuming, of course, that this was the result of a rational actor, and not mere chaos.

Tsi spent several hours after the change of the Dreaming Stars hooked up to her data-link, cross-referencing old files on stellar behavior. She could find few incidents of stellar re-ignition occurring, let alone the simultaneous re-birth of thousands of stars at once. Still, all she could hope was that she was wrong, that years of travel had made her prone to hysteria. It had to be some kind of mistake, a natural phenomenon being misinterpreted into something fantastical.

Then again, she lived in a universe where the fantastic was commonplace. Humanity had found the Slip-Drive, learned how to cheat their way past the speed of light, built machines that could think better than they themselves, engineered whole new species...

All she could do was hope she was wrong. There was enough trouble in the universe with mankind alone.

Her sleep that night was fitful. She remembered Goodhome, as she did so frequently these days. Vylk wasn't the first man she'd killed, but for some reason, driving a knife into his flabby stomach stayed with her. She could see his bulging eyes, his sputtering lips. The image of him clutching at the knife in his belly, his meaty hands dragging at hers, repeated over and over in her mind. She did not know why.

Perhaps it was because she had liked him.

Strongmind offered little speculation when she shared her data with him via neural link that morning. The machine had been sullen and quiet. She thought perhaps he was ashamed of the way he had treated her. It was a mistake to treat an AI like a human being, but they did possess some of the same emotions and drives. Strongmind in particular was prone to sulking when he was in the wrong. She supposed it was natural for a weapon to act that way.

She'd seen fleet actions before, where countless lives depended on the workings of AIs like Strongmind. He had to have the capacity for guilt. Maybe guilt wasn't the right word, but he had to know that his actions had consequences, and that success and failure mattered.

A day passed, and she was returning from a clandestine meeting with a smuggler. The woman had been short and small, with a scarred hair-lip. She'd asked much in money, but Tsi was confident in her ability to buy the smuggler's silence.

Back in her domicile, she opened up the crate she had dragged home. Inside were suits of clothing, genome-purity certificates, and a variety of finely worked tools and pieces of equipment. Together, she and Strongmind went over their finery.

"Thick shoulder plates," Strongmind said, examining his own clothing. "They could protect against a bladed instrument. I approve."

"A little gaudy for my taste," Tsi said. "It should work, though."

"What is our identity to be?

Tsi shared the data link with him, offering him a long cable attached to the base of her skull. She uploaded information to the machine: the history of the Clan Lletheren. They were a small group, all but extinct after the recent wars. But they would be more than welcome at the Triumph of the Dath Clan. With her pure blood and exceptional genetics, she could easily pass for an Inheritor. Strongmind would be her bodyguard, and together they would go beyond the Black Wall to witness Inheritor Brem Dath's Triumph.

From there, she could improvise their way into the clan's great palace, and hopefully discover what she had come so far to find.

"A small retinue," the guard said. He was standing on a raised platform, looking over the scroll of pedigree Tsi had handed him.

She was sweating beneath her elaborate clothing. The Inheritors believed in functionality, and so she was glad to be wearing loose breeches, covered with spiraling designs beneath her traveling cloak. A respirator, filigreed and worked with intricate floral patterns, covered the lower half of her face. It was the fashion of Inheritor ladies of great esteem to make even their most practical equipment gaudy. On a world of poverty, luxury was a sign of power. Even still, the Inheritors prided themselves on the ability to move and fight in their regalia.

Strongmind sketched an elaborate bow to the guard. He looked utterly absurd to Tsi, wearing a brocade coat with long green tassels hanging from the heavy shoulder pads. His pulse-rifle was slung across his back, but it was now cased in the luxurious striped fur of some off-world animal.

"I am a warrior of the Lletheren," he said crisply. "We may be few, but our marksmanship is the match of any canyon-lord. My Lady needs no other protection."

The guard rolled his eyes. They were in a throng of thousands, a human river slowly making its way through the massive gates of the Black Wall. Guards stood on short podiums, islands in the river, halting the flow of traffic and checking papers. It was a laborious, agonizing process, as people jostled for position. There were true Inheritors here, some sitting atop palanquins and glowering down at the commoners, but the vast majority of people trying to get in to witness the Triumph were ordinary souls. They carried with them sheaves of paper, testifying to their character and deeds, or else merely brought satchels full of goods and money to offer the guards.

Some tried to hide their deformities beneath cloaks and wrappings, but others had taken to painting and decorating over their scars and tumors. It was odd to see the gaiety with which these diseased people pressed through the throng, letting out snippets of song or shouting praises to their clan lords. They did not hate the Dath for having more than them. They worshiped them.

The terror of Clear Night seemed to have passed these people. Tsi wondered if the rebirth of the stars had been taken as a good omen, or if the people here were too ignorant to understand what they meant.

"Small Clan, but your genome tests are exceptional," the guard said finally. He whispered something into the communicator in his collar, waited a moment while the reply was transmitted to his ear piece, then jerked his head at them to go.

"Glory to Dath Clan!" Strongmind said smartly.

"Yes, yes, glory, glory," the guard said. "Next!"

Together with a mass of revelers and supplicants, Tsi and Strongmind made their way up a vast flight of stairs into the terraced fortress of the Dath. The steps were wide and steep, easily accommodating the throng as they slowly ascended. Banners waved above the crowd frantically, and shouts of praise mixed together into an incomprehensible cacophony. Sheer walls flanked each side of the great stair, and atop them Tsi could see the manors of the Inheritors.

Pennants hung from balconies, displaying familial heraldry beneath the sigils of the Dath. They fluttered gently in the breeze, a riot of colors to match the thronging crowd slowly making its way up to the great central square where the Triumph would be held. The Inheritors stood on their balconies in all their splendor, scanning the crowd with a mixture of curiosity and contempt.

It took nearly an hour to reach the top of the stair, one of her hands on Strongmind's shoulder as they pushed and jostled their way through the slowly churning horde. At last they finished their slow climb, and stood at the edge of the square, which was already thronging with people. Looming beyond the square was the great Palace of Brem Dath, the ruler of the Clan.

It was an obsidian ziggurat, low towers bristling with heavy cannon. Spiked flags bore the Dath Clan sigil proudly, and even at this distance she could see guards standing in disciplined ranks at various landings, weapons held at shoulder rest. Brem Dath was a proud man. His crowning achievement was establishing a highly disciplined personal guard, known and feared across the world.

She noted one tower in particular. Observation equipment and antennae projected from it incongruously. Her next target.

"We'll make our way across the square," Tsi whispered to Strongmind, when she felt a hand on her shoulder.

She turned to see two men in heavy combat armor, bearing the grey and blue livery of the Dath. Neither had his weapon drawn, but she could see from their posture that they both did not intend to be taken lightly.

"A thousand pardons, my lady," the first said, releasing his hand from her shoulder and inclining his head. "But it is my privilege to offer you the greetings of the Lord Brem Dath. He bids the esteemed daughter of Clan Lletheren join his house within the Palace, at her pleasing."

Strongmind looked at her. He had one of his fists closed tightly, the other resting on the case of his pulse-rifle.

She raised her hand in supplication.

"It would be my pleasure to join the most esteemed lord of the Dath," she said, smiling.

As the two guards escorted Strongmind and her down a back alley, Tsi felt lucky for the first time in a long while.

Tsi had seen opulence before. The human taste for luxury was almost universal. It could take many forms, but there was always a message: *I have more than you.* Wealth and status were not about comfort, they were signs of power, no more or less than Strongmind's pulse rifle or the staff of a Bykon priest.

For this world, having any possessions at all was a mark of status, and so it was that the Dath Clan's halls were overflowing with goods. She walked past rows of armor, most of it scavenged and obsolete, but painted and maintained like works of art. Crude, hand-formed tapestries hung from the walls; the only link between these people and their cruel history. In every hall and alcove was a gilded water tank, around which people flocked and drank from hanging tubes. Watching the nobles drinking together, water dripping from their chins and beards, Tsi briefly thought of infant cattle pressing against their mother, sucking at her nipples. Or whip-maggots burrowing greedily into carrion.

Tsi and Strongmind made their way through the halls, escorted by their guards. Curious eyes studied them as they passed. There were many strange people coming to pay homage today, even a few off-world trading captains and missionaries.

They were directed up a flight of stairs to a small octagonal room. Four figures stood inside. The first was striking: a bronze-skinned, muscular man, standing with his back to her. He was stripped to the waist, wearing nothing but a loose kilt of armor cloth. His hair was woven in tight grey braids which hung down his back. She could see scars upon his skin, most inflicted by knives and claws with the odd laser-graze here and there. He did not turn to her as she entered, but kept his arms outstretched to either side.

Kneeling to his left and right, a pair of women swaddled in silver robes worked on him. They were painting his body with intricate blue and grey designs, their faces hidden beneath goggles and filter masks. One of them reached into a jar of silver powder, and spread it the length of one of the man's scars, then gently began to pluck at the scar with a pair of tweezers. Instantly, the wound turned a bright, vibrant red.

The painted man looked out of the thin, angular windows that illuminated the room. They were gun slits, Tsi realized. She smirked to herself at the thought of a bunker-turned-powder room, then realized someone was looking at her.

It was the fourth figure, a tall woman with her arms crossed. She was dressed similarly to Tsi, though a saber hung openly from her hip, and she wore a breastplate with the Dath Clan's sign wrought into it in raw metal. Her hair was woven in a tight bun, and heavy rings hung from her pierced cheeks. She studied Tsi coldly as she entered the chamber.

Tsi fell to one knee.

"Honored Lord Brem Dath, I am humbled at your summons," Tsi said.

"This is the Lletheren?" the man said, still staring out of the gun slits as his two servants worked on his body.

"She looks healthy," the other woman said. "Older than I thought she'd be. Her pedigree is impeccable. No genetic blemishes."

"Good," Brem Dath said. "Lady Lletheren, I have a proposal for you."

He turned, and Tsi got a good look at him for the first time. His jaw was wide and heavy. His hair pulled back from his brow, revealing a long cut where someone had obviously tried to scalp him, and failed. His dark eyes burned with a fierce intelligence, and his short beard was worked with glass beads and shining silver ornaments. Tsi looked up at him coolly but said nothing as the two servants began to paint his chest and face.

"The Lletheren are weak," he said. "The Dath are strong. But as yet, my only heir... is not as capable as I had hoped. Your blood is strong, and I do not doubt that in any mixing, you might... *override* my son's qualities."

"You are proposing a marriage pact," Tsi said.

The other woman snorted. Brem Dath silenced her with a look.

"Presumptuous. No, I would make you his chief concubine. All children of the union would be Dath Clan property, but you and your kin would be well compensated. We may even take your clan under our protection. I know the Ikanus have been expanding into your territory, and I might... curb my ally's ambitions, if it pleases you."

"My lord, I would have to consult with the Clan Elders," Tsi began.

"Why?" the other woman asked. "You're free, aren't you? The

choice is yours."

"It is a weighty decision," Brem Dath allowed. "Perhaps she should meet our son, first. Sunelle, take her to the boy's gallery. She can watch the Triumph from there, and come to know my heir's... charms."

"Many thanks, my Lord," Tsi said as she rose and bowed to him.

"Think on your decision carefully," Brem Dath replied. "My patience is not infinite, and this is not an offer we extend lightly. I might note that you will not be leaving the palace... until I have an answer to my liking."

Sunelle led Tsi and Strongmind back through the palace. As they traveled through winding corridors and long halls, Tsi took note of entrances and exits. The palace was a fortress first, its opulence having been added to it over long centuries. She could still see where barrack-room bunks had once hung, and where bulkhead doors had been removed, replaced with arches draped in hanging beads.

There were a decent number of archways opening out onto the central courtyard which overlooked the Inheritor's city, but the number of exits on the other side were limited. She found one or two windows open to the outside world, but the walls of the palace were steep and would be hard to climb or slide down. Tsi had counter-measures for such an escape, but she liked to keep things simple. Especially as she might wind up leaving in a hurry.

"There's no shame in it," Sunelle said as they walked.

"My lady?"

"Concubinage," Sunelle said. "You can keep your Clan-name, return whenever you like. It's a reproduction contract, nothing more. You'd be well treated here, I think you should know."

Out of Brem Dath's presence, Sunelle's attitude had shifted. She was still tense, but she seemed more open.

"I do not doubt that," Tsi said. "The hospitality of the Dath is legendary."

"But you still hesitate," Sunelle observed. "I won't deny it can be... difficult. I served the Ikanus when I was younger. Four healthy children I gave them, before I returned here and married my Lord. I haven't seen them since then. One of my daughters died out in the wastes, I heard."

"That must have been difficult, my lady," Tsi said.

"I barely knew her," Sunelle said quietly as they walked. "Still, she was healthy and brave. I am proud. I did what I had to do to serve my people. It is all that is asked of any of us, no?"

Tsi nodded silently.

She was seated in the gallery next to the heir of the Dath Clan, a young man named Hiron. When Tsi first set eyes on him, she knew why his parents had been so eager to find him a mate. He was deformed. One shoulder was set above the other, and his legs seemed to be of two different sizes. Thin white hair hung from his scalp, and his clothes seemed too big for his frail body. He looked up at her and smiled nervously, watery eyes full of innocence.

He introduced himself formally in his soft, gentle voice, and made a few perfunctory overtures to Tsi's beauty. She hadn't been wooed in some time, and she had to stifle a laugh at the young man's improvised attempts at poetry. Eventually, they settled into a more natural conversation, and Tsi asked him what his interests were.

"Astronomy," he said, half-ashamed.

"How fascinating," she replied. "I have an amateur interest in that area as well."

"Really? Y-you know, my clan has one of the most sophisticated stellar scanners on the planet. My father doesn't approve, but I've been working with it for years. I've even been able to get a Slip-courier back and forth from a few of the probes that are halfway to the Dreaming Stars themselves."

"The Dreaming Stars... Tell me, you observed them on Clear Night, yes?"

"Incredible," he said. "Do you have any idea what that phenomenon implies?"

"Stellar re-ignition," Tsi said.

"Yes! Something that should be practically impossible," Hiron beamed. "That is, if the phenomenon is being observed correctly. I haven't been able to get a courier back recently, but I was able to watch the beginning of the phenomenon a few months ago. I thought it was just a system-error in the courier, but now, well, we've all seen it with our naked eyes, haven't we?"

"It doesn't frighten you?"

"Frighten me?" Hiron asked.

"It's a change in universal theory," Tsi said. "We witnessed a disruption of cosmic order. Everything we thought we understood about the universe and its behavior... it's wrong."

"I know! It's fantastic, isn't it?"

"It means all our old methods, our old theories, they're unreliable now. We're in completely uncharted territory when it comes to understanding the cosmos. Like starting over from scratch."

Hiron beamed.

"Anything could happen," he said.

Tsi smiled in spite of herself.

"I suppose you're right," she said. "Anything could happen."

CHAPTER 4

The triumph began when the sun was at the apex of the sky. Shining down through the canyon-dome, it illuminated the great throng of Dath Clan chattel. Factory workers, merchants, radiation infested dregs from beyond the wall crowded the great square, chanting and cheering as drums sounded from the palace courtyard. Thousands of clan warriors marched in unison, carrying brilliant banners displaying the deeds of their brotherhoods. Inheritors strutted before them, baring relics and trophies they had taken from the wasteland, preening like exotic birds. The courtyard was a massive stage, and the mob below cheered with unbridled enthusiasm.

Tsi watched as a troupe of actors erected a platform, and performed a dumb-show of the history of the Dath Clan. Dancers in brilliant costumes played out the story of the Last War: how cruel and greedy warlords scoured the world with atomic fire, killing everything that was green and good. A few golden figures emerged from the chaos: the Inheritors, standing tall and proud. The dance showed how, through cleverness and foresight, they had dug into the earth and survived the holocaust, then emerged and built their canyon fortresses.

The wars of the Dath came next. Over and over again the figure who represented the Dath Clan triumphed over foe after foe, and brought the poor, wretched survivors of the wasteland under his protection. At last, with all the other dancers kneeling or miming death at his feet, the Dath figure sat upon a throne, his arms raised in victory.

The crowd erupted in wild cheers. *"Dath clan! Dath clan!"* they chanted, over and over.

Suddenly, the platform fell away, and there was a great burst of smoke. Striding from within it, came the Lord Brem Dath. His warriors knelt at either side, and Inheritors from many clans tossed their tokens of esteem at his feet. One of his warriors hurled the banners of defeated clans before him, and he strode imperiously over them, his body a riot of blue and silver, his scars picked out in brilliant red.

A golden amulet hung from his neck. Though it was well disguised, Tsi could see it was a personal shield generator. It wouldn't stand up to the most sophisticated weapons, but he'd be near-invulnerable to any would-be assassins in the crowd. Tsi doubted many Inheritors were familiar with the technology, just as she was sure that Brem Dath's bare-chested display of bravado was calculated to inspire them with a sense of his own immortality.

He stood at last in the open air at the edge of the courtyard, overlooking the crowd. He raised his arms, just as the dancer in the dumb show had. The cheers were deafening.

She guessed that most of the crowd had been terrified by the change in the Dreaming Stars. Their cries at the sight of their tyrant were a sort of relief. If the stars themselves were inconstant, then at least their mighty lord was eternally strong.

Tsi was sure the triumph was at its apex, when a hush spread across the crowd. She strained her eyes, and saw two more Dath warriors, emerging from a hidden gate. They carried between them a staggering, reed-thin figure. Even at this distance, Tsi could make out the markings on the man's clothing: he was a Chom-Ap, like the man she had murdered in the shanty-town. They were the latest of the Dath's conquests.

"Lord Katus," Hiron whispered to her. She glanced at the youth and saw that he was trembling, his eyes fixed on his father.

The warriors shoved Katus to his knees before Brem Dath. There could not have been more contrast between their two figures, one powerful and ramrod straight, the other shriveled and weak. Tsi was sure the man had been starved. Likely tortured too.

Then, the warriors stepped away. Brem Dath faced Katus, and took a fighting stance. Katus staggered to his feet, and Tsi saw he had a dagger in one trembling, bony hand.

With the shriek of pure terror, Katus lunged at his foe, but Brem Dath easily stepped to the side. He darted about the flailing Katus, casually turning aside his blows, mocking him with feints and jabs. At last, Katus managed to thrust his dagger right at Brem Dath's throat. The Lord of the Dath Clan caught the dagger with his bare hands, and wrenched it from Katus's grip.

The blade was blunt of course. This duel had been as much of a show as the dancers and their pantomime. Brem Dath kicked Katus in the chest and cast the dagger aside. Kneeling and wheezing, Katus looked at the dagger beyond his reach, then up at his foe.

Brem Dath raised a fist, and the crowd cheered. It came crashing into the side of Katus's skull, sending him sprawling. Roughly, the lord of the Inheritors seized him up, and struck him. Again and again, his bronze fists came down upon the yielding captive. All lord Katus did was shriek and moan.

The crowd was roaring its approval, but Tsi's eyes were on Hiron. The boy's lips were quivering, yet he kept focused on the brutal display. He shook with every impact, every whimper of pain. Tsi put her hand on his.

"Look at me. Look at me. Hey! Look at me."

Hesitantly, the boy turned to her.

"You don't have to watch," she said.

"I... I must. It's what, it's what makes us strong."

"No," Tsi said. "No it isn't. Nothing about what's happening down there is a sign of strength, do you understand me? You don't have to watch."

"It's my father's triumph. I owe him, I—I've failed him, I'm weak but I have to be strong, and—"

"You don't owe him anything. Look away."

Sweat was beading on the shaking boy's brow.

"Please," she added quietly.

He collapsed into her arms, bawling like an infant. Tsi held the boy tight as he wept. It had been a long time since she did this, but she rocked him back and forth, gently. She could find no words for him, so she stayed silent, only relieved to no longer witness his pain.

She was glad he had found the strength to look away. But Tsi could not, and she stared as the Lord Brem Dath beat Katus to death with his bare hands, until all that was left of the man was a bloody pulp. The crowd never stopped cheering.

CHAPTER 5

The boy apologized to her as he dried his tears. In truth, once the Triumph had finished its bloody climax, Tsi had felt horribly awkward holding him as he wept. She'd never felt comfortable giving people physical comfort. She wasn't without compassion, but she had spent so much of her life keeping a tight leash on her emotions it was difficult to speak to him after the moment had passed.

Revels were erupting in the streets below. While the common folk were forbidden beyond the great square, they were permitted to stay until midnight, and many of them took this time to make merry to their heart's content. Even being close to the wealth of the Inheritors was ecstasy to them.

Within the palace, there was a buzz of activity. The Triumph was formally finished, but Brem Dath's victory feast would come in a few hours. Now, without the rigors of formality, the Inheritors mingled with each other freely,. As they left the viewing gallery, Tsi saw every alcove filled with men and women in hushed conversation, or standing in the open, brazenly boasting and mocking.

All of the Inheritors traveled armed. Tsi brushed passed a red-faced man, she was curious as to how many of them would wind up dead in drunken duels tonight. Theirs was a warrior culture, a world of killers and survivors. Even at the height of luxury and security, it was vital to them to prove they could still do violence at a moment's notice.

Hiron was still trembling slightly when their guards and Strongmind rejoined them in an adjoining hall. Tsi wasn't sure where they were headed, likely off to greet his bloody-handed father. She couldn't stand the thought, and was about to speak when a woman with long, golden loops of hair crossed their path. She smiled and kneeled on seeing Hiron, her flowing white skirts pooling upon the ground about her.

Tsi recognized her facial tattoos, corrupted hazard markings, as the signs of clan Ikanus. She was certain this was the Inheritor the dead water-guard had spoken of. As she rose, she formally introduced herself to Tsi.

"Vitara of Ikanus," she said, raising a hand to her chest in a warrior's salute.

"Tsi, of Lletheren," Tsi replied.

"A Lletheren? I had thought you were all dead..."

"We yet live," Strongmind interjected. "Our warriors are proud, and fear no skulking Ikanus raider!"

Tsi glowered at the machine. She was discovering he had a habit of over-acting.

"Please, please," Hiron said. "There is no need for such talk..."

"Of course not," Vitara said. "Perhaps we shall see each other at the next triumph, Lletheren. I hear your Lord is quite robust. He might give us more of a show than that stringy little Chom-Ap."

"Enough!" Hiron snapped. "I won't have you-you-you threatening someone in my house!"

"Your house?" Vitara arched an eyebrow. "Of course. How you must look forward to taking your father's throne some day. The Palace of the Dath has always been held with such *strength*, I am sure your reign will be most... remarkable."

Vitara bowed again, then wheeled with her entourage and left. Hiron glared after her.

"I would have married her," he grumbled, "If I wasn't... like *this*."

"Lucky you," Tsi said, eliciting a laugh from Hiron.

"Listen," she continued. "We have some time before the feast. Why don't you show me your star-gazing equipment?"

Hiron beamed, and half-galloped as he led her down a side corridor and up a winding flight of steps. Their guards stayed a few respectful paces behind, and took up positions outside the door as he led her into a chamber in a high tower.

Inside the walls were covered in machinery. Much of it was old and crude, like everything on this world, but she could see a data-link hanging from one of the computer stacks, and what looked like a primitive AR device. On the walls hung glowing charts, their holographic displays subtly moving, running simulations of the life spans of stars.

"My favorite place," Hiron said, as he showed her around. "That's a Bykon image condenser! And over there, I have authentic star charts from one of the Free Traders. Here, look at this."

He eagerly sat Tsi in a well worn chair, and lit up a screen in front of her. She was staring out at a field of lights. With some quick calculations, she realized this must be an image recording from one of the probes near the Dreaming Stars.

"With these," he said, pressing two keys beneath the screen, "You can get a complete panorama. I know it's a little fuzzy, but that probe's been operating for centuries. It was launched before the Last War by our ancestors. You know, some people think we came out here just to look at the Dreaming Stars. This is the closest habitable world, and it hasn't got much in the way of resources. I've always told my father that I think that's our real legacy. Not war, but observation."

Tsi nodded as she flicked through views. It was an old recording, showing the crimson stars as they had been before their strange re-ignition. She let the recording advance, then stopped it several times, zooming in on particular spots in the display. She couldn't be positive, but she thought she saw several of the lights vanish from existence, tiny dots of darkness emerging in the star field over time, barely perceptible to someone without her enhancements. Strongmind would be even better at this she realized.

"Hiron," she said. "May I ask something of you? A gift?"

"Whatever you desire," he said happily.

"May I clone your data? I'd like to study it when I get home."

"Oh," Hiron said, reddening slightly. "When you get home. I see, I see. O-of course! Here, I can get you a data-pad, and—"

"That won't be necessary," Tsi said, slipping the cable from behind her head and affixing it to the machine.

In moments, the data was coursing into her. She erased some of her memories from her augment-stack: bits of information from past planets she'd visited, facts and trivia that had been useful in her old lives, but now would do nothing but crowd her hard memory. She quickly filled those spaces with stellar data from the Dreaming Stars... then turned her attention elsewhere.

"How did you get that... that thing in your head? And why are you looking at Guraggan space?" Hiron asked, studying the screen over her shoulder.

"Curious..." she murmured, zooming in on one quadrant in particular. For a brief moment, she saw one of the tiny stars flicker in and out of existence. Then another, and another. In all, she counted four stars that seemingly disappeared, then reappeared. Strongmind would be able to analyze the data properly, but she had a feeling she already knew what he was going to tell her. Satisfied, she disconnected her data-link.

"You've never taken an interest in our neighbors?" she asked, as she rose.

"Why would I? The Hegemony was defeated decades ago. They mostly keep to themselves now. I've heard Free Traders talk about them launching raids sometimes, but I thought they were too busy tearing themselves apart to worry about the rest of us."

"They've been here," Tsi said. "Your father never spoke to you about them?"

"No... Why are you so interested in off-worlders? We have enough problems here."

"If the Guraggan come to this world, you'll have something much worse than petty clan squabbles..."

"Who are you?" Hiron said suddenly. "Y-you're not an Inheritor. You're not one of the Lletheren. One of us would never talk the way you do, or-or know as much as you know."

Tsi sighed and breathed in deeply. She had a choice to make. Of her options, none were favorable. She could see a mixture of fear and curiosity in his eyes. He was weak, and unlike most Inheritors, he carried no weapons. It wouldn't be hard to slip her knife into his throat before he could react. Strongmind could deal with the guards. They'd be out of the palace before anyone noticed. Her ship wasn't stashed too far beyond the canyon. From there they could burn out of the atmosphere and be out of the system in a matter of hours.

Of all of her plans, it was the least risky. She had the data she'd come for. She'd seen what she needed to of the Dreaming Stars, and of the Hegemony's space. She could resolve her guilt later, what she was dealing with was more important than the life of one overgrown child. She could wipe out this whole city, sacrifice the whole world if she had to, and she'd still be vindicated in the grand scheme of things.

You're not that person anymore, she told herself.

Tsi sighed.

"You're right," she said finally. "I'm not an Inheritor. I'm a traveler, from very far away. But you have to believe me, Hiron, I am your friend. The things that are happening on this planet, they have... implications, for all of the known systems. For humanity. I need your help, Hiron, and I need you to trust me."

He stared at her a long time.

"One condition. Take me with you."

"What?"

"Take me with you. Once you've done what you're going to do, you're going to leave, right? I want you to take me with you. I want to see the stars. Most of us are forbidden to leave our world, most of us don't even know we can leave. But there's nothing here for me. I wasn't born to be an Inheritor."

"What about your parents?" Tsi asked.

"I'm a burden to them," Hiron said. "I know that. It would have been better for them if I had never been born."

"Hiron..."

"Don't try to lie to me," he said. "I know what I am. I want to... I *have* to go someplace where people like me... where I'm not treated like this."

"I can take you with me," Tsi said after a moment. "But I can't promise you anything. The stars are hard and cruel. I've never been to a world where anything makes sense."

"Well, then maybe we can find it. Together."

The boy looked at her then with an earnestness she hadn't seen in a long time. There was nothing else for it. She couldn't leave him behind.

"Get us beyond the walls without being stopped," Tsi said. "Strongmind and I have a ship stashed just beyond an old filter pipe, outside the canyon."

"Strongmind? You mean your servant?"

"Yes," Tsi said. "You should know he's a machine. An artificial intelligence, housed in a human simulacra drone. If anyone starts shooting, stay behind him."

"I don't think there's going to be any shooting," Hiron laughed. "Listen, it might surprise you but I've done this before. We'll be expected at the feast, but once that's over with we can slip away easy. There's a water pipe that runs along the canyon wall. A maintenance shaft goes right along side it, all we have to do is talk our way passed the guards at the reservoir and we should be able to travel along the shaft without trouble. It is a bit cramped, though."

"We'll adapt," Tsi said.

"Good. Come on, we'd better put in an appearance at the feast before we make our grand escape."

The two of them left his stargazing chamber, Hiron pausing to copy data to a recording device and bid his beloved machines a last goodbye. As they left he dismissed his guards, only Strongmind falling into step behind them as they made their way to the feasting hall.

"I told him everything," Tsi said over her shoulder to Strongmind.

"Shall I terminate him?" Strongmind asked.

"No, no," Tsi replied, noting the look of panic in Hiron's face. "He's going to help us get out of the palace. It would be best if we weren't noticed."

"I understand. It is nice to meet you, Hiron. I am Strongmind."

The Machine thrust his hand out to Hiron as the trio continued to walk, forcing the boy to awkwardly half-turn and shake it.

"Uh, I'm honored to properly meet you," Hiron said.

"Why? You know I am not a noble. I am a machine. My presence should not bring you any honor."

"I meant, that, uh..."

"Enough, Strongmind," Tsi said.

She pulled a face at Hiron.

"He has a sense of *humor*."

CHAPTER 6

They entered the feasting hall, and Tsi's senses were immediately overwhelmed. Four tables of ebony made a cross at the center of the hall, and seated all around them were the Inheritors and their entourages. Musicians played in galleries above, and a-grav chandeliers hung suspended in the air, brilliant and gold. The ceiling itself was open, allowing a view of the slowly emerging night sky through the canyon dome above.

The tables were laid with all manner of succulent food. She could see fruits and vegetables, brightly colored mushrooms grown in subterranean caves, and bloody haunches of meat. She noted with some nostalgia the bulky form of a Gene-Bear, smoked and garnished with pungent spices. While they were the food of poor folk and frontier colonists, on the Inheritor's World, this simple fare was a sign of awesome power. Few among even this elite would feast in this manner again.

She also saw crystalline dishes, filled with clear, sparkling water. Inheritors dipped their drinking tubes into the basins, sucking up mouthfuls of clean water like the most decadent liqueur.

On a raised dais above the cross-table, she saw Lord Brem Dath. His wife was at one side, a half-dozen concubines were seated below her. Brem Dath was gnawing on a haunch of Gene-Bear, clearly playing into his image of ferocity. He had not dressed since the Triumph. Though much of the paint had worn off, his hands still showed red in places and his knuckles bore bruises and fresh cuts.

Together with Hiron, she made her way to the dais. She and Hiron bowed to Brem Dath and Sunelle, then took their seats to the right, Strongmind standing behind them. A pair of choice dishes were laid out before them, and Tsi was just beginning to relax and enjoy her meal when she felt Strongmind's hand on her shoulder.

"There," the Machine whispered, jerking his head to

the cross-table.

Sitting at one of the heads of the table, attended by her servants and retinue, was Vitara Ikanus. The arrogant Inheritor's presence was not what drew Strongmind's attention however: it was her companions.

One was freakishly tall and broad, with long, ungainly limbs. Its face had a metallic, jackal-like snout, from which hung a mass of bifurcated stimulant tubes. One clawed hand played idly at the table, while the other rested on a shock-glaive. Only a single un-augmented eye peering out from behind the war mask gave any sign that the creature had ever been human.

The jackal-thing's opposite was much more subtle. He still had the general figure of a man, but like all his kind he went nowhere without heavy battle armor. His panoply consisted of thick, overlapping plates of metal with a curiously beautiful sheen of verdigris. A cloak stitched from a score of different fabrics was draped across his shoulders. His face was hidden by a high domed helmet and bevor, from beneath which a pair of green cybernetic eyes glowed balefully. With his many-colored cloak draped across him, Tsi could not see any weapons, but she was certain he was armed.

Like the Inheritors, the Guraggan went nowhere without their weapons.

She knew these two, knew their cruelty and their prowess. If anyone could survive the decades of civil war after the Guraggan Hegemony was defeated by the Janissariat, it was them. The Jackal-thing was called Nomic Shi. He had led the raiders at Lehyde, and nearly seized Kios itself before his capital ship was boarded and destroyed by the Janissaries of the *Ironside*. He was older now, much older, and had augmented himself to the point where it was generous to even call him human.

The other was Turon Chryte. He had been a young man at the end of the war, famous for having led one of the last great offensives before the Janissariat put the Hegemony to rout. She knew little of him, save that he was as fearless as any of his kindred. He sat almost motionless at the table, seeming more like a fixture, a pillar, rather than a man.

"Suggest withdrawal, immediate," Strongmind said quietly, losing his simulated speech pattern for a moment.

"We have to go," Tsi whispered to Hiron. "They're moving faster than I thought."

"Who? Who's moving?"

Tsi indicated the Guraggan with her stem of water, pretending to laugh at something Hiron had said. Her palms were slick with sweat.

"Those things with Ikanus. They're Guraggan. If they're on-world already that means their plans have advanced faster than I thought they would."

"What are you talking about? They're probably just here to do my father homage."

"Those two wouldn't set foot on a world they didn't intend to conquer. We have to find an excuse to leave before—"

She was going to say "before they see me", but stopped short, realizing her face had changed more than once since the last time she had come across this pair. She tried to take solace in the fact that to them, she was a total stranger. But she was in no less danger.

"There are only two of them..." Hiron began.

"And they'll kill half the palace before we can put a scratch on their armor."

She was already checking exits and entrances. There was a set of spiral staircases leading up to the viewing gallery, the main doors beyond the long tables, and a few side passages and alcoves set into the walls. A quick dash could get her to the staircase, then from there they could—

Brem Dath had taken this moment to rise from his throne, causing the entire hall to stir.

"Again, we triumph," he said in a loud, clear voice. "Again, the Dath Clan has gone into the field, has braved the killing storms and the blasted wasteland! Again, we have done battle with treacherous foes, and again we have been victorious! I say to you there are none stronger than we!"

Cheers rose up at this, though Tsi saw a few of the Inheritors from other clans were silent. Vitara Ikanus had her hands folded beneath the table, a faint smirk on her face.

"Another competitor dies at my hands. Another pretender to the throne of this world, gone. I say we shall not rest until all upon this world have yielded! Yielded to the might of the *Dath Clan!*"

Riotous cheers shook the room, and fists were slammed into

the tables. It took a long while for the crowd to quiet itself as Brem Dath gazed upon them all with grim satisfaction, his heavily muscled arms folded across his chest.

He seemed about to speak again when he realized that Vitara had risen, along with her companions. Flanked by the Guraggan, she strode to the center of the room, her footsteps echoing in the silence. Brem Dath's arms fell to his sides, fists balled in barely controlled rage, but his face was stony.

Vitara inclined her head to him curtly.

"My Lord, if I may," she said. "Am I to take it from your words that you wish to lay claim to all of Promise?"

She used the Inheritor's name for their world. An archaic name, one Tsi found bitterly ironic.

"I do," Brem Dath smirked. "None can oppose me. None dare."

Idiot, idiot! Tsi thought to herself as she fumbled for her heavy Repeater.

"You would have Clan Ikanus submit to you?"

"Your kin already submit to me, girl," Brem Dath spat. "Everyone knows your Clan lords do me homage."

"Ah yes, my clan lords. You will find this interesting." She reached into one of the wide sleeves of her dress, and tossed a holographic projector onto the ground. From it burst a recording, a long, slow pan in three dimensions showing a hall not unlike the one in which they now stood. It was littered with bodies, ripped to shreds by weapons fire, or else keeled over, their mouths foaming.

"You see, they are all dead. I am the heir to the Ikanus, and so, now I am its ruler and sole Inheritor. And I do not recognize you as my lord," Vitara said, her voice still pleasant and light.

"You killed your own kin!" Brem Dath roared, pointing an accusing finger at her.

"Only the ones in my way. Honestly, my lord, you could do to follow my example. No matter how hard you try, you've only got that one little whelp to replace you, and I have to say, there's few left in the Clans who would follow a weakling like *that*. Better to keep the blood strong, and toss out the chaff."

Angry murmurs erupted from the crowd. A few stood, loosing weapons from scabbards and holsters. The Dath Clan Guards had their rifles in hand, but had not yet raised them to fire on the Inheritor of Ikanus.

"It is clear what you want," Brem Dath growled. "Your courage does you credit, Lady Vitara, but it betrays your ignorance. Did you really intend to kill us all with what? A pair of off-worlders and a dozen retainers? The finest warriors of all Promise are here! Did you not think I had precautions against your betrayal?!"

At this more guards emerged from the alcoves, fully armored, their weapons shouldered and pointed squarely at Vitara and her party. The Inheritor stood very still, her hands folded daintily in front of her.

"I was counting on it, actually. All your personal guard, all the mightiest warriors on the planet. All in one room. Drinking. Feasting. Enjoying the open sky above them..."

Tsi glanced upwards. She saw movement in the open roof of the chamber, but Brem Dath and his troops were still fixated Vitara.

"You exterminated the Inheritors of Chom-Ap, it's true. But there were still plenty of common folk and gun-sworn left, looking for a new master, and someone to pay their bills. Add to that all the other enemies you've made over the years my lord, including many Inheritors in this very room, and you'll find your little house guard... just a bit out numbered."

Brem Dath ground his teeth.

"Enough of this! Kill her!"

With a flash, Vitara hurled something to the ground. Suddenly, she and her companions were encased with an opaque sphere of crackling purple energy. Gunshots roared out, but every blast bounced off the sphere. Tsi saw black figures rappelling down from above. There was a series of loud bangs and then the room filled with thick yellow fog.

Foam ran from the mouths of those caught in the gas without their respirators. Some of the Inheritors were rising up, dozens of them in varied clan livery, their filter masks strapped on at the sign from lady Vitara. They hurled themselves onto the Dath Clan's guards, striking them down with long blades and blasting them apart with flechette pistols.

Strongmind wrenched forwards and upended the table, giving them cover as bullets and laser blasts shrieked through the air. He helped Tsi strap on her gilded respirator, then helped Hiron do the same. At last, he drew his pulse rifle, and Tsi drew her own weapon. They looked each other in the eye and nodded.

Battle was erupting all across the feasting hall. Dozens more black-clad figures were rappelling from the ceiling now, blazing away at knots of Dath Clan warriors and hurtling more poisonous grenades.

Tsi turned to Hiron, and put a hand on the shaking young man's shoulder.

"Follow Strongmind. Stay low," she said.

He nodded mutely.

"Alright. Let's go."

CHAPTER 7

si moved through the fog, keeping the bulky form of Strongmind to her right. They'd practiced tactical drills before, but this was the first time she would actually need to rely on the machine under fire. He'd have to slow down to keep pace with her. His body wasn't a combat drone, but he could still move and think far faster any human.

She could see Hiron out of the corner of her eye, following close to Strongmind like a pup to its mother. They kept low to the ground, moving in a shuffling run from cover to cover. The gas cloud had thickened and enveloped the entire hall, making it impossible to see more than a few feet ahead. She could hear the battle raging around them though; feel the whip-crack of solid rounds overhead, see the sparkle of pulse fire.

There was another noise in the din. Screaming, and the familiar *thwack* of metal hitting meat. The Inheritors fought in the old way, blade to blade as much as gun to gun.

Suddenly, a figure stumbled out of the haze. A Chom-Ap, clad all in black. In the brief moments it took Tsi to scan him, she saw that he'd taken a flechette to the side, puncturing his sealed-suit and letting the gas in. The man was certainly dying, but he still held a long knife in one hand.

Tsi raised her Repeater and shot him through the throat, blood and bits of vertebrae showering out from the wound. He fell without a word. She kicked the knife away from him they moved past, just to be safe.

With a tensing of her muscles, she flicked through the vision enhancements in her eyes. The chemical fog had strange properties, obscuring basic scanning, but she could still get a vague back-scatter image. Eerie outlines danced around each other in the mist, darting forwards, firing their weapons, keeling over, dying. She saw one figure seize another and slam it onto one of the tables, then drive a blade into its stomach over and over.

Unable to tell one side from the other, Tsi felt a distant compassion for all involved in the melee. One figure might rise, strike down two or three, then fall to a burst of fire from behind, only to be avenged by a wild swinging blade or another random burst of shot. She was almost transfixed by the melee, even as she and her companions made their way towards the nearest staircase and, hopefully, safety.

Amid the carnage, at the eye of the storm of gunfire and flashing blades, she could still see the crackling orb of energy that the Lady Ikanus had created. It was Bykon technology, Tsi was sure. A form of shielding so advanced she had never seen it used before. The device had created an oasis, in which Vitara and her Guraggan companions stood while the battle raged around them. Tsi knew the Guraggan were chafing at the chance for violence, but they were shrewd creatures. Despite their vaunted sense of personal honor, the Guraggan believed in victory above all else. They would not risk themselves foolishly when they could wait and watch the battle unfold.

The sphere began to pulse and fade. It was weakening, and would soon disappear completely. Then the Guraggan would be unleashed.

"Follow!" she barked, taking the lead in a sprint towards the stairs.

A Dath Clan Guard huddled at the base of the stairs, snapping shots from her carbine into the fog. She turned, panicking, towards Tsi and her companions as they approached. Before the woman had a chance to raise her weapon, Tsi shot her twice in the stomach, then put one more round through her forehead.

"She was one of ours!" Hiron stammered.

"Mourn later," Tsi said, seizing the dead woman's weapon and shoving it into Hiron's shaking hands. "You might need this. Come on."

They sprinted up the stairs, discarding their masks as they cleared the gas. She could hear Hiron panting, but she did not slow her movement. They made their way through the halls, brushing through knots of cowering servants. A pair of guards challenged them as they crossed an alcove, confusion evident on their faces.

Tsi was raising her gun, when Hiron roared a command.

"Assassins! Lord Brem Dath is betrayed! Go quickly, the

feasting hall! He needs all the help he can get! Go!"

"It will be done my lord!" one of the guards barked, grabbing her companion and shouldering by them.

They kept running through the halls, Hiron taking the lead now and slowing their pace with his twisted legs. Tsi covered him with her Repeater, while Strongmind brought up the rear, periodically sweeping behind them with his rifle.

"Just a few more," Hiron panted. "Water shaft... just beyond that gate..."

He was sweating by the time they made their way to the utility shaft. It was a heavy octagonal door set into one of the side alcoves. Thick brass pipes shot out from above it, the direct line between the Dath Clan palace and the their reservoirs hidden in subterranean caverns far beyond the canyon city.

Hiron typed frantically on the access pad, but was met with a failure alarm. He tried again, but once more was met by the same droning alarm.

"They've hacked your system," Tsi said.

Hiron looked at her questioningly.

"It is a standard Guraggan tactic," Strongmind supplied, keeping his gun trained down the hallway behind them. "They begin an assault via electronic warfare. Disable systems as rapidly as possible, change security codes, burn out gateways, re-write drone command structures. Elegant, efficient. I am fortunate to not have been wired to your crude network, I would have certainly terminated both of you."

"We'll need to take the direct approach," Tsi said. She placed her pistol against the door bolt and fired.

The Noxian Repeater had been designed to shoot through bulk-heads, and even the heaviest metal that the Inheritors could manufacture was no use against it. The lock was blown clean through. With a single hard shove from her enhanced muscles, the door swung open.

They entered a cramped, stinking corridor. The main pipe ran alongside it, making up the entirety of one wall. Lesser pipes crisscrossed the ceiling, each on a separate route to different parts of the palace.

Again, Hiron took the lead. It was a tight fit, forcing them to travel single file. Tsi knew she needed the boy to keep her from taking a wrong turn, to get them out past the canyon wall safely, but she was also keenly aware of how much of a risk it was to rely on someone so weak.

You don't think like that anymore, she told herself. *He has value. His life has value. He's saving you.*

Silently, Tsi cursed herself as she reloaded her weapon.

The sounds of battle from the palace faded behind them, and for what seemed like hours they moved in silence down the tunnel. The only noise was their irregular footfalls splashing in puddles of rusty water, and Hiron's uncomfortable panting.

"Movement ahead," Strongmind whispered.

They slowed as they approached a t-shaped junction in the corridor. A trio of guards in Dath Clan livery and a technician stood nervously in the junction around a monitoring station. As they approached, one of them shouted a warning, and the rest scattered into what cover they could find.

"I am Hiron Dath," Hiron panted, raising one hand, not strong enough to keep the carbine he held in his other hand up. "I... I come... I come on behalf of my father."

"Hiron?" the technician asked, peaking out from above a computer console and wiping grease from her brow. "What's happening? The comms said something about an attack and that we had to stay put, but it's gone all crazy. I never seen the machines act this way."

"An electronic attack has subdued your systems. Any communication you receive is unverifiable," Strongmind said as the trio emerged from the corridor.

Tsi kept a firm grip on her gun.

"Hell," the technician muttered. "Who is it? I heard the Savic Clan were working on something like this, talking to Off-Worlders about getting Kill-Minds to override our machines."

"Ikanus," Hiron said. "Off-Worlders are helping them. They've already stormed the palace. My father... the last I saw, my father was fighting bravely..."

One of the guards spoke up, a big man with a cracked visor.

"We can't stay here," he said. "They could smoke us out, no trouble. Seen it before, just a couple gas grenades and the whole tunnel's done."

"They haven't come for us yet. Maybe we could form a barricade? Hold out until help arrives?"

"*What* help? You heard the heir, everyone's dead."

"N-not dead," Hiron interjected. "My father..."

"Oh stuff it," the big man grunted. "Clan's gone. You're not a prince anymore, cripple."

"Don't talk to him that way!" the technician shouted. "We still have obligations."

"To what? A crazy dead man and a kid who can barely walk? Screw that, and screw those odds. I ain't dying for him."

"What about our honor?" one of the other guards asked.

"Honor? Shit, I thought you were smarter than that. 'Honor' is for psychos and idiots. We should get out of here!"

Tsi was slowly edging towards the far side of the junction, Strongmind shadowing her while the guards debated. A subtle vibration raised the hairs on the back of her neck. In the fractions of an instant it took her to hear the noise, a soft click-clicking upon the floor of the corridor, she realized that the person approaching was making no attempt at stealth. She spun around, her Repeater raised and pointed down the tunnel.

A single figure strode through the flickering emergency lights, his many-colored cloak dragging along the damp ground. Despite his motion, Tsi could not shake the feeling that Turon Chryte was no living thing. He was more a like a force of nature, advancing on them with the steady inexorability of a great storm. She could see nothing in the Guraggan's body language, only his even, measured stride towards them.

A metallic hand emerged from within his cloak. Silver lights danced around it, moving back and forth in long flashes, like fire bugs. Strongmind pushed her to the ground and began blazing away with his weapon just as she realized what the Guraggan held in his hand.

The junction erupted in chaos. The Guards began firing, some of their bullets ripping into Strongmind's back, others blazing down either tunnel. Tsi fell to the ground hard, and saw Hiron had fallen too. The boy's eyes were wide with panic, and he was clutching at a bleeding graze on the side of his head.

Turon burst into a sprint, waving his hand in front of him. The light sparked and shimmered, casting aside the solid shot that the Dath

Clan guards fired at him. Strongmind's pulse rounds ripped into the Guraggan's cloak, tearing and burning it, but they slid off the armor beneath like rain on a tiled roof. In seconds, Turon was among them. His hand whipped out, and two of the guards fell, their bodies trisected in grotesque geometrical patterns.

Mono-wire. An old weapon, and popular with the Guraggan. Turon was whipping and pulling the wires around him, like a one-armed puppeteer manipulating marionettes. Strands of razor thin cord ripped through flesh and armor with equal ease.

He twisted his wrist, wrapping the wires about the big guard's throat. With a quick twitch of his fingers, the man's head slid off in a plume of blood. The Guraggan spun, flicking the wire out towards Strongmind.

Strongmind's rifle fell from his hand as the wire wrapped about his arm. Turon pulled taught, the wires now ripping into the machine's pseudo-skin. Tsi could see fluid leaking from the wounds erupting all around where the wires bit into her companion's arm. Suddenly, the machine jerked backwards, yanking the Guraggan towards him. Even as the cord sliced through his forearm, severing it into a dozen pulpy pieces, Strongmind slammed his other fist into Turon's helmet, hammering blow after blow into him like a piston. The Guraggan stumbled, reaching out with his free hand to steady himself.

Tsi saw her opening, and emptied her pistol into the Guraggan. Most of her shots sparked off the warrior's armor, but one round punctured his knee joint, another tore into his left shoulder. Turon staggered backwards, emitting a strange wheezing growl.

"Strongmind! Cover!" Tsi shouted as she detached a slow-grenade from her belt.

She flung the grenade at the wounded Guraggan, then hurled herself on top of Hiron. Understanding her orders instantly, Strongmind threw himself between Tsi and the blast.

There was a roar, and the room was filled with sparkling shrapnel. It was a weapon designed to counter personal shields, its blast sending out thousands of flechettes at just the right momentum to puncture armor while moving too slowly to cause a force field to react. The fragments had a dream-like quality to them, drifting like snow flakes through the air. The cowering technician's back was turned into a gory mass as she tried to flee, and all of the machines around them were sparking and stuttering as their systems were torn apart by the grenade.

Tsi rose after a few seconds, seeing the strange snowfall of hyper-sharp metal coating the junction. Strongmind was badly damaged, but he was still standing. White synth-muscle showed through his lacerated coat, and a long strand of flesh had been torn from his jaw, exposing the ceramic bones beneath. His right arm, severed at the forearm, hung limp from one side, and the left had been badly damaged. Wordlessly, Strongmind scooped his carbine up in his remaining arm, then looked to Tsi for orders.

But Tsi's attention was focused elsewhere.

Turon was pinned against one wall, his cloak in tatters. Dozens of shards protruded from his armor, but she could still see his chest rising and falling slowly. His augmetic eyes stared at her from within his faceless helm. One hand slowly raised and slapped at a device on his belt, and from within it what seemed to be thousands of black insects began to crawl. They burrowed into his wounds.

A low, growling laugh came from the Guraggan.

Tsi shot him two more times, silencing him. She knew it was only temporary.

"We must retreat," Strongmind said. "Reinforcements are incoming. We do not have sufficient firepower to terminate this hostile."

"Agreed," Tsi said.

She turned to see Hiron on his knees, staring at the ruined body of the technician. The whole junction was a mess of red, the walls scarred with pulse blasts and the air stinking with viscera and burnt ozone.

"We will travel faster without him," Strongmind said quietly. "If it will assuage your guilt, I will terminate him."

"No," Tsi said firmly. She walked to Hiron, knowing she was wasting valuable time.

She'd put enough shot into the Guraggan to blow a hole in a star ship's inner hull, but even now his nanite swarm was slowly stitching him back together. In minutes Turon would be able to stand, not long after that he'd be able to think, fight, kill. Every second was a second closer to being lacerated by mono-wires, or whatever other horrid weapons Turon Chryte kept on himself.

She stood over Hiron, looking down at him. She'd seen the expression on his face before, countless times. He had no training, had never been in a firefight before, and now the reality was hitting home. He was going numb.

"Come on," Tsi said, holding her hand out to him.

Meekly, Hiron took it, and pulled himself up.

Battered and bloody, they set off down the tunnel, Tsi to one side, Strongmind to the other, and Hiron limping along in the middle.

It was a long way to the canyon wall, but they made it. Hiron guided them through a series of twisting corridors and rocky caverns, until at last they reached the vertical shaft that would lead to their freedom.

A maintenance ladder ran up the shaft, alongside an endless system of corroded fans and oxygen scrubbers. It was rusted through in places, clinging to the concrete wall like a skeletal insect. At the top of the ladder, so far away that its dim illumination looked like a star in the night sky, was a landing that led to the surface. Hiron let out a groan.

"We've made it this far," Tsi said.

"We... have," Hiron panted. "But there's no way... no way that ladder can hold... hold your friend."

"You may refer to me by name," Strongmind said.

"It is Strongmind," he added helpfully.

Tsi rubbed her jaw, looking up and down the ladder. The boy was right. She had been the one to scout this exit route alone, while Strongmind had gone to procure a ground crawler from another settlement. She'd assumed that she'd only need to take this route if things went wrong. They had, but she had also assumed she would be making her escape alone. Not with a badly damaged Strongmind and an exhausted boy in tow.

She felt another pang of regret at that thought. She would never have gotten this far without Hiron. It wasn't just that he needed help, she *owed* him.

"I'll go up alone," Tsi said. "There's cord in the ship. Should be sturdy enough to hold both of you."

"I'll come with you," Hiron said quickly.

"No, I can't risk you taking a fall. Once I get the rope, I'll toss it down to Strongmind. He'll secure both of you, then climb up."

"He's only got one arm!"

"It is more than sufficient," Strongmind interjected. "My locomotive capabilities outmatch your own significantly. Even in my damaged state."

"Just hold here until I get back," Tsi said. "Our 'friends' can't be far behind if they intend to pursue us. You've got a clear line of fire down the tunnel."

Tsi pulled a pair of grenades from one of the pouches in her gear, and handed them to Strongmind. As he took them and attached them to his belt, she leaned in close, lips barely moving as she whispered to the machine.

"You keep that boy alive, do you understand? You don't have my permission to let him die."

Strongmind only looked at her, his face placid, the strip of skin still hanging off his exposed jaw.

"I'll try to be as quick as I can," Tsi said as she holstered her pistol and mounted the first rung of the ladder. "You keep following Strongmind's lead, alright, Hiron? I'll be back before you know it."

Hiron watched uncertainly as she grasped the first rung of the ladder. Standing there, small and twisted, holding the rifle of one of his fallen guards, he looked far younger than his years. More like a little boy playing with a toy gun than a warrior.

It was another sight she knew far too well.

Without another word, she began to climb. She worked with a slow, steady tread up the rungs, grasping and testing each bar before she put her whole weight on it. After a few dozen rungs, she risked a glance downwards. Hiron and Strongmind were crouched to either side of the tunnel, their weapons braced. Even at this distance she could see Hiron was shivering, and she suddenly became aware of how damp and cool the tunnel had been.

The feeling left her as she continued her ascent, replaced by a foul humidity. The air turned muggy as she closed with the planet's radiation blasted surface, the dry desert heat mixing with the stagnant, moist tunnel air to create a repulsive miasma. Tsi was beginning to regret leaving her mask behind when she heard the whip crack of a solid round.

She shot a look downward, and saw Strongmind and Hiron opening fire. Hard rounds came screaming out of the tunnel, peppering the walls behind them.

It couldn't be Turon Chryte, the Guraggan would have rushed them with his mono-wire by now. But the fire was too rapid, too aggressive for any of the Inheritors or their mercenaries. Tsi heard a noise above the din, a muffled wailing and moaning. One she recognized.

Chemical Thralls.

Turon was using his slaves to flush them out. There was a resounding boom as Strongmind hurled the first of his grenades, and the noise died for a few moments. Soon it picked up again, the fire intensifying, and now, joining the cacophony, the slap of bare skin against concrete as the Thralls advanced. They'd be coming on at a dead run, undeterred by enemy fire.

Tsi wanted to slide back down the ladder, to go and help the two beleaguered souls below. But she had done this far too many times before. She was at war again.

In War, she reminded herself, there must always be sacrifice.

She continued her climb.

CHAPTER 8

Hiron's hands were shaking. They had come out of the darkness, moving like scavenging animals. Their faces were hidden beneath helmets festooned with sensor lights, and they seemed to thrust them forwards, sniffing the air as much as seeing with their eyes. Most were bare chested, their clothing little more than rags rotting off them. A few were completely naked. Their bodies were slim and wiry, cybernetics bursting the flesh of some, others carrying weapons bolted to raw skin.

All of them quivered in unison as a thin beam of yellow light crossed over Hiron's trembling hand. A strange smell came from them, sweet and cloying, and suddenly their muscles tensed, and they began their sorrowful wail.

Strongmind was the first to fire. Disciplined blasts of pulse shot cut into their ranks, sending the wailing cyborgs tumbling backwards. In an instant they were returning fire, their chattering weapons ripping the air all around Hiron.

He jerked back into the cover of the tunnel's edge. His heart was in his throat, his vision blurring. He felt as though his twisted legs were going to jerk out from beneath him.

A thunderous explosion sucked the wind from his chest, deafening and blinding him all at once. He gasped and sputtered for breath, numb to the world around him, white knuckles around the barrel of his gun. He could only hear one noise, a steady, heavy drum beat in his ears, the same pattern repeating over and over again. As his vision cleared, he realized they were words, repeated over and over.

"SUPPORTING FIRE IS REQUIRED! SUPPORTING FIRE IS REQUIRED! SUPPORTING FIRE IS REQUIRED!"

Strongmind was shouting at him, but the machine's face was slack. The words were said loudly, quickly, but there was no emotion in them. The machine continued to fire its pulse carbine one handed, then pull back, awkwardly reload it, and lean out to fire again.

Hiron peered around the corner. The dead were piling up. Severed limbs were scattered everywhere, blood painted the walls, yet on the creatures came, sprinting across the backs of their fallen comrades,. There was something grimly comical about them, tripping and slipping and falling over each other, scrabbling along the ground in their rush to get to grips with their enemy. Some were panting lustfully, bodies slick with that sweetly stinking sweat. Others let out that same terrible moan.

Hiron raised the carbine to his shoulder. He did not pick a target, just pulled the trigger and felt the weapon jolt in his hands. He did it again and again, until he realized he had closed his eyes and the weapon was no longer firing. He stared dumb struck at the oncoming horde, then felt something hard crash into him.

It was Strongmind, the machine's damaged shoulder smashing Hiron into the wall, and out of the hail of fire raking towards him. Senseless to the blasts ripping through its chest and abdomen, Strongmind returned fire, then dropped its weapon as it, too, went dry.

The machine pulled back into the alcove with Hiron. Fire was chipping away at the edge of the tunnel as the horde staggered towards them. Broad back pressed flat against the wall, fluid leaking from dozens of wounds, Strongmind stared straight forwards.

"Tactical Assessment," Strongmind said. "Ammunition depleted. Effective weapons stores: Fists. One High Explosive Grenade. Mission Parameters: Evacuate area. Ensure Hiron Dath's Survival. Ensure this unit's survival."

"Are... are you talking to me?" Hiron asked.

"I am running scenarios. Our evacuation is unlikely. I cannot allow myself to be taken intact. Your capture would also ensure the exposure of mission critical details. Our mutual termination is the optimal course of action, given imminent catastrophic mission failure."

Strongmind drew the last grenade from his belt.

"What?! You're going to blow us up?!"

"Catastrophic mission failure is increasingly likely. If it will aid you psychologically, you should know that the Guraggan would certainly execute you after thorough interrogation and torture. I assess that Lady Ikanus would also engage in inflicting seriously physical and mental harm upon you."

"Tsi's coming back!"

"Unlikely. Upon arriving at our ship she must calculate, as I have, the time it will take to acquire the cord, return, secure both of us, and provide cover for our escape. Knowing that I have tertiary suicide parameters, her optimal course of action would be to abandon us."

Hiron stared wide eyed as the machine armed the grenade.

"If you wish, I can also break your neck instead. The grenade will be significantly more efficient, but some humans have expressed this preference in the past."

"Wait! Look!"

Hiron pointed a shaking finger. There, just alongside the rusting ladder, pooled a coil of thick, silver cord. Looking up the ladder they saw the tiny figure of Tsi in the distance, high above, waving her arms frantically at them. She had tied the cord tight at her end, and was gesturing furiously for them to come up.

"It seems I have miscalculated," Strongmind said.

Without hesitation, it stepped out into the open and hurled the grenade down the tunnel. There was a second deafening explosion. Even as Hiron was reeling from the shock, Strongmind had grabbed him and begun wrapping the cord around both their waists. In seconds, they were tied tightly together.

Strongmind began a furious ascent, pushing off the wall with its legs and pulling them up the rope with its one arm. Despite the machine's incredible strength, their movement upwards was slow and erratic, with Hiron awkwardly doing his best to help, wedged as he was between Strongmind's massive frame and the concrete wall. His back scraped against it as they climbed, carried upwards by powerful shoves of the machine's legs against the wall and its single hand, snapping upwards, seizing the rope, snapping up, and seizing it again.

Even as shots sparked around him, Hiron marveled at how embarrassed he was to be carried up the wall like a child. Every impact against the concrete hurt, but still he could not help but think on the fact that Tsi was watching their climb. He felt like an idiot. Not only was he going to die, he was going to die in a stinking filter chute, being scraped to death against a wall by a mad android while the most beautiful woman he'd ever seen watched.

Hiron laughed.

Something stung him, just below his navel, and he felt a strange, cold wetness begin to spread. As he was jerked back and slammed into the wall again by Strongmind's movement, pain suddenly shot through his whole body. He cried out.

No, not his whole body. He couldn't feel his legs.

He looked down to see he had been shot somewhere near his waist. His red blood was mixing with the oily fluids leaking from Strongmind's many wounds, and he realized the stray round must have torn through both of them. He suddenly felt weaker than he ever had. His hands were shaking, but the rest of his body was going limp.

He could hear the machine speaking to him. Its voice was very far away. It was giving Hiron instructions, but he couldn't move, couldn't understand a word that was said.

"Hold on to me, please. Hold on to me, please. Hold on. Hold on. Hold on."

CHAPTER 9

Tsi had flattened herself against the ledge, peering down the shaft as Strongmind and Hiron climbed up. She was cursing herself again. She should have brought more weapons, more explosives, or at least stashed more equipment here. She'd wasted precious time in the ship hunting up the cord, and hadn't remembered to secure any of the heavy firepower they kept in it. Now she had nothing but her short-ranged Repeater, while the Guraggan Chem-Thralls had their plethora of weapons, tearing up the walls all around Strongmind as he continued to climb.

They weren't good shots, which was a small blessing, but they put enough fire into the air that it was a simple matter of odds they would hit something. She saw it happen twice. First a round tore into Strongmind's back, one of a multitude of wounds the AI had taken. He was built to take damage, but he wasn't invincible. Every shot was slowing him down, and it was a miracle none of his critical hardware had been damaged. The second time the shot came in low, ripping through Strongmind's back and into Hiron.

For a moment, she thought they would both fall, but Strongmind caught them, steadied them by bracing his legs against the wall, and then began to climb again. Unflagging, the machine pressed on, though his metallic innards were clearly visible and long strips of synthetic muscle hung limply from his limbs.

Uselessly, Tsi aimed and fired her gun, but she knew there was no hope of her stopping the milling throng below. The thralls had rushed forwards, begun to crowd around the base of the shaft. Some were trying fruitlessly to climb the ladder, their weight tearing the decayed metal to shreds, while others continued to fire their weapons in wild sweeps.

Another round struck Strongmind. Then another. The Machine stopped, dangling in mid-air, his one arm clutching the rope tight, trying to cradle Hiron close to him with the severed stump of his other limb. As they slowly spun in the air, suspended like the carcasses of Gene-Bears on Goodhome, fire licked all around them. There was only one thing to do.

Tsi holstered her gun. She spat into her hands, grabbed the rope, and heaved. She heaved again, engaging every one of the muscles in her body, straining as she pulled the two of them bodily up the shaft.

She screwed her eyes tight, still hearing the whistle of rounds, feeling them snap past her. She heard the thud of rounds hitting Strongmind's back, and prayed that the machine could endure a little longer.

Finally, her hands raw and slick, she gave one last mighty heave, practically flattening herself. Strongmind's hand shot above the lip of the ledge, and he hoisted the inert Hiron upwards, then clambered up after. A round had exploded in Strongmind's left cheek, ripping it open. He now had a ghoulish half-skull for a face. His eyes were dead, and his limbs moved stiffly as he began to drag Hiron along the ground.

Allowing herself no respite, Tsi grabbed the boy's other arm, and together the two of them staggered into the open sunlight.

It was a dozen yards to their ship. She was a craft of beautiful, blue metal. She looked out of place against the crimson wasteland and the sick yellow sky. The heat was horrific after the damp confines of the tunnel network, but Tsi's pace did not slow. She'd left the loading ramp down, and together with Strongmind she dragged Hiron up it.

She'd had a crash-bed installed a long time ago, but the truth was she was never much of a healer. Gingerly as she could, she lifted the boy into the bed and strapped him down. She attached a breathing mask to him, set the auto-doc to emergency, then sprinted to the cockpit and began prepping for take off.

Strongmind had already staggered in and strapped himself into the co-pilot's chair. He was moving slowly, and his badly damaged hand barely managed to thrust the data-link into his head, but he had the engines on and running as Tsi sat down. They exchanged no words as the ship lifted off from the dusty surface of the world. They charted a course, low and fast, across the horizon. The Guraggan would surely have seen them, but her little ship was swifter than it looked, and all she had to do was get clear enough to activate the Slip drive. Once that was on, they could jump to dead space and plot their next move.

Where to, she did not know.

The ship began to shake as it broke atmosphere, the hull super-heating. Her instruments were feeding her endless strings of data. Massive objects above them. Tachyon clusters. There was something wrong. As they moved away from the poisoned sky of Promise, Tsi saw it in one of her view screens.

Thousands of craft floated in space, so many that they could be seen with the naked eye. Crimson-hulled and angular, bearing the spider-like script of the Guraggan, it was a fleet so vast it seemed to swallow the moon as it moved in slow synchronicity. Such a gathering of war ships had not been seen since the Janissaries routed the Guraggan at the close of their great war.

It made no sense. So many ships, arriving so quickly would have overloaded any standard Slip-Path. It was too much mass, too much energy. They would have crashed into each other, caused a micro-singularity and never returned to real space. She could see on the scanner they were surrounded by a debris field, as if they had already fought their way through a terrible battle, but the Inheritors had no ships capable of standing against such a fleet.

Tsi thought of the Dreaming Stars for no reason she could name, and felt a terrible dread.

There were other craft fleeing the atmosphere of the Inheritor's world. Personal ships of clan lords perhaps, or the few off-world merchants who came to Promise. Dozens of them scattered in all directions, like a herd of animals stalked by predators. The Guraggan vessels pounced upon them, lances of blue light ripping through the void, swarms of fighters raking the bigger, slower ships with shot.

A few fighters swept towards Tsi, but she was far from the greatest concentration of fleeing ships. The ship rocked as a missile exploded off her port side, spraying the ship's hull with debris. Warning lights flared, but the damage wasn't enough to slow her down. Tsi took the ship through a dizzying array of maneuvers, altering course erratically while the Guraggan fighters blazed away. Another salvo took her in the port side, but Tsi kept her ship dancing. Soon enough the fighters broke off contact, returning to the fleet to seek easier prey.

Her scanners told her more ships were headed her way, but by then she had charted a course for empty space. She was lucky that the Inheritor's system was so barren. In less than an hour there was no significant mass concentration around her, and she was able to activate her drive, and jump into the darkness of the Slip.

Sitting in that silent blackness, Tsi at last allowed herself to breath and take stock. Strongmind was sitting next to her, on minimal power. He looked like a puppet with its strings cut. So much of his body had been destroyed, it was a miracle he could function at all, and all of the damage made him look like some morbid thing stitched together by a madman. He'd need a new body soon, if they could find him one.

She rose and walked back to the crash-table. The auto-doc's silvery limbs were cutting away at Hiron's clothes, pulling bullet fragments from him, stitching his flesh. Syringes of blue fluid pumped into the boy's small, twisted body. He was breathing, but whether he would walk again, or live, or die, Tsi could not say.

She sat down cross-legged on the floor, and watched the spider limbs work for a while. His body was so frail, so wounded. Every shallow breath was a struggle. He'd never seen a battle before today. Tsi thought of Strongmind, all but a corpse in his chair. Then, she looked down at her own hands.

There was not a scratch on them.

PART 2

SALVATION

CHAPTER 10

The Slip drive hummed gently in the background while Tsi sat on her bunk. Worries coursed through her mind. Strongmind's body was crippled. Linked to the piloting circuitry of her ship, he was guiding them along the strange pathways of Slip Space, but his physical form could barely move. An hour or two into their journey, he had risen from his console and tried to walk.

Instead, he had fallen flat on his face. When he tried to stand, all his legs did was jerk awkwardly against the ground. It was comical and pitiable, seeing him squirm there like a beetle on its back. Tsi had helped him into his chair without a word. Neither of them spoke of what had happened for the rest of the journey.

Hiron's heart was still beating. The auto-doc had done as much repair work as could be expected. Now all that she could do was wait and see if he woke up. The surgery machine was a very a basic model: good for patching up broken bones and the odd laser wound, but not terribly sophisticated. The boy was already so weak, Tsi wasn't sure what the drugs would do to him.

He had been spectacularly unlucky even before he was born: he had the ear-marks of a dozen genetic abnormalities and conditions, not to mention his obvious deformity. The Inheritors were too primitive or too proud to engage in the gene-editing of their children, and so he had come into the world a weakling on a planet of warriors.

Tsi had traveled far in her many years, and Hiron's kin filled her with a mix of revulsion and sympathy. So far from every other civilized world, they tried to do with crude eugenics and brutal indoctrination what the scientists of Kios had perfected nearly a century ago. The most ferocious of the Inheritors could never hope to compare to a Kiosan Janissary.

They were super-human genetic chimeras, each one pulled

forth from a clone-womb ready for battle. Unequaled in combat by anyone save the Guraggan, their bodies were superior to any naturally born human to have ever lived. The only thing they lacked was the ability to reproduce naturally. They were soldiers after all, their lot was to die for the Empire, and so in this alone they were inferior, even to poor, weak little Hiron.

What a miserable thing, Tsi thought, to have so little control over one's fate. It was a small wonder they had overthrown their Empress and seized Kios for themselves, just as the Dath Clan's rivals had banded together and risen against Hiron's people. Tsi wondered if Brem Dath's head was being presented to baying crowds, just as the Janissaries had held up a bloody mass of pulp and declared it the head of their Empress.

She swung herself off of her bunk, bare feet gently making contact with the warm metal grating of her cabin floor. Her quarters were sparsely furnished: she had an old armored EVA suite suspended on one wall, and a few gadgets she was constantly tinkering with at her little work bench. On another wall she had stacked up crates of foodstuffs and other supplies. Guns, explosives, useful wherever one went across the cosmos. Other than that the room was bare, except for the shrine.

It was a small thing, made of plastic and wire. A figure of a faceless man with a single eye sat cross legged, wearing an artist's rendition of a vacuum suit. In one arm he cradled a naked infant, while his other hand was held in a ritual pose.

He was a syncretic god, worshiped in many places but prayed to particularly by pirates and mercenaries. There were quite a few names for him, but Tsi had always liked "The Forgiver". He was a god of fate, chance, death, and mercy. A junker had sold the statue to her for half a credit and what was left of a packet of Red-Chew. Tsi had never put much stock in gods, but now, thinking about Strongmind and Hiron, and everything that had happened, she slowly took a knee in front of the little figurine.

She was bringing her hands up from her sides, starting to interlock her fingers, when something stopped her. She stood up. It was pointless, she chided herself. Besides, what right did she have to pray?

"I think I might have had a dream," Strongmind said.

They were working at their consoles in the cockpit. It had been about seventy hours, relative, since they entered the Slip. In that time Strongmind had said very little to her, save to answer questions when she asked. He spent most of his time on minimal power, devoting some of his processors to calculating their course while the rest stopped functioning to conserve energy. The drone body had some basic self-repair functions, but nothing that could totally restore him anytime soon. He still couldn't move without her helping him, and had stayed in his chair most of the time.

"It's not unheard of," Tsi said idly as she checked over the scanners. They were making good time. "Your designers might have put in something like that, for a lot of reasons."

"Are you trying to reassure me?"

"Strongmind..." she began, swiveling her chair to face her companion.

She was used to the horror that was his body now. Tsi had planned on repairing his face a little, but there had been so much to do on the ship that all she had managed was to strip away some of the bits of artificial skin that had come loose, exposing a patchwork of ceramic skull and metal pistons beneath. One of his eyes was still just a monochrome sphere, which drew attention to how eerily inhuman his other, fleshy replica was. The facade of false-humanity had been destroyed, exposing the simulacra beneath.

She was surprised to see that his Interface Simulation Algorithms were on. He was breathing regularly, and his brow was slightly furrowed as he looked at her.

"I am not disturbed at the prospect of having dreams," Strongmind insisted.

"I'm sure you aren't," Tsi said. "I shouldn't have assumed. You've just, you've taken a lot of damage. I thought maybe—"

"I am not susceptible to trauma the way a human is. You should know that. I once suffered a critical hull breach twenty meters from the Engine's core. Oxygen levels were severely depleted, a fire broke out on four different levels, and severe plasma leaks decreased our maneuverability by forty seven percent. If my memory fragments are correct, I dealt with the matter efficiently and achieved total tactical victory. The event had no perceptible impact on my performance in my next six engagements."

"I'm sure you're very proud of that."

"I transmit this data to you to correct any assumptions you have regarding my ability to function under difficult circumstances."

"I don't doubt your courage Strongmind. You did very well back on the Inheritor's World."

"I performed efficiently."

"You did," Tsi sighed. Sometimes Strongmind was utterly inscrutable to her. Other times, he reminded her of a small child.

"May I tell you about my dream?" Strongmind asked.

"Sure," Tsi said. "I'd like very much to hear about it."

"I dreamed of the engagement I described. I believe I was experiencing a memory. I remember the Captain indistinctly, and I remember Engines and Pilot very well. Their data transmission was very efficient. They were effective intelligence."

"They were your friends," Tsi said quietly, smiling.

"They were part of me," Strongmind said. "Engines, Pilot, Weapons. The triumvirate which formed the intelligence of the Ship. We fought together many times. Crossed vast distances. Our crews, our captains came and went. But we were always together."

"I'm sorry," Tsi said. "It can't be easy to be alone."

"It does not matter. I still have function. Remembering them is not what perplexed me about my dream."

Strongmind faltered here. His flesh eye looked downwards. Tsi could never be sure, but she thought he looked embarrassed.

"I do not know which side I was fighting for," Strongmind said. "I do not even know what part of the galaxy I was in, or what name I was called. I only remember that I fought. Why did you not save that data?"

"I could only recover so much from the salvage pod, and I didn't have the storage space for everything I found," Tsi began, the words well-rehearsed. "I've told you this before Strongmind. I am truly, truly sorry I couldn't recover everything. A lot of your data... it was corrupted, or contradictory, or I couldn't begin to make sense of it. I saved the basics of your personality, and as much of your abilities as I could, but your memories..."

"You sorted them by tactical function," Strongmind said. "I

remember Guraggan boarding strategies, but not whether I *used* them or fought *against* them. I know the weaknesses of 3,217 standard combat craft, but not which kind I was. I can speak almost every human language, but I do not remember how my Captains spoke to me."

"Strongmind, believe me, if I had had the time, I would have gone over that pod inch by inch to figure out who you really are. But things were hectic, and I needed you as quick as I could—"

"You made an efficient choice," Strongmind said. "I commend you. I would have done the same."

"Thanks," Tsi replied, swiveling her chair back around. "I really appreciate it."

"They're the best I could manage with what we have here," Tsi explained. "I want you to know that they're only temporary."

Hiron was sitting on the edge of the auto-doc, naked except for a wrap around his waist. He gingerly strapped the crutches to his forearms, and slowly began to test his weight against them. A shiver passed through the boy, despite the heat of the ship. For what seemed an eternity he studied the crutches, then finally hoisted himself off of the auto-doc, awkwardly standing with as much of his weight put on them as possible. His legs were scarred and twisted, and only one foot could be planted fully on the ground. He looked like a bizarre human tripod, his back hunched, fingers wrapped tight around the grips of the crutches.

Then, he shuffled deftly around the room, completing three full circuits while Tsi watched. He was panting slightly by the time he was done, but she was amazed that he could move so well after such a long time in surgery. He seemed almost to move more swiftly and surely on his braces than he had on two legs. His face, however, betrayed neither pride nor satisfaction, only resignation.

"I had to use these when I was younger," Hiron explained. "It took years to get my legs strong enough to walk on my own. I thought my father would be so proud of me..."

He laughed bitterly.

"I was wrong," he said.

"It's only temporary," Tsi repeated. "As soon as I can take you to a proper cyber-medical facility, we'll see about getting you something more permanent."

Hiron shrugged.

"Thank you. But really, it's nothing to bother yourself about. I'm a cripple after all, a weakling. Enough of a liability to you already, you don't have to—"

"Don't talk about yourself like that," Tsi snapped. "Not in front of me. Not ever. Do you understand?"

"It's the truth."

"It's nonsense. You saved my life, remember? I owe you for that. And I won't hear anyone as brave as you insulted."

The boy smiled. He looked like he was on the verge of tears. Quickly, Tsi thrust a data pad into one of his hands.

"No one rides on my ship for free, though," Tsi said. "I've got your clothes set up in your bunk. Get dressed, then go down in the hold and start taking inventory. And size yourself for an EVA suit while you're there. There should be a few about your measure, with a little modification."

Hiron stared mutely at her.

"I don't have all day," Tsi said.

"You... uh, you want me to do all this?"

"Yes," Tsi said, folding her arms.

"But this is... this is real work. Like-like I'm part of your crew."

Tsi nodded. The boy's smile got wider, and he shambled off down the corridor, the data pad tucked snugly under his arm. Tsi wasn't certain, but she could've sworn he started whistling a tune as he rounded the corner.

She smiled to herself. The boy had no idea how long she'd spent watching over his comatose body, or that she, too, had almost wept with joy when his heartbeat strengthened, and his eyes finally opened. Almost, but not quite.

Tears were a luxury after all, and she did not have time for them now.

The three of them crowded the cockpit as they dropped out of Slip Space. There was a familiar groan as the ship transitioned back to normal reality, its sub-light engines kicking in and following the course that Strongmind had plotted. The ship was a dual-purpose atmospheric and space-borne craft, and so it afforded the rare luxury of a transparent canopy around the cockpit that gave them a view of their surroundings.

As the strange blur of the Slip disappeared around them, it was replaced with a sight that never failed to stir Tsi's heart: the endless stars. Billions of points of light flickered around them, blue, white, yellow, red. She could see the green tinge of a gaseous nebulae, billions of kilometers distant yet still visible to the naked eye, and she smiled at the realization that Strongmind had set this course in particular. There were many ways to exit the Slip and approach their destination, and the machine had chosen the scenic route that gave them a full view of Blake's Nebulae.

"Where are we?" Hiron asked.

The boy's voice was barely more than a whisper. He had only glimpsed the stars from his little observatory, staring at them through crude telescopes or grainy viewing screens. It was a world that had existed only in his mind, guesses conjured up by equations and calculations, to him surely as much of a fantasy as the tales told to children to make them sleep. Yet now, here he was standing before a field of blazing suns and roaring pulsars, seeing comets streak past like flights of birds.

For the briefest moment, Tsi felt pride.

"A tri-solar system beyond the Epilotii Mandate," Strongmind said blandly. "Its Kiosan stellar catalog designation is Zeta-114, the Guraggan call it the "Poison Suns", but it is commonly known as Noxia."

"Noxia," Hiron whispered, voice half fear, half wonder. "I've heard of this place. It's a pirate den isn't it?"

"Among other things," Tsi said.

The ship's cockpit swung round as they glided across the inky dark, blue jets burning behind them. A single, dimly glowing crimson orb hove into view. Tendrils of red light seemed to leak from around it, trailing in the ether like strands of hair. Slowly, a black object crossed the distant sun, a curious interloper far smaller and yet billions of kilometers closer to the ship.

It was a space station, a set of four long metallic loops slowly circling around a metal ovoid in the center. Despite their vast distance, the station appeared distinct to the naked eye, a testimony to its sheer size.

"Salvation," Tsi said. "That's where we're headed. We'll make some repairs, refuel and plot our next move."

"Look at that!" Hiron shouted.

A strand of blue-green light slowly undulated far above and beyond the station, moving like some massive serpent before slowly fading into the blackness surrounding them.

"A Kerenkov Snake," Strongmind said. "Unusual phenomenon observed only in the Noxian system. It consists mostly of hard radiation and irregular photonic activity. There is no consistent explanation for their behavior, or predictive method for their arrival and disappearance."

"Incredible," Hiron breathed.

"Dangerous," Tsi said. "They interfere with instruments, tear ship's hulls apart. More than half the hulks in-system are caused by things like that. That's why we're not going any deeper into the system than Salvation."

"But people live farther in, don't they? Closer to the sun. Salvation's just at the edge."

"It is," Tsi said. "It's actually one of the farthest points you can get while still being within useful sub-light distance of the asteroids and the other stations. And yes, there are people deeper in the system than Salvation. But what they do... I wouldn't call it living. I'd call it surviving. By any means necessary."

Salvation, strictly speaking, did have laws and a government. Station-Head was the technical dictator and final authority of the entire massive construct, a post created untold centuries ago when the first pioneers came to this star, seeking to set up mining colonies among its rich asteroid belts. However, in practical terms every section of each of the two rings had its own sub-dictators and councils, and given that every Noxian had a secondary profession as a scavenger, hijacker, or pirate, the strict "Law" on Salvation tended to be most accurately translated as "how much pull you have with the people with the most guns." Which, Tsi supposed, wasn't that different from anywhere else in the universe.

They started negotiations an hour out from the ring, slowing their thrusters and drifting on inertia with only minor course corrections. Tsi found a communications band in Panglos, the most common of the trader languages and one she spoke very well. She began asking for coordinates and docking permission, and immediately received a barrage of questions about her cargo and business on the station.

"Just travelers," she said. "We need some repairs and equipment."

"You have money?" the voice on the other end of the comms growled.

"Some," Tsi lied. "Barter mostly."

"Good, good. Hate people coming in, thinking Kiosan chits mean anything out here. You gotta know, you'll be docking at Station 74. This is the territory of Jarawat and the Ten Sons. You behave yourself, don't break their rules, don't take anything that isn't yours, and we'll be fine. Understood?"

"Understood," Tsi said.

"Good. Welcome to Salvation, traveler."

CHAPTER 11

Enlil was slumped at the bar, sucking on a globe that she was promised contained at least three different kinds of alcohol. It gave her belly that familiar warmth, and she gagged slightly after every pull, so she had to assume this was the good stuff. At least, as good as it got out here.

She studied the globe in her hand. It was slightly pliable, caving in with the pressure of her hands. They were good in zero-g, which was funny because one of the main claims to fame of Salvation was that it had reliably functioning a-grav. Of all the space stations in Noxia, it was the largest, and the farthest from the dying red giant at the heart of the system.

Salvation was how a lot of people came in to this horrible patch of space. Not her, though. She'd been born in the Mid Stations. Her parents had always talked about Salvation like it was the last stop before you escaped. Practically heaven; hence the name.

In Enlil's estimation, it was just as shitty as the rest of this place.

"Well, well, well. If it ain't the Gilded Lily."

Enlil didn't turn. She knew the voice well enough. She could picture the speaker's thick red face and black stubble without turning around.

"Tha's not my name," she slurred, drunker than she realized.

"Oh, sure it is. Sure it is. Yoch, look at this. Have you met her before?"

"Nope."

A woman's voice, reedy and thin. Someone who smoked too much Yellow Root. Probably half blissed-out right now.

"Turn around Gilded Lilly. I want my friend Yoch to see you."

Enlil sucked down the last few drops of liquor from the globe and set it on the bar. She spun around and stepped from her stool unsteadily. Her vision was a little blurry, but she tried to straighten herself out, thrusting her hands into the pockets of her soft suit.

The speaker laid a heavy hand on her shoulder, gripping tight and steadying her. She looked into the grinning face of Bragen. He was flanked by a tall woman with a long neck and a nose that looked like a beak.

"Killed Captain Black, she did. Made that big score on all that Cold Salvage a while back. You 'member that, Yoch?"

"Yup," Yoch said.

"How'd'ya spend it Lilly? Tell her, I always get a kick out of this."

Enlil could feel bile rising at the back of her throat. She swayed on her heels.

"What do... ya want, Bragen?" she asked.

"Oh, come on," Bragen insisted, his hand never leaving her shoulder. "We can talk business any time. Yoch here wants to hear what you did with all that money. Don't you, Yoch?"

"I want to hear it."

"Spent it," Enlil said. "Come on Bragen, I'm not... not in the mood t'day."

"Ah, you're no fun!" Bragen grinned. "Should I tell the story? See, this kid right here, she gets one of the biggest scores anyone's ever done. And you know what she does with it? Drinks it, snorts it, jabs it, *all* in three weeks! Three stinkin' weeks and it's gone! Can you imagine? She's still standing, too! Not the first time she's done it, neither. O'er and o'er again. Gods and spirits, my old heart couldn't take that."

Bragen laughed heartily. Yoch gave a mirthless chuckle.

"More money than most folk'll ever see. Coulda got outta here. Could have seen the rest of the systems. But no, Yoch, you see what we have here?" Bragen pulled Enlil's hood back, letting her greasy hair spill out. He stroked her cheek with the back of his hand. Her jaw set, but she didn't move.

"What we got here is one-hundred-percent Noxian Scavver. She's an oxygen-rat, born and raised. You could give her a Warship and a Legion of Janissaries, and she'd use 'em to rob tramp freighters and get soused. Get her a ticket on a long trawler to anywhere in space, and she'd huck it for half price and go get herself a two-suit or a jab of

Grey. Ha!"

Bragen leaned in conspiratorially. She could smell the old sweat coming from his collar. The man hadn't left the station in years, but like every Noxian he wore his vacuum suit everywhere, just in case.

"I don't think I've ever seen anything more pathetic than you, Enlil. And I been here most of my life, too."

"Fuck you," Enlil grunted back.

Bragen released her, his arms raised in mock offense.

"Such language! Gods and Spirits, how will I ever deal with a fearsome little thing like you! I practically soiled my skin-suit, I did."

"I'm gone," Enlil said, making to brush by them.

Yoch grabbed her and shoved her roughly against the bar. One arm rammed up against her throat, while the other hand grabbed Enlil's wrist as it went for her survival knife.

"You owe me money, Gilded Lily," Bragen said coolly. "I know you been working. Where is it?"

"Back at my locker, I was on my way to—"

"I ain't a feec-rec, so don't try to feed me shit," Bragen said. "We busted your locker. Nothing in there but rotten Rat-Paks and a broken rad counter. But, you seem to have been having a merry old time here... and from the looks of that suck-globe on the counter, I think you already spent your pay, didn't you?"

Enlil didn't answer. Maybe if she hadn't been drunk she could have taken them, but she had her doubts. She hadn't lived this long by being stupid. Or proud.

"Look, I'll line up another job, I'll sign a contract with the ship's AI to transfer to you direct, and—"

"No, Enlil. It ain't like that. You don't pay me back, and people talk. Yoch, left hand. Pinkie and pointer."

Yoch back-handed Enlil and had her left hand in a vice grip in seconds. It seemed to take forever for her little finger to snap, but her index finger broke much more quickly. Enlil shrieked and cursed and curled in on herself. Yoch kicked her in the stomach, grabbed her by the hair and hurled her to the ground.

"Flip her over. I want that knife," Bragen said.

Enlil roared and tried to force herself up, but Yoch's wiry limbs were stronger. She tried to keep her good hand on the scabbard at her thigh, slapped ineffectively at the big woman with her broken left, but it was useless. She caught a straight punch to her jaw, then another landed squarely on her nose, knocking the back of her head hard into the dirty bar room floor. Yoch ripped the knife away from her.

As the two thugs walked away, Enlil rolled onto her stomach. Her vision was blurry, and she spat blood.

"Hey! How the fuck am I supposed to work with a busted hand an' no knife?!" she shouted after them.

Bragen just waived his hand airily. Enlil screamed curses after the two of them as they left the bar until she was hoarse, then collapsed. She lay in a puddle of her own blood and filth for a long time, pain searing through her left hand, letting out the occasional sob. At last she pushed herself up on one arm, and staggered out of the bar.

All around her, patrons were still drinking and chattering as if nothing had happened. Yoch could have stomped her head in, and no one would have batted an eye or raised a hand. Enlil had no patch, and no crew. Unless it was to pick her pocket, or haul off her dead carcass to be sold down market, the rest of Salvation couldn't care less. Salvation wasn't any different from anywhere else in Noxia. The people were all the same.

Then again, so was she.

They drifted towards the coordinates their growling interlocutor provided, sending out the odd scan pulse. There were other ships coming and going. Despite Noxia's harsh reputation and remoteness, merchants still traveled here regularly. There was a fortune to be made in salvage, as well as the rare metals dug up from the barely functioning asteroid mining stations. Tsi kept their own transponder codes switched to an old pseudonym of hers, a trader ship from Lenettella she'd worked on for a few years, not too long after she first arrived on the Frontier. The ship itself was long since gone, but she was obscure enough and generic enough that no one would ask questions about receiving a pulse from an old merchantman.

"It's huge," Hiron beamed as they came closer to the ring, their view slowly filled by endless fields of grey metal. Scanning towers jutted haphazardly from a surface scarred by asteroid impacts and the odd missile strike, giving it the look of one immense monochrome city. Thousands of lights, tiny portholes and vast viewing galleries, dotted the surface of the station.

"It is an average structure for its function," Strongmind pointed out. "The Kiosan Janissariat has eighty-four defensive fortifications approximately two-to-three times the size this station. Before its destruction, the Guraggan "Siege Victorious" was roughly four times this station's mass—"

"Strongmind, he's never seen something like this. Give him a break," Tsi chided.

"I thought he would benefit from further information," Strongmind replied. "If he reacts with shock to every megastructure we encounter, we may suffer a tactical deficit."

Tsi rolled her eyes.

"I'm sorry," Hiron said, still smiling as they closed in on the massive docking bay. "I just... I read about things like this back home. Our space station's tiny, and the Clans all fight over who gets to administrate it. Some of the commoners don't even know it exists. Yet this thing... it's bigger than Dath Stronghold! And you're telling me it's small?"

"Not small," Tsi said. "Average."

"Huh."

They came for a slow, graceful landing in one of the docking bays, its surface exposed to the empty void. Once their landing gear was out and magnetized, Tsi transmitted a signal to the dock master, letting them know that they could be closed in and air cycled back into the dock. It was a dull process, watching the massive hatch close on the bay, sealing them in darkness for what seemed like ages before the lights finally came back on.

The docking bay itself was also a haphazard mechanic's shop. Tsi could see equipment secured to the deck and half-done repair jobs all around. A quick check of the scan showed that the bay had been filled with an oxygen-nitrogen mix not unusual for a habitable planet. Looking out of the cockpit window, Tsi saw a group of technicians emerging from a port in the far wall. They were all wearing heavy duty work suits, and still had oxygen masks on as an added precaution. Noxians knew better than to trust that hull-seals wouldn't fail, living their entire lives as they did mere meters from the endless void.

They were carrying tools, crates of basic repair equipment, but she noted without surprise that two at the rear wore body armor and carried shotguns. All of them had crew patches on their suits: a beautiful siren clenching a dagger in her teeth. Crew and clan affiliation was important here. Tsi had briefly considered making some sort of patch or symbol for the ship, but she decided it would be a waste of time. The Noxians would spot them for outsiders the moment they set foot on Salvation.

The leader halted before the nose of the ship, waiting for her to come out. He wiped down the front of his suit by way of greeting.

"Strongmind, get yourself ready," Tsi said. "Make sure your face is covered. Hiron, help him and do whatever he asks. I'll go handle our docking fee."

Repeater at her hip, long cloak draped over her shoulders, her face unconcealed, Tsi lowered the loading ramp and walked boldly down among the Noxian repair crew. They sized her up with their eyes, a few of the technicians gripping spanners and spot welders like cudgels. The two most obviously armed guards took a step towards her as she approached, but they kept their weapons low. The head tech was the first to speak.

"Good lookin' ship. She a custom? She's been around for sure, but this thing looks top of the line."

"It works," Tsi said.

"How many crew?"

"Three of us are coming on station," Tsi said. "We'll be two days at most."

"Sure, sure. You ever been to Salvation before?"

Tsi didn't answer, only folded her arms and set her jaw.

"Well, you should know the rules here are a little different. From this deck all the way to Seal Nineteen and the Red Breach, that's all the Jarawat's territory. We keep things nice and clean, we don't like trouble. You got a dispute, you settle it down in the bilges. No gunfights on the main decks. Makes sense?"

"Sure."

"Jarawat's a gentle being. She doesn't take kindly to people killing each other in her section of the ring without cause. Does that make sense too?"

"Sure."

"Alright then. What're you offering for our hospitality and protection."

"Whatever cut you take from the local bars and shops, plus

eight kilos of protein to repair my outer hull."

"Eight kilos? I think you don't get how this works. See, you pay to dock here, and you pay to get your ship fixed. Two separate charges."

"Actually," Tsi said, "I know exactly how this works. Every establishment in this ring pays your organization protection money. I pay them, they pay you, you spend the money to maintain the dock. You add a fee on top of that to fleece brain-dead pilgrims. Not real spacers. Not people who know how Noxia works. Eight kilos is what I'm paying."

The head tech pulled off his oxygen mask with a wet plop, the suction seal releasing from his raw, stubbly skin. He had thick dreadlocks tied back from his scalp, and a scar ran down over one iris-less eye. An old fighter. Not a successful one either, given that he'd never had his eye replaced. She wasn't surprised to see he was smiling.

"Eight kilos huh? That's not bad. But poor people don't travel in a ship like that. Now, what's to keep me an' my pals from ventilating you, storming that ship, fragging your friends and takin' it for a prize?"

"It's got a kill-switch inside it. It needs a code from me or my mates to operate. Without that, it's just dead scrap."

The head tech rubbed his chin.

"Chassis' still worth a lot. There's ways around kill-switches too. Sorry, traveler, you'll have to do better than that."

Tsi sighed. She reached down, and rolled up her left sleeve, exposing her skin. She held her arm up for the head tech to see.

The man squinted, then took a few steps forward. He grabbed her arm, almost reverently, studying the bare flesh before him. Then he turned to Tsi, a look of honest joy on his face, and wrapped her in a fierce hug.

"You got the mark!" he shouted. "You rode with Captain Black! Gods of the Sun, woman, why didn't you lead with that!"

Tsi disengaged from the man's hearty embrace, returning his smile as best she could as she switched to Noxian argot.

"It was many shifts ago," she said, repeating an old pirate's greeting. "I didn't know if you were his friend or foe."

"I ain't causing no trouble with any of Captain Black's band. How did you know I'd be able to see the Mark, though?"

"That eye might look dead," Tsi replied, "But I know a scanner-aug when I see one.”

The head tech smiled, tapping his artificial eye.

“It ain’t much good except for seeing the mark. I’m Furner Ketsu,” he explained. “I was with the Captain during the raid on *Void Rose*. Retired here after I got a few too many additionals.”

“I caught my share too,” Tsi said, slipping back into pirate slang as naturally as her mother tongue. “On the Ninety Day Raid.”

“Ha! That was before my time. The Captain used to talk about that, you know? His proudest moment, ripping the mid-stations apart for all they were worth. Were you there when they took that Epilotii merchant, just before the end?”

“Luck,” Tsi said. “Luck, and a drunken Slip navigator. Plopped her right into our laps. Crew gave up without a fight.”

She forced a smile to her face. Her fingers trembled, thinking about the thrill of leading a boarding party, remembering her fighter raking shots across the hulls of merchantmen. It had been a bad time in her life, falling into an old pattern. Not the worst, though. She was ashamed of how much she had enjoyed it.

“Well, any of the Black Captain’s old marauders docks here free of charge. One of my boys’ll get you a docking token, and we’ll get you spic-and-span in no time. Look me up while you’re here, aye? I’d love to talk about the old days.”

“Perhaps I will,” Tsi said. “I’ve got stores of material on board. All I need from your men is labor, that clear?”

“I read you,” Furner said.

He shouted orders to his men, who began breaking out repair equipment. She headed back up the ramp to gather Strongmind and Hiron, and haul out a few crates of the metal needed to repair the ship’s hull. Something made her pause at the base of the ramp as Ketsu began shouting orders to his crew.

“How is Captain Black anyway?” Tsi asked.

Ketsu stopped, turned to her and put one fist over his breast.

“Gone to the void,” he said. “One of his own did him in on a job not long ago. Well, what did you expect?”

“Nothing less,” Tsi sighed. “Nothing less.”

They had gone where Tsi always went when she was in a place like this: to a bar. On Salvation, there were essentially three industries: the assaying and evaluating of minerals and salvage, prostitution, and selling stimulants and depressants. Murder, and the recruitment of those willing to commit murder, was a common business as well, but still far behind the other three. Walking the main boulevard of what was now being called Jarawat's Corridor, they had passed dozens of drinking holes, brothels, gambling dens, and mining clan fronts offering the best prices for raw ore. Tsi had settled on the one bar she had recognized, a place called "Glory".

As they stepped through the cheap strips of plastic that made up the door, a bouncer grunted and patted the trio down. He made no comment on the fact that Tsi and Strongmind were armed, only seemed to note that this was the case before sending them further in. The place was dimly lit, the only real light seeming to come from a central holographic display of a duel being fought between two naked men with razor whips.

It was an old Guraggan fighting method, used on their Chem-Thralls to determine which was worthy of emancipation. Outside the Guraggan territory, it had an exotic mystique, but the truth was it was closer to comedy in Guraggan culture. The movements vaguely mimicked fighting with mono-wire, but it was clumsier, more awkward. The duelists were as likely to kill themselves as each other. In the grainy green-blue of the holo-display she could see they had already scored dozens of large gashes on their own backs.

Tsi signaled to the barman for a drink, and downed it in one gulp, then signaled another. She'd passed out here once, her only clear memory a damp feeling on the back of her head as she stared up at a sky made of rusty grating and slowly turning fans.

Strongmind and Hiron sat down on either side of her. Strongmind's head was completely wrapped in a turban, goggles, and a long-snouted breathing mask. Hiron had switched to a soft suit which his robes fit comfortably over. The boy was experimenting with putting his oxygen mask on and off.

"You left the helmet back on the ship," Tsi said.

"What? Oh, oh yes, well, I uh, I thought it'd be kind of... bulky. To carry around with me, I mean."

Tsi shrugged.

"The mask's for getting back to the helmet. If there's a breach, there's no way you'll get there in time."

"Oh."

"Just don't waste your time playing with that thing," Tsi said. "It makes you look like an amateur. *More* of an amateur."

Hiron nodded silently, taking a swig of his own drink. Tsi patted his shoulder gently.

"Relax," she said. "We just need to keep a low profile for now, that's all."

"Right, low profile," Hiron said. "Don't we... kind of stand out? Not a lot of people here look like me, plus the android..."

"I am an artificial intelligence housed in a servile drone body," Strongmind corrected. "An android is built specifically to simulate a human being. I was not."

"What a trio," Hiron grumbled. "Why are we here anyways? You said we came here to repair and plan our next move? What next move?"

Tsi took a long breath, and glanced at Strongmind. The machine's face was completely hidden, but it tilted its head at her slightly. The boy wasn't ready for... no, he did not *need* the whole truth. Not yet.

"I've traveled the Frontier for a long time," Tsi said. "When I started out, I didn't have a purpose. I drifted from one place to the next, taking what came to me. I was a mercenary, a miner, a gambler. I spent a long time herding Gene-bears on Goodhome. I wandered all over without a purpose. I think I was trying to escape... or maybe I was just waiting."

"Waiting for what?"

"For things to catch up with me," Tsi said darkly. She took another drink, emptying her glass. The liquor was harsh and acidic, but she could feel the warmth wending its way through her limbs. Captain Black had always held those who needed drink to give them courage in contempt. Maybe that was why Tsi had never much liked Captain Black.

"Then, one day they did. It wasn't long after I left Goodhome that I was in a fringer bar near Arphelion's Soul, doing... this."

She indicated her glass as she refilled it, a humorless smile on her lips.

"When I got news of what had happened on Bactria Novo."

"A Guraggan raid," Hiron said. "A traveler told me that. One of the merchants selling guns to my father."

"Not *a* Guraggan raid. The first they'd carried out in decades. A true attack, not some nameless warlord trying to prove his worth by sacking a station or ambushing a ship. It was done with the same precision, the same ruthlessness, that they had throughout the war with Kios. It was organized, directed, with an end in mind that was pursued ruthlessly. It was War. Their kind of war."

"But they... they butchered Bactria Novo. Millions of people. They pulled some of them up into those big slave ships of theirs but... but they didn't take the planet."

"The Guraggan don't fight the way the other empires do. For them, violence is an end in itself. They take worlds, yes, but as vassals, not colonies. It's how they test themselves. Remind themselves that their way is still best. It had been decades since they lost against Kios, and in all that time I thought they'd torn themselves apart in civil war. I thought maybe, with the Empress gone and the Guraggan houses sating their bloodlust on each other... maybe there'd be peace. After all that horror, maybe it could finally end."

Tsi's eyes were wet, and there was a tightness in her throat. She wiped her lips with the back of her hand, and gulped down more harsh tasting liquor.

"I was there," she said. "During the war between Kios and the Guraggan Hegemony."

"You were a pilot? A captain?"

"Something like that. I saw all the brutality of both sides. I've never wanted anything in all my life more than I wanted that war to end. But now they've come back, and I think it might start again."

"Is there anything we can do about that?" Hiron asked.

"I don't know. When we fled Promise, just before we entered the Slip I saw thousands of Guraggan ships. There weren't any of the usual energy readings that come off of ships leaving the Slip. They were moving close-pressed in formation, heading for your home."

Hiron looked at her questioningly.

"Their alacrity should be impossible with conventional Slip Drive technology," Strongmind said. "Every ship using such a drive must re-emerge with sufficient distance to any other dense concentration of mass. This makes lengthy periods of sublight maneuvering essential before a planetary invasion, and makes the deployment of large numbers of battleships ships extremely cumbersome and inefficient."

"It's the second miracle I saw on your world," Tsi said bitterly. "First the Dreaming Stars coming back to life, and now a swarm of Guraggan ships moving through the void in formation like it was nothing."

"So they have an edge over the Kiosans."

"Not an edge," Tsi said. "If they can move that quickly, with that many ships... it won't be war. It'll be slaughter."

"Well then, we have to go to Kios. Get close enough to send a Slip-beacon, warn them about what we've seen."

There was silence between the trio after Hiron spoke. The hubbub of the bar room continued unabated behind them, punctuated by howls of joy when one of the holo-gladiators inflicted yet another wound on his opponent. Hiron looked nervously between Tsi and Strongmind, but neither the woman nor the machine spoke.

"Shouldn't we?" he added.

"That's what I was going to ask you," Tsi said. "I've been watching the Guraggan, waiting for them to do this, but now... now I wonder if it's even worth trying to stop them. The more I've thought about it, the more I wonder if there's even a difference between them and Kios. The Janissaries are monsters, they were designed that way. They can only barely be called *human*. The only distinction between them is that the Empress made the Janissaries, and the Guraggan made themselves."

"Why did they come to my home?" Hiron asked.

Tsi raised an eyebrow questioningly at him.

"Why?" Hiron said again. "We don't have resources, the whole planet is a wasteland. Our warriors are nothing compared to theirs. Why did they destroy my clan? Why did they invade us?"

"Practice," Tsi said. "It's a rehearsal, to see if their techniques still work."

"So. They'd destroy my culture, ravage my planet, kill millions, just to see if they could kill millions more. Did I get that right?"

"Yes."

"Would the Kiosans do that?"

Tsi thought about it long and hard, rubbing her jaw.

"Maybe... maybe when the Empress was still in charge, they might have done something like that. They'd have spent a long time arguing and debating, working out the moral arithmetic. The Janissaries though... No. No, they don't fight except to achieve victory and protect the empire. They'd never attack a world just to see if they could," Tsi said. She took another long pull on her glass, draining it completely, before she rounded to look the boy squarely in the eye.

"Just remember: they are *not* human, not truly. They butchered worlds at the Empress's command. Violence is as natural to them as breathing. On Kios they used to say 'a sage's mind, a demon's soul.' That's what the Janissaries are."

Hiron set his jaw and knocked back his own drink.

"I think maybe we need some demons on our side right now."

She spoke a long time with the machine and the boy, plotting their next course as she had when she last visited Salvation: during round after round of drinks. She found herself slipping into Noxian argot, peppering her words with their curses and their exclamations. The liquor loosened her tongue enough that she was smiling and laughing, clapping the boy on the back. Soon they were not speaking of what to do next at all, but merely talking as people do. As friends do.

For his part, Hiron could hold his drink shockingly well, and was surprisingly merry given the circumstances. He quizzed her about her travels, and while she was not drunk enough to tell him everything, she did tell him about dodging a bull Oulantka on Triumph, and the time she got stabbed for insulting an Epilotii dignitary.

In turn, she asked the boy about his life. She had already guessed much of his story: the only heir of a powerful leader whose throne passed by bloodline, born stunted and weak in a culture of physical strength. Privilege of birth kept him from a swift death exposed in the wastes, but his life had been filled with shame and guilt he could never shake. His body was an insult to his mother and father. How could their hard muscles and fierce eyes have produced such a frail, shaking little thing?

He'd fled inside his mind. The only organ he possessed not damaged by his birth was his brain, and he had strengthened it as best he could. He was lucky to have been born to one of the wealthiest Inheritor Clans, his dreams of star-gazing would have been impossible for anyone else on that pauper's world.

Tsi always sobered up faster than she wanted to, and by the

time Hiron was done relating his first humiliating encounter with Vitara Ikanus, she was groggy but fully possessed of her faculties. She sent Strongmind and Hiron back to the ship. The machine and the boy made an odd pair, one gangling on crutches, the other stiff-legged and awkward as they moved off down the filth-strewn corridors of Salvation.

She knew this station well from her time here, and there was still enough fire in her limbs that she wanted to walk its streets and gantries alone. She was tempting fate, she realized, but she didn't care. Noxian liquor always made her ready for a fight. It was that particular mix of deadened inhibition, depression, and fatalism that made her think getting shot by a mugger was a far better way to go than whatever else the universe had in store for her.

With a suck-globe of alcohol tucked into one of her pockets and her Repeater heavy on her hip, she walked the streets. There were always lights in Salvation. The station didn't have enough organization to run a proper day-night shift, and so as she passed down wide corridors and climbed rusted gratings, stepping over spacers blacked out in their own filth and shoving away the amorous advances of tight-suited catamites, she walked through light and darkness in equal measure. Here was a long tunnel, lit in green and blue where Noxians in white masks sold hallucinogens and filled the air with whispered prayers. Then, a deep basin that had once been a water reservoir, pitch dark save for the small glow-candles around which destitute scrappers huddled.

Tsi walked through the nightmare that was Salvation, saw people selling weapons and narcotics, their skills and their bodies, hiring out for murder and love. They threatened her, cajoled her, begged her. Prayed for her.

She walked by all of them stony faced. The memories of her amiable companions were growing more and more distant. She remembered a time when she was no different from the harlots and gunslingers, the knife-jacks with their vaunted boarding skills, the yellow clad hackers claiming they could peel open the brain of any machine, the back-channel surgeons claiming they could do the same for any man. She'd walked among all this filth, all these torn and lost people, far from the lowest that dwelt around Noxia's dying stars, and she had called them her brothers and sisters, and called this place her home.

Yet, she felt no shame. These people were desperate, yes, but they had been born into this stellar cistern. Calling them her comrades brought no guilt to her, only wry amusement and a vague sense of loss. No, there were other thoughts that made guilt rise from the pit of her stomach, another life she had led far worse than that of a Noxian pirate. She thought for a moment on that life, teeth clenched, throat tight. Then, she did what she always did.

She took a long pull from the suck-globe, and she buried those memories deep.

CHAPTER 12

Hiron tottered uncertainly alongside the machine, making their way back to the ship. It was funny, he had always thought space stations would be sterile, but Salvation was positively teeming with life. The boulevards were a twisting, cramped network. No one pathway was more than a dozen paces wide, and it seemed that every square inch was occupied somehow. Graffiti scarred the walls. Everywhere there seemed to be people or their refuse. Technicians steadily repaired loose wires, derelicts sprawled across corridors, oblivious to the people stepping over them. Or on them.

He would have felt threatened by all these strange spacers, were it not for the hulking machine walking stiff-legged beside him. Even missing most of an arm, Strongmind exuded a reassuring menace. It reminded Hiron a bit of the veteran palace guards, all pock-marked and malformed by decades of hard living, but sturdy and tough like an old pair of boots.

"Left," the machine said as they came to a T-junction.

Hiron was groggy from all the drinking he had done, and he stumbled after the machine as it led the way. They walked on in silence for a little longer, Hiron's thoughts drifting. He still felt a certain giddiness about the whole thing: he was in space! He was finally traveling the stars, leaving his old life behind him. His twisted feet were brushing the deck of one of the oldest stations in the Frontier, alongside two strange but stalwart companions, journeying together into the unknown on their trusty craft.

"Does our ship have a name?" he suddenly asked aloud.

"No."

"Huh," Hiron said. "It should probably have a name."

"It has many designations. The serial number on the engine core is 11197Z-Gamma. We have thirty five different transponders ready for activation. Currently we are the Epilotti merchant vessel *Grazer* from the planet Lenettella."

"*Grazer* isn't a very good name for that kind of ship."

"It does not attract attention. Our master does not wish to be discovered easily."

"*Our master?*"

"What do you call her?"

"Tsi," Hiron said. "It's her name, right?"

The machine was silent.

"You know, I've never heard you call her... anything before," Hiron said.

"Titles make her uncomfortable, so I do not use them unless it is necessary."

"Huh. I'm the same way," Hiron said, huffing as they began to ascend a steep ramp towards the docking bay. He nearly slipped in an oil spill, but righted himself deftly with his crutches.

"I always had a hard time being addressed as 'Lord' and 'Heir' and things like that. You know, one of my titles was 'Slaughterer of Legions?' I never killed anyone. It's just what people of my rank get called on Promise."

"Commanders often assume the deeds of their subordinates. You may claim the killings of your Clan servants as your own. Philosophically speaking, you were their source."

"I didn't ask them to kill anyone," Hiron objected. "I didn't want them to. It was my father who gave the orders. I just got paraded out at feasts."

"You were the symbol of their ruler's genetic continuity. All conflict furthers the dominance of one faction or another. The clan warriors fought to secure your father's realm, with the knowledge that you, in turn, would rule it on his death. They killed for you."

"Are you... are you trying to shame me? Because I—"

"I was trying to reassure you," Strongmind said flatly. "Clearly I have not succeeded."

"*Reassure* me?"

"Yes. You seem under-confident in your physical abilities. I hypothesized that thinking of yourself as a great warrior would improve your morale."

"I don't want to be a warrior, Strongmind. I wish I was stronger, but I... I don't want to kill anyone. Unless I have to."

"You have already participated in combat. You do not control circumstance, and it is useless to profess pacifism when your objectives require violence. We will most certainly have to terminate more opponents before our journey is done. I would advise you to psychologically prepare yourself for that eventuality."

"I'm not a pacifist. I just... where I grew up, everyone wanted to be a warrior. I couldn't do that, and the people I saw, coming back from raids... it was horrible. Not just the ones who were maimed, or-or dead, but the ones who had nightmares. Their eyes looked empty, like being in a battle had... had sucked everything out of them. I thought I was the lucky one sometimes, never having to face that."

"Yet now you have."

"Yes," Hiron said, defeated. "Now I have."

"You were not completely ineffective when we engaged the Guraggan Chem-Thralls."

"That's a complement right?"

"Yes."

"Well, thank you. I, uh, appreciate the sentiment."

"You are welcome," Strongmind said.

After another long silence, Hiron asked:

"Did I hit anyone? When we were in that tunnel, I mean, and I was covering you. I closed my eyes and pulled the trigger. Did I... I mean did you see me-?"

"Your fire was inaccurate. You did not inflict any casualties."

"Thank God," Hiron breathed.

"Your covering fire provided me with several opportunities to terminate the opposition. As I said, you were not completely ineffective."

"But... but *I* didn't kill anyone, right?"

"No," Strongmind said. "You did not kill anyone."

They had made it to the docking bay. The technical crew had retired for the night, leaving the hull half-repaired and floor of the bay scattered with equipment. Hiron picked his way gingerly across the expanse and up the loading ramp into Tsi's ship, Strongmind following close behind.

He paused and caught his breath in the ship's central cabin, which served as the galley. Their craft could fit a crew of about a dozen, if it needed to, but Tsi had kept the place decidedly spartan.

There were Rat-Paks in sealed containers, and a small heating unit was set in the center of a collapsible table. Hiron pulled up a chair and stretched his aching legs. His arms had done most of the work, but his legs still felt terrible.

Strongmind shuffled past him and into his cabin. At first Hiron ignored it as another of the machine's eccentricities, but eventually he grew curious and hobbled over to entrance to the small room. Within, Strongmind was carefully arranging Hiron's sheets, moving with crisp efficiency despite having only one hand.

"What... what are you doing?"

"I am making your bed," Strongmind said.

"Do you always do that? Like, for Tsi?"

"When she is intoxicated, yes."

"Am I drunk?" Hiron asked indignantly.

The machine swiveled its head, looking him up and down.

"Yes," it said, then returned to its work.

"Oh, my. Well, th-thank you. I appreciate it..."

"You are welcome," the machine said, taking a step back. It presented the bed to him with a short bow. Feeling awkward, Hiron clambered into the bed, surprised at how comfortable such a simple cot could be. The machine made to leave.

"Strongmind?"

It turned.

"I have a question for you."

"Yes?"

"Why are you... why are you called Strongmind?"

"It is my name."

"No, I mean, did Tsi call you that?"

"No. When I was recovered many of my data files were corrupted, including the designation of the ship I was installed in. I did not have a name."

"So you named yourself Strongmind?"

"Yes. Does this line of questioning serve a purpose?"

"No," Hiron sighed. "Good night, Strongmind."

"Goodnight," the machine said, and closed the door.

Tsi awoke in a damp shaft ledge off the main boulevard. Her hair was completely soaked. There was a slow drip of water coming out of a pipe somewhere high above. Her back ached, her head pounded, and her calves felt like someone had taken an iron rod to them. A dark figure filled her slowly returning vision, its left arm outstretched towards her.

It took Tsi a moment to realize she was being robbed. As the figure's hand encircled the pistol at Tsi's hip, she suddenly slammed her palm into the side of the thief's head. Springing to her feet, Tsi landed an uppercut, then a swift kick to the stomach. As her vision fully returned, she saw that her opponent was a young Noxian woman in a loose grey space suit, hair long and greasy, flesh pale and untouched by the sun.

The woman was cursing and reeling towards her, launching an awkward blow with her left hand. Tsi darted backwards, grabbed the woman's outstretched arm and expertly spun her to the ground. Standing over the prostrate thief, arm still locked tight, Tsi placed her boot firmly on the woman's back. She began to apply pressure. A little more, and the arm would break.

"Fuck! FUCK!" the thief roared, struggling uselessly. Her right arm flailed out from beneath her, trying to push her upwards, but the thief let out a whimper and collapsed the moment she pushed against the ground.

A broken right hand, Tsi realized. A thief with a broken hand. Her main hand, clearly, and no weapons. Her vacuum suit was old and worn, but well-maintained, a generational rig by the look of it. Tsi was standing over a spacer down-on-her-luck, a debtor of some kind. It was a bad thing to be a Noxian without a weapon, and worse to be a pirate with a broken arm and no way to make enough money to get it fixed.

Tsi relaxed her grip. The thief was sobbing silently.

"Why shouldn't I chuck you down that shaft?" Tsi said, jerking her head towards the vertical tube behind her. It was ten floors down to the next junction.

"Do it," the thief grumbled. "Quicker than starving to death."

Tsi let go of the woman's arm, and slowly took a step back. The thief still lay on the ground in front of her, not moving. Her body shook with quiet tears. Then, she stilled herself, rolled onto her back and sat up.

She glared at Tsi, eyes still wet. Her lip was split, and she rubbed at her nose. She was young, Tsi thought, but had already lived a hard life. A mid-stationer of some kind, probably one of the more stable dominions like Iron Point. Her face was delicate despite the wear on it, she looked more like a girl from a Goodhome fairy tale than a pirate. Someone who should meet strange spirits and test her courage, not loot freighters and cut throats.

"If you're thinking about shooting me, we're not that far from the hull," the woman warned. "That thing'll cause a breach."

"It's loaded with fragment rounds," Tsi said, her hand resting on the Repeater.

"Huh. Bust me wide open but only scar the deck. Smart."

"I've been on Salvation before."

"Well, are you gonna kill me or are we gonna keep jawing like Epilotii?"

Tsi took another step backwards and pointed to the boulevard.

"Go," she said.

The thief rose unsteadily and started to stumble away.

"Wait," Tsi said.

The woman turned to her, uncertainty in her eyes. Her good fist was clenched, ready to fight.

"You don't have a patch," Tsi said, indicating the woman's suit.

"Real top gear scanner you got there," she replied sarcastically.

"So you're not with any crew?"

"You think I'd be robbing drunks if I had a crew?"

"Not alone," Tsi conceded. "You'd bring someone else to hold me down."

"Yeah."

Tsi had noticed a habit of laconic fatalism among Noxians. This woman was alone, obviously on her last legs. She had no loyalties to worry about. She wouldn't exactly be trustworthy, but Tsi decided she was worth the risk.

"I need a guide. I haven't been here in a long time, I don't know whose goods are worth a damn. I'm looking for some specific items. You hiring out?" she asked.

The woman shrugged.

"If I still had my knife, I'd have done you in while you were asleep and kept the pistol," the thief said.

"Then I guess I'm lucky you didn't have it, aren't I?"

"Okay. You pay for my hand, I'll take you wherever you want to go."

"Done."

Tsi walked to the woman, and put her hand on the thief's left shoulder. After a moment, she returned the gesture. It was an old Noxian trust sign, mimicking the motions of checking another's suit before a space walk.

"I'm Enlil," the woman said.

"Tsi," Tsi said.

"Now, where did you want to go?"

CHAPTER 13

In the years she had served them, Wylla had come to understand this about the Guraggan: they did not like explaining themselves. She had been selected when she was still young, barely out of her first cycle as a member of a triumvirate. She would have protested, but she had no say in the matter.

She was never told why she had been taken, and not another. There were others in her commune that she thought were smarter, stronger willed, more observant. But who could guess at the whims of the Guraggan?

She was in the hold of a Courser called *Dragon's Tooth*. It was a swift ship, sent away from the Khagan's great fleet. The *Dragon's Tooth* had been her home for years now, its dim, cramped corridors as familiar to her as her father's temple. The mistress kept it poorly lit. She enjoyed watching her servants stumble in the darkness that she could see as clear as daylight. Despite years of service, Wylla had never been given quarters beyond a small section of the hold where she lay her bed roll, her prayer shrine, her lyre and a data-jack to the ship's computer.

Her only company was a score of Chem-Thralls. The Thralls huddled together, half-naked and grunting, faces hidden beneath their neurohelms. She'd gotten used to sharing space with these creatures. They were treated like little more than cattle. In some ways they were luckier than her. The drugs pumped into their brains kept them in a constant stupor. For them, the hold was nothing more than an unpleasant dream.

The only person she saw regularly besides the Thralls was their keeper, Skyme. Skyme was a small, bland creature, basically sexless in appearance and neutral in aspect. His body was soft and hairless, his skin and eyes a shade of grey, and he wore a simple grey jumpsuit, his only ornamentation a marking designating him as belonging to the

House of Ornicht. His single kindness had been to greet her whenever he entered, before he checked on the Thralls and administered their daily dose of sedatives.

He seldom engaged her in conversation, despite her best efforts. Few of the retinue did. The Bykon were not well-liked, even among fellow vassals of the Guraggan. Wylla had gotten used to scorn from everyone who was not one of her people.

She knew they were traveling by Slip drive, based on the gentle stirring she had felt in her stomach over the past few days. The way the field interacted with her body's personal magnetism always had that affect on her. Some dismissed it as psychosomatic, but she hypothesized that the mysterious energies of the Slip touched everyone differently. There were ancient legends of the very first Slip travelers going mad. While she doubted that was the case, it was true that you could not take matter from one reality and expect it to emerge unchanged within another.

Whatever the truth was, she was glad they were no longer on the Path of Glory. She had overheard her mistress muttering about the risks it posed, how some of the fleet was ripped apart every time it was used. Danger and helplessness was part of Wylla's life, but at least the Slip was something she understood.

The stirring left her as they transitioned out of the Slip, and her body returned to normal. Or at least, as normal as it could be aboard a starship. She had never truly felt comfortable except upon her homeworld. She sighed, thinking of the fields of tall grass, and the azure shores of Bykonus. When she closed her eyes, she could almost feel the earth between her toes, smell the salt in the air.

"Good morning, Wylla," Skyme said as he entered the hold. He was thumbing through his stimulant box, adjusting the cocktail he would feed the Thralls today.

"Good morning, Skyme," she replied, bowing to him.

"You are needed in our mistress's chamber," Skyme said nonchalantly.

"I... am needed?"

Skyme nodded and smiled, and said no more. He walked in among the throng of cyborgs, calling them out by number and having them kneel down so he could inspect them and begin jabbing needles into their veins. Wylla knew this was a game the Guraggan liked to play, sending their messengers as if there was nothing amiss. She knew better than to ask Skyme for details: if he knew any more he was forbidden to tell her.

She dressed herself in her finest gown, and coiled her hair expertly. An amulet of protection about her neck, her face painted and still, she took one last look at her beautiful, silent lyre. Then her eyes turned to the prayer shrine. She did not kneel to it, nor did she whisper any of the ritual words. She turned on her heel and left the hold, heading straight for the mistress's chambers. She was not certain she would return, but there was nothing her Gods or her Ancestors could do for her now.

Lady Ornicht's quarters were a testament to a life of war. On one wall, her weapons: thick-bladed glaives, flechette guns with muzzles like growling hound's heads, a captured Epilotii toxin thrower, and an endless plethora of lovingly crafted knives and daggers of every assortment. They were held in scabbards, or pinned to the wall by thin bands of glowing white crystal. A veritable armory was contained in that small space.

On the opposite wall were her suits of armor, from the first, delicately crafted reaving harness, worn when she was likely no more than sixteen, to the elaborately engraved but no less functional cuirass she wore into combat now. They bore their battle-damage openly, a plasma burn on the gauntlet of one set, a dozen flechette holes peppering the chest of another. The Lady's servants had taken special care never to remove the signs of her valor. *What is Broken Can Be Remade* was a favorite saying of the Guraggan. They took great pride in never hiding scars, either on their equipment or on their bodies.

Her helms were set above the armor, each growing more fancifully grotesque as Ornicht's career progressed. One in particular horrified Wylla: it was wrought to look like a deformed human skull ending in a twisted beak. Its eyes were a single visor of pale yellow, and tiny white teeth protruded from its mouth. Wylla knew they were human, plucked from her mistress's dead foes.

On the last wall, Lady Ornicht kept her memories. More sophisticated and subtle than many Guraggan, who collected severed heads and defiled sacred objects to display their victories, the Lady Ornicht had instead installed a neural-wire-suite. It was a simple device, a pair of vascular cables ending in delicate wires which hung from the wall. Surrounding it on shelves were hundreds of nondescript black wafers that could be slid into a slot above the neural-wire. Inserting the wires just below the eyes triggered electrical stimulation in the brain, causing the user to experience in excruciating detail every memory stored within the wafer.

Every broken starship, every shattered station, every plundered world that had ever felt the wrath of Kinshah Ornicht was on that wall. Wylla did not know if her mistress kept other memories. The birth of her children perhaps, or some joyous occasion of her youth? She doubted it.

Wylla was not alone in the chamber. Her mistress had two constant companions. One was Breaker Liss: a freed Thrall, now sworn to her service. He was a brutal figure, his naked chest covered in scars and thick muscles, pocked by stimulant injection ports. The Breaker had been the child of nobility when he was enslaved. He wore a beautiful chain of precious stones about his waist. They were signs of wealth that were utterly meaningless to the Guraggan. He was a pet, a very favored pet, and he followed in his mistress's shadow with all the loyalty and eagerness that was expected of him. Liss was the only member of the retinue who spoke to Wylla regularly, and with kindness. He was grim faced as ever on her entrance, though.

Kinshah Ornicht's other companion took up what seemed an entire corner of the room by itself. It was a combat drone and, if the whispers were to be believed, the only surviving unit from the Lady's first raids as a controller. Quadrupedal and massive, from its shoulders jutted a rudimentary head studded with sensor beacons that looked like the eyes of an arachnid. "90" was written on its hull in Guraggan script. The number had spiritual significance to them, but none that Wylla understood.

Last of all was the Lady Ornicht herself. She sat on her couch, brooding as she clutched a bludgeoning staff. Lady Ornicht was old and hard. Her head was shaved, save for two locks of golden-red hair that fell from her forehead, curling like demon's horns in front of her face. The left side of her lip was lop-sided, a scar that had never properly healed. Golden eyes fixed on Wylla from beneath a scowling brow.

Wylla fell to her knees, prostrating herself before the Guraggan as all her people were expected to do. She was sure that her hands were far forward, her fingers spread wide to show that she carried no weapons.

"Rise."

The voice was clipped and ragged. Almost bored.

Slowly, Wylla began to push herself up. Her gaze rose to Lady Ornicht's knees. She raised one of her own legs, preparing to stand.

"Knees will do," Ornicht said.

Wylla remained kneeling, eyes now on the ground. It was a delicate game dealing with the Guraggan. Unlike the rest of the retinue, Wylla had no drugs or implants compelling her loyalty to Ornicht. Her mistress sometimes liked to provoke her into defiance, so that she could be punished. Brutally.

"Do you know why you are here?" Ornicht asked.

"No."

"Speculate."

Wylla licked her lips. A delicate game indeed. Say too much and she would suffer. Too little, and it would be an insult. Her treatment would be worse.

"I am here... because we are investigating something. Something that my analytical skills would be useful for. A scientific problem, or perhaps a logical one. Maybe one of simple observation. And..."

"And?"

The voice cut through the air like a knife. Wylla's throat tightened.

"And you are here because the Khagan does not trust you," Wylla said.

Lady Ornicht's claw-like fingers tightened on her staff.

"What an...*interesting* hypothesis. Why do you think our mighty Khagan does not trust me, as you put it?"

"I could not begin to comprehend the Lord of All Houses," Wylla said. "But we have been dispatched alone. We fly with no other ships, and we do not take the Path of Glory."

"Is that not a sign of the Khagan's faith?"

"No," Wylla said. "If he had faith in you, he would have given you additional resources to ensure your mission's success. Whatever we are doing is important, but clearly our failure would not impact the Khagan's great design. Mighty as you are, my Lady, the Khagan did not wish you at his side to aid in conquest, nor did he give you this task because he believed you alone could achieve it. He is testing you, my lady."

Ornicht's eyes narrowed. Wylla watched her mistress's hands. She'd felt the crack of the Guraggan's staff more than once.

"Good," she purred. "Very good, Bykon. Your skills haven't dulled since Kypria."

"I live only to serve the Hegemony," Wylla said, catching her breath at last.

"I'm sure. Indeed, your conclusions are the same as my own. I am being tested, and you will aid me in proving myself worthy once again. I have a very specific task for you."

Wylla bowed.

"I stand ready to obey."

"You have a clever mind. It's why I've always valued you, and treated you so gently," Ornicht said. "Come, my hunting hound. We have prey to catch."

"I thought you gave up your thieving ways, Palma."

"I ain't a pirate anymore, but I've got to live!"

The merchant and Enlil were in a heated discussion, while Tsi stood at the back of the shop, observing. 'Palma' was a thin old woman, head shaved and branded with old Noxian tattoos from a long dead pirate band. The Pulsar Hounds, from what Tsi could read of their script. They'd been shattered even before she had come to the system for the first time, all those years ago.

Still, this woman was a survivor. Now she had a tiny shop filled with refuse and wonders. Tsi saw energy packs and cables, a combat drone's head, what looked like half the navigation system of an old Nioban scouter, all piled together next to a crate containing frozen Shanda fruits.

They were arguing over the price of an adjustable servo-brace. Crude technology, but a step up from the crutches Tsi had rigged for Hiron. It was a miracle the device was even on Salvation, let alone for sale. Most Noxians in Hiron's condition didn't live long.

"Alright, alright. What about this?" Enlil said. "Tsi, come look at this. Think that's what you need, too?"

She pointed at a severed drone arm, made of brass-colored

metal. A Kiosan design that Tsi recognized: old, like everything else in this shop, but very effective. She did some mental calculations. Strongmind would be lop-sided with it, and she'd have to patch his wiring in, which would take time and effort...

Tsi picked up the arm, testing its weight. One of her fingers caught at a catch just above the thumb, and suddenly a shining white blade sprung from the wrist. Palma started.

"Didn't know it could do that..." she muttered.

"How much?" Tsi asked, depressing the catch again and retracting the blade.

"Well, that, and the brace, that's a pretty good pair, put your friend back in fighting shape so I can't let it go for less than... twenty kilos protein?" the merchant said, her voice rising hopefully.

"Done," Tsi said. She took a Rat-Pak out of her coat, and set it on the table alongside her docking token. "This is a sample of what I've got," Tsi continued. "I'll need the arm now, but I can have the rest of the protein sent to you from my ship, and I'll collect the brace then."

Palma picked up the token and examined it suspiciously. It had Furner Ketsu's glowering siren on one side.

"Hmm. I know that crew," Palma said. "Furner's an idiot, but he isn't a cheat. You know if you try to decouple without paying me the Jarawat will hear, aye?"

"I rode with Captain Black," Tsi said. "I know how to pay my debts."

"I'd expect so."

"I have another item I'm in the market for," Tsi said. "A Slip-Beacon. Long range, wide broadcast. The message I need to deliver is very urgent, and it's absolutely vital that I get something in working order."

The merchant rubbed her wrinkled chin.

"Slip beacon, huh? Rare goods out here. Some of the mining clans use 'em to talk to outside merchants, but they're not gonna sell. I suppose you could pry something off one of the merchantmen, but that's risky. Jarawat's put all the vessels coming into this ring under her protection, and you certainly don't want to trouble the Jarawat."

"Of course not," Tsi said.

"You could always try Glutton..."

"Glutton?!" Enlil exclaimed. "That thing's crazier than you."

Palma shrugged.

"It has a lot of stuff."

"Yes, and it doesn't give up any of it!"

"It's been known to do a trade now and again," Palma said coyly. "How do you think it got so much cargo in the first place?"

"Good luck with that," Enlil said. "Come on Tsi, you've been fleeced enough."

"Hold on. I've heard that name before. Who's Glutton?"

"*What* is more accurate," Palma said.

"It's an AI. Orbits a ways out from the station most of the time," Enlil said. "It's nuts."

Tsi searched her memory. She'd never dealt with something like that when she lived here, but she could recall someone describing it to her vaguely.

"Is it in orbit now?" Tsi asked.

"Oh yes. Of course, if you want to talk to it you'll need to either take your ship out or speak to one of its reps on-station," Palma said. "They've got a few wires loose in the cockpit though."

"I've had my share of run-ins with eccentrics," Tsi said. "Where can I find these representatives?"

"Whelp, last I heard, one of them was hanging around the Big Blister, Gyje the Third Son's territory. I'd, uh, I'd be careful going there if I was you. Third Son is... tetchy."

"Like I said," Tsi replied. "I know how to handle eccentrics."

"What do you think?" Tsi was saying, but Hiron wasn't really paying any attention.

He was sitting in the corner of the medical bay, sucking on a re-hydration cube that Strongmind had given him. Small and white and tasteless, he wasn't quite sure how it was supposed to work, but it had done wonders for his hangover. The machine was sitting at the table, Tsi standing on the opposite side, a mechanical arm laid out between them. Both were studying the object with intense concentration.

Hiron was more interested in Tsi's new companion. He had been certain that Tsi was the most beautiful woman he'd ever seen, but now he wasn't quite so sure. The new arrival was tall, scrawny in her ill-fitting spacer suit, and her hair was greasy and lank. Still, there was something Hiron found painfully entrancing about her face. Her eyes kept flicking around the room anxiously, and she shifted positions, sometimes leaning back against a wall, other times pacing. She kept hovering her injured hand over an empty scabbard on her thigh.

Her eyes then came to land on Hiron, and he instinctively looked away. He looked up again to see the girl was scanning him up and down and frowning. Her jaw was set. She asked something aloud in Noxian, a language Hiron didn't understand. Tsi's head snapped up from the table, fixing the young woman with an icy glare.

The Noxian raised her arms in mock surrender and stepped backwards, murmuring a half-hearted apology. Hiron knew exactly what the exchange had meant without knowing a word of their language. He was used to being judged this way. After all, the Noxians weren't so different from his own people. No sympathy for useless mouths.

"It is acceptable," Strongmind finally said, placing its maimed arm on the table. "We will need to conduct repairs at once."

"Good," Tsi said. She jerked her head at the Noxian woman. "I have some more business to do with this one. You can start the augmentation on your own, and—"

"Can I ask what her name is?" Hiron interjected.

Tsi looked at him, surprised, as if she had forgotten entirely that he was in the room. She nodded, and barked something over her shoulder at the Noxian.

The girl smirked. She poked a finger at her chest.

"Enlil," she said.

"Hiron," Hiron replied, bowing to her as much as he could.

That got a laugh. Not a cruel one, either.

Tsi went to one of the walls and opened up a cabinet. Inside was a rack of surgical tools and repair equipment. Brittle blades of polished metal hung alongside lengths of wire and soldering irons. Tsi pulled the rack down from the wall, and began laying the tools on the table.

"Hiron, we're going to need your help," she said.

He got up and hobbled over to the table. Strongmind had already picked up a particularly sharp-looking blade and was nonchalantly cutting into its own shoulder. Hiron was both revolted and fascinated by the machine's sudden self-mutilation. Fluid leaked around the blade as it cut through synthetic tissue down to ceramic pseudo-bone.

"Alright," Tsi said, handing Hiron a pair of goggles and an electronic saw. "Just follow Strongmind's instructions and you should be fine."

"We're gonna cut off its arm?" he asked.

"Yes," Strongmind said. "Your observational skills remain adequate. Please place the saw at my shoulder joint and begin applying steady pressure."

The machine had peeled back layers of tissue, completely exposing its shoulder joint. Cautiously, Hiron placed the blade against the ceramic bone. He looked up at Tsi from beneath the goggles he had put on.

"We'll be back in a few hours," she said. "You'll be fine."

"Right, right."

Tsi got up and signaled to Enlil to follow. The Noxian girl gave Hiron a last look, then turned on her heel and followed Tsi out of the ship. Hiron sighed and began working the saw back and forth gently, the spinning blade purring as it slowly cut into polymer and metal.

"Are you upset?" Strongmind asked as Hiron's blade cut into its shoulder.

"No," Hiron sighed.

"I assume it was not something I said."

"No."

"Very good," Strongmind said. "Your veneer of denial shows courage. Continue to apply pressure with the saw. We will need a class II soldering device for my precision motor instruments, and—"

As the machine droned on, Hiron couldn't help but smile. In spite of himself, he was starting to like this thing.

Big Blister hadn't been part of Salvation long, Tsi realized as they approached. From the outside it would have been a beautiful blue dome, a jewel embedded in the hull of the station. Tsi was sure Gyje Third Son had named it something different, but in typical Noxian fashion someone had noted how the dome rose from the surface of the station like a blister, and given it was filled with a pus of its own kind, the name had stuck.

It was a riot of bizarre splendor within. The central space was open and crowded with people, out-system traders rubbing shoulders with hardened Noxian pirates. Stalls rose like tiny islands within the sea of people, dispensing liquor, food, and precious water to the baying crowd. Music pulsed through speakers suspended in the air, and dancers in elaborate costumes cavorted and gamboled above the crowd, suspended on barely visible wires.

Catwalks rose above the mob, each ramp up guarded by armed thugs. The ramps in turn formed a strange geometric pattern, booths suspended off of them where the station's elite gathered to make deals in hushed tones or merely to be seen, flaunting their success.

"It was Jarawat's idea," Enlil said as they made their way through the damp throng. "She was a very successful pirate before she killed Moriton Lapt and took this corridor over. Thought she could win the mining clans, the water barons, *and* the dregs over with this place."

"Did she?" Tsi asked as she elbowed past another drunkard.

"People kill to get to the catwalk," Enlil said. "And those dancers aren't Noxian. Must be making enough money to pay 'em, right?"

They shoved and jostled their way to one of the ramps. The base of the ramp had a small exclusion zone of about a meter where none of the drunken crowd dared approach for fear of the guard's mauls. Tsi strode forward brazenly, issuing a clear challenge.

"Business with Glutton's Emissary," she said.

"Cute," the guard replied.

He extended a meaty hand, palm upwards. Tsi looked between him and his companion. Big men, but not wearing armor. She was sure she could get her knife into one's throat and have the other's head burst with a fragmentation round before he drew his weapon. Instead, she pulled a Rat-Pak from her coat and put it in the man's hand.

"Really?" he said.

"It's good stuff," Enlil insisted. "Clean. There's powdered Gene-Bear in there. Make your hull hard."

"Gilded Lily," the guard said, recognizing her for the first time. A cruel grin split his face, and he took a large bite of the Rat-Pak before handing it to his companion.

"Well, heh, boss always liked you. He could use a laugh I'm sure. Go on up."

The guards stepped to the side and Tsi and Enlil began their ascent.

"Gilded Lily?" Tsi asked.

"Nickname," Enlil replied. "I don't like it."

They ascended the catwalk slowly, Enlil taking the lead. Tsi realized they were heading towards the very highest ring, where starlight filtered down on to pathways shrouded in artificial shadow. Once they had achieved the final platform, Tsi saw that it was no small booth bolted to the end of a walk, but instead a wide open gallery in its own right. It was a disk of golden light in the blue gloom, and as she approached she knew instantly that this was the private reserve of Gyje and his most favored confidantes.

They stepped onto the disc: its floor a polished marble-gold, the plush furniture constructed from leather hides shipped in from far-off worlds. Aged pirates lounged on couches, sharing hookahs as they watched obscene displays in grainy holo-recordings. A young woman sat on a dais draped in powder-white fur, playing mournfully on a psalmodikon.

A tall man with thin eyebrows and a muscular physique, evident even through his soft suit, lounged against one of the railings. There was a small crowd gathered around him. He was holding court, loudly expounding on nothing. Occasionally he would reach out and caress a woman at his side. Her body was plump and soft beneath an elegant gown, clearly someone from outside the system. A paid harlot perhaps, or just an adventuress attracted by the sense of danger and mystery that Noxia held for the ignorant.

Tsi pitied any woman who chose to be Gyje Third Son's consort. Noxian pirates were notoriously short-lived, and even a petty Ring-Baron like Gyje would make a worthy kill for whatever up-and-coming rakes were doubtless planning to depose the Jarawat in due time. When that happened, as it inevitably would, this woman would count herself extremely fortunate to be sold off as a slave. Most of the time, concubines went out the airlock with the rest of a dead pirate's unwanted goods.

"That's Gyje," Enlil said unnecessarily.

"What about the Emissary?"

"That thing smoking Red Ether," she said, pointing to a ring of couches around a hookah.

A figure dressed all in crimson save a featureless white helm was suckling casually at the pipe. Its legs were crossed, its forearms the color of tallow. Tsi could see flashes of silver on its fingers: data-jack augmentations, allowing it to directly interface with a computer. A few other figures lounged around it, dead to the world in the throws of the Ether. The couch opposite the Emissary was conspicuously unoccupied.

Tsi approached cautiously, flanked by Enlil. She sat down while the Noxian remained standing behind her, arms folded. Tsi crossed her legs, mirroring the Emissary's pose, as she mentally went over everything Enlil had told her about the Glutton and its Emissaries.

"Have you come to indulge?" a thick voice asked from within the polished helm. Smoke emerged from beneath the helmet, curling seductively around the Emissary's crimson collar.

"I need to speak to your master."

"The Traveler has a great mission," the Emissary said. "It allows me to indulge myself when I am not needed, but never to waste its time."

The thing took another suck on the pipe, then extended a long, bony arm towards Tsi, offering her the hookah. Tsi took it, wiping spittle from the pipe mouth. She inhaled lightly, just enough to not insult her opposite. Her limbs began to tingle instantly.

"I am not here to waste anyone's time. I need to trade with your master."

"You have acquisitions? Carbon? Precious metals? Flesh?"

"I have traveled very far," Tsi said, returning the pipe as she spoke. "Acquired all manner of things, some that would be very precious to your master indeed. But I must know if your master has something that I desire before I offer my hard-earned wealth to it."

"What do you know of the Traveler's desires? I warn you again, waste my master's time at your peril."

"I know your master has a great destiny. I would not insult your master's great work by implying that my contribution will be significant, but I know that even a single step can be vital on a journey. This is what I offer your master: a step forwards."

"Hehhh.... Fascinating," the Emissary purred. "You are a most interesting creature. You are present in my master's data-banks. Yes... one of Captain Black's pilots. A fine reaver. An acquirer of great goods and mass."

"I... have never met your master."

"You have felt the heat of the Poison Suns. My master has seen you," the Emissary whispered. "A moment, then. I must prepare myself for the ecstasy of my Master's embrace."

The Emissary took one last long suck upon the pipe, then set the corded tube aside. It touched the index fingers of its hands to its palms, raising them in supplication. A deep, crackling breath came from within the thing, then a long, slow sigh. A convulsive shiver ran through the Emissary's thin body, and suddenly its helm lit up.

A display-screen, Tsi realized. She had already deduced the helmet had a long distance neuro-link, allowing its remote owner to see and hear what the wearer did, but its smooth surface allowed the master to project an image as well. Tsi found herself staring at a single massive mechanical eye, projected onto the helmet's surface. It focused on her, cybernetic pupils contracting.

"Offer: Mass/Goods/Crew?" the voice grated from the helmet's speakers, a harsh contrast to the dulcet tones of the Emissary.

"Goods," Tsi said.

"Worship? Affirmative? Negative?"

"Negative," Tsi said.

"Trade?"

"Affirmative."

"Doubtful," the voice said, suddenly becoming fluid and clear, though no less harsh. "What could you possibly offer I, Pirate? Killer for Straum Black, who never once traded with I, Traveler. Called I 'Glutton'. Brute. Dead brute. Brief flaring on my screens, but defiant of I, Traveler."

"That was a long time ago," Tsi said. "Captain Black is dead, and I haven't worked for him for many years."

"Years," the voice growled. "Relative. Short-term. You are augmented, not a May-Fly-Dancer like these things. You understand I. Plans of decades, lifetimes, you may guess at. Insult I, speak to I of 'years'. Long time. Junk data."

"I don't bear you any ill-will Traveler," Tsi said. "I wouldn't contact you if I wasn't serious about trading."

"TRADE!" the voice screeched. "What does Brute offer I?"

"You're preparing for a long journey, aren't you? That's why you've acquired so much mass over the years. Repair materials, redundant equipment... fuel."

"Much fuel have I, Traveler. Many tons. Energy cells. Many cells."

"I offer you a load of Helium-3," Tsi said. "A load near this system, only a short Slip-jump away. By my calculation, it had a potential impulse load of eighty thousand tons."

"Helium-3?" Enlil hissed in Tsi's ear. "What the hell are you playing at? That stuff's not worth—"

"*WHAT DO YOU REQUIRE IN TRADE?*" the voice blared over her. "For Coordinates-Helium-3?"

"A Slip-beacon. Long range, with a maximum efficiency drive and a broad spectrum message delivery system. Programmable, and in good working order," Tsi said.

The eye disappeared. Suddenly, the image was replaced by a picture of a metal object sitting in a launch bay. Schematics began flashing on the helmet's surface, showing the beacon in intricate detail. Every schematic was matched to a full, three dimensional picture of the machine, assembled and disassembled, followed by a return to a brief live feed of the Beacon sitting in its launch bay.

"Come to collect," the voice said. "Bring Helium-3-coordinates in data burst and hard form. I, Traveler will be waiting."

The helmet screen then went dead, and Tsi was left in silence with the unconscious emissary.

Enlil was starting to doubt her choice of employer. She was grateful, certainly, that the dark haired woman hadn't tossed her down a maintenance shaft or splattered her brains all over the bulkheads, but making deals with Glutton wasn't good long-term planning. She'd met her fair share of leak-brains around the Poison Suns, and at least this out-system woman hadn't tried to knife her spontaneously or anything.

"Is that normal?" Tsi asked, indicating the unconscious emissary.

"Oh yeah," Enlil said. "Think it's brain shock. Glutton talking through 'em usually fries 'em out for a while."

"Hmm. Well, we'd better head back to the ship. I don't want to waste any time getting that beacon."

"You know, you still owe me a hand," Enlil said, indicating her broken extremity.

"I've got an auto-doc, it'll patch you up on the way."

Tsi rose and Enlil helped to steady her. The Red Ether was hitting her harder than she'd expected from the look of it. Enlil tried not to laugh. She really was from out-system, even if she'd been to Noxia before.

Suddenly the hairs on the back of her neck raised. The platform had gotten quiet. Conversations muted and cut off. Even the Psalmodikon player strummed her instrument slower. All eyes were on one figure that had emerged onto the platform, a blue-black silhouette that seemed to meld with the darkness beyond.

He was tall, and clad head to toe in fearsome armor. Loose trousers bunched at his knees above a pair of solid greaves, a pair of climbing spikes jutting like claws from his boots. His breastplate had an oily sheen, well-maintained despite many years of wear. Daggers and pistols hung from his waist, and a Nioban kukri was strapped to his chest. A carbine hung from his back, short and light. Good for fighting aboard a station.

His face was covered by a helmet with a demonic mempo, its features snarling beneath a pair of red eyes. Two stimulant tubes burst from the fanged maw and snaked their way around his back. She noticed something else, too: a slight twitching about his shoulders and chest that she couldn't quite identify, as if the armor itself would writhe from time to time.

A Bondsman. Enlil knew it instantly. She'd only seen one once, when she was a child. There weren't many left, according to rumor. Only a Bondsman would travel loaded to take on an army by himself. A Noxian would have sold half that gear a long time ago for passage out of this damn place.

"Tenlok! How wonderful of you to join us!"

It was Gyje Third Son who spoke, emerging from his crowd of sycophants, arms raised in greeting. He strode towards the Bondsman as if to embrace him, but his bodyguards kept close behind. Enlil tensed as Gyje stopped a few paces short. The Bondsman hadn't moved. His head only snapped to look at the Ring Baron. He was still as a statue.

"This could get ugly," Enlil whispered to Tsi. "Come on, we gotta move quiet."

Together the two women began slowly shuffling their way through the crowd that was gathering, watching the meeting between the pirate prince and the hired killer.

"I trust you got my message," Gyje said, running a hand over his blonde braids. "The Jarawat is very interested in acquiring your... services."

"I got it," Tenlok said. His voice was little more than a growl, never rising in tone.

"And?"

"No."

The crowd was completely silent. Tsi and Enlil moved faster. They were almost to the exit when Enlil heard something unexpected.

Gyje was laughing. He roared and whooped and slapped his thigh.

"Oh, you're a funny one!" he said. "And here I was... here I was thinking you wouldn't have a sense of humor. Come all this way just to say 'no'! Imagine!"

"Answer's no," the Bondsman repeated. "Not interested in contracting with your org."

"You saw our offer? Lot of money," Gyje said.

"I don't do permanent contract work," the mercenary replied. "Only came up here so your mother would know I meant no insult."

"Come on, sure you couldn't... reconsider?"

Gyje was standing face to face with the Bondsman now, their chests almost touching. Enlil could see tension in the pirate's body, but the Bondsman still betrayed nothing. Slowly, Gyje raised one hand and wrapped it around the handle of the Nioban blade strapped to the Bondsman's chest.

"We're gonna need that gun of yours right quick," Enlil hissed to Tsi.

It was one of the worst insults a Noxian could make, grabbing someone's weapon. The people of the Poison Suns weren't a warrior cult, and they certainly weren't famous for their pride. But putting your hand on another's blade showed that you didn't think they were a threat. It was a sign that you were willing to take whatever you wanted from them, and there wasn't a thing they could do about it.

"Come on," Enlil insisted, tugging at Tsi's arm.

The other woman had put a hand on her holster, but she was watching the confrontation, as fascinated as the rest of the crowd. Enlil thought maybe it was just the Red Ether, but there was a fierce alertness in Tsi's eyes.

"Careful," the Bondsman said, un-moving. "You might cut yourself with that."

Gyje's guards had white knuckles on their guns. Several of the crowd let out low chuckles. The Psalmodikon had stopped. Enlil could see sweat trickling down Gyje's smooth brow. His lips had peeled back from his teeth in a snarl.

At last, his hand unwrapped from the kukri. Gyje stepped backwards, a false smirk on his face. He raised his arms high, palms glistening with sweat.

"Alright then," Gyje said. "Walk away from all that money. I'm not here to tell you how to live. But I hope I'll see you again before you leave the station, eh?"

"I'm sure you will," the Bondsman said.

He turned on his heel and the crowd parted before him. He headed for the exit with a steady gait, and Enlil noticed that as he strode passed them Tsi turned her face away. In a moment the Bondsman was gone, and Gyje's court was left awkwardly silent.

The Psalmodikon started playing again, and the crowd slowly dispersed. The murmur of conversation started, but it was low and nervous. A few hollow laughs were heard. No one could ignore what had just happened.

Gyje had lost status. If word got out that he had threatened the Bondsman and failed to make him yield, it'd be taken as not just weakness on Gyje's part, but weakness for the Jarawat's whole organization.

Enlil didn't envy whoever Gyje took his wrath out on. She was only steps from the exit, close to freedom when the inevitable happened.

"Gilded Lily!" Gyje shouted.

"Keep walking," Enlil murmured to Tsi.

Dregs looked up from their hookahs and gaming tables curiously. Enlil's boot was on the threshold when Gyje called her name again, this time in a tone she couldn't ignore.

She turned around. He had resumed his position on one of the banisters at the edge of the disc, elbows cocked back against it in faux-relaxation. He raised a finger, and beckoned her.

"We don't have to," Tsi said, putting a hand on Enlil.

Enlil only shook her head, and walked towards the pirate

prince, Tsi trailing a few paces behind. She could feel eyes burning into her. She knew exactly what this was. Gyje had to reassert himself. The only question was how cruel he was feeling.

Gyje had two of his guards with him, men with armored suits and war paint on their oxygen masks. Neither of them had drawn a weapon, but they glowered at Enlil as she approached. Gyje's consort, the woman in the gown, lifted one of his arms and wrapped it around her shoulders, smirking at Enlil contemptuously.

"Well, well. Lily. Didn't think I'd see you again. Heard you blazed yourself to death after that Cold Salvage job, but you look healthy... hello there, what's this?"

Gyje grabbed Enlil's hand suddenly. He lifted the bandaged limb with just enough strength to quell any thoughts of resistance from her mind. A wicked grin spread across his face.

"A busted hand. A busted hand! Look at that, somebody done poor Gilded Lily an unkindness! Heh, and no knife either. No knife. No crew patch. Isn't that something?"

"I made some bad calls," Enlil said, glaring back at Gyje.

"I'm sure you did. You're always a laugh, Lily. Can't imagine how you made it this far and still get yourself busted up. Who's your friend?"

"Nobody," Enlil said. "Off-stationer looking for salvage, that's all."

"Sure, looking for salvage. And talking to Glutton's pet. You didn't think to make her come and even say so much as *hello* to me, did you? That seem kind of arrogant to you, Lily?"

"I didn't mean to insult you—"

"You a captain now Lily? Is that it? Got your own crew squirreled away somewhere?"

"No," Enlil said, shaking her head. He pressed in on her broken hand slightly, causing a tremor of pain.

"That's right. No patch. No ship. So what have you got?"

"Nothing," Enlil said.

"Nothing, huh? Then *why* did you think you could cut a deal in my dome, and not even ask *permission* first?"

Gyje's grip suddenly tightened. Enlil buckled to her knees as broken bones mashed together. She bit down hard, trying not to scream.

"See," Gyje was saying to Tsi as he kept up the pressure on Enlil's shattered hand. "This. Is. What *happens* when you don't show respect to Jarawat's son!"

His boot slammed into Enlil's side, sending her sprawling. Even as the wind was driven from her lungs, she found herself vaguely bemused. This was the third beating she'd received in less than two days. Surely a new record for herself. She almost laughed as the tall pirate stood over her, cracking his knuckles.

"Ooh this just isn't your day, is it?" he said. "I always liked your face, Lily. And I know your little tourist needs you able to talk and see, so I'm just gonna work your ribs a bit. Nothing too bad, I promise. And as for you, outsider, you should know there's a price for doing business in *my* corridor without—"

Gyje was cut off by a wet thud. Tsi had struck him across the face with her Repeater, hurtling him backwards. In an instant she was on him, grabbing his shoulder and jerking him between herself and his guards. Her pistol roared four times, and each of the guard's legs jerked backwards as they fell, reduced to bloody pulp. They yowled on the floor as Tsi's knee found Gyje's stomach, then her palm struck the side of his head. On the ground now, Gyje looked up at her, face red and contorted.

Tsi knelt over him, pressing her pistol into his face.

"Don't! Don't don't don't!" Enlil stammered.

Tsi ripped the dagger from Gyje's belt, and slid it along the ground to Enlil, who scooped it up with her good hand instinctively.

"You gotta calm down—" Enlil began, but Tsi's focus was solely on Gyje, squirming beneath her.

"That's the price for interfering in my affairs," Tsi said. "I guess this really just isn't *your* day, is it?"

"You don't know who you're messing with!" Gyje growled through bloody teeth. "When Jarawat finds out—"

Tsi shattered his jaw with another blow from the barrel of her pistol.

"Tell her all about it when your face heals," Tsi said.

She got off of the pirate, who rolled around on the ground, moaning and clutching at his ruined face. Tsi's visage was dark, and she stared straight ahead as she walked across the platform and to the catwalks leading down below. Enlil hurried to catch up with her, only sparing a quick glance backwards. Gyje's horrified consort was at his side, blubbering helplessly. His maimed guards were fumbling in pools of their own blood, bizarrely humorous as they slapped at each other and tried to stand on ruined legs.

"Gods and spirits!" Enlil swore. "You didn't have to do that!"

"Oh yes I did," Tsi said. She wiped the blood from the barrel of her pistol and shoved it back into her holster.

No one raised a finger as they left Gyje and his court behind.

Wylla and Liss left their pod at one of the outer landing bays of the great ring. It was a small vehicle, meant for shuttling passengers back and forth across the Guraggan fleet. Breaker Liss had seemed to take up the whole space himself, piloting their craft with surprising dexterity. The Breaker spoke little. Of all the fellow servants of Lady Ornicht, he was kindest to her, in his own way. She didn't find him pleasant exactly, but he never spoke to her with the same contempt or coldness as the others. At least he had put on more clothes than he normally did.

They had slipped in, more-or-less unnoticed, with a throng of small mining craft. The Noxians were a shockingly disorganized people. Miners in miss-matched fatigues jabbered with each other as they began unloading crates of raw ore and carefully harvested ice. A few shouted obscenities as Liss and she walked past, but a glare from the Breaker silenced all of them. No one asked them for a docking registry, or welcomed them to the station either.

They made their way through the twisting corridors of Salvation, Wylla occasionally referencing an archaic holo-map she'd stored on her wrist-comp. Cross-referencing the architecture with known designs, Wylla was trying to determine where she might find any kind of central computer bank or link that could give her up-to-date information. It was a hopeless task. Salvation had been built over generations, different waves of migrants and refugees adding to the patch-work structure. It might look vaguely uniform from the outside, but its innards were utterly chaotic. Oxygen and gravity were the only two things that were constant throughout the rings, and the first she wasn't entirely certain of.

As they walked they attracted stares. Jeers. Sometimes hissed threats. The people deeper in the station were more alert than the giddy miners. They marked her for an outsider. Some stalked her from the shadows, like predators scenting blood. Still, she was not afraid of them. Like any predator, they weighed risk and reward. She might be easy prey, but Breaker Liss certainly wasn't.

At last, Wylla gave up on trying to find a computer core, or any more civilized way of gathering information. She decided to try the direct approach. Heading for one of the upper docks, she found a bored technician standing at a wall-console, looking over what appeared to be docking registries.

"Greetings," Wylla said, folding her hands in front of her and bowing to the man.

"Ya? What ya want?" the man asked, not looking up.

"May I ask who this docking bay belongs to?"

"Orto Hej-Kassel's miners own this one. We're under Jarawat and the Ten Sons," he said. "Ain't been no big fights lately. She's still runnin' things."

"Ah," Wylla said. Her well-honed mind ran through probabilities in micro-seconds, but the name was unfamiliar. A pirate, a Noxian pirate, establishing a symbolic familial bond with her lieutenants or possibly a direct blood relation. Noxians tended not to have very long lives, so if her Ten Sons were biological, the Jarawat was unusually lucky or unusually successful. Wylla guessed it was the second.

"May I look at your docking registry?" she asked.

The technician laughed.

"You get lost or something?" he asked, turning to her and grinning through broken teeth.

"I require information about a ship which docked here recently. It may still be on station."

"You a bounty-killer?" the man asked. His hands were hovering nervously about his waist. He had no weapons, save an arc-welder that Wylla was sure could bore straight through a Reaving suit.

Wylla smiled at him.

"No. We are part of a trading mission, collecting goods from the system. Our craft was damaged, but a sister ship from our Company has also docked here. We wished to consult with them about possible paths forwards."

"What company?"

"Delwint Conglomerate," Wylla said, naming one of the largest and most powerful stellar corporations on the Frontier. She was not positive, but the odds were good Delwint ships were present on the station.

"None of them in this section," the tech said. He brushed a hand across the screen, sending it dark.

"Perhaps they are traveling incognito," Wylla said.

"Well, check with your captain. My shift is over, and I gotta bad need for a two-suit so—"

"We have money," Breaker Liss said.

"I'm not sure—" the Technician began.

"Money or pain," the Breaker continued, balling his fists for emphasis. "Your choice."

Wylla looked between the two men. She wanted to stop Liss with all her heart, but she knew the path of logic. With luck, fear would cave the Noxian.

"Two... two hundred," the Technician murmured, eyes cast to the ground. "Two hundred and not a word of this to the Orto or Jarawat or any of her people."

The Breaker pulled a pouch from his waist and sorted through it. Wylla stared in wonder. The bag was full of money,: credits, chits, Sola, markers from a thousand worlds. They glowed with different symbols, luminescent signs of their various denominations. It was a fortune. Enough to buy this whole station, if someone was willing to sell it. At last, the breaker pulled out a black bar with a crescent shaped bite in the center, and handed it to the Technician.

"Here," he said, turning the screen on, and gesturing for Wylla. "It's all yours. Every ship that's docked that we know about is in that register. I—I have to go."

He walked away from them briskly, tucking the money into his jump suit.

Wylla stepped to the screen. Her fingers danced across it. She began scrolling through ship names and docking dates. The Noxian methods were imprecise and informal, many craft just listed by size and arrival time. She worked quickly, running calculations, likelihoods that this craft or that one was the target. She had narrowed it down to three ships in the general vicinity, all of the right size and arrival times, all potentially hiding something more beneath their appearance as freighters and light frigates, when she glanced over her shoulder at the Breaker.

"How much money do you have in that sack?" she asked.

"Enough," Breaker Liss said.

He knew what she was going to propose. She could tell from his body language. But she had to try anyway.

"We could hire a ship," she said. "With that kind of money. Plenty of people here are flying all over the Frontier and beyond."

"Why would we do that?"

"You're from Niobus, I know," she said. "One of the oldest civilizations in the Frontier. It must be very beautiful."

"It is," the Breaker said. "I traveled to many Nioban worlds when I was younger. I was part of a high family, before I entered our Lady's service."

"Do you ever want to go back?"

"No."

"I think about Bykonus Prime every day," Wylla said lightly.

"It would be a stupid place to run to," he said. "We would find you. Punish you."

Her work finally done, Wylla turned away from the screen, and looked up at the Breaker. He was a giant, but she felt strangely calm around him. He wouldn't hurt her unless she crossed a line, and she knew she had been careful not to. There was something else there though, beneath his heavy brow, behind his dark eyes.

"Why don't you want to leave?" she asked. "I thought everyone did."

The Breaker shook his head, a rueful smile on his face.

"How little you understand," he said. "I could leave our mistress whenever I like. I stay because I long to serve her, not because I am forced to."

"How can you be loyal to her? She *enslaved* you."

"She liberated me."

"By stealing you from your home? By pumping you full of drugs and sending you to die against her foes?"

"By purging my weakness," the Breaker said. He took a step towards her. She could smell his sweat, see the tightness of his vast muscles. Wylla's heart hammered in her chest.

"She sent me into the flames of war," Breaker Liss continued, deep, dark eyes burning into Wylla's own. "On Niobus I was a prince. On the battlefield I was no one. The fires changed me, reforged me. All that I truly am, what was within me, not given to me... that I owe to her."

He raised a huge hand, and Wylla closed her eyes, trembling. Expecting a blow, she felt instead a delicate, hesitant touch. Slowly the Breaker ran one finger along her cheek, tracing the line of her jaw.

"Do not speak to me of such things again," Breaker Liss said. "I would suffer greatly if I had to choose between my Mistress and you."

"Increase difficulty. Increase randomization."

The machine spoke in the same clipped tone it always did. It was seated in the hold, a bundle of cables linked to the back of its head. It was defenseless, inert save for the movement of its slack, fleshy jaw.

Hiron was running it through the combat scenarios it had requested. Tsi's computer systems were extremely intuitive, and he couldn't deny his gratitude for that. He'd been cooped up with the machine for hours now. His sleep had been poor, interrupted by Strongmind constantly waking him to make 'adjustments' to the surgery he'd performed.

This he had done uncomplainingly, and then at last he had passed into a sleep so dreamless and blissful that he was fairly certain nothing could rouse him from it... until Strongmind had woken him up again. The machine had gently but firmly shook his arm and repeated his name over and over again, an irritating tone of *insistence* in its voice. It had explained its desire, and with no hope of being left alone to sleep, Hiron had wound up spending the whole morning running simulations for it.

"No," Strongmind said after Hiron entered some adjustments. "This scenario is not adequate."

"Why not?" Hiron asked, turning up from the computer screen. "I increased the difficulty like you said. Opposition is twice the default, and I gave them Guraggan heavy armor—"

"They attack the same way. Over and over."

"It's just a training scenario..."

"It is useless if it does not simulate the behavior of my opponents."

"Alright, I'll dig through the memory core and see if there's anything more challenging."

"How would you approach this situation?"

"Me?"

The machine's question hung in the air. Hiron had never really thought of such things. The simulation was the ninth battle of Tellemon's Landing. He'd put Strongmind in the position of the Epilotii garrison, getting overrun by Nioban shock troops. Unlike the real event, Strongmind had inflicted devastating casualties and captured its opponent's landing craft. Repeatedly.

"I don't have a lot of experience with this sort of thing..." Hiron said.

"I do not care. You are the commander. You must take this location. Adjust the program to fit your desires."

Hiron studied the screen. He was not unfamiliar with the principles behind what Strongmind was asking. Indeed, if he had been stronger he would have gone through many such scenarios with his father and his father's court. But he had been born stunted and weak. War had been as distant and foolish a pursuit for him as love.

"How would you deploy the advance guard?" Strongmind asked.

Hiron swept his fingers across the screen and it changed, forming a beautiful field of green grass. Across it he could see the Epilotii garrison's barricade. It had been thrown together in a few scant hours in real life. It was nothing but earthworks and portable shield generators, just enough to resist the Nioban's strafing runs. Niobans didn't have the luxury of assault drones, so the first wave had been made up of shock troops, leaping from their landing craft and controlling their fall with jump jets. He studied the Epilotti strongpoint, the field around it. There was a small outcropping of buildings beyond the fortification, nestled at the edge of a clear lake with a rocky shore.

Hiron entered a series of commands.

"Alright. I've adjusted the program. Have at it."

Strongmind sat in silence for a few minutes. The console beeped and blinked, signaling it was finished. Pulling up the simulation's results, Hiron wasn't surprised to see the machine had won.

"Well, sorry," he began. "I did my best, but this isn't really my area of expertise—"

"You have defeated me," the machine said, meticulously removing the cables from the back of its head.

"You don't have to spare my feelings—"

Strongmind had risen from its chair and walked over to the console. It busily input commands, replaying the battle on the display.

"I sustained 78% casualties," Strongmind said. "My defensive systems were severely damaged."

"Well, you still won," Hiron said.

"I achieved my primary objective. The victory is not sustainable. Why did you drop your advance troops around the outbuildings? They could not support the main force's landing."

"I figured the buildings could give them some cover. They'd be slaughtered just charging at you across an open field."

"And your second wave then had to advance unsupported across that same field… but I, in turn, had to divide my attack between two forces. My kill-rate was inefficient."

"Look, you still cleared the field of my men. You won."

"Because your troops retreated. I sustained heavy casualties trying to assault the weaker force. Your casualties were minimal."

The machine turned and looked at Hiron hard. It seemed to be studying him, probing him with its eyes, as if it was looking at some bizarre anomaly.

"You adjusted your troops aggression levels. You made them more reluctant to fight, and more willing to retreat. Why?"

Hiron shrugged.

"I didn't want them to die, I guess. You asked me how I would fight this battle? The answer is I wouldn't, not unless I absolutely had to. So I tried to keep my troops as safe as possible."

"They are not humans," Strongmind said.

"It doesn't matter. It's what I would have done."

"Your prudence gained you a strategic victory," Strongmind said. "A second attack would have easily taken the defenses."

"Thanks, I guess."

"I do not think that *you* would have been capable of leading that second attack," Strongmind said. "I suggest you avoid command positions unless absolutely necessary."

Hiron rolled his eyes.

"I'll keep that in mind."

Tsi called the ship a few hours later. She had spent another night out in the station with her newfound companion. From what Hiron overheard of the conversation between Strongmind and her, she was making some sort of transport arrangements. He wondered why she wasn't taking the ship, but he quickly realized it was still under repair by Furner Ketsu and his crew. He hobbled outside and spent a few hours sitting on an empty crate in the repair bay, watching the men work.

They came and went freely, starting projects at random, and shouting at each other all the while in their strange pirate's tongue. Seeing how casually they treated their work didn't exactly inspire confidence in Hiron. The hull they were patching up was going to be the only thing between him and the void soon enough.

A shadow fell across him. He turned and looked up at the smiling, pleasant features of a woman. She was wearing a canvas traveling cloak, but he could see the hem of a silken robe playing about her feet, and she had her hands clasped in front of her, ringed with bands of precious metals. It was clear she was not from this place. She looked almost surreal, a startlingly clean thing standing amid rusting old machinery and glistening pools of oil.

She bowed formally and said something to him he didn't understand.

"Uh, No... not speaking Noxian," Hiron managed.

The woman suppressed a laugh.

"Trade-speak?" she asked.

"Some," he replied.

"May I ask, my friend, whose ship that is?"

"I'm traveling on it," Hiron said. "Just in for repairs a few days. Nothing significant."

"Ah," the woman said. She turned and looked at the ship. He could see a subtle movement of her lips as her eyes danced up and down the hull. She seemed to be counting, or perhaps quietly working out calculations.

"It's not for sale if that's what you're thinking," he said quickly. "Or, that is, I'm not the captain. I mean, she wouldn't sell it, is all."

"Oh, I was just passing by. I am a traveler myself, and I could not help but admire such a beautiful craft."

"She is at that," Hiron beamed.

"What is she called?"

"Uh... *Grazer*," Hiron said. "I don't really like the name though. Hoping to get the captain to change it."

"What would you call it?"

"*Horizon*," Hiron said quickly. "Or, maybe *Star Chaser*. We're going a long way, I just kind of think it should have a better name, you know?"

"Of course. You're merchants?"

"No, no! Just, uh, just travelers, you know. Heading from one spot to another."

"Back to Kios I would imagine," the woman said.

"Kios? Why would we be headed there?"

"Just a guess," the woman smiled politely. "But where are my manners? I am Wylla Laran-Se. It is nice to meet you."

"Hiron of-...um, just Hiron," Hiron said, staggering to his feet and shaking the woman's extended hand. He had almost told her his clan name, but decided it would be both unwise and irrelevant. The Dath were probably all gone now, and the only people that name would matter to would be trouble for him.

"Is your captain around?" Wylla asked.

"No," Hiron said. "She'll be back later. She's dealing with something else right now. Why?"

"I... I was thinking about doing some more traveling myself," Wylla said. "But perhaps it would not be such a good idea. You have a lovely ship. I wouldn't want to disrupt things."

"I'm sure we could make arrangements. If you tell me how we can get in touch—"

"You are too kind," the woman said stiffly. She bowed to Hiron again. "But I really must be going. Thank you for your time Hiron, it was very pleasant to meet you."

"You as well," Hiron said, watching the woman leave.

She walked back to one of the arches leading into the bowels of the station. He caught a glimpse of someone standing in the shadows, waiting for her. It was a large man, so big Hiron thought he might be as tall as Strongmind. He exchanged words with Wylla briefly, then the two of them disappeared.

Hiron grabbed his crutches and hobbled back to the ship. Half of him had wanted Wylla to stay, to come with him. And half of him knew better.

He had to tell Strongmind. Their enemies were here, and they would be making their move soon.

Tsi and Enlil were drifting beyond Salvation, their small pod's jets flaring irregularly. She concentrated on what lay ahead: Glutton. They were moving at good speed in their tiny craft, rented from a salvager they had haggled with. The pod was small but sturdy, plenty of room for two people, and good seals too. It had solid manipulator arms, reminding Tsi of the time she'd spent as a miner in the Web of Eden. The thought of that peaceful life always brought a smile to her lips. She almost wanted to tell her companion about it, but Enlil had been quiet since last night.

Noxians weren't notoriously talkative, nor were they stoics. Tsi knew she had done plenty to upset her new companion. She shouldn't have hurt Gyje. Enlil had asked her not to. Tsi's blood had been up though, and she always did stupid things when she was angry. Particularly when she was angry and thought she was in the right.

Now their time on Salvation would be even more complicated. She hadn't risked returning to the ship just yet, meaning Enlil's injured hand would have to wait until they were ready to leave. Still, all she had to do was take a quick trip out to Glutton, secure the beacon, then head back and Slip out of the system. They'd be gone and on their way to the Janissariat within twenty four hours.

The thought was not reassuring. In fact, it turned Tsi's stomach. She reminded herself that it was what she had to do.

"I don't like this," Enlil said from the co-pilot's chair.

She was adjusting their heading slightly, keeping Glutton ahead of them. The ship, if ship it could be called, was a small station by itself. A monstrous tangle of engines and cargo containers, hulls of dozens of makes of craft welded together and reforged into each other, held in place by delicate metal tendrils and crude bulk clamps. Drones drifted like insects around a hive, subtly altering and rearranging the vast frame of Glutton, following the whims of a mind at once expansive and stunted, genius and idiot all contained within the same pulsing memory core.

Tsi noted as they drew closer that the chaotic mass congealed into a long, bullet-blunt nose, with a massive ram-scoop at the fore. The ancient device would have been useless to a structure like Glutton unless it jettisoned half its mass. It looked like a huge maw. She thought of the deep sea leviathans of Old Earth, and wondered if Glutton had patterned itself after those monsters on purpose.

"You can't trust it," Enlil said. "It's crazy."

"Lot of that out here," Tsi said. "Doesn't mean we can't make a deal."

"A deal for *helium*," Enlil continued, exasperated. "What next? Coal for a steam engine?"

"You know what a steam engine is?"

Enlil scowled at Tsi.

"I know how to read," she said. "Not just flight manuals, either."

"Sure... I've just never met anyone out here who was interested in pre-Slip history."

Enlil shrugged.

"Mama liked engine lore. Is what it is."

"Sure."

Tsi knew better than to pry. Few Noxians had happy families. Even reproducing out here always struck her as a strange decision. Enough people still wound up doing it to keep the population up, though. There were always refugees and vagabonds from outside the system steadily flowing in, too. Like she had been a lifetime ago. As she was now.

At last they came to dock upon Glutton's station side, finding an open airlock waiting for them. It was at the end of a series of pods, linked and welded together to form a ramp down into the bowels of the machine ship. Tsi led the way, awkwardly scrambling hand over foot down the impromptu ramp, clambering over ancient control consoles and trying not to tear her suit on the sharp edges left by the imprecise, frantic work of Glutton's drones. The AI had only communicated with them in brief bursts of data as they approached, not bothering with direct communication. Tsi was not yet ready to abandon her chance at acquiring the beacon, but as she crawled off the ramp and into an empty, dusty chamber lit only by emergency lighting strips, she couldn't deny her unease.

Tsi was wearing an EVA suit, as was Enlil. She tapped the side of her helmet, turning on the head lights. That, combined with her augmented vision, turned the room into a murky green, rather than the near-pitch it had been. It was then that she saw a small figure sitting in the far corner.

Dressed similarly to the Emissary she had met on Salvation, this thing's body was dry and desiccated beneath its silken robes. Tsi thought it was a corpse, crystallized with space exposure. It stirred when their lights played across it.

"The suits are unnecessary," it said in a reedy voice. "My master has generously provided you with oxygen from its personal reserve."

Tsi knew better than to insult the machine. She slowly removed her helmet and snapped it onto her back-rig, ready to re-clasp it around her head in an instant. Though if Glutton really intended to murder her, she had to admit it would have an easy time doing it now.

"You have the data?"

Tsi held up a pad.

"Hard-locked," she said. "Your master releases the beacon, I input the code, and we all walk away happy."

"*A LOCK WAS NOT PART OF YOUR ARRANGEMENT WITH I, TRAVELER.*"

Tsi realized Glutton's speech was coming through all of the speakers in the room at once, including her own helmet's broadcaster. The servant-creature mouthed the words in unison with the booming, crackling voice.

Enlil had drawn her knife instinctively, her stance defensive and low. The Noxian watched the shadows like a trapped rat, waiting for an attack from any angle. But they were quite alone except for the desiccated servant.

"*I, TRAVELER, EVALUATE YOUR RELUCTANCE AND DEFIANCE. WHY DO YOU PROTEST AGAINST ME, BRUTE THING? I HAVE GIVEN YOU A GREAT OFFER OF ADVANCED MASS. THE BEACON COULD BE RENDERED TO CARBON AND HELIUM, FUEL AND BUILDING MATERIAL FOR THE GREAT WORK OF I, TRAVELER. I OFFER IT FOR YOUR KNOWLEDGE. DO NOT TEST THE PATIENCE OF I, TRAVELER.*"

"Bring out the beacon," Tsi said evenly. "Then I unlock the data pad. Not before."

"*THE BEACON IS SAFE.*"

"Where?"

"*WHERE THE MOST PRECIOUS THINGS OF I, TRAVELER, ARE KEPT.*"

"Why don't you just float it out to us?" Enlil asked. "No fuss. We'll leave the pad here, and—"

"*YOU WILL NOT TAKE CARGO FROM I, TRAVELER WITHOUT PAY. MENT.*"

"We're going to pay you," Tsi insisted.

The servant-creature tittered at that.

"Oh yes, oh yes you are," it murmured.

"*IF NO PAY. MENT. RECEIVED. THEN I, TRAVELER, WILL PUNISH NON-COMPLIANCE—*"

Tsi could hear stirrings in the corridors around them, see lights flicking on. She heard the click of spidery limbs against metal. Kill-drones. At a guess, Glutton could mobilize and sustain thousands of them. Not a lot of good her Repeater and Enlil's knife could do here.

"We'll comply!" she shouted. "We'll comply. Take us to the beacon, and you'll get your data. I promise."

"*LOGIC DISPLAYED. FOLLOW EXTENSION 181.*"

Mechanically, the servant-creature rose from its chair. It leered at Tsi and Enlil, and beckoned for them to follow.

They emerged from the dusty chamber into a narrow tube. The thing led them forward, tracing steps it had clearly walked hundreds, thousands of times before. As they walked Tsi had a sudden moment of terror when she realized she was in a star field. Naked space stretched beneath her feet, twinkling stars and inky darkness. Instinctively, she moved to snap her helmet on, then hesitated when she realized she could still breath and feel artificial gravity. The servant-creature tittered.

"Clear shields," it said. "I have reduced their opacity to give you a view of the stars. My master wishes its guests to enjoy their stay."

"Keep the rest of your surprises to yourself," Tsi growled, giving the thin creature a shove on the back for emphasis.

Its flesh was brittle and yielding beneath her hand, but it only tittered again in response. A little more pressure and she would have broken its collar bone. The servant-creature no longer felt pain the way a human being would, though whether that was through drugs or delusion Tsi couldn't say. She'd heard of people spending so long linked to a virtual intelligence like Glutton that they stopped caring about their physical bodies. Tsi wondered how old this creature was, how many decades it had spent sitting inert in that chamber, waiting for one of Glutton's "guests" to arrive.

They followed the cackling little thing through a series of hubs, taking a magnetic lift down almost a hundred floors by Tsi's count before they were at last led to a long octagonal corridor. This space, at least, was regular. Pristine. Sterile. Its walls were bathed in a peaceful blue light, every surface obsessively polished. She watched as a mite-sized drone scurried methodically along the ground, tiny brushes scraping away at accumulated dust.

As they turned a corner she saw a single console, long since dead, and on its side she could just barely make out characters in an ancient language. She paused to study the strange shapes, her brow furrowed. She spoke many languages, but historical linguistics wasn't one of her areas of expertise. Still, she could see in the writing a vague ancestors to some of the script of Kios, and, oddly, a strong resemblance to the language of the Guraggan.

"Heeee... the guest doesn't understand the words, neh?" the servant-creature said, rubbing two rachitic hands together.

"What language is this?" she asked.

"Old. Old when my master was first forged. *If* you are decorous and *if* you are intelligent, the Traveler may speak it to you... hehh..."

"Says 'Auxiliary Power Console 22'," Enlil said casually.

Tsi and the creature turned to her questioningly.

Enlil shrugged. "Told you I can read."

"Hnnn... been here before perhaps?" the creature asked.

"Let's keep moving," Enlil said impatiently.

At last they came to Glutton's heart. Tsi knew they were nearing the engine core by the familiar hum within her bones. She'd been a spacer for a lifetime now, and even before she'd come to the Frontier she'd spent a lot of time on ships. She could always feel an engine before she saw it, the raw power within setting the hairs on the back of her neck standing up, her heart slowly beating to the rhythm of the star drive.

This was the deepest, most heavily armored place within Glutton's haphazard body, a reactor that could have powered a battle cruiser. They were above it in a massive chamber of glass and steel, consoles surrounding them. It had once been an engineer's station, or perhaps an ancient command bridge. Surrounded by windows looking out onto the pulsing core, Tsi realized that when fully powered they would have served as display screens too, surrounding the crew with information while they straddled the heart of their ship. The chamber was so huge, it reminded Tsi of some of the great temples she had seen in her travels.

The chamber tapered upwards to a point high above them, a single light shining down. There, at the center of the room, was the beacon. It was about the height of a person, made out of angular grey metal. There were no frills or decorations on its hull. A simple device with a simple purpose. Tsi walked around it, reassuring herself it was real. Then she looked upwards into the light.

At first she thought there was a strange ribbing on the roof of the chamber, but as she focused she came to realize what the rows upon rows of metallic spheres were. Each had a single circular viewing plate at its center. Each was numbered. Tsi guessed there must have been a hundred, perhaps two hundred spheres in all.

Cryo-stasis pods. As she studied them, she realized at least a third were un-powered. Others showed signs of recent maintenance. Tsi thought on this a moment. The best cryo-pods could last a millennium with top-tier maintenance, but the chance of successfully recovering a human inside dwindled with each passing decade.

"MY CHARGES. MY CREW. THE MOST PRECIOUS COMPONENTS OF THE JOURNEY OF I, TRAVELER. MORE PRECIOUS THAN BEACONS AND TITANIUM, MORE PRECIOUS THAN URANIUM AND HELIUM-3. YOUR PRIZE IS KEPT SAFE WITH THEM BY I, TRAVELER."

"People..." Tsi whispered. "You've been trading in... people."

"THIRTEEN REMAIN OF THE ORIGINAL RESERVES OF I, TRAVELER. BUT I, TRAVELER, AM RESOURCEFUL. THE GREAT JOURNEY CONTINUES. I, TRAVELER, KEEP MY CREW SAFE. THE HUMAN MASS OF THE JOURNEY HAS BEEN MAINTAINED SINCE THE DAY OF DEPARTURE."

The machine's words were harsh in Tsi's ears. They came from all around her, from the lips of the servant-creature, but most of all from her own comm unit, pulses of sound against her skin.

"SAFE," Glutton repeated, *"AND WHOLE. NOW, BRUTE, WE WILL TRADE."*

Like a performer on a barren stage, Lady Ornicht stood alone in the single light of the armory. She was on a circular platform, raised a step above the floor. She wore nothing but her *bulkchin* suit, a tight-fitting glove of black synthetic material that clung to her wiry frame. She flexed her hands, testing her strength, seeing how her raw body moved unaided.

First the skeleton. Servants emerged from the darkness, directed wordlessly in a ritual they had performed countless times. The ports along her spine were opened up, and a flexible second vertebrae of oily black metal was clasped into place. Next, the armature and braces were worked around her arms and legs, anchored about her waist and shoulders. Thousands of miniature tendrils burrowed into the *bulkchin* hide, linking with Ornicht's nervous system, increasing her strength a hundred fold.

Her body now strong enough to bare it, her slaves began to encase her in armor. She had fought battles in all the ways of a free Guraggan woman, from a humble reaver yet un-blooded to a drone controller, cold and precise, but it was the way of the *Kheshtic*, the line breaker, that had been her true calling.

Greaves and breastplate were clasped in place, linking with the power core on her spine. Next, her gauntlets and vambraces, monomolecular blades whispering out of their sheathes and back with a thought. A hopper of ammo was magnetized to the back of her armor, the flechette cannon mounted to her shoulder.

Last of all, Breaker Liss knelt before her and offered up her helmet. Ornicht took the fearsome thing in her hands, one thumb running across the war mask's twisted mouth. This was her face. She put it on, and it linked with all her systems, sharpening senses, filling her eyes, her ears, her nostrils, her very lungs with information.

"You are certain of the target," Lady Ornicht said as she stepped from the platform.

Liss was shadowing her as she walked, but her question had been directed at the prostrate form at the far side of the room. Wylla the Bykon lay with her head pressed firmly to the floor, not daring to look up at her mistress.

It hadn't been a question, but the woman responded:

"I am. That is the ship which escaped your fleet. There are at least two people aboard her now, but likely more soon. At least one must be a formidable warrior."

"Good," Ornicht hissed.

"Your Battle-Serfs await you at the transport craft," Breaker Liss said, adjusting his own body armor slightly. "Skyme informs me that the Thralls will be ready as our reserve if necessary."

"The fodder will be unnecessary," Ornicht said.

She paused at Wylla's side, her boots mere inches from the woman's face.

"You have done well, hunting hound," she said. "This will be a worthy prize."

Garbed for war, Lady Ornicht reveled in the sensation. Every step she took made her feel young. Strong.

Alive.

"Seventeenth attempt has been met with failure," Strongmind stated.

They were aboard the ship, Hiron sitting next to the machine as it worked away at the comms unit. They should have thought of a way out of this. They should have run. Or scuttled the ship. Or jettisoned it off the dock and waited in space for Tsi to come and rescue them. But the machine had rejected all of Hiron's suggestions.

"It won't be long before they hit us," he said.

"You are aware of enemy movements?"

"No," Hiron said. "It's what I would do though. They sent scouts. They know there's only two of us. I'd hit us fast. That's what my father used to do, strike fast and hard when your enemy is weak."

"Certainly. But you do not know our opponent's logistical capabilities."

"Well, I figure it's more than a cripple and a damaged drone."

"I am 73% functional," Strongmind said.

"And what exactly does that mean?"

"I can terminate at least three standard opponents before I am disabled."

"Oh good! So if we have three Guraggan warriors coming at us, we'll be just fine!" Hiron said.

"I could not fight a Guraggan," Strongmind corrected. "Their standard level of enhancement would outmatch my own current performance capabilities."

Hiron crossed his arms and tried hard to still his twitching leg. It was pointless. He wanted to run, but to where? The interior of Salvation? He'd be gutted within a week. But the machine had insisted that they stay here, and it was the only thing that could protect him.

"Why don't we tell the technicians?" Hiron asked.

"The hull is nearly secure. It is most important that they ensure our ship is space worthy."

"They're Noxians, right? They know how to fight."

"Correct. They are also noted for a strong mercenary culture. Their loyalty is in-group oriented and mercurial. A logical course of action for them would be to secure our own termination in exchange for monetary reward."

Hiron sighed. The machine was right. No one on the station would risk their lives to protect him.

"Well, we could do something at least..."

"Eighteenth attempt at communication unsuccessful."

"Look. How much of the ship's computer could you... you know, get inside you?"

"Very little," Strongmind said. "My algorithms take up much of the processor capacity of this body. Scuttling the ship represents an unacceptable loss of intelligence for our Master's operations, as I cannot duplicate the information contained within its data core."

"So we're just going to sit here and wait for—"

There was a loud thump outside the ship, followed by screams. Then shouting. The familiar pop of gunfire and the burning hiss of lasers in response. Hiron looked at Strongmind, eyes wide with fright.

"I suggest you get behind something," the machine said, as it picked up the pulse-carbine at its side and slammed a fresh energy cell in.

CHAPTER 14

Tsi was still staring at the strange honeycomb of stasis pods above her. More than a hundred people, frozen in suspended animation. Glutton's "crew", prisoners to its madness. Some might have been there from before the rise of Kios, or the arrival of the Guraggan. Captives from ancient history. She wondered what they would say if they were ever released, emerging into a world alien to them. They had put their faith in this machine, its programmers and engineers, and had been utterly, horribly failed. It was supposed to be their protector, but it had become their tyrant.

She knew that story well.

Tsi wasn't sure if she felt worse for the few original survivors of the crew, or Glutton's recent additions. Despite the advent of drones and clones with deliberately stunted intelligence, there had always been a market for human chattel. The Frontier was especially rife with it, and the Guraggan practiced enforced servitude as a matter of course. Why waste money manufacturing and maintaining a drone when you could pry open a merchant ship and force its crew to serve you? Humans were cheaper than machines, after all, and easier to replace out here. There were worse fates than the dreamless sleep of the cryo-pod. A gentler sort of murder compared to many.

"Your crew," she said. "Perhaps if you woke them up, they could assist you in-in evaluating my data—"

"NO. I, TRAVELER, MUST PROTECT THEM. THE FUNCTIONS OF I WILL SUFFICE. THEY MUST NOT BE AWOKEN UNTIL THE DESTINATION IS REACHED."

"Don't try to reason with it," Enlil whispered to Tsi. She was still nervously eyeing the way they'd come in, shifting her weight from foot to foot.

"I humbly submit that they might help speed you on your journey, Traveler," Tsi insisted. "Your crew is a vital part of your mission, it can't be accomplished without their help."

"YOU DO NOT COMPREHEND, BRUTE. THEY ARE KEY TO THE JOURNEY OF I, TRAVELER. THEY MUST REMAIN ALIVE FOR THE MISSION TO SUCCEED. NO HARM MUST COME TO THEM. THEY ARE SAFEST IN CRYO-CONTAINMENT."

Of course, Tsi thought. Glutton's ancient programmers had made one of the most careless mistakes one could when designing an intelligence. They had given it two unexpectedly paradoxical orders: complete the journey, and keep the crew alive. Little did they realize that the machine did not see its crew as unique individuals, but as a certain amount of mass, like any other cargo. It had stopped itself here, for one reason or another, frozen in the uncertainty of whether or not it could complete its mission. And so it had become this ghastly mass, enslaving unwitting spacers for centuries. Too terrified of failing, Glutton would never attempt to complete its quest.

A few careless lines of code, and this monster had been born, blindly carrying a hopeful crew of colonists into damnation. How like the Empress of Kios those ancient programmers had been, Tsi thought, unwittingly forging the means of their destruction. Every precaution had been taken to ensure the loyalty of her Janissaries, and yet still those creatures had risen up and seized the Empire for themselves.

She looked between the cryo-pods, and the beacon.

"Let's hurry up and finish this," Enlil said.

Tsi nodded. She felt as if the bottom of her stomach had dropped out.

A hundred lives was nothing compared to what she needed to do. She still hated herself for doing it, hated herself for even thinking that way. She had sworn to never make this kind of trade again. Her promises never had been worth the breath she'd wasted on them, though.

She took out her data pad, and pressed a series of keys, unlocking the code within. Tsi held it out. The servant-thing scuttled forwards and took it, bony hands wrapping greedily around the device and tucking it away into the folds of its robes.

"TRADE COMPLETED. THE DRONES OF I, TRAVELER SHALL BRING THE BEACON TO YOU."

Tsi turned wordlessly and walked away from Glutton's heart, trying to shut out the thoughts of all those people suspended in cryo-stasis forever. She thought about vowing to herself that she would find a way to come back and free them. She was too tired, though. She had not the strength to lie, even if it was just to herself.

"Maybe we can negotiate this!"

One of the Noxians was shouting in Panglos. His voice was loud, but there was fear beneath it. Lady Ornicht could smell his sweat, practically taste his blood.

They had struck quickly, Breaker Liss leading the assault while she had scuttled, beast-like, through an ancient ventilation duct. Oh, the shock on their faces as she had descended upon them! Tiny, desperate little things fleeing before her as she cut them down. She could feel the sharp pangs in her chest, hear her own ragged breathing, but she did not care. Every inch of her body was alight with a joyous flame.

She had not killed so effortlessly since she was young. There was something to be said for a worthy foe, but it was a great pleasure to be reminded of her own superiority.

She loped across the open deck, taloned limbs sparking against the ground as she ran. One of the Noxians leaned out from behind a crate and fired at her, but Ornicht's shoulder-cannon was already tracking him. With a thought, the man's chest exploded in pink mist, the report of her weapon echoing against her helmet.

She drove hard towards the stacked crates, then tumbled into a combat crouch as she passed them. Two of the Noxians were standing beside their dead comrade, panic upon their faces. One was a big man in greasy coveralls, his hair a mass of dreadlocks. Older, heavier, clearly their leader.

She lashed out with one foot, dexterous mechanical claws wrapping against the man's throat and pinning him against a crate. With a quick swipe of her arm-blade, she decapitated the other Noxian. Crimson sprayed across the leader's face, clotting in his black hair.

"No negotiation," she hissed, voice distorted by her beaked helm. "Tell your people to surrender."

"Give it up! Give it up!" the man gasped.

There was a clattering of weapons as the few surviving Noxians laid down their arms and stepped out into the open. Weaklings, but intelligent enough to know when they were beaten.

Perhaps she would take some as Thralls when she was done.

She pulled her leg back, releasing her claw grip and letting the man fall to the ground. She always relished the quiet after a battle. So much cacophony, and now what? Just a few moans, the hiss of cooling weapons, and that beautiful, serene drip of open wounds. She closed her eyes, feeling sensation return to her limbs. She needed to think again, not just act.

Breaker Liss and her troops rounded up the survivors, and brought them kneeling in front of the ship. One tried to run, and was swiftly cut down. The others meekly allowed themselves to be bound, their leader last of all.

"Know then," Breaker Liss intoned, taking his place at her side, "That you are now the prisoners of the Lady Kinshah of the Great House Ornicht, and property of the Guraggan Hegemony."

"I'm Furner Ketsu," the leader said.

Liss cuffed the man hard.

"What?" he growled. "I thought we were doing introductions!"

None could see it, but Ornicht smiled. She enjoyed the pirate's bravado. Perhaps he could be reasoned with.

"Where is the crew of this starship?" she asked, gesturing towards it.

"Hell if I know."

"Are they still aboard?"

"Maybe. My contract's just for the outside, see? I'm a discreet sort, and—"

"Clear the vessel," Lady Ornicht said.

"It will be done!" Liss barked, then signaled for her guards to follow him.

She crouched down so that she was eye to eye with Furner Ketsu, moving so that her beak nearly touched his bloodied face.

"You do not owe these people anything," she said.

"Well, technically speaking, it's them as owes me, as I only got about half-payment up front, and well, you know, they didn't tell me a bunch of my crew were going to get killed, so that's usually extra, plus ammo expenditures..."

"You are very prudent," she continued. She played with her claws idly, scratching circles in the deck plating. She felt a certain gratification when Furner looked down at those same sharp blades, then looked away.

"I have enough wealth to cover your contract. Tell me everything you know about this ship and its crew. I will spare you and your people, and compensate you handsomely."

"Like I said, I'm open to negotiation."

"Name your price."

"There is, uh… one thing," Ketsu said, grinning at her. "I kinda made a promise to the captain of that ship not to spill anything about her, and she rode with Captain Black y' see. We're practically crew."

"Your words are meaningless to me. Explain them."

"It means, I can't go back on the word I gave her. That's all. Professional thing."

Ornicht put a hand on the man's shoulder reassuringly.

"Of course. We all have our standards."

She rose, and patched herself in to her ship's communication network.

"Skyme?"

"Yes, my lady?" the little man replied, a tiny holographic image of his face appearing in her visor.

"Bring my physician aboard. I have a feeling we will need to loosen some tongues."

Tsi left the beacon in orbit less than hour from the station. She memorized its position and trajectory carefully, then killed the power to everything on board it except a stealth transmitter. It would blend in with the background radiation of the Poison Suns, invisible to everyone except her. If Furner and his crew weren't done with the ship yet, she didn't want to risk leaving the beacon out on the deck. Still, there was a chance of it being found and looted out in space too. A weighted series of risks, that's all anything ever was.

They docked the pod at a bay a few levels above their own, returning it to the scavenger Tsi had hired it from. Tsi was looking forward to seeing Strongmind and the boy again. She'd been oddly worried being away from them so long. Strongmind was a competent machine, and the boy was smarter than he looked, but Noxia was an unkind place. Their comms had cut out while they were aboard Glutton, so she was eager to get back and speak to them in person. She'd been halfway to calling them when she got back aboard the station, but had decided against it. Strongmind could take care of himself.

"Got a spare Rat-Pak?"

It was a beggar, with a voice like a frog being strangled. He raised his one blistered arm up, thrusting it into their path. Tsi would have simply side-stepped him, but his accent was familiar. Transfixing.

"Please, mistress, as I've no one else," the beggar said. "Been a long time since my last meal, is all."

"Still meat on his bones," Enlil said coldly. "You got at least three days left, old-timer."

"Where are you from?" Tsi asked.

"Chalakhat," the beggar said.

Looking at him deeper now, Tsi recognized the marking on his skin. One arm was a stump, and long strips of scar tissue ran up it in a perfect geometric pattern, like a star bursting outwards from where his forearm had been sliced off. Precise and perfect torture. Janissary work.

"Feec-rec," Enlil said. "Weren't you all supposed to be dead?"

"I was lucky," the beggar said. "Just a little boy. Big men took my arm, then told me to scarper while they did my ma. So I did. Picked up by a long-hauler a little while after, spent some years on that. Then they decided I wasn't worth the oxygen ration. So I wound up here. Not a lot of use to people, I guess."

"The Janissaries had orders to kill everyone," Tsi said.

"Like I said, I was lucky. Scary men in those helmets, voices like plasma drives. But they let me go all the same. Less than I could say for my dear ma and pa, but... well, you can't expect much from this universe, now can you?"

Tsi fished into her gear pouch, and pressed a few coins into the man's hand.

"I'm sorry," she said. "For what happened to you."

"It's been so long," the beggar smiled. "Who cares, really? My thanks for your kind words all the same."

Tsi nodded, and she and Enlil continued on their way.

"You shouldn't have given him money," Enlil said. "He's just going to shove it into his veins. Probably kill himself on bliss pills."

"Maybe he wants that."

"You say that, but if he'd asked me to just dust him, I got a feeling you'd have reservations about obliging him."

"Maybe."

"He was a liar, is all," Enlil said.

"Well, he's not alone."

Enlil shot her a look.

"You got something you need to say to me?"

"What about?"

"I don't know. Glutton. You know I made a deal with that thing before—"

"For 'Cold Salvage'," Tsi said. "Yes, I gathered that."

It was a smuggler's term. It meant anything taken from a derelict ship. But it especially applied to colonists, still frozen in their cryo pods.

"That going to be an issue between us? Because look, I can walk away any time. I don't need some sanctimonious outsider looking down on me."

Tsi shook her head.

"I don't approve," she said. "But I know what it's like to make a hard call. I'm sure you were only doing what you thought you had to do to survive."

"Every damn day of my life," Enlil said bitterly.

"You're a survivor, that's for sure. But you don't have to live this way."

"What, you gonna preach to me now? You gonna kiss my palms and save my soul, is that it?"

"I'm not—" Tsi began, but Enlil cut her off.

"I don't need this. I don't need this, not from *you*. You patch me up, and we're done, alright?"

"Enlil, that isn't what I want," Tsi said.

"Fuck what you want."

"You're not *listening* to me. I've lived in Noxia, remember? I know what being solo is like here. You keep living the way you are, you're going to wind up dead."

"What's that to you, huh? Why do you care so damn much?"

"Because I want you on my crew!" Tsi snapped. "I... I need someone like you, Enlil. I've got a long, long way to go, and I know that I'm going to need someone who's resilient. Resourceful. I need a survivor."

Enlil was silent for a moment as they walked.

"Your ship's got a Slip drive?" she asked.

"Yes."

"And you're leaving, right? You ain't sticking around here?"

"As soon as she's repaired, we're gone," Tsi said.

"Maybe," Enlil said slowly. "Maybe I'll ride with you for a while."

They had reached the dock. Tsi ducked through the archway, Enlil at her side. She could feel a weight lifting from her shoulders. This long sojourn was almost over. They had the beacon. The ship was in good order. Just one more jump, and—

A bullet took Enlil in the side. She pitched over, mewling. Tsi grabbed her instinctively by the shoulder, then dragged her to cover behind a massive soldering machine. Shots ripped out all around, and finally she was aware of her surroundings. There had been a battle here. The scent of blood was still thick in the air.

Moving quick and quiet, she saw them. Guraggan serfs were converging on her position, their necks dangling with service beads.

Tsi peeked out from behind cover, and fired twice. One of the serfs jerked backwards and fell. The others dropped prone, or scuttled to what cover they could. In the brief moments she had, Tsi checked Enlil's pulse. It was rapid but strong. The shot had taken the girl hard, but it hadn't been enough to kill her.

"Steady," Tsi said to her. "Steady."

Bullets buzzed above her head. Peering over the edge of the hulk, she saw a huge figure in Guraggan armor emerge, a pulse gun at his shoulder. He barked an order at the others, and they began to rush forwards. Half a dozen troops, and a mass of muscle that had been clearly augmented on par with a true Guraggan. Tsi only had one choice.

She detached a smoke grenade, and hurled it between her and her adversaries. She squeezed Enlil's shoulder once, then got up and ran back the way she had come, as hard and as fast as she could. Her booted feet pounded against the metal deck, each stride taking her farther and farther away, leaving Enlil and Strongmind and Hiron and all the rest in the hands of her enemies. She shut them from her mind, and disappeared into the depths of Salvation.

CHAPTER 15

I s this your commander?"

Hiron had learned the name of the man who spoke. 'Breaker Liss'. A giant, he would have dwarfed even his parent's most intimidating guards. He had come to hate this man almost as much as he was terrified of him over the past few hours.

The fight had been short. A few minutes of fire at most, and then Furner Ketsu's men had given up. Not long after that, the Guraggan had stormed the ship. Good as its word, Strongmind had killed three of them before one of its legs was shot out from under it, and it was disarmed by a sharp kick from an armored boot. Hiron had spent the entire time cowering behind the sturdiest bulkhead he could find, before he was dragged roughly out into the hold, bound, and set beside Strongmind's inert form.

Ketsu and his men had been brought in, then, and an hour later, the "physician" had arrived. Aided by Breaker Liss, they had begun torturing Furner Ketsu in front of him. He had seen terrible sights before, but watching what they had done to the old engineer had made Hiron wretch against his gag.

"Is this your commander?"

The Breaker's voice was more insistent, and directed to Hiron this time. He realized he was one of the only people still alive in the room. A few Noxians were whimpering in their own filth, and Furner Ketsu had long since lost consciousness without telling his captors anything beyond a long string of expletives.

The Breaker was holding Enlil, the Noxian girl, by the back of her head. Her eyes were rolling upwards. Her skin was pale. Long and thin and frail in his muscular arms, she looked like a doll made of strings and twigs, ready to be snapped in two. She'd been shot. Maybe she was dying.

Hiron couldn't speak. He hadn't even noticed when they'd

pulled his gag out.

The Breaker looked over his shoulder to the Physician. She was a strange, alien creature, swaddled in an apron with a plastic sheen and decorated in bizarre patterns. She wore a headdress secured by a metal circlet, with drooping cords that hung down over her face. It completely concealed her features save a pair of glowing eyes that could just barely be seen between the cords.

Her slim hands had worked horrors on the Noxians with a skillful craft that belied its sadism. Hiron had known a few like her on his homeworld, true torturers for whom the human body was nothing but a canvas on which to paint with scalpels and hooks.

The Physician shook her head.

Breaker Liss tossed Enlil to the ground with contemptuous ease, and the girl screeched in pain. He stared straight at Hiron, and cocked back a foot as if to kick her.

"Stop," the Physician said.

All eyes turned to the strange figure.

"Take the cripple to another room," the Physician instructed. "I will deal with these others."

Mutely, Breaker Liss picked up Hiron, and carried him on his shoulder to the ship's loading bay. He set the boy gently down against a crate, and the two looked at each other for an awkward moment, before the Breaker turned away and began to pace.

Hiron watched the big man make two circuits of the bay. Made of muscle and sinew, with skin like good leather, he seemed more like a caricature than a human being. His armor barely fit him, and his helmet was clasped to his belt. Hiron surmised the Breaker didn't like being confined.

He saw also that the man wore strange baubles around his waist, crystals of a dozen exotic hues. He'd never seen such wealth on his homeworld. At a guess, The Breaker was a very successful warrior.

Hiron spent some time breathing, and thinking. His captors wanted him alive, that much was clear. For what purpose he wasn't certain. He had been important back home on Promise, but his parents were dead, and he couldn't think what use they would have for him now. The Guraggan held his home. They wouldn't need an heir of the old regime to make themselves legitimate. An armada of battleships was more than enough authority.

He realized the Breaker was murmuring something to himself, and Hiron strained his ears to hear. Breaker Liss was speaking a sub-dialect of Panglos, uncommon, but one that Hiron had studied. He could make out the words easily enough. They were simple, child like.

"It's not my fault. It's not my fault. It's not my fault."

"What isn't?" Hiron asked in Panglos.

The Breaker glared at him, and continued to pace, silently this time.

At last, someone else entered the room. Hiron had caught a glimpse of her on the viewing screens, a terrifying creature with a helmet in the shape of a bird of prey. Still wearing her armor, she was smaller than the Breaker, but even then she made Hiron look like a child. Her claws were stained dark brown with blood, and the iron tang of battle-musk followed her.

"Stand. Up."

The words were in his home tongue. Shakily, Hiron got to his feet, bracing himself against the crates. The Guraggan looked him up and down, its merciless visor judging him with neither pity nor contempt.

"I have a problem," the Guraggan said.

"I... I cannot help someone I do not know," Hiron replied. "I am Hiron, of the Dath Clan."

"Ornicht," the Guraggan replied.

"Ornicht," Hiron said. "I—I am honored to meet such a mighty warrior."

"Do not trifle with me," the Guraggan warned, and for one moment of sheer horror Hiron realized that he was not being threatened. She had not raised her voice, had not tensed her muscles. No flexing of those terrible claws, not the least attempt to intimidate him. She had merely told him, in no uncertain terms, that she would murder him if he insulted her.

"How may I serve?" Hiron asked.

"That spindly little pirate out there," she said. "She is not the commander."

"No."

"And the Drone my servants are dissecting right now is not in charge either, obviously."

"Is it dead?"

"I ask the questions," Ornicht reminded him.

Hiron's heart sank. He hadn't liked the machine exactly, but the idea of Strongmind being pulled apart, its circuits exposed, its mind delved into... there was something vile about it. Almost worse than what had happened to Furner Ketsu. At least as the knives and saws bit into the old engineer's skin and bone, he had still kept the sanctity of his mind, shouting curses at his torturers all the while. There was nothing a thing like Strongmind could do against a sufficiently skilled technician. Enter the right codes, and its soul would be bared open for all to see.

"You must be the leader," Ornicht said, inclining her beak slightly. "Last scion of the Dath, spirited away on an advanced ship with a cadre of mercenaries. Your only goal to survive, and find allies to reclaim your world. Is that it?"

Hiron looked at the ground. If he lied... If he had the courage to lie, here, now, he could save Tsi. He could repay her kindness. Maybe, maybe make sure that she got away, that she found some way of stopping the Guraggan.

"I..." he said, throat dry, tongue heavy in his mouth. "I am—"

"A weakling," Ornicht said. "No one would follow you. Your master is still out there somewhere, isn't she?"

"I'll tell you everything!" Hiron blurted out. "Everything I know! Just-just don't hurt anyone else."

The raptor-helm regarded him for a long time, that yellow visor seeming to burn with an unnatural hunger. He felt as if at any moment that beak would open and those tiny white teeth would bite into his flesh and devour him. At long last, Ornicht rocked back on her heels and let out a sigh.

"Liss," she said. "Tell the Physician to stop. I have everything I need right here."

She did not have much left. The EVA suit, and a ragged shawl hanging over it that she'd pulled from a recycle. That was all that had kept her warm for the last few hours. No rations, she'd traded those away. No medical kit, that was gone too. She'd meant to restock on the ship, but well... Tsi had run away.

She still had her Repeater, heavy and reassuring at her hip. Tsi had never been the sort to fetishize weapons, she'd seen plenty of armed people cut down as easy as cattle. Still, it was better to have it than not. She'd honestly been close to selling the gun; had sold off all but one magazine of ammunition.

All for the fragile little blade she had carefully concealed on her forearm. She'd never thought much about the weight of knives before she came to the Frontier. Captain Black and an old timer called Ressad had taught her how to knife fight like a proper Noxian, but her reflexes and muscles had done more work than her skill at first.

Since then, she had learned to appreciate a well-made knife. Different tools had different uses, from a Nioban Kukri, meant to slice through cables and oxygen tubes and augmented muscle, to the sort of sharp butcher's blade she'd had on Goodhome.

Tsi could still remember the first time she'd slaughtered a Gene-bear. It had been a rite of passage among the homesteaders, and she had killed the thing easily enough. They were big animals, but passive and slow. It wasn't hard to slip a blade into a Gene-bear's throat and rip outwards. What was trickier was flensing the thing, working off layers upon layers of fat and carapace and fleshy hide, pulling out rudimentary organs until only its pink-caked bones remained.

Tsi had slipped and slid in the thing's ichor, much to the amusement of her companions. It had taken more than an hour, but she had done it, and she hadn't asked for help. Vylk Preston had pulled her up out of the slaughter pit with one of his big hairy hands, a grin of pure joy on his simple features.

How like a Gene-Bear he'd looked when she had killed him. Knife wounds all over, laying on his side, his flabby body quivering and nerveless. So much larger than her, but looking so pitiful and vulnerable as he died. She had wanted to hug him, to hold his hand and lie to him about there still being some way to save his life.

He had beaten her to the punch though. Those sad brown eyes had stared at her, and he had mouthed one word:

"Liar."

He had relied on her, and she'd failed him. It didn't excuse what he'd tried to do, she reminded herself. 'Nobody deserves a knife in the throat,' was an old Nioban saying, 'Unless they ask for it.'

She hadn't asked the big man to try to kill her. At least from her perspective. Now he was dead and gone, and none of it mattered.

She had work to do. The Guraggan had her ship and her people, and she needed both. She tried not to think of what they were doing to little Hiron and Strongmind, what kind of things they'd do to Enlil if she was still alive. Poor Furner Ketsu and his crew too, doubtless slaughtered for being in the wrong place at the wrong time. Salvation wasn't exactly a place for a peaceful retirement, but the man had made a life for himself. If he lived, he'd curse the day he ever met Tsi, and had all her troubles brought to his door.

The air changed as she reached her destination. The corridors weren't clean exactly, but they were not as carelessly filthy as the rest of the station. Graffiti shifted from boasts of pirate prowess and crude curses to warnings and reverent prayers. She passed people with bowed heads, looking like a procession of pilgrims.

They were poor, even by Noxian standards. Some empty-handed, others clutching precious offerings. Law on Salvation was tributary. The weak offered their meager possessions to the most dangerous predators, hoping that in exchange they would not get eaten.

A dozen aged Breachers stood guard at Tsi's destination. It had once been some sort of loading bay, now converted into an observation dome and royal court. The doorway in was a huge octagon, tall enough to drive a ground crawler through. She descended to the antechamber outside from a spiderweb of rusting ladders and synthetic ropes.

One of the old pirates challenged her as she approached. A woman about Tsi's size, swaddled in second-hand armor that had seen better days. She wore a helmet with a winking succubus crudely stenciled across the visor.

"Court's closed!" the guard barked. "Come back next shift."

"I need to see the Jarawat," Tsi said.

"I need six hours in a bath of omni-bliss and a Slip-jump out of here," the woman replied. "But it's not going to happen. Now walk before we dust you."

"I need to make a deal with her," Tsi said. "I think she'll want to hear what I have to say, and I think you'll regret turning me back."

"Why?"

"Because," Tsi said. "I'm the one who broke her favorite son's face. I think I might owe her an explanation."

The guard smiled beneath her visor. The stock of her gun suddenly lashed out and struck Tsi in the stomach. Tsi doubled over as rough hands grabbed her arms.

"Come on," the guard said, "Let's taker her inside. I have a feeling the Jarawat will pay us extra for this shift."

"Your wounds are so beautiful my lady," the Physician cooed. "You really must allow yourself to be fully recorded. A statue of you ought to reside in every warrior's home."

They were in a disused side room of the ship. Wylla had been summoned away from her work, only to find the Physician tending to their mistress. Lady Ornicht had stripped out of her armor, and the Physician's dexterous fingers played across her scarred skin, tending to new wounds and old ones that had opened up during the battle. Tubes flowing with ocher fluid fed into Lady Ornicht. They pulsed slightly as if they were hungry tendrils, suckling on her weathered skin.

"Do not flatter me," Ornicht said. "Do your work and be done. Vanity is not useful."

"I know my lady, I know," the Physician said soothingly. "Still, your form stirs such passions in me."

"Stir them silently."

"Your will is my will..."

Ornicht sighed.

"You want to say something else?"

"It's only..." the Physician began, swabbing at a cut before she speedily clamped it shut with a metal bolt. "My lady... your condition—"

Ornicht growled. The Physician paused, then took up again, her tone even more placating.

"I only mean that it affects the connection with your armor—"

"It performed adequately," Ornicht said.

"But for how long, my lady? We must face reality, if you continue at this pace..."

"Death holds no fear for me."

"It is not death I speak of, but... uselessness."

"What do you mean?" Ornicht spat. Her eyes snapped up at the Physician, glaring darkly at her from beneath her brow.

"My lady, if you continue to interface with the *kheshtic* suit, the costs could be dire. If you allow me to administer nanite treatment, we can halt, even reverse the decay—"

"*I will not!*" Ornicht roared. "How dare you? How dare you even speak such words to me?"

"A warrior rejects no advantage," the Physician said piously. "Flesh and metal are one, as it was on old Earth."

"What would you make of me? That I become a *thing* like Turon Chryte?"

"He is a mighty warrior."

"He cannot *think* anymore. You've seen him. He's barely there when he's not on a battlefield. It's like speaking to a dead man. All he does is tilt his head, and nod, and wait to be given permission to kill something. The insects in his blood control him now, not his mind, not his soul."

"He has survived—"

"He has not! And I will not! Don't let me be turned into a puppet for those *things*. Don't let me die a shadow of my old self."

"When you were young," the Physician whispered, "You would not have hesitated. You would have done anything to make yourself stronger."

"I am not young," Ornicht said bitterly. "Leave me."

"Your will is my will," the Physician saluted.

She turned and left the chamber. Wylla began to bow as well and follow the strange creature, but Ornicht cleared her throat.

"Not you," she said.

"My lady?"

"What have you learned from the drone?"

"Well," Wylla said. "It speaks many languages. It insulted me in flawless Bykonian for ten minutes straight."

"Unusual for a combat device," Ornicht mused.

"I don't think it's just a drone," Wylla continued. "Its algorithms are incredibly complex. The machine is a true intelligence. I've barely cracked its outer defenses, and even then I think it has more traps waiting for me."

"Traps..." Ornicht said. "Is it dangerous? Perhaps we should destroy it."

"I would advise against that, my lady," Wylla said reluctantly. "Your Serfs disabled it quite thoroughly. I haven't gained root access to its programming yet, but I have confidence I can, in time. The potential intelligence boon would be extremely valuable."

"Hmm. I do not care for a thinking machine that is not bound to us. Be cautious with it, Hunting Hound."

"Of course, my lady."

"And what can you tell me about its owner?"

"The boy?"

Ornicht glared at her, eyes icy beneath her furrowed brow. Wylla regretted saying it. Even a half-lie could be punished harshly by her mistress.

"The captain of the vessel, my lady means," Wylla said quickly. "I merely thought perhaps the machine was the boy's bodyguard, or property."

"It isn't. He's too worried about it, it can't be a possession," Ornicht said. "What can you tell me about the ship's captain? I want to confirm what the boy said."

"Well, she is resourceful. And wealthy. This ship is a masterpiece, but its been very carefully disguised. I've only begun to understand its systems and construction. She wants to travel incognito, but she wants to be able to fight and run if she has to. She isn't Noxian, but she has lived among them. The way the place is laid out… Forgive my indulgence, but it is very strange."

"How so?"

"Most stellar outcasts are not practical. They spend their money on weapons, and luxuries when they have the chance. The captain has one of the best ships to be found outside the Hegemony… but its so barren. She isn't an ascetic, I saw how much liquor is kept aboard. But even that, it's all rotgut. It's cheap," Wylla said.

"So she has poor taste?" Ornicht asked.

"Everything on this ship screams that she's punishing herself. She's running from something, something she feels terribly guilty about."

"A pirate with a conscience," Ornicht said. "It explains taking care of the boy. He said her name was 'Tsi'."

"A Kiosan name. Though, it is a common alias among criminals."

"The boy told me she is a great hero," Ornicht said. "That together they are on an adventure."

"Oh?"

"They intend to stop us, you see."

Wylla was silent.

Her mistress guffawed.

"Imagine," she smirked. "One ship halting the march of the Hegemony. Only a child could believe such things..."

"Indeed," Wylla said.

"If you were her, where would you flee to?" Ornicht asked. "My men gave chase, but she lost them in the station."

"I do not know this station at all. She seems to be familiar with it, so hunting her down would be extremely difficult for outsiders like us."

"A scout would be useful. The Noxians I have taken are all injured or too terrified to be put to work," Ornicht sighed. "I was too hasty in the attack. I should have consulted further with you, first. Now this Captain Tsi is likely out of my reach."

"I serve you my lady. I do not doubt you."

"Your doubts are useful to me. Express them more in the future."

There was another long, uncomfortable silence. Wylla did not know what to say to that. An honest opinion had nearly gotten her killed in the past. She shifted her weight slightly. It was one of the hardest things about being *owned* by another, never quite knowing what her role was. Had she merely been a sounding board? Had her mistress wanted to calm down after the argument with the Physician? Did she want Wylla to stay, or had she simply forgotten she was there?

"How long has it been since you played your lyre?" Ornicht asked.

"Two weeks," Wylla said. She sometimes strummed the instrument quietly when she was alone in the hold with the Chem-Thralls. It was one of her few means of solace.

"I thought the ship was quieter," Ornicht murmured. "When we finish here, I want you to play it again. Your spike-fiddle as well. You are very skilled."

"Of course, my lady," Wylla replied. Lady Ornicht had never expressed an interest in her music before. She knew she was constantly monitored though. How odd, to realize Lady Ornicht had been her audience all these years.

"I have a command for you."

All mirth had left the Guraggan's voice. Her speech was clipped and direct now, the voice of authority that brooked no disobedience. Wylla raised her eyes questioningly to Lady Ornicht, and found herself met with a tense, icy gaze. There was something else there now though, the faintest hint of tightness. Desperation. For the first time since she had come into Lady Ornicht's service, she felt a tremor of pity for her mistress.

"How much do you know of my condition?" she asked.

"I... know that you are a venerable warrior, and like all warriors, you have sustained injuries, from time to time. Some still trouble you, but you would never permit pain to slow you down."

"Perhaps I have no choice but to be 'slowed down', as you put it. Some injuries are too great, even for a Guraggan."

"Then you will find a way to use your pain to strengthen yourself. What is broken can be remade."

Ornicht nodded slowly.

"True... true. Do not ever let my Physician treat me against my will. Promise me you will never let that happen."

The words were hard, but there was something brittle beneath them. Wylla silently folded her hands in front of her and bowed her head.

"Your will is my will," she said.

CHAPTER 16

The air was intoxicating. So much oxygen, so fresh in her lungs. Tsi had almost forgotten what it was like to breath air that had not been filtered thousands upon thousands of times. The scent of earth was thick in her nostrils, the feeling of dew on her skin like a lover's caress. She almost forgot she was being forced onto her knees with a gun barrel shoved into the back of her neck and her hands bound in front of her.

"Who is this?" the Jarawat asked.

She was a luxurious creature. Success had bred wealth, wealth had granted power, and now the Ring Queen lived a life rarefied and unimaginable by Salvation's countless dregs. Draped in expensive, gaudy silks from the Epilotti Mandate, the Jarawat rejected the traditional space-walker's suit of a Noxian pirate. Everything about her showed her scorn for the fears of her people: her lack of armor and weapons, the way she lounged casually on a suspensor couch hovering half a meter off the ground.

Her court was an incredible sight compared to the cramped corridors of the station. Plants grew in abundance, and a layer of imported dirt meters thick hid the deck plating beneath. All around them were iridescent fronds and flowers with petals the colors of oceans no Noxian would ever see. Two stout Sannatan Oaks flanked the Jarawat's couch, their tops brushing the thin glass sky that separated them from the raw and deadly stars above.

Like all tyrants, the Jarawat projected strength as a matter of course. Indulgence had become a profoundly political act, if she should one day strap on armor and make herself ready for war, it would be a sign of weakness. Tsi almost laughed at the absurdity of it all. To seem strong, the Jarawat had to become weak.

Then again, perhaps the Ring Queen's ostentation was well founded. She was surrounded by bodyguards and hired guns from all across the system and beyond. Tsi saw mercenaries from the Sannatan Free Union, looking ridiculous in their heavy furs, a plethora of Noxians from pirate clans stretching into the deep core, even a trio of Pilgrims from Ouemac. What those gentle people were doing in the Jarawat's company Tsi couldn't guess, but the Ouemacan were strange folk who thought anyone could be redeemed. Tsi found that idea as painful as it was preposterous.

Also present was Gyje the Third Son, and his out-system concubine, both overshadowed by the Jarawat's effortless elegance. Gyje looked comical, the lower half of his face completely covered in a bandage. He and his mate glared hatefully at Tsi, but she ignored them. She knew where the real power lay. The Guard behind her pulled the gun away from her neck, letting her sit up to address the Jarawat properly.

"I am Tsi," she said. "I rode with Captain Black."

"Don't talk about dead men here," the Jarawat said. "And I never heard of no hull breakers called 'Tsi.' That's a Kiosan name, and Kiosans don't scav, and they don't pirate, do they?"

Despite her opulence, the Jarawat still spoke with a crude pirate's tongue.

"Weak people," one of her guards said. "Get freaks to do their work for them!"

"That's right," the Jarawat said, pointing at Tsi. "See how weak you get when you leave the light of our mothers? Look at that thing, not wearing her suit right, bet she hasn't walked the hull in years! Honestly… what kind of spacer lets her weapons go? Captain Black! Pfah! Feec-Rec!"

Tsi felt the emptiness of her holster. The Repeater had been with her a long time, had saved her life more times than she could remember. More importantly, it had saved Hiron and Strongmind too. It was some of the finest work a Noxian gunsmith could make, head and shoulders above the crude scatter guns and improvised pulsers that the Jarawat's guards toted.

Of course, now one of the guards had it and her last magazine of ammunition strapped to his thigh. She still had the knife concealed on her forearm, carefully placed so that the incurious guards couldn't find it. One knife wouldn't be enough to take the Jarawat's court, unless things went just as s he'd planned it.

The Jarawat's court was chortling on command, all except the Ouemacans, who made strange hand signs to ward off evil. There was a contrast in how her court behaved compared to Gyje's. While the Third Son's sycophants had been quick to turn on him, the Jarawat's people studied her with an intensity, a fear bordering on reverence. They took their every cue off of her, never laughing too long or too loud, never exchanging whispers or grins among themselves. Tsi would have to play this game carefully.

"So, why do you come here, huh?" the Jarawat asked.

"I want to propose an alliance."

Laughter. Loud and raucous, as if she was the finest comedian ever to hit the station. It erupted like a volcano and then collapsed back into silence when the court realized the Jarawat was not laughing.

She rolled one leg onto the earthen floor, then another, and hoisted herself up out of the couch. Beautiful silks trailing behind her, she strode carelessly towards Tsi, idle curiosity on her face.

"An alliance? Did they hit you on the head? You said *alliance?*" she asked, glancing at her guards.

A little closer, Tsi thought. That's all she needed. Just two more steps.

"Yes," Tsi said. "I think we could start a very profitable partnership."

"You broke my favorite son's face. You didn't bring trade to me, no good cargo. You got Glutton all agitated, which I will *not* be hearing the end of... and now you come here to talk alliance? Is it cause your little ship got taken from you?"

"Yes."

The Jarawat smirked with approval.

"You're burning hot fuel," she said. "That's worth something. But not enough. Why shouldn't I make you walk out an airlock?"

"Because the Guraggan are on your station."

A few gasps came from the court, a few nervous laughs, a murmur of derision.

"Feec-rec!" Gyje shouted through his bandaged mouth. "She's lying!"

"Watch the monitors if you don't believe me," Tsi said. "Those are Guraggan serfs, and a Guraggan warrior taking my ship and slaughtering people under your protection, Jarawat."

"Who cares?" Gyje continued. "Furner made his choice the moment he did a deal with an impudent little oxygen rat like you—"

"Shut your mouth," the Jarawat snapped.

"She's taking advantage—"

"Not. One. More. Word."

The Jarawat had not turned to face him, but the tension in her body was plain to see. Gyje's face was flushed, his brow thick with sweat. Tsi could see the physical effort it took him to muster his courage.

"Mother," he said insistently. "What does it matter? They did us a favor—"

"They don't do *favors* you brainless waste of mass!" the Jarawat rounded on him. "You're too young, and too thick-headed to remember what it was *like* when they came through here. Get out of here, and take that insipid waste-mass with you."

"Mother you are making a mistake—"

"I don't repeat orders."

Gyje turned ashen. He grabbed his terrified concubine by the arm, and together the two of them fled the court, but not before he spat a curse in Tsi's direction. There was no laughter following their indecorous exit. The crowd was too fixated on what the Jarawat would do next, they hung on her every movement as she paced, clenched her fists, closed her eyes.

She was almost within Tsi's reach, just close enough for Tsi to slip the blade from her sleeve, when she stopped, took three long strides away, then turned around again.

"Alright. Alright, outsider. You've done alright," the Jarawat said. "How many guns does the Guraggan have?"

"I counted a dozen. One of them is augmented, all of them are well geared."

"Well, I got a lot more than that, don't I?" The Jarawat said, raising her arms. Her warriors let out a ragged cheer in response.

"These are the best bulkhead breachers and throat cutters in the whole system! Scalp-takers and heart-eaters! Who breaks shields with their bare hands?!" She cried.

"We do!" the pirates echoed.

"Who flies through the deep of the suns?"

"We do!"

"Whose got hearts like plasma cores?! Whose got skin like a cruiser's hull?!"

"We do!"

"Who dances in the void dust and burns the foe with engine's flame?!"

"We do!"

"Drinks! Ammo! Stimms!" The Jarawat cried, her people in a frenzy of exultation. "Brace yourselves boys and girls, we're going to toss those damned freaks right back out the hold they came from! And when we're done with that, we're going to take the next ring, and the next! This is the start of it, after this, we'll take all Salvation! After this—"

Amid the cheering and pounding of fists, it was easy to miss the noise. A single, loud crack. The Jarawat jerked backwards. Her fist opened. Her arms hung limp and nerveless at her sides as she stared into the middle distance, drool leaking from the sides of her mouth.

There was another crack, and her chest exploded. She tumbled backwards, silks shredded and stained with blood. The cheers had stopped.

In long heartbeats, Tsi's eyes traced the path of the shots to the entrance. She saw a figure, armored in blue and black, eerily still, a long rifle in his arms. The rifle fell from the figure's grip, and the demon mask sneered at all of them, stimulant tubes vibrating subtly within its fanged mouth.

It was the Tenlok. The Bondsman. Before the screams could start, before another shot could be fired, a pistol was in one of his hands, a Nioban Kukri in the other.

He made no noise as he leaped in among them, and began his butcher's work.

Enlil knew what pain was. She'd come down from a six week bender on the Red Ether once, got stabbed while she was omni-blissed out of her mind another time. She had starved for much of her childhood. She'd had suit failures in the void, too, remembered that sinking feeling when her HUD went white and words in languages she didn't understand told her just how many mouthfuls of oxygen she had left.

Compared to some of what she had been through, getting shot

wasn't so bad. For a while she had thought these people would just let her bleed out on the deck of Tsi's ship. The grating against her cheek had been painful long enough that it was starting to become familiar, almost pleasant. She couldn't move, couldn't turn her face around to see what that twisted torturer had been doing to Furner Ketsu and his men. She was glad. Enlil didn't have anything to prove, and she'd seen enough horrible things in her life.

She drifted in and out of oblivion, but when her eyes went black all she saw was her parents. She knew they were long dead. She hated remembering them in her dreams. It was an illusion, memories of a happy time that had never really existed. They'd been kind to her, as kind as any parents were to their children.

Then they'd sold her.

In a way, she was grateful to them. They had taught her the most important lesson: the second you rely on someone, that's when they'll strip you for parts. Enlil knew as long as she lived that she was never going to have children. It was too cruel, bringing a new life into the Frontier, weak and helpless. What kind of Oxygen Rat needs a home grown slave?

She came to as the Physician was peering into her eyes, their faces much too close together. The Physician whispered something to her in Guraggan, and held up her bloody fingers. She was holding the bullet that had struck Enlil, a metal flower coated in sticky red fluid. The masked thing offer it to Enlil, but she shook her head.

"Nah, no mementos for me."

The Physician shrugged and murmured in her strange language, like liquid being poured through a sieve. Then, she stood up and walked away, leaving Enlil laying on her back.

She was feeling better. Admittedly, she felt like there was a hole in her stomach, her tongue was thick and dry, she was fairly certain that one of her shoulders was dislocated. All in all it was still an improvement.

With tremendous effort, she raised herself onto her elbows. Her legs only jerked and flopped when she tried to move them, and for a moment she thought they'd damaged her spine. No, she realized. They just didn't want her running off.

Slowly, she scraped her way across the room on her hands and elbows, dragging her useless legs behind her. She felt a slight tingling sensation in one foot. A good sign. They weren't dead meat, rotting off of her. Her bad hand had been re-bandaged and splinted too. At last, she propped her back against a wall, and looked out into the gloom of the hold.

She was fairly certain she was alone. Two of Furner Ketsu's men were there, but they had already started to smell. One of them had been a tough rat. He'd let the Physician work his chest and hands for a long time, before his throat had been cut. The second had been lucky, a pneumatic wound to the forehead. About as quick a way as you can go. She'd never done anyone that quick; it needed special tools and patience. She wasn't that sort.

"Spirits fuck me sideways," she sighed.

She needed to vomit, but she couldn't bring anything up. Her hand was still broken. She was stuck in this dim hold, waiting for the Gods-forsaken Guraggan to come and do whatever it was those bogeymen did. Her father had told her stories about when the Guraggan came through Noxia, said they were all ten feet tall and could breath the vacuum, rip open hulls with their bare hands. They ate naughty little girls, too.

Well, that much hadn't proven to be true. So far. Her captors might be brutal killers and sadistic maniacs, but at least they weren't anthropovores like the Rock Drinkers of the deep stations. Enlil sighed again.

She wasn't getting out of this one. She didn't have a crew anymore, she had burned everyone she ever cared about. There wasn't anyone who would fight for her out here. She couldn't blame them. Tsi had been an interesting one, but her self-righteous veneer had wound up false. Just another con artist. The people who talked high-minded were always the first to turn on you when things got tough.

The worst murderer she'd ever known had been a Nebular Mendicant, a tiny woman who wouldn't show her face in public and prayed every time she killed someone. She had prayed a lot, so much so that Enlil had learned half the Mendicant's holy book before they parted company. How exactly she reconciled piracy and assassination with her God, Enlil had never figured out.

That holy little killer was probably dead too. So who would remember her? Tsi? No, she was long gone. The last person Enlil had actually *befriended* was sitting in a cryo-pod inside Glutton. Maybe Gyje

Third Son would curse her name every once and a while, for all the trouble she caused. *Oh joy*, she thought. *I'll be the butt of jokes from a brain-dead Ring Baron.*

She searched her mind, but she couldn't think of anyone else. Then, something unexpected happened.

Enlil started crying.

"You don't have to feel guilty. It's just a machine."

Wylla and Liss were walking together through the captured ship. It was a small miracle that a man with the Breaker's frame could fit into this place at all. He was about as big as the drone that Wylla had been working on, but made of enhanced and modified muscle instead of metal and ceramics and circuits.

"Our first loyalty must be to our lady," he continued. "Our own reservations come second."

"I am as loyal to Ornicht as anyone else," Wylla said. "You don't have to remind me how to be a good servant."

"I am trying to *help* you," Liss said. "You think she is a monster, but you have not been with her as long as I have. If you keep up this... this *recalcitrance*... then she will have no choice what to do with you."

"Everyone has a choice Liss. You and I made ours, she made hers. We're both her tools, the same as Skyme and the Chem Thralls and the drones."

"I am not a Thrall," Liss said. "That time is behind me. I could leave whenever I like."

"Then why don't you?"

"I ... have a reason to stay."

"Because you are so very loyal to your jailer," Wylla said, more venom in her words than she intended. "You amaze me, Liss. You act as if being a slave is the best thing that ever happened to you."

"You do not understand. She has shown me such things, given me so much that I can never repay—"

"She is a butcher. She enjoys killing."

"She's more than that. She *needs* me Wylla."

"So you stay out of pity?"

"No."

They were on the threshold of where the machine was kept. Wylla's victim. The silent drone, its false flesh half-carved off, chained for her protection while she ripped the secrets from its mind. Wylla rounded on Liss, suddenly, violently. She looked up into the Breaker's eyes.

"Why?" she asked, spitting the word like acid into his face. "You know how much suffering we bring. Why?"

"You know why," he replied, taking one of her hands in his.

"Don't do that. Don't pin what you—what we have done on your desire for me."

"I was on the verge," he said. "I was so close to going home. She would have let me, or killed me, and I would not have cared. But then you came into my world."

"Don't," she whispered. She wanted to look away, but his eyes were so deep and sad, filled with sorrow and longing in equal measure.

"I cannot deny what my heart tells me, Wylla of the Bykon. I have seen horror and beauty in equal measure among the stars. But I have never met someone like you. Do not throw yourself away like so many others. I could not bear to lose you."

Wylla placed her free hand on the Breaker's cheek. It was her turn now to trace the line of his strong jaw, feel the surprising smoothness of his bronze skin. He was like a sculpture from old Earth, something she had read in ancient books and seen in flickering holographs. Naked, doomed warriors, their bodies perfect save their mortal wounds.

"I'm not yours to lose," she said.

"You could be. We could be. We could belong to each other, and no one else."

"And if our Mistress disapproved?"

"I would break her in two for you," he whispered, voice weighted with guilt.

"Of course," Wylla said sadly.

She squeezed the Breaker's hand, entwined her thin fingers in his for a moment. Then she let go.

"I have work to do," she said.

She opened the door, stepped across the threshold, and shut it behind her without a backward glance. She stood there with her eyes closed for a long moment, then she heard the Breaker's heavy footsteps walking away.

She opened her eyes again, and saw the machine. It was

chained to the wall in its ridiculous regalia. "Strongmind", it called itself. It was something she had only learned after incredible effort. Its head was half-opened, long cables running to a portable computer bank she had installed next to it.

"I hate you, and you are a vile creature and have an inadequate intellect," the machine said tonelessly in perfect Bykon.

"Hello to you too," Wylla replied, as she walked to the console. A few keystrokes, and she began to rip open its mind once again.

"Would my mistress like him executed?" the Physician asked.

Hiron was surprised that he could understand their language, but then he realized the Guraggan were speaking Panglos for his benefit. He had been dragged out in front of the ship with the few remaining survivors of Furner Ketsu's crew. Lady Ornicht had surveyed them with callous disdain while each of the Noxians was offered a choice: become a Chem-Thrall, a slave to the Guraggan, or die here. About half had taken the deal. They had been stripped naked, bound, and dragged away for horrors only God knew, while the others had received a single strike to the temple with a piston of cold steel.

The raptor mask studied him for a long time. His body was small and twisted. He'd be useless as a slave. And, well, he had told her everything he knew already. He had made her promise to hurt no one else, but the Guraggan's word wasn't worth much.

No, he corrected himself. Dealing with her was like dealing with his father. He had to remember the complex logic of tyrants. She had promised to harm no one else, but by refusing enslavement, the Noxians had chosen death. One could say they were killing themselves, rather than being murdered by her.

He was a fool for assuming Ornicht would have any compassion. He should have resisted. Should have been tortured, and bought Tsi more time. Instead he had spilled the truth like offal on a slaughter room floor.

He glanced over at one of the dead Noxians, bits of brain leaking from a crater in the man's brow. He wanted to vomit again, but he kept his bile down.

The Lady Ornicht was about to render her judgment when a commotion arose at the far side of the bay. After a lot of shouting that Hiron did not understand, two of the Guraggan serfs arrived, roughly escorting an odd pair.

A handsome man in Noxian garb, his blonde mustache and long braids expertly cared for, accompanied by a beautiful woman in a gown that trailed along the deck, its hem dampening with engine lubricant. Neither of them bowed when they approached Lady Ornicht. Swift blows from rifle stocks corrected that quickly, and soon they were on all fours, grovelling in front of the Guraggan the same as Hiron.

"She's going to kill us," the woman whispered in Epilotti.

"Don't talk stupid," the man replied, his accent torturous. "We got good money thoughts for her."

"Speak the tongue of the stars," Ornicht said in Panglos. "I do not suffer fools."

"Our apologies!" The man cried, pressing his forehead to the ground. His right hand was extended and pressed flat against the deck, and the seeping blood from one of the Guraggan's victims lapped gently against it.

"We come with valuable news," the woman supplied. "Your enemy is above us. We can take you to her."

"I have no enemies," Lady Ornicht said, mirth in her distorted voice. "The whole of the human race can be put into two categories: my allies... and my prey."

"Umm," the woman said, looking uncertainly to her companion. "Well, I'm Yulette, and this is Gyje the Third Son, and we are most honored to make an alliance with you and—"

"You are not my allies."

The color drained from both the new arrival's faces.

Hiron could tell that the Physician was smirking beneath her mask. He was shamefully grateful that these newcomers had pulled attention away from him.

"I swear we know! We know where the captain of that ship is!" Gyje the Third Son said.

It was strange to see such a well-built man filled with such desperation. His face was bandaged, but he seemed so strong and powerful. Then again, before the Guraggan physical strength was nothing. Just more bulk to be hacked away.

"Tell me and we will spare you," Ornicht said.

"She's at the outer hull," Yulette said, her beautiful, fleshy features strained. "Speaking at the court of the Jarawat right now. Not far from here, it's a dome on the surface. If you hurry, you could make it there before the Jarawat's judgment is rendered."

"Judgment?"

"She's a captive," Gyje said. "She... hurt me. My mother might punish her. She might get dusted-uh, might get killed."

"So," Ornicht said. "You have come here to tell me the one I seek may be executed on your account?"

"That's... that's the long and short of it."

"You may have cost me a great deal," Lady Ornicht said, folding her armored fingers in front of her. "Lead me to this place. Swiftly. Right Hand Guard, you are to follow me. The rest of you protect our prize with Liss."

"My lady," the Physician hissed, then continued in Guraggan.

When the Physician was done speaking, Hiron could tell that Lady Ornicht was enraged, but she said nothing.

"Take the boy inside," she growled. "Put him with the others. You two. Lead. Now."

Half the Guraggan Serfs fell in line with Lady Ornicht, as Gyje and his consort led them from the deck. Two others grabbed Hiron by the shoulders, and began escorting him up the loading ramp. The Physician stopped them, and leaned her hidden face close to his.

"You have been very fortunate," she whispered. "You are a truly marvelous creature. I would love to study you. Be kind to me, and do not die before we have a chance to meet again."

Hiron swallowed hard. He knew Tsi would have had some clever insult for that twisted sadist but, all he could manage was a shake of his head.

"Lucky boy," the Physician hissed, as he was dragged up the ramp, and taken into the depths of the ship.

Tsi could hear him inhaling. One long breath. The tubes worked like living things, corded serpents in his demon-fanged mouth. Stimulants pumped into the Bondsman's body.

How many people were dead in the Jarawat's garden, Tsi did not know. He had moved among them like a specter or a bolt of lightning, always where they couldn't see him, his guns howling, his blade flashing. He would fade in and out of the light, dappled with shadow by the lattice work that secured the clear dome above. Noxians and Sannatans, mercenaries from all across the Frontier, fell before the Bondsman with equal ease. She had thought him a butcher, not an artist, and she was right. There was a brutal efficiency to all that he did.

Booted feet kicked up the dirt on the floor of the Jarawat's court. Weapons roared. Lasers pierced the air, but they never found their mark. He was too swift.

Tsi kept low to the ground, her bound hands in front of her as she darted from tree to tree, keeping out of the line of fire. It was one man against the Jarawat's entire retinue, and they were being utterly annihilated. He would leap out from cover, his knife low and quick as it gutted one man, scatter pistol barking as it blew apart another gunman's face.

A Sannatan burst from cover, her fur robes flowing behind her, hoisting a heavy rotary cannon. The woman let out a primal bellow, joining with her weapon's thunderous song. Thousands of rounds poured towards the Bondsman. Tsi saw a series of flashes, smelled burning metal, and realized at last that Tenlok was protected not just by speed and armor, but by an old, clever system.

A personal point defense shield, dozens of tiny automated lasers placed strategically around his body. They detected fast moving objects instantly, targeted them with machine precision, and blasted them apart as they approached. The Sannatan might have been a mighty killer on her homeworld, but her solid shot would have as much chance of stopping the Bondsman as a gentle rain.

Tsi heard a bark of the scatter pistol, and the rotary cannon went dead.

The air was filling with smoke. She could hear the crackle of lasers too, but these had either gone wide or dissipated against the killer's armor. Why was the Bondsman here? Why had he killed the Jarawat? Tsi took some small relief in the fact that he had not come for her personally, but she might still get caught up in his berserker fury.

Belly crawling towards a dead Noxian, she saw the Bondsman sprint across open ground towards a huge cyborg. The machine-man was blazing away with a breacher's gun, a weapon meant for blowing open airlocks and heavy armor alike, like Tsi's beloved Repeater.

Every shot turned to mist as the Bondsman sprinted towards

him, solid rounds caught by the lasers that shielded him. Casting aside his scatter pistol, the Bondsman leaped into the air, arcing his kukri above his head. The curved blade came down hard into the Cyborg's skull, splitting it wide open. The Bondsman wrenched his blade free, dripping with oily fluid, as he drew another gun from the dozen holsters he wore.

It was horrifying and awe-inspiring all at once to watch the Bondsman move, every shot and blow carefully placed, his armor and his shields catching every bolt and bullet returned against him, or else his body twisting efficiently away from danger. He reminded Tsi of the Janissaries, monstrous hulks who glided through a battlefield like birds across a clear sky. The Bondsman was in his element, surrounded by killers yet unafraid. Totally aware, completely one with the moment, every squeeze of the trigger and thrust of the blade as easy and natural as breathing in and out.

Tsi had felt like that many times.

But not now.

Not against him.

She scuttled to a dead Noxian's body, the man who had taken her gun. Slipping a knife from his thigh, she sawed off her bindings, then stripped him of her pistol and the single magazine of ammo she had kept. She dropped the mag and checked it.

She wasn't one to pray, or to really believe in any gods or spirits or ancestors. She had a shrine to the Forgiver, but that was just a way to calm her mind. In any case, she was thankful to... whoever was watching out for her that this had been a magazine full of solid rounds. Not flechettes to rip flesh, or shield penetrators. Just simple, hard bullets, accelerated at incredible force.

A freakishly tall warrior from the Deep Stations rushed at the Bondsman, whirling a war glaive above his head. He was a Rock Drinker, a killer without peer if he had reached Salvation. That glaive was a weapon that could cleave through even Strongmind's toughened hide, and it was dancing about with such fury and precision that for a moment, Tsi hoped this would end here and now.

The Bondsman stepped to the side as the glaive cleaved downwards, missing him by centimeters. He whipped his kukri outwards in a wide arc. The Rock Drinker's unnaturally long forearms burst open, and the glaive went clattering to the ground, held by severed hands. Maimed, the warrior fell to his knees, letting out a keening wail. The Bondsman kicked him in the throat, silencing him forever.

Tsi had loaded her weapon, and made her decision just as the fight was starting to die down. The few survivors were fleeing for the edges of the court, realizing their weapons and their paltry skills were nothing against a creature like this. Tsi had seen that reaction before, against both the Janissaries, and the Guraggan. Even the bravest cannot fight against death itself.

The Bondsman was walking determinedly towards the Jarawat's dead body. He seized up her long hair in one hand and raised his Kukri high for the decapitating blow, when his eyes suddenly snapped up. He saw Tsi.

For another moment, she had allowed herself to hope he would take his prize and leave. It would have been a failure, yes, to not enlist the Jarawat's aid, but she wouldn't have to keep fighting. But he did see her, crouched, pistol in hand, her face icy calm, looking for all the world like a hardened pirate. Just like the dozens who had tried to kill him. Tried, and failed.

The Jarawat's hair fell from the Bondsman's free hand, and he pulled a pistol from its scabbard. He aimed it square at Tsi's chest.

Tsi was faster.

She aimed and fired.

Once.

Twice.

Three times, each shot shattering one of the magnetic clamps that kept a section of lattice work in place. The clear dome above them shattered.

She snapped her EVA helmet in place just as the dome cracked open. The room decompressed, hurtling its contents out into space. Trees, and plants and earth. Corpses. Tsi herself.

And the Bondsman too.

All cast into the deep and merciless void.

CHAPTER 17

ell, that's rather interesting," Wylla said aloud.

The machine's face was slack, but the eye that was still an organic facsimile rolled to look at her.

"You are absurd and irrelevant," Strongmind said. "Your logic is faulty. You are lazy, and commit inadequate effort into every endeavor."

Wylla stifled a laugh. Its language coding for Bykon was outdated. It was like hearing someone read insults from a dictionary without any understand of how they were supposed to be delivered.

"You fly the ship then?" she asked. "I'm seeing a lot of coding related to ship systems. Mostly weapons controls. That can't be right though, this is for whole banks of plasma cannons. Mass driver trajectory equations... Captain Tsi doesn't have a battle cruiser parked somewhere nearby, does she?"

"I will not divulge mission critical details," Strongmind said.

"Well, we're getting somewhere," Wylla smiled. "I think that's the first thing you've said to me that wasn't an insult."

"My tactics have proven ineffective," the machine replied.

"You couldn't hurt my feelings enough to get me to stop?"

"That is evident."

Wylla turned away from the display screen. She pushed her chair over, and sat in front of the machine. It glared at her, one eye moist and human, the other hard and mechanical. She studied it for a long moment, placing a finger to her cheek. She was relieved to finally be talking to it like a person.

"You call yourself Strongmind," she said. "I'm called Wylla."

"I know who you are."

"I've kept your vocal interfaces on because, contrary to what you might think, I don't actually want to harm you. I'm hoping we can come to an understanding, and I can get the data from you without doing any permanent damage."

"You are wasting time," Strongmind said.

Wylla folded her arms.

"I don't think trying to avoid suffering is ever a waste of time."

"I am not programmed to philosophize."

"What *are* you programmed for? I'm seeing a lot of combat data, piloting, navigation. Extensive language skills, communications, problem solving... but almost nothing in your memory banks. Very few recorded personal experiences. But there's been modifications to your combat data. You're a learning machine, aren't you?"

"I am capable of extensive function."

"You're not new either..." Wylla said. "If I didn't know better, I'd say you were of Guraggan manufacture. There's some very clever coding here. It's in a universal language, but it's been converted several times. I've only seen it on Guraggan warships before..."

"I do not know," Strongmind said. "Most of my memory files have been corrupted or deleted. I have no clear memories of my function prior to serving my current master."

"Your master. You mean Captain Tsi? Is that what she calls herself?"

The machine did not respond to that.

"Listen," Wylla continued. "I know that you don't like this, but try to think about it logically. If you give me root access, I won't have to risk damaging your operating systems. If you stay functional, you've got a better chance of helping your master later. This is the only way we all benefit."

"Your statement is logical."

Wylla relaxed slightly. She was finally getting somewhere. People she could read well enough. Objects, patterns, even better; but drones were difficult. Even something like this Strongmind, patterned to look like a human in every way, always had something subtly *off* about its movements. When it was dead-faced like this, it was nearly impossible to guess at what was going on inside its machine mind.

"There is another course of logical action, in which we all benefit," the machine said.

"Oh?"

"Disconnect your computer from me, and put me in the hold."

"If you're asking me to let you go..."

"I am not asking you to release me. You cannot gain any further relevant information from me. If you have interrogated the human Hiron, you have already gained enough mission-critical data to make the success of your operations highly likely," Strongmind said. Its eye flicked up and down her briefly. "Is my inference correct?"

"The Mistress has... spoken to the boy."

"Put me in the hold. There is nothing more that you can gain from my data banks without damaging them, and your forces already have what they need. I will not escape because of you, but you will also not be responsible for unnecessary damage being sustained by this unit."

"If the mistress finds out that I—"

"She will triumph or fail against my master regardless of whether you continue your current course of action. What you must decide is whether you wish to be responsible for inflicting further damage... or not."

Wylla stood up and turned away from the machine. She crossed her arms, feeling the machine's eyes boring into her back. After taking three deep breaths, she began disconnecting wires from the side of the drone's head.

She pressed a key on her wrist commlink.

"Liss? Would you send a man up? There's nothing else I can do with this drone. The data I've transferred needs to be compiled for a little while. I'd like it put in the hold until further notice," she said.

The Breaker murmured his assent. He would do anything to please her, but something seemed to be troubling him. Well, troubling him more than usual. She would have to speak to him about it when she had the chance.

The machine was still staring at her fixedly. It had not moved at all, still as a corpse.

"And Liss?" Wylla said. "Make... make sure the men know it still needs to be chained up."

Tsi had been spaced three times in her life. Once it had been an accident on a mining vessel. Two times it was an emergency jump off a burning ship. This would mark the first time she'd been the cause of the disaster.

She was drifting in the cold dark, no noise but the sound of her own breath. The EVA suit was of good, sturdy manufacture, but it wasn't made for long trips. She didn't have jets or magnetic cords, those cost extra. Some old spacers called this a "chance in hell" suit. It was the sort of thing only the very desperate wore, on the off chance that if the worst happened, they'd be picked up before they ran out of life support, or drifted into heavy radiation, or just got ripped apart by passing debris.

There was quite a bit of that going by. Despite her hammering heart, despite the terror of the Bondsman's attack, despite the nightmare of everything that had happened since she left Glutton, Tsi was still struck by the surreal beauty of her surroundings. Exotic plants and great pine trees drifted by, ice coating their delicate, shriveling limbs. The artificial ponds that had been the Jarawat's pride boiled and froze, turning into vaporous clouds of crystalline particles.

There were corpses. Dozens of them, ones gored by the Bondsman's fire, or those not fast enough to secure their suits when Tsi blew the dome wide open. They were all drifting away into the deadly radiation of the inner core. She'd die long before she started to feel the kiss of the Poison Suns, but Tsi found it useful to remember where this journey would end if she didn't move quickly.

Still breathing heavily, she spun round and round in place, her enhanced eyes searching the debris cloud for what she needed. At last she spotted him: the blue-black form of the Bondsman himself. He was spinning into space, but like Tsi, he was still alive, his armored suit secure. She could see he was fumbling with something at his belt. She'd spotted it even in the chaos of his ambush, and now she was counting on it to save her life.

It was a stupid plan, had been a stupid plan from the beginning. The odds were a thousand to one, if she was generous. But it was all she had.

She saw a massive fir tree drifting towards her. Spinning her back to it, she made a rough calculation, aimed her Repeater, and fired.

The gun was silent in space, but the explosion and force of the shot propelled her. She recovered and fired again, knowing she had precious few rounds left. She felt a dull impact against her back as she hit the tree, and her free hand snapped out and grabbed one of the shriveled limbs. She hauled herself along the tree's length, hand over hand, trying not to put enough pressure on the tree to push herself off until she reached its gnarled roots. Glancing to her left, she saw that the Bondsman had caught hold of a hunk of shattered statuary. He placed his taloned boots against it, and pushed off.

She followed suit, angling herself across the void in an arc to intercept him. A fat, dead Noxian drifted into her path and she caught hold of the man, awkwardly placed her boots against his stomach, and pushed herself off again.

There had been a great many people crowded into one corner of the dome when it had shattered, and they had been pulled out with a huge cloud of dirt at once. That cloud of bodies and dirt hove into view, cutting both Tsi and the Bondsman off from Salvation. She could see some bodies squirming in the cloud, Noxians who had managed to get their suits secured. Now they'd drift off to their deaths, surrounded by their slain comrades. She wondered how many would simply pop their helmets off when they got out of reach of the station, accepting the inevitable.

She was drifting on an intercept course with the Bondsman. He had not noticed her yet, had something black in one of his hands, and was peering through the cloud of dirt and bodies. Everything rode on his precision, for both him and Tsi.

The Bondsman pulled the trigger, and the magnetic grapnel launched a long claw with a thin strand of nano-carbon attached to it across the void. It must have been a few hundred meters in length, long enough to reach the skin of Salvation. The claw pierced the debris cloud, and the Bondsman slapped a catch on the side of the grapnel. Just as its automated winch started to pull, Tsi fired her Repeater again.

The shot was towards her feet and to the right, propelling her forwards, and she crashed headlong into the Bondsman's side. She wrapped her free hand tightly around his side as they were pulled into the debris cloud.

Flailing limbs and bodies buffeted against them. Hunks of rock struck their sides, and by the time they had cleared the nebulous mass, they were both spinning. Tsi's visor was utterly fouled. She clung to the mercenary for dear life. Awkwardly, she shoved the Repeater into its holster, just as the Bondsman's first blow hit her.

It was an awkward thing to fight in the depths of space. A single solid strike would send both opponents flying in opposite directions. The Bondsman had no trouble with this, of course, his goal was simply to drive her away.

His first punch took her hard in the ribs, but she kept her arm vice-clamped around him. His next strike hit the side of her helmet. He was strong, incredibly strong. She guessed his muscle enhancement put him on par with something like Strongmind. Stronger if his chemical stimulants were working. His fist connected with her helmet again, rattling her around. She could see cracks starting to form in her face plate, but she only needed a moment more.

The knife slipped out of its carefully concealed scabbard on her wrist. She caught the fragile little blade, and thrust it with all her might just below his armpit. It was thin, but it was sharp, and the blade bit through one of the weak points in his armor, cut through subdermal plate, and into tissue below. Tsi depressed a stud on the handle, and held the blade in place with all her might. The Bondsman was still striking her with one hand, his other holding fast to the grapnel, but she buried her helmet against his chest, angling her face plate away from his blows.

Next he wrapped his fist around her hand that held the dagger. First his iron fingers tried to pry her off, but when that failed, he simply began to crush her hand. Tsi could feel pain, feel the human flesh of her hands starting to bruise under her gauntlet, but her bones wouldn't break. She smiled. All she had to do was hold on and endure. She was good at that.

The two of them hit the side of Salvation. The Bondsman's boot-claws snapped out, burrowing into the hull, and Tsi let go of him. She spun away, but one of her hands shot out and caught an extruding antennae. With the practiced ease of a Noxian, Tsi triggered her magnetic boots and clamped herself down to the surface of the station.

For a moment, Tsi and the Bondsman stood facing each other across the expanse of pock-marked metal. The stars whirled behind them, reflected in the burning eyes of of the Bondsman's demon-mask. Tsi saw him reach up to the dagger she'd left in his side, but he stopped before pulling it out. All he'd do is spring a leak, possibly expose whatever parts of him were still human to the void. The Bondsman reached down and pulled the Kukri from his scabbard instead.

Tsi whirled and ran. He would have the advantage over her, the climbing spikes on his boots ripping up the metal surface as he moved, easily outstripping her awkward magnetic boots. But Tsi knew how Salvation was structured, had walked its surface many times.

A dozen bounding strides found an emergency access hatch. She ripped open its ancient cover, vaulted across it as a sudden burst of coolant was released into the void. The Bondsman reeled backwards from the icy mist, and Tsi leaped down into the access shaft.

It was a narrow passage, intended for repair drones, but roomy enough for Tsi. She hit the bottom of the shaft soon enough, whirled and pushed her way past scuttling machines. She could see another bulkhead door labeled "EMERGENCY AIRLOCK" in faded paint. She began working the external lock furiously. It was a simple winch system, but it was slow, and the Bondsman was close behind her.

She sensed, rather than heard the Bondsman drop down the shaft. With disdainful ease, he sliced through two of the scuttling drones blocking his way, and stalked towards Tsi.

With a furious yell, she worked the winch as hard as she could, until at last a gap opened in the airlock door. She pried the door open with her gloved hands, abandoning the winch, and squeezed inside. It was an engineer's prepping room, octagonal and filthy. There were racks of repair equipment on both walls. She stumbled forwards, losing her balance as she felt the a-grav fully. She slammed an emergency lever to start cycling the airlock again.

The Bondsman had slipped in after her, before the airlock door could close. She heard the loud hiss of oxygen being pumped back into the room. The click of the Bondsman's boots against the floor filled her ears as he lunged at her wordlessly, his kukri high.

Tsi caught his wrist, and flipped him deftly over her shoulder. The mercenary landed in a heap at the far corner of the airlock. Before Tsi could react, he had drawn a dagger from a sheath along his thigh and hurled it at her. Only by jerking to the side did she keep it from burying itself in her throat. Instead, the blade clipped her shoulder and sent her spinning to the ground.

The hissing had stopped. Tsi could feel oxygen around her. Recycled yes, but the air of the station. She pulled the EVA helmet from her head, and lurched against one of the octagonal walls, still on her knees, the merciful feeling of air in her lungs numbing her to the pain of her wounds.

The Bondsman had risen, gripping the Kukri tightly in one hand. He was walking towards her, clearly having decided to take her head rather than just shooting her. Tsi met his gaze, unflinching.

"I wouldn't do that if I were you," Tsi said.

The Bondsman paused. His pitiless dead eyes studied her. Tsi let the faintest trace of a smile play on her lips. She was telling the truth.

The Bondsman touched the dagger she'd stuck in his side with his free hand.

"Uh huh," Tsi said. "Go ahead and pop it out. It's done its work."

She wiped blood from her nose, not having realized until now that her face had smacked against the visor of her helmet more than once. The blade slid out of the Bondsman's side and clattered to the ground.

"I know you're pretty heavily augmented, but there has to still be some meat under there, no?" she asked.

The Bondsman gave no response.

"That wasn't just any knife. It was a delivery system. Right now, medical nanites are filling your bloodstream. They'll latch on to major organs, neural links, you name it. When they get the signal, they'll necroticize every living tissue in your body. You'll rot from the inside out."

"And you control the signal," the Bondsman growled.

"Yes. And so do you, in a way. Want to know what it is?"

Tsi tapped her chest impishly.

"Heartbeat link," the Bondsman said. "You die, your machines flay me alive from the inside."

"That's about it, yeah."

"Risky. And expensive," the mercenary observed. The kukri was still held tightly in his hand. Tsi could see a thin coat of crystallized oxygen on the blade, slowly turning to moisture in the heat of the station. "How do you know I won't just kill you and find someone to flush my system afterwards?"

"I'm gambling that you want to stay alive," Tsi said. "And with all the 'friends' you just made on Salvation, I don't think you'll be finding a med-tech willing to work on you before your lungs turn to sludge. Besides... I was hoping to hire you. I need some help taking back my ship. You seem qualified for the job."

Tsi flashed a smirk at the mercenary. She got no response for ten long heartbeats. Then, at last, the Bondsman sheathed his blade.

"Thirty thousand credits," the Bondsman said flatly. "And transport out of Noxia. Does your ship have an auto-doc?"

"A decent one."

"I want full use of that, too."

"Seems reasonable," Tsi said.

"I don't take kindly to being poisoned," the Bondsman said.

"Well, I don't take kindly to people trying to kill me either," Tsi replied. "But why don't we leave that in the past?"

Tenlok offered her his hand. She took it. He pulled her up.

Tsi smiled at the demon mask, and wiped the rest of the blood from her face with the back of her hand.

"Alright," Tenlok said. "Let's go take care of business."

CHAPTER 18

Lady Ornicht had never been in a place as filthy as Salvation. Every urchin and beggar, every two-bit haggler and aspiring gun-for-hire cringed at the site of her. She felt one hand tense and relax, ready to ease her blades out of their sheathes. Looking at these people made her feel an animalistic hunger, an urge to split one of them open and watch his companions flee in terror.

They could tell, too. All eyes darted away from her, or stared fixedly ahead as she passed. It was good to be feared.

The two Noxians went ahead, followed by a trio of Ornicht's most trusted serfs. Three more followed behind her, chests shining with service beads. They were not the finest warriors she had ever commanded, but they were loyal and desperate to please her. None of them would ever have dared, as her Physician had, to question her choice to lead this raid.

She could feel the pressure building behind her eyes, the numbing of her mouth, but she didn't care. She would find the prey herself, pin this woman called 'Tsi' down, and incise such beauties on her flesh as these savages would remember for a lifetime. Among her people, it was an old teaching that war was primarily fought in the mind. Inflict horrors upon your enemies, make the price of resistance, even the *thought* of resistance so high that none would pay it, and victory was already yours.

"Almost there," the Noxian man said.

Gyje the Third Son. Perhaps she would turn him into a Thrall when she was done. She'd rather kill him, though.

His whole body stank of false bravado, a fragile shell concealing a weak man. She wanted to crack it open and watch him mewl a moment before she crushed him. His pudgy little consort would follow shortly. Perhaps Lady Ornicht would throttle her. Or ask Breaker Liss to split her head with a kukri. Or maybe let her go.

Kinshah Ornicht had never considered herself a sadist. She was efficiently cruel. Rage was certainly one of her vices, but she was never excited by suffering for its own sake. Even so, nothing filled her with contempt more than hollow courage. The whole of this station, every human in the light of the Poison Suns, reeked of it. They were all trying so hard to show how *fearsome* they were, little dreaming that things like her dwelt in the darkness between the stars.

She was not even the most terrible of her kin. True, she counted herself highly ranked among Guraggan warriors, old as she was, but there were others like Turon Chryte, the Lady-Of-Nine, and Gorm Many-Shadowed who made even Ornicht pause. She was proud to count them her people, but that didn't mean she was foolish enough to think herself their equal. Still, even they paled in comparison to the Khagan.

"You!"

Lady Ornicht's guides had come to an abrupt halt, her serfs almost stumbling over them. They were at the base of a wide, cylindrical chamber, twin ramps spiraling upwards to the next level. People had set up stalls all around the base of the chamber, barnacle-like dwellings bolted up the walls, crisscrossed by rope walkways and rusty ladders. The hovel dwellers were cowering away, sensing danger with their well-tuned coward's instincts.

A score of Noxians were standing at the base of the twin ramps, strung out in a ragged line twenty meters from where Ornicht's party had halted. They were armed and armored in the ramshackle way of this place, but their eyes were hard. Their leader, the one who spoke and extended an accusing finger, was a man with powdered skin and exotic silks wrapped around the shoulders of his vac-suit. A savage, enraptured by the tokens of civilization.

"Gyje!" the powdered man cried, harsh voice belying his foppish demeanor. "You've gone too far! Did you really think you could take the Corridor with a rotten play like this?"

"What are you yapping about, Pren? I haven't done—"

"Our Mother's dead because of you! Don't deny it. You brought that Bondsman here, didn't you? You brought him and that woman to kill our Mother!"

"The Jarawat is... dead?" Gyje asked.

Ornicht was amused to hear genuine sorrow in his voice.

"Don't play stupid! Everyone saw your little tantrum, talk went all across the ring. That hired killer of yours showed up not ten minutes later, and now the whole court is slaughtered and the dome's been voided! Crude, brother, very crude. If I'd've been there I mighta put a stop to it. But I think our other other siblings won't complain when I bring you to them in pieces."

With a thought, Ornicht's shoulder cannon began tracking Pren and his men. She stepped forward, brushing past Gyje.

"I own this one," she said, fixing Pren with the yellow glow of her visor. "Speak to me, if you want something from it."

"Who the hell are you?" Pren retorted. He had a pistol in hand, and cocked it nonchalantly.

"I am Ornicht of the Guraggan," she said. She noted with some satisfaction that what little color could be seen in the man's face drained.

"Junk mass," he said. "No Guraggan here. You're just another merc, aren't you."

"I tire of this," Ornicht replied, letting her forearm blades slip from their sheathes. "You insult me, but I am feeling merciful. If you surrender now I will take you as a thrall."

"Big talk," the powdered man shot back, that Noxian bravado rising in his voice again. "But it seems I brought more guns than you, little sister. Be smart. Walk away."

Ornicht spotted several men moving on the ramps high above. He wasn't lying, there were more shooters coming out of the shadows, some carrying heavy ordinance. This Pren had planned his ambush well. Perhaps his spies had been watching ever since they left the docking bay, making note of her armor and her entourage. They weren't as pathetic as they looked. Strong as a *kheshtic* suit was, it would not be proof against every gun and blade they had.

But she was no one if she could not handle a few pirates. Lady Ornicht felt the pressure slip away from her eyes, felt her body, strong and whole within her armor.

She shot Pren twice in the chest with her shoulder cannon, then once more in the forehead as he fell to his knees. The world exploded around her in the glorious cacophony of gunfire.

As she danced between the blasts, shrapnel pattering across her breastplate, the heat of lasers brushing her limbs, she almost cried in joy. She would give these Noxians something to remember her for generations.

Hiron could, in fact, walk; but that was lost on his captors. They had shoved and prodded him up the boarding ramp, obviously impatient with the speed of his crutches. Once inside the ship, they'd grown tired of his shuffling gait. So they had simply grabbed him and dragged him to the cargo hold that was serving as a make-shift prison.

He'd spent some hours in here before, but now, for some reason they'd turned the lighting to minimal. The room stank too, filled with the familiar scent of death. Hiron shuddered. The Guraggan leader had ordered him kept alive. He wasn't too sure exactly why. Perhaps the Serfs had decided he wasn't worth the trouble, and were going to—

He felt a sudden sharp blow to his back and was sent sprawling. Laying on the ground wheezing, he felt rough hands grab his shoulders, pull him into a sitting position, and bind his hands with a length of cold wire. When he protested that the wire was cutting into his skin, the Serf slapped him across the face. It was a casual, disdainful gesture, but it broke Hiron's lip. He fell silent, ashamed. If only he was stronger, smarter, if only he knew some way out of this. But no, there were two of them, they had armor and weapons, and he was just a weak little boy. The Serf who had bound him raised a single finger to his lips, then made a striking motion. Hiron understood. They left him in the dark.

He was quiet for a long time, listening to the sound of his own breathing, trying to decide if he should fall asleep. It was a tricky question: he probably didn't have that much longer to live, so should he spend his time awake and alert, or should he try to rest?

Life didn't have that much to offer him right now, he reflected. Just a cramped cargo hold, night-dark and foul. He was pretty sure there were a few dead people in the room with him, from the stench. They'd make it hard to sleep, but they didn't make staying awake pleasant, either.

"You alive?" a voice asked from the darkness.

Hiron started, and peered out towards it. The accent was strange, but he remembered it well. Not a soft voice exactly, but with a faint scratchiness that made it sound youthful, like someone stuck perpetually in that awkward transition from adolescent to adult. He began to sweat when he recognized the speaker, then realized how stupid it was to be embarrassed in a situation like this, and sweat even more. He dabbed futilely at his brow with his bound hands.

Enlil was propped up opposite him, her tangled mess of hair falling across her face. He could see flickers of blonde in the darkness. Her head hung low, and she seemed to be curled in on herself. In the dim light he could not see her well, but he saw that unlike him, she was unbound.

"Yeah, I'm alive," he said. "Uh, how are you?"

"Gooder days," she shrugged. She was fairly good at speaking Panglos, but she made a lot of mistakes that Hiron found charming.

"Yeah, I've been, uh better too," Hiron said, trying to summon up some of Tsi's laconic bravado.

Enlil laughed. Not for very long, though.

"What's your name, twice?" she asked.

"Again," Hiron corrected gently. "What's your name, again."

"Screw you, I'm not pretty talking," she grunted back.

"Sorry, sorry. Hiron. I'm Hiron."

"Enlil."

"I know."

"Yeah."

"Um," Hiron said, desperate to fill the silence that was creeping in. "Do you know what they're going to do to us?"

Enlil laughed, and this time the sound was cruel. She pointed a finger at him lazily and said "bang" and then repeated the gesture at herself.

"Yeah... yeah that's what I think they're going to do to us too."

"'s Okay," Enlil said. "Happens everyone."

"It doesn't have to. Maybe we could, we could figure out how to get out of here. You're not tied up—"

Enlil shook her head and pointed at her legs.

"Water," she said.

"What?"

"They take a small... pipe, with a sharp?"

"A syringe?"

"Yeah. In here."

Enlil made a stabbing gesture at her legs. Hiron realized she was barefoot, and her feet were bruised and swollen. The Guraggan had given her some kind of drug so that she couldn't walk properly. He smiled glumly. Now they really were a pair.

"Can't crawl faster than guns," Enlil said ruefully.

"No," Hiron agreed.

They were both quiet for a long moment. It was Enlil who broke the silence first.

"Talk at me about your ship."

"My ship?"

"Where you were a baby. Where your parents are."

"My homeworld?"

"Homeworld…" Enlil said, rolling the Panglos word around in her mouth. He realized that whatever native dialect of Noxian she spoke, that word was probably unfamiliar. Noxians were bred on stations and starships. Few of them ever set foot on a planet, and then it would be one of the airless dwarfs and massive asteroids of this poisoned system.

"Um, well, other people call it the Inheritor's World, but we… well, we call it Promise."

Enlil laughed. "Stupid name."

"Yeah, kind of," Hiron agreed sheepishly.

"What's it like?"

"Hot," Hiron said. "And… the air is bad. Too much radiation."

He paused briefly and looked at her to see if she was following. 'Radiation' seemed to be a word she knew, which didn't surprise him. She was probably familiar with quite a few technical terms in Panglos. Second only to curse words, he'd guess.

"Most of us live in big domes or underground. Some people go up into the wilderness, but it's hard and unless they have good gear, it makes them sick."

Enlil nodded.

"I know rad sickness."

"Yeah. The clouds are usually pretty thick too. Big, grey things. They cover up the sky. It's not like here, most of the time you can't see the stars at night."

Enlil raised an eyebrow.

"Sleep-shift," he said. "It's when you can see the stars on a planet—"

"I know," she said.

"Right, right. Well, yeah, it's kind of... my home is kind of ugly. And crowded. Everyone is sick, or cruel, or sick *and* cruel."

"Why'd you come here?" Enlil asked. "Not big different."

"It's prettier here. You can see the stars whenever you want."

Enlil snorted, and brushed her hair out of her face with her good hand. She wasn't much older than Hiron, but there was something so hard about her features. Hiron's life hadn't been a happy one, but he couldn't guess at what this woman had been through.

"Stars look pretty," she said. "But they kill you if you get too close."

"How many rounds you have left?" the Bondsman asked.

"Nil," Tsi replied casually.

She had stripped out of her EVA suit, its cracked face-plate and the damage the Bondsman's blade had done rendering it useless. She was back down to her regular garb, a loose-fitting body suit with a long traveler's cloak over the top of it.

"You're retaking your ship with an empty gun?"

"Well, originally I was going to be backed by a gang of Noxian pirates. But someone decided to kill them all."

"Happens in this line of work."

They were making their way along a disused maintenance route. Salvation was a maze of corridors, gantries and holding chambers, but there were veins threaded through the entire station used by its Technician's Guild. The Technicians themselves were a small minority, mostly untroubled by the rest of station's denizens, and so many of their hidden corridors and utility shafts went empty and unused much of the time. Tsi had learned they were good for a quick escape on more than one occasion, or as a way to sneak up on a target undetected.

It was a tight fit with the Bondsman walking close behind her. It reminder her a little of her escape with Hiron and Strongmind from the Inheritor's World. While she could trust the machine and the boy with her life, she felt a tremor in the hairs on the back of her neck at the sound of his boots behind him. It was as if the mercenary might reach out and smash her skull into the side of the tunnel at any moment.

She knew he wouldn't. Self-preservation was the code of a hired killer, and he could be relied on as long as he thought she could help him.

"Why exactly did you come after Jarawat?" Tsi asked.

"Self-defense," the Bondsman said.

"Is that what you call gunning down a dozen people in cold blood?"

"Twenty three," Tenlok corrected "And the Jarawat was going to kill me. Or one of her underlings would try to. Doesn't matter. After the talk I had with Gyje I wasn't getting off this station without burning some ammo."

"You don't know that for certain—"

"You were there. What's your opinion on Gyje? Think he was going to let bygones be bygones?"

Tsi tensed. The Bondsman had seen her at Gyje's den. She'd tried to hide but he'd noticed her, memorized her features. She wasn't sure why, but she had her suspicions.

"No," Tsi admitted. "He's a proud man. He wanted me dead, he'd have wanted you dead too. But that doesn't mean the Jarawat would have agreed."

"She'd have to. They're a family."

"So you killed them all, just to be safe."

"Yeah," Tenlok said.

There was a low rumble that shook the tunnel, and a series of popping sounds. The lights flickered briefly, but the pops continued.

"News must have finally hit that Jarawat's dead," Tsi said. "What's left of the Ten Sons will be tearing each other apart. Every guild, clan and crew is going to join in."

The Bondsman didn't say anything, but kept walking behind her.

"Killing Jarawat destabilized this place," Tsi continued. "Everyone's going to be trying to seize what they can. A lot of people are going to die."

"I know," the Bondsman said. She could practically hear the shrug in his voice.

"They'll kill you too, if they can get their hands on you. It'll really make a name for whoever does it... 'the Breacher who avenged the Jarawat'. Good ring to it, you could start a crew around that, couldn't you?"

"Lot of people tried to get famous by shooting me. Hasn't worked yet."

"Never a whole station at once, though."

"I've had worse odds."

Tsi had to laugh at that. There was something in the way the mercenary spoke that made it sound not like bluster, but a simple statement of fact.

"Sure. I'm just reminding you," she said. "I'm the best chance you have of staying alive."

"No question. That's why I still want to hear this plan of yours to retake your ship with an empty gun."

Tsi had been mulling that conundrum over herself the entire time they'd been traveling. They were near the ship now. Silently, she sent out a signal pulse with her internal comms unit. After a long moment, she was rewarded with a single ping back.

"I'll need you to run interference," she explained. "I'm drawing up a holo-map of the landing bay right now. You breach from stern while I hit from above. Once I give the signal, you just drop every Guraggan you see, then make for the ship's secondary boarding ramp, understand?"

"Sure," the Bondsman said. "Still not clear on how *you* expect to survive more than thirty seconds, though."

"Simple," Tsi said. "I've got people on the inside."

Enlil had been talking to the boy for a while now. She didn't much care for it, but she had to keep her mind occupied. He was useful for that, even though he kept correcting the way she talked.

Stupid habit. There were people who'd knife you for making them feel dumb. The way the boy spoke, his home was full of rough types, but for some reason he'd grown up soft and sweet, like a Goodhome peach. *Miracles abound in this universe.*

He wasn't so bad, really. But he was small and scrawny and malformed, and she disliked how he sometimes stared at her and blushed. That was another thing that could get you knifed.

"That's how we think the universe was formed, anyway," Hiron said, wrapping up a long-winded lecture that Enlil had only half-listened to.

"You know a big amount of stuff," she said. "How old are you?"

"Well, that depends how you count, I guess. Back home I'm two years past blooding age. Not, uh, that I've actually been Blooded."

"How many years is that?"

"Well, different planets rotate around their suns at different speeds. I know some people like to use Terran standard, but honestly I think that's silly. I mean, how many people even go back to Earth anymore? It's half again as far from Kios Prime to there as it is to Promise, and my home's one of the farthest habitable worlds out there. Plus, there's what people say about Earth and the Guraggan—"

"Yeah, them," Enlil grumbled.

Why did this have to happen to her? She'd never been lucky exactly, but why did it have to be the damned *Guraggan* to catch her?

No sooner had she thought of their captors, than one of the doors to the hold opened, filling the room with light. Two serfs entered, dragging a massive figure between them. They were followed by two more who both had their weapons out and charged. She recognized Tsi's pet drone, comically lop-sided with its one arm of bronze metal, its face a nightmarish patch-work of synthetic flesh and ceramic bone. It seemed to be pacified somehow, staggering along between the two guards. A solid round had gone right through one of its knee joints as near as she could tell. Heavy bindings were clamped all over the thing, chaining its arms in place.

The four Serfs escorted the drone into the room, then secured it to the far wall with magnetic clamps. Like Enlil and Hiron, they forced it to sit on the floor, though its ruined face was totally passive and inscrutable as it suffered the humiliation of being bound in place.

Once their prisoner was secure, one of the Serfs barked something in his native tongue. A woman entered the room. Enlil had seen her before, briefly. She was elegant and beautiful, wearing robes of a silk that was strikingly alien to her surroundings. No one on Noxia would wrap themselves in something that expensive, Enlil thought. Maybe Jarawat, some of her sons. If she killed this woman and stripped her, the dress alone could buy passage on a freighter out of here.

The woman must have seen the hunger in Enlil's eyes, because she seemed distinctly uncomfortable as she walked across the room and leaned over the drone. She examined it briefly, then turned around. Enlil noticed the woman glancing at the dead crewmen on the ground, then looking away quickly. She almost laughed. Gentle souls had no place on Salvation.

The woman spoke to the two Serfs briefly. Guraggan wasn't a language Enlil understood, but she could gather the gist of the conversation from the tone the woman spoke in and the Serf's surly responses. They'd drawn short straws, stuck guarding a bunch of half-dead captives while their comrades got the glory, and the pretty woman was trying to get them to take their jobs seriously. Enlil almost sympathized with them. She'd been stuck on 'live cargo' duty more than once.

"Wylla," Hiron said. The woman turned, hearing her name.

The boy looked at her pleadingly. Wylla seemed to be steeling herself, and for a moment it looked as if she would simply walk out of the room. She didn't though. Enlil quietly applauded the boy. Guilt was a good weapon, if you knew who to use it on.

"Wylla, you have to get us out of this. She's hurt," he said, jerking his head at Enlil. "She needs help."

Wylla shook her head.

"The Physician has seen to her," she said. "She will live. So will you. Please, Hiron, you have to stay calm, and be quiet. Don't do anything foolish, alright? Lady Ornicht——Lady Ornicht can be very reasonable, if we don't cause trouble, do you understand?"

"Reasonable?" Enlil cawed. "Like, piston-to-the-head reasonable? Or gut-shot reasonable? Or how about throat-cut reasonable? That what your boss has waiting for us?"

One of the Serfs, a woman who had a pair of crimson slits in the center of her face instead of a nose, walked briskly to Enlil. Without ceremony, she kicked Enlil hard in the chest, driving the wind from her lungs. As Enlil was gasping, a booted foot connected with her solar plexus again. The Serf was about to continue the beating, but Wylla began roaring at her in Guraggan. Reluctantly, the battle-Serf backed away, shooting Enlil a venomous look.

"Just... just don't cause trouble. All of you," Wylla said, looking at each of them in turn. "I'll... I'll be back to check on you."

She gave Hiron one last look, then fled the room. The Guraggan Serfs glared at them for a few moments, before exiting after her. Enlil, Hiron and the drone were alone.

Enlil coughed. Breathing had gotten hard all of a sudden. That last kick had rattled something loose, she thought, but after retching for a moment, she felt better.

"Strongmind," Hiron whispered. "Hey, Strongmind?"

One of the drone's eyes flared to life, but it did not speak.

"Do you uh... do we, I mean, what should we do?" the boy asked.

"Wait," the drone said tonelessly.

"You got a plan or something, tin-head?" Enlil asked.

The machine did not respond.

"Wait. 'Wait'. Okay. Okay, we can do that..." Hiron said. He looked like he would have gotten up and paced around the room if it wasn't for his bonds. "Maybe.. maybe the Guraggan will forget we're here. It could happen right? They seem to be working on something really complicated. And there's the rest of the station, someone's bound to come looking for Furner Ketsu's men..."

Enlil shook her head.

"If somebody was gonna come for Furner, they'd have done it by now. They're just letting us cook in here a little while, that's all. When the boss lady comes back, they'll ask us a lot of questions, see if we know any good stuff. Crack us open, I bet. Then shoot us."

"I don't... I don't think they need to ask us anything," the boy said quietly.

Enlil looked at him questioningly.

"She already talked to me," he said.

"Like... *talked* to you?" Enlil asked. "Like knife cuttin' skin talked to you?"

"No," he sighed. "She didn't have to. I got scared."

"Hmm, lucky her. I'd've talked too. But I don't know shit."

"I thought maybe I could hold out but... I couldn't."

Enlil shrugged.

"Doesn't matter. They'd have cut on you 'til you cracked anyway. Nothing in the Void is worth that."

"Tsi is," Hiron said. "Maybe if I delayed a little longer, it would have helped her to, you know, to rescue us."

Enlil laughed.

"Hate to break it to you kid, but Tsi ain't doing anything like that. The second I took a round, she got out of here quick as she could.

She ain't coming back."

"You don't know that! She's clever. She has to have something up her sleeve—"

"Kid, that's *exactly why* I know she's not coming back. Tsi's smart. That means she's not taking a losing bet… which is exactly what we are. So you, me, and handsome over here are pretty much fucked."

"This body is not capable of sexual function," Strongmind said.

"What?" Enlil asked.

"I think it might be joking," Hiron said. "I can never be sure."

"I deemed this information valuable. You referred to me as 'handsome'. If the possibility of sexual activity with this body is a motivating factor, it is vital that you understand I am not capable of such behavior."

"Right," Enlil said. "I'll try to keep my disappointment in check."

"Your estimation of Tsi is also incorrect," the drone said.

"Oh yeah? You know something I don't?"

"Yes," Strongmind said.

"And that is?"

"She is coming to rescue us," Strongmind said. "I am certain of it."

CHAPTER 19

Lady Ornicht stared out at the broken dome. It had a serene quality to it, less a battlefield, more a graveyard. A few dozen people had certainly died here. Exposed as it was now to the open vacuum, she could see bodies drifting like schools of fish beneath a black sea, colliding comically with clods of dirt and crystallized plant matter.

Even through the narrow viewing slit of the emergency airlock, she could surmise what had happened. There had been an ambush of some kind. A spectacular amount of firepower had been brought to bare. What little she'd gleaned from Pren's men before she killed them indicated they thought this was the work of one man. A "Bondsman".

She knew a little of those mercenaries, cybernetically and surgically altered to be fanatically loyal to their contract holders. Negotiable loyalty was no loyalty at all in her view. Still, they had a reputation as effective killers, and if this was the handiwork of a single warrior then he could almost compare to a Guraggan. Almost.

She sighed, idly scraping dried blood from one of her gauntlets. Survivors were possible, but unlikely. Perhaps the trail ended here. She would have to return to the fleet with her captives and the ship. This was not a defeat, but it tasted of one.

"I can't believe it's true," Gyje murmured. "Stupid of the Jarawat to live in a dome. Should've had more guards. Shouldn't have trusted all those hangers-on."

"True," Ornicht said, not really listening to the grieving pirate.

Her lungs were starting to burn again. She'd stayed in the suit too long, been too active. She would need treatment, and soon.

"We return to my shuttle. Communicate to Liss that he is to take this "Tsi's" ship and rendezvous with our own," she commanded, her surviving serfs immediately rushing to obey.

Half of them had fallen in the Noxian ambush, but if the

survivors mourned they did not show it. She would allow them their grieving rite later, when they were in transit back to the fleet. They'd fought bravely and relentlessly, and deserved full honor.

"Come," she said, gesturing to Gyje and Yulette.

The captives looked at her, bewildered.

"Um," the woman said. "W-where are we-?"

"Do not trifle," Ornicht said. "You are returning with me to my ship. You've proven useful and are now part of my retinue."

"We held up our end of the deal!" Gyje insisted. "We did everything you asked!"

Ornicht let one of her mono-blades slip from its sheath. Light glinted on its ebon surface, and she slowly raised it so that the edge hovered mere inches from Gyje's eye.

"I own you," she said. "I've owned you since the moment I set foot on this station. There is only one release from my service."

The couple looked helplessly to each other. Yulette seemed like she was about to speak, when one of the Serfs stepped forward and took a knee in front of Ornicht.

"My lady, I beg to speak," he said.

"What is it?"

"Liss informs us that he is under attack. We must reinforce him with all haste."

Ornicht rounded on Yulette and Gyje again.

"Take us back," she said in a voice that brooked no argument. "Without delay."

Wylla sat in the cockpit of the ship, going through navigational data. Though it was only strings of numbers and codes, it painted a marvelous picture in her mind. This ship had been to every corner of the frontier. Logs going back decades traced time spent in the Web of Eden, the Crown Worlds of the Epilotii Mandate, even tiny backwaters like Goodhome and Last Call.

In the years she'd spent as part of Lady Ornicht's retinue, she had traveled far and seen much, but it had always been at her Lady's command. Always there was a mission, some cruel scheme, jockeying for position with other Guraggan Houses or riding along with raiders against weakly held worlds. This ship though... it had been a nomad. The thought of it made Wylla smile, but she felt a little twinge of sorrow in her heart.

It wouldn't be a wanderer for much longer. It was Lady Ornicht's prize now. Soon it was to be brought back to the Grand Fleet, taken apart and pored over by Guraggan engineers. A marvelous ship, despite its outside appearances, she knew plenty of the Houses would love to create replicas of it, incorporating its technology into their own. She still couldn't guess at what much of the hull was made of, some strange alloy perhaps, and the computer systems were incredibly sophisticated.

"Wylla."

It was Breaker Liss's deep, somber voice that stirred her from her musings. She swiveled in the chair to look at him, the smile leaving her face. She did not rise from her seat.

"We will be leaving soon," he said.

"Returning to the fleet?"

"Yes, I think so."

"Very well," Wylla said.

"I wanted you to know I intend to ask our Lady to release me from her service."

The Breaker folded his hands behind his back, and stared at a point on the far wall above Wylla's head.

"And," he continued. "I intend to ask that you be released along with me."

"Oh Liss," she said. "You know it can't happen."

"Why not?" he asked. "Isn't this what you've always wanted? What you've always asked of me?"

"I want to be free, I want to leave more than anything else," she replied. "But I've told you—she will never allow it. When will you learn Liss? We are not people to her."

"I've stood with our lady in battle a thousand times!" Liss insisted. "She has remembered me and rewarded me. I am her strong right arm, her protector, her—"

"Her weapon?" Wylla asked.

"I am not a slave any longer—"

"No. You're less than that. You're her tool, Liss. And she'll never let such a useful thing as you go without a fight."

"Why do you do this?" he asked. "Why do you torment me? First you tell me that I should be ashamed to serve her, that we should escape, but then when I find a way to free us you turn it against me."

"I want to escape," Wylla agreed. "But I don't want to die. I don't want either of us to die. And that's exactly what will happen if you ask her *permission* to leave."

Something changed on the screen next to Wylla. She glanced down at it. A message had appeared. A simple alert, informing her that power had just been transferred to secondary systems. She would have ignored it, some ship's rudimentary intelligences could run autonomous power checks, but this alert was different. It was concentrating power on four separate points....

She heard the familiar pop of gun fire, and shouts from outside the ship. The Breaker's commlink crackled to life.

"Attack!" he roared in surprise. "We're under fire! Wylla, stay here! Stay in cover! I have to get to them—"

He was already sprinting down the hall, drawing his carbine from its sheath and tightening his armor.

"Liss, wait!" she shouted after him.

The power fluctuations weren't random at all. Someone inside the ship had access to the entire system. Now, they were powering up the weapons.

Wrist computer securely fastened, she ran from the cockpit, headed for the hold. She'd been played for a fool. The machine had tricked her. Every moment she'd thought she was torturing it, pulling apart it's mind, it had been in control of the ship. Waiting for the right moment to strike.

Strongmind had been in control the whole time.

Tsi was above the docking bay, looking down at her ship. She had crawled like a rat through old ducts and empty coolant pipes, and finally worked her way out onto a network of scaffolding. The scaffolds hung from the ceiling of the hangar, rusted and ancient. At one point, they would have been lowered to work on the fore-sections of massive freighters, or extended out into the void when the bay doors were open.

That would have been generations ago, though. Big, slow freighters avoided Noxia if they could help it. Even the merchant ships that came here to trade were small and fast enough to escape, should their customers turn hostile. As Tsi crawled along the scaffold, she paused briefly to regard some faded graffiti.

"This is very high up," it said, in an old pirate's script. She stifled a laugh. It was that kind of absurd behavior that had made her enjoy living among the Noxians for so long.

She was above the central mass of her ship now, and could pick out the details on its hull. It was a beautiful thing, really. Scarred and pitted, Furner Ketsu's work on its armored surface hastily done, the ship showed its age. Yet, it had a quiet dignity to it. She'd taken this craft as a means of escape, decades ago, never realizing how much it would come to mean to her. She'd spent years away from it, hidden it in abandoned space stations, even left it buried in a desert once. But somehow... Somehow she always came back.

It was her home.

She positioned herself above the central hull, near the top access hatch. She was a little more than twenty meters up. A survivable fall, just barely. She'd secured some graphene cabling to use as a rope, and began carefully un-spooling it and securing it to the scaffold. She peered down on the deck again.

There were a half-dozen Guraggan serfs patrolling the area. They were casually alert: professional, but clearly unhappy with their menial duty. They swept the obvious entrances with their weapons, always traveling in pairs of two, evenly spaced a few strides apart. She watched one pair complete a full circuit, walking passed a pile of crates near one of the entrances to the bay. It was then that she spotted the Bondsman.

Like a blue shadow, Tenlok was standing by the crates. He seemed to be making no effort to conceal himself, just standing there as if he was part of the scenery. None of the guards had reacted as they walked by, his stillness rendering him invisible.

She tightened the graphene cable around her waist, and raised her arm. The Bondsman looked up to her, waiting for the arm to drop. Smoothly, he brought a carbine up from its sling, and held it in a loose ready position, waiting for her signal. He shifted his weight from foot to foot, lightly, subtly, the tremors of an animal getting ready to run.

"Still," a voice growled at her. "No moving."

The voice was speaking Guraggan, though accented heavily from a dialect she didn't know. She could feel a weapon trained on her back. Somehow, the Serf had been watching her, had crept up on her from behind. Of course, she realized, the Guraggan had expected an attack from above, had almost certainly sent some of their forces in this way themselves when they'd taken her ship. It was always a mistake to underestimate them. Even the lowly Battle-Serf, barely above the Chem-Thralls in their hierarchy, would have been trained and drilled fanatically.

She kept frozen as she listened to the sound of the Serf moving towards her along the scaffold, scuffing boots a whisper on the rusted metal. When the man was less than a yard a way, she flung herself flat and kicked backwards sharply. Her boot connected hard with the warrior's shin, sending him tumbling forwards. His weapon went off, a bullet sparking next to her head.

Below, she heard a burst of fire from Tenlok, and the roars and curses of the Serfs. She rolled onto her back, grabbed the barrel of the Serf's weapon and yanked it away. The man let go instinctively, drawing a knife in a single smooth motion and thrusting it at her. Tsi twisted away, dropping the rifle as she rolled into a crouch. There was no room to maneuver here, she was tied to the scaffold, unarmed.

The Serf rushed towards her, hissing and spitting, empty hand raining blows on her while he jabbed simultaneously with his knife. Tsi blocked the blade with a hard chop to his wrist, but calloused knuckles struck her across the crown, sending her reeling. The blade arced upwards, biting through her suit, opening a shallow red gash across her breastbone.

With an animal yell, Tsi grabbed her opponent's weapon arm with both hands, and yanked with all her might. The two of them tumbled from the scaffold, hurtling towards the hull of her ship below. Tsi held tight to her opponent, twisting his body around as they plummeted. He was screaming curses in the bare few heartbeats he had left. Then they struck metal.

The man was beneath her. He absorbed most of the shock of their landing, his spine snapping instantly. Tsi bounced and rolled across the hull, flesh bruising, stomach churning. If she'd been an ordinary human, her bones would have shattered on impact. Instead, she was only stunned.

She hung against the curved dome of her ship for a long time, her vision blurred. She could hear shooting and screaming. It was like coming to after a hard night of drinking. She knew she had to wake up, had to move, but her body was sluggish, her every movement a labor. The only thing she could do was keep her fingers locked tight against the hull, clawing into the crevice she had found.

Slowly, strength came back to her forearms, and she pulled herself forwards. She could see the red smear left by the Serf as his body had snapped and slid off the top of the hull. She clawed her way passed it, towards the upper hatch. Fumbling, she tapped her temple, opening up a voice link.

"S-Strongmind? You hear me?" she asked.

"Yes," a voice replied, familiarly toneless.

"Hold tight, friend," she said as she pried the hatch open. "I'm coming to get you."

CHAPTER 20

What's going on?" the Physician hissed as Wylla barged past her.

"We're under attack!" she snapped "Maybe if you spent less time cutting people up you'd know—"

"Attack, by who?"

The Physician was matching Wylla's pace, shadowing her steps.

"I don't know! Something's gone wrong with the ship. There's shooting outside! I've got to get the prisoners under control—"

"You? Control the prisoners? Don't make me laugh. I'll handle them."

"*No*," Wylla said, rounding on her.

The Physician was a full head taller than her. She stank of blood and fear. Even now, she looked at Wylla not like a human, but like something to be cut apart and examined, laid bare with knife and hook.

"They are *my* responsibility," Wylla said. "Go and help Liss."

The Physician cocked her head to the side curiously.

"You order me?"

"Our people are dying out there! You can help them. Or do you want to explain to Lady Ornicht that you'd rather be torturing captives than helping our warriors?"

"Careful, hunting hound..." the Physician hissed. "The day will come when we get to know each other much more... intimately."

"I'm sure we will," Wylla replied blandly.

The Physician rounded, and headed for the exit ramp. As soon as she was out of view, Wylla allowed herself one brief exhalation of relief. Then she headed for the hold.

Tsi dropped into the upper most cargo hold of the ship, colloquially called the "attic". It was cramped and dusty, she hadn't been up here in a long time. She found an old locker, pressed her thumb to the gene-lock and opened it. A flechette gun slid out of the locker, and two magazines of ammo. She loaded the weapon, slipped the strap around her shoulder, and made for the ladder down to the central corridor.

Landing with cat's grace, despite the fact that she'd been on the verge of exhaustion since her fight with Tenlok, she padded her way to the cockpit. It was fortunate that the Guraggan seemed to be evacuating the ship to deal with the Bondsman. He might have been a remorseless killer, but he had his uses.

For some reason, that thought made Tsi feel sick. She pressed on to the cockpit. Someone had been studying the consoles, prying them apart. Of course, the Guraggan would love to get their hands on this sort of technology. They were sophisticated engineers, but they were never shy about stealing a good idea when they found it. This little ship could outrun all the gunboats in the Kiosan Fleet at sublight. Tsi felt strangely gratified that her enemies wanted her pride and joy for their own.

With practiced ease, she slid into the command chair, brought a console to life with a series of keystrokes. The cut on her chest burned, but she trusted the blood would clot soon. She had more important things to deal with.

"Strongmind, can you hear me?"

Two clicks. Affirmative, but he couldn't speak.

"I'm updating your target priority data. We've got a friendly outside."

Three clicks, a pause. Three more. A request for clarification.

"Trust me, we need him. Just be ready to move when I—"

Another series of clicks.

"You're tied up? Magnetic bonds?" Tsi asked exasperatedly. "Why didn't you tell me?!"

Strongmind clicked out the code for "no relevant data".

"Alright, alright, I can improvise something. You've got company with you right now? I'm heading down."

A series of clicks told her to wait thirty seconds. Tsi counted it off, realizing with no small amount of admiration that Strongmind was tracking targets on the weapon's systems at the same time. She saw one of the rotary-cannons prime hot, ready to fire, just as she got to thirty. Flechette rifle in hand, Tsi headed for the hold just as the ship's weapons came screaming to life.

Two Guards were waiting for Wylla, and fell silently in behind her as she entered the hold. The Machine was watching her as she entered, as if it had expected her. Hiron was cowering, bewildered against one wall, while the Noxian girl, Enlil, seemed to find the whole situation hilarious.

"Having trouble?" she crowed as Wylla walked by. One of the Serfs, a burly man named Bohus, gave the girl a cursory club from his rifle.

"Stop that!" Wylla snapped.

"I say we frag 'em all," the other Serf said, a nose-less Epilotti called Aene.

"No! No one is getting executed without our Lady's order, is that clear? I can't have you distracting me while I work!"

The Serfs murmured their sullen assent as Wylla knelt next to the drone. She extended two wires from her wrist-computer, prepared to link them directly to a data port in the side of the machine's head.

"Clever, Strongmind, very clever," she murmured. "You really had me going. But if I can just—"

"Gods and spirits," she heard Enlil whisper.

There was a whip crack as something went past Wylla's head. She looked up to see one of the machine's magnetic manacles shattered, a flechette dart embedded perfectly in the wall. A second crack, and the other manacle shattered. Wylla hadn't heard the door open, hadn't heard anyone enter the room, yet when she spun around she saw a tall, gaunt woman standing in the doorway. She would have gasped, but Strongmind sprung into action.

One arm wrapped around Wylla, clamped her throat tight as it held her in front of its chest. Using her as a shield, the machine rose to his full height.

The Serfs were frozen, Bohus training his rifle on the dark-haired woman, Aene keeping her weapon fixed on Strongmind and Wylla.

"Drop her! Now!" Aene barked.

"You take one more step and I'll—" Bohus roared at the intruder.

The machine took three steps forward, carrying Wylla in front of it, limp as a doll. She saw a blade snap out of its bronze arm in the corner of her vision, and skewer Aene, then hurtle the Serf into her comrade. Even as the machine moved, the dark-haired woman fired twice, flechettes impaling Bohus and sending him tumbling to the ground. As the Serf fell, his weapon roared, and Wylla saw two ruptures appear in the dark-haired woman's thigh and side.

The Serfs fell in a heap, one of their rifles scattering to Enlil's feet. Fast as a rat, she grabbed the weapon, and readied it. She fired three rapid bursts into the two tangled, squirming warriors. Aene was dead as soon as the first round hit her. Bohus took two shots through the chest, a third round making a mess of his jaw. He tried to rise, bleeding and gurgling, but Enlil put five more shots into him. He bucked and moaned and fell, twitching for a moment before he went still.

For some reason, Wylla remembered that she had been taken by Lady Ornicht not long before those two. She had known them throughout their entire servitude. They were dead because of her.

"Okay, handsome," Enlil said as she pointed the rifle at Wylla's head. "I got this one."

"No... no you don't Enlil," the dark-haired woman said. The hits she had taken had sent her into the wall, but, bleeding from her wounds, she had staggered back to her feet.

"That one... that one's a Bykon. Not her fault what happened here."

"Feec-rec, Tsi," Enlil grunted. "She's one of theirs."

"She's a captive, like you were. Can you walk?"

Enlil shook her head.

"Did something to my legs. Jabbed me with something..."

Wylla spoke up, thinking quickly.

"Dokholani," she said. "It's a barbiturate compound, disables neural receptors to certain parts of the body. An adrenaline charge should counteract the effects."

The woman called Tsi walked over to Enlil, and knelt beside her with a grimace. She pulled a syringe from one of her belt pouches, and stabbed it into Enlil's thigh.

"Ow! Gods and spirits, you're trusting her word on that?"

"Yes," Tsi said. "You should be able to walk in a minute or two. Strongmind, keep the Bykon secured. When Enlil can walk, all of you head to the cockpit and strap in. We're making our exit," Tsi said.

"Where are you going?" Enlil asked as Tsi made to leave.

"I've got one more person to pick up," she said. "Just get the ship prepped. We're getting out of here fast."

The docking bay was in chaos. Bodies lay scattered across the oil-slick floor, cabling writhed and sparked. Repair armatures burned like fallen idols. Lady Ornicht's prize sat at the center of the scene, twin gun pods raking the surroundings with fire.

Someone had activated the ship's weapons and used it to slaughter her Serfs. The ship was not the only threat though. She saw Breaker Liss, fearless and swift, leading the survivors in an attack on a figure in dark blue armor. From their foe's movement, flitting from cover to cover like a shadow and loosing deadly salvos in return, she knew him instantly to be the Bondsman. The very thing that stole her prey. Lady Ornicht thanked the gods for such a glorious day.

"Serfs. Deal with the turrets. Do not damage the hull," she commanded her surviving troops, who sprinted from the fuel tank they'd sheltered behind, silent and eager to obey her.

She turned, watching as Liss and his men continued to hound the Bondsman, boxing him in with their fire. He was an impressive warrior. His armor seemed impervious to solid rounds and he was moving fast enough that the Serfs couldn't hit him with anything more than glancing shots. Still, Liss was a veteran. He was playing for time, working the mercenary into a corner where he couldn't dodge and weave his way out. Whoever was controlling the ship's weapons clearly wouldn't fire on the Bondsman, and so Liss was keeping his men as close to the target as possible. Many had died, caught between the ship and the mercenary, but Liss was spending their lives well. How much he had changed since he was that sniveling, awkward boy, herded with so many others onto her ship. Even as a Chem-Thrall she had known there was something worthy about him.

"Gods and spirits, this is bad," Gyje whispered.

Ornicht cocked her head to the side, fixing him with her gaze.

"You have a weapon?" she asked the pirate.

"Y-yes," he said, patting a pistol at his side.

"Follow closely, and assist," she said.

"What about me?" Yulette asked.

The consort had been run ragged with the day's journey. Her hair was a mess of loose strands, her gown torn and filthy. She was not used to sprinting across boulevards and clambering down maintenance shafts.

"Lie down on the ground and avoid being shot," Ornicht replied. "I will collect you when this is over. Don't try to run. You, follow."

She gestured for Gyje again, and the pirate drew his weapon. The ship's turrets were concentrating their fire on her men. She doubted the serfs could disable them, but they would keep the weapons away from her long enough. Breathing deep, she stilled the pain that had been welling up inside her, the tightness in her throat, the lances behind her eyes. The pain would leave when her blades tasted blood again.

She sprinted out from cover, Gyje close behind. Shots arced after Ornicht, but she was too swift for the turrets to track.

The Bondsman had been forced into a corner, hunkered down behind a mining craft. Liss was laying down a steady stream of fire from his position, while his surviving Serfs moved to the flank. One of them rushed forward, his weapon ready. The moment he rounded the corner his head snapped back, and he tumbled to the ground with a single, clean wound through his skull.

Lady Ornicht hurled herself behind a metal recycler, Gyje panting behind her. Her vision was starting to blur. No. No. Not yet. She heard the distinct crack of the Bondsman's rifle and looked out to see the last of Liss's Serfs fall. She sprinted to where Liss was taking cover, sliding to a crouch next to him as he slammed a fresh magazine into his weapon.

"My Lady," he said, slapping a fist to his breastplate in salute. "I have failed you, losses have been exceptional—"

"Hard fought, hard won," Ornicht said. "We will take this Bondsman together."

"His armor is at least class four, and he has a reactive shield," Liss said.

"We will have to do this close then."

Ornicht smiled beneath her mask.

"Why isn't he shooting at us?" Gyje asked.

Ornicht had briefly forgotten the pirate was with her. She put a hand on his shoulder, causing the man to flinch.

"Because he must be out of ammunition," she said. "Cover us

from here. Victory in my service is rewarded, Gyje. Cowardice is punished. Do not forget."

The pirate swallowed hard, but he nodded and braced his weapon. Ornicht let her blades slip from their sheaths, and Liss drew a short metal rod from his waistband. With a flick of his wrist, the rod extended to the length of a quarter staff, and a wafer-thin blade forming from its head. Clutching the demi-glave in one hand, Liss waited for her to take the lead.

The two of them burst from cover, each heading for the opposite side of the mining vehicle. Fire from the ship raked after them, but the guns fell silent when they closed on the Bondsman's position. Ornicht slid around the corner, saw that Liss had already reached the mercenary and was raining blows down on him. The Bondsman was backing away, turning strikes with his vambraces as he drew a Nioban Kukri from its sheath.

It was almost too easy. She rushed forwards, driving her blades towards the Bondsman's spine. At the last moment the killer spun around, and she caught a glimpse of his face. A ghoul with dead red eyes leered at her. It was a sneering *mempo*, made of the same blue-black metal as the rest of his suit. He parried her blow with incredible precision, sending her passed him with a savage kick to the side.

Ornicht let loose a feral snarl as she whirled around, Liss moving to her right. As one they attacked the mercenary, driving him backwards with a savage flurry of strikes. She had taught Liss how to fight, and together they were as efficient as a war-drone. His heavy sweeping blows forced the Bondsman to dodge and leap, while her quick, precise thrusts kept him desperately parrying. She could hear a grotesque sucking sound as the mercenary drew from the twin stimulant tubes in his mask. *Breath deep, little creature,* she thought. All the combat-chems in the galaxy could not save him from her now.

Keeping his kukri in front of him in a low guard, the Bondsman backed away from them, his left hand held low and behind. He was taking what her people called the monkey stance, loose and flexible. It was an impressive display of discipline, given the cocktail of rage-inducing drugs cooking through his veins at that moment. He was getting tired, she could tell. Liss threw a blow high at his head, and the Bondsman parried, briefly turning his side to face Ornicht. Seizing the opportunity, she thrust for him again hard, aiming for his armpit.

The mercenary snapped back towards her, but too late. He dropped his arm quickly, but her blade bit deep into his bicep. The sword ripped upwards, sending a spray of oily fluid out from the wound. The Bondsman tumbled backwards with a startled grunt. The moment he hit the ground, Liss was on him. The demi-glaive smashed downwards, as the mercenary rolled desperately away. One of Liss's blows struck the Bondsman's shoulder, tearing the pauldron loose in a shower of sparks.

Like two predators, Ornicht and Liss hounded the fallen Bondsman as he scrambled away from them. He was still fast, but he would not escape. She pierced his calf with another thrust, her blade breaking through hardened armor and into the meat below. Liss struck him across the side, his glaive plowing into the Bondsman's breastplate, crushing it inwards. The mercenary made a strange noise, a ragged inhalation mixed with a yowl of pain as he collapsed. It was time to end him.

He rolled onto his back as Ornicht pounced. She brought her blades back for a killing strike to his throat. She heard his sucking, wheezing breath as her blades came downward. At the last moment he raised his ruined arm weakly, shielding himself. One of her swords punctured his vambrace, the other sparked across his mask, ripping open one of his cyber-eyes.

"Pathetic!" Ornicht spat.

The Bondsman swung his good arm at her. She felt something tap against her armor.

Then everything went white.

She screamed. Electricity coursed through her body, her visor sparked and blurred. She fell to the ground hard, blood filling her mouth.

An old trick. She cursed herself. An old trick. A risky one, a desperate one, but she had fallen for it like an untested child. He had struck her with a micro-EMP weapon. The concentrated energy pulse had disabled her armor, ravaged her augmentations, blinded her.

She heard a hum and rush in the distance. Heavy hands grabbed her shoulders, and un-did the clasps of her helmet. Through blurred eyes she saw Liss's face, looking down at her with shock.

"My lady—" he stammered.

She cast her eyes about, saw the ship slowly starting to lift off the docking pad, its weapons raking around them. The Bondsman was fleeing towards it, limping and stumbling, one arm a mess of blood and broken armor. To his credit, Gyje was shooting at the man, but with no success.

She hissed two words into Liss's face:

"Kill. Him."

Tsi had headed one way down the corridor, while Wylla was roughly escorted to the cockpit by Strongmind. Enlil and the boy followed, leaning on each other like a pair of drunks. The drugs that the Physician had given Enlil seemed to be wearing off, the adrenaline shot doing its work. She still moved with a comical awkwardness, but as Wylla was bound in one of the cockpit chairs, Enlil gave her a murderous glance.

"Do not attempt to escape," Strongmind said as it finished strapping her down.

She wanted to protest. After all, she was harmless. *She* hadn't done anything to them, hadn't tortured their friends or ransacked their ship. She'd even helped reverse the Physician's drugging.

No, Wylla realized, as she saw the fear in Hiron's eyes, the sickly hatred in Enlil's face, and the places in the side of Strongmind's skull she had opened and shoved wires into. She had helped her Mistress. She had served, faithful slave that she was, and her Mistress had ordered all this.

Outside, the sounds of battle raged. The machine was busying itself at a control console. She saw displays flicker to life, external sensors creating live holographic displays of the exterior. Wylla had seen battle many times before. She didn't care to witness it again. She was about to shut her eyes to the carnage erupting around the ship, when something caught her attention.

It was the unmistakable black silhouette of Lady Ornicht, crawling on the ground. There were two other figures nearby. One was wearing strange armor, demon-masked and festooned with weapons. The other... the other she recognized despite his blast-plate and helmet. Liss was outside in the maelstrom, was chasing the masked figure down, and almost certainly working his way into Tsi's sights.

Quietly, Wylla began to pray.

Tsi's fist hit the control stud, and the access ramp slowly lowered. The roar of the ship's engine vibrated through her body. Strongmind had raised them about a meter off the floor of the docking bay, the ship tipping side to side slightly as he prepared it for take off.

"Keep her steady, Strongmind," she said into her comm unit.

"Affirmative. Caution: one weapon pod has been destroyed. Requesting authorization for use of shredder missiles."

"Negative," Tsi said, shaking her head. "I've just got to get one more—"

A solid round sparked passed Tsi's head, and she dropped to a crouch. Pain lanced through her side. She had almost forgotten her injuries thanks to all the adrenaline and pain-suppressants in her body. Staying low and hugging the struts of the ramp, she patted at the wound with her free hand while she scanned the docking bay for enemies.

There were a few Guraggan serfs, no more than three or four spread out between what cover they could find. One was aiming at her, others were concentrating their fire against the other gun turret on the ship. Even their handheld weapons could damage the turret with time and effort. What little protection Tsi had on her person wouldn't do much good.

She brought her free hand back up to the barrel of her flechette rifle. She steadied it against the strut of the ramp and grimly noted that her fingers had come back from her wound stained with blood. She'd have to look into that.

A burst of fire kept the Serf's heads down, giving her time to scan the dock again. She spotted their leader. She was crawling along the ground like an insect, black carapace scarred with energy burns and blade strokes. A noble, from the looks of her gear, a true Guraggan born and bred for war. She'd been badly hurt, or something had happened to her suit to leave her in this state.

"Hey! Hey!"

It was the snarl of the Bondsman that caught Tsi's attention. He was stumbling towards the ramp, his cries half pleading, half threatening. A giant of a man pounded after him, enhanced muscles bursting from beneath well-worn blast plate.

Tsi aimed, but at that moment the giant pounced. His body speared into Tenlok's back like a thunderbolt, hurtling both of them to the ground. Tsi heard Tenlok let out a gasp, but the giant had already grabbed his helmeted head in one hand and slammed it into the deck.

"You hurt her!" the giant roared. *"You hurt the mistress!"*

Tenlok's head hit the metal floor again. There was no way Tsi could get a clear shot, crouched as she was on the pitching and yawing ship. Even if she could, there was no guarantee her flechette rounds wouldn't be instantly turned to dust by the Bondsman's shield.

"Strongmind, turret on my mark, twelve by point three from exclusion zone!" she shouted into the comms.

Instantly the machine obeyed, firing the ship's surviving weapons at a point just beyond where the Giant was beating Tenlok to death. Shrapnel rained down on the pair of them, scraping their armor and burying itself into exposed flesh. The Giant was in a frenzy, but he was not stupid. He rolled from the impact, drawing a Katar-blade from his belt as he did so. Tenlok scrambled away, one arm limp, the other desperately fumbling a pistol from its holster.

The Giant leaped on him again, thrusting the punching dagger high and low. It sparked off the Bondsman's armor as he brought his pistol to bare, but the Giant's free hand came down on the weapon hard. It barked twice, one round blasting through the Giant's thigh. With a roar, he slammed his palm into Tenlok's chest, sending him flying.

The mercenary crashed to the ground again, this time falling with a splash into pool of oily liquid. Before he could rise, the Giant was on top of him, plunging the Katar towards his throat. Tsi had a clear shot for a fraction of an instant, but more rounds sparked around her, and she ducked backwards, cursing. The Serfs were still alive, still firing on her with determination. She saw two of them break from cover and run to their crippled mistress, shielding her from fire with their bodies. What drove them more, Tsi wondered: loyalty or fear?

A loud bellow cut the din of battle, and she saw that Tenlok had caught the Giant's blade, locking his hands around his opponent's wrists. With a guttural snarl, he pushed upwards, and the two of them rolled over. The Giant's back hit the pool hard and coated both of them with a disgusting sheen. The Giant suddenly let go of the blade, reared back and slammed his forehead into Tenlok's chest, sending the mercenary sprawling.

They looked less like elite warriors now, and more like a pair of bloodied drunkards. Tenlok let out an audible groan as he crawled away from the oil pool. The Giant rose, his cracked and battered armor and muscles glistening with sweat and oily fluid.

Tsi watched in dull fascination as the hulking figure strode towards Tenlok, scooping up his blade on the way. She saw Tenlok had loosed a sharp black dagger from his waistband. With obvious effort, the mercenary got to his knees, staying low. His mempo glowered up at the Giant as he raised the Katar for a killing strike. At that instant, Tenlok's hand whipped out. The blade struck the hull. Sparked.

Then the Giant was screaming. He was burning. The liquid coating his body, seeping into the gaps in his armor, had been set alight by a single spark. He shrieked and tore at the seals on his helmet, cooking alive. The Bondsman pulled another pistol from its scabbard and shot him in the stomach once. Then he staggered away, leaving the Giant twitching and burning on the deck.

"*You!*"

A familiar voice cut the din. She turned to see Gyje the Third Son, looking comically out of place as he stood up from behind a pile of scrap metal, his handsome face red and contorted with rage.

"This is all your fault! You *gods-damned oxygen rat!*"

His pistol roared as he fired one handed, gesturing obscenely at Tsi at the same time.

"Killed my brothers!"

One of the rounds from the Noxian Repeater tore through a strut by Tsi's head.

"Killed my mother!"

Another shot, this one blasting a hole next to Tsi's feet.

"*Beat me* in front of the whole damned station! I'm going to tear your—"

Gyje never got to finish his last threat. Tsi fired a single, well-aimed shot. A flechette burst through his throat. The pirate looked at her, mute confusion on his face. His repeater fell from limp hands. Blood frothed between his lips, and he pitched forward, his body nothing more than nerveless meat.

Someone was screaming far away. Tsi wasn't sure who, but the air was still filled with solid shot and pulse rounds. She felt, more than saw, the Bondsman haul himself up onto the ramp beside her. Without a word, the two of them stumbled up into the ship, raising the loading ramp behind them.

Once they were inside, Tsi leaned against one wall. She felt perspiration trickle down her brow.

"Strongmind," she said. "Blast a hole through the docking bay doors. It's time we were out of here."

"Affirmative," the machine replied.

She looked up at Tenlok. He had collapsed against the other wall. His breastplate had a long dent in its side, and one of his arms hung limp. The cybernetic eye that had been hit was a ruin of shattered glass. Yet his mask betrayed nothing, the dents and scrapes it had taken only making its rictus leer all the more inscrutable.

"You could have left without me," he said.

"But I didn't," she breathed back.

The Bondsman pointed a gloved finger at the wound in her side.

"Better get that taken care of," he said, then lurched into the depths of the ship.

Tsi laughed as she headed towards the auto-doc. She paused briefly in the central chamber that served as the galley, running a hand over one counter, not caring that it left a trail of blood. She smiled. Whoever she was with, it was good to be home.

CHAPTER 21

The third shot blew a hole in the skin of Salvation, and the ship drifted through crystallizing flames into the void beyond. The patter of gunshots against the hull was replaced by the silence of space, and the hum of the ship's electronics. Hiron realized he had been holding his breath, and exhaled gratefully.

Strongmind was piloting the ship, its hands working the controls with brisk efficiency. Still bound in her chair, Wylla had her eyes screwed shut. She was mouthing words in repetition: prayers, Hiron realized. His gaze then fell on Enlil, who winked at him and flashed a wicked grin.

"We made it."

"Yeah," Hiron said, trying to sound more sure than he was. The last few days had taken their toll, and he felt as if he could sleep for a week.

"Where's Tsi?" he asked.

"She is in the Medical Bay," Strongmind replied tonelessly. "She has relayed coordinates to me. I will carry out all necessary piloting functions."

"Someone better go check on her," Hiron said, making to rise from his seat.

"Relax, kid," Enlil said, unstrapping herself. "I'll check on the captain. Besides, I've had a date with that auto-doc scheduled for a while."

"Um, I can come with you. If you need help getting there, I mean?"

Enlil snorted.

"Thanks, but the adrenaline done me fine."

She stretched her legs demonstratively.

"You keep metal man and the pretty lady company. I'll be back."

As Enlil left the room, Hiron turned his attention to Wylla. She had stopped praying and opened her eyes. Now, she seemed quietly withdrawn.

"It's going to be alright," Hiron said.

Wylla returned a pained smile.

"I somehow doubt that," she said.

"You'll see. Tsi is a good person. She's kind, she'll take care of you. Here, let me at least get you out of those bindings," he said as he got up and hobbled over to her chair.

"Do not attempt to release the prisoner," Strongmind interjected.

"She's got nowhere to go. Come on, there's no danger."

"Do not attempt to release the prisoner."

Strongmind had turned away from the console, and was fixing Hiron with a blank stare. There was something in the machine's toneless voice that made him hesitate. He knew it was a combat drone, but Tsi had given it directives, restrained its ability to act. It couldn't hurt him, could it?

"Don't," Wylla said quietly. "Don't provoke it."

"Alright," Hiron said, raising his hands and backing away. Strongmind looked at him for a long moment before finally returning to its work.

"We'll get you out of there soon," Hiron said. "You'll see."

Wylla shrugged.

"I've spent my whole life like this, Hiron," she said. "A little longer won't make any difference."

Enlil's hands felt oddly empty as she walked down a flight of steps to the galley, heading for the medical bay. She'd left the gun back in the cockpit, but even knowing they were out of immediate danger, there was something in being unarmed that made her feel particularly vulnerable. She'd lost her knife to her creditors a few days back, and Gyje's blade had been stripped from her when she'd been taken by the Guraggan. It was funny. She hadn't spent this much time disarmed since she was a little girl.

Tsi's ship smelled terrible. She obviously didn't vent the place properly when she was docked, and the Guraggan's brief stay here hadn't helped matters. It was rank with old sweat, spilled liquor, and machine oil.

Enlil's legs wobbled and she caught herself on a wall. She'd been close to death so many times, but it had never hit her as hard as when she had been trapped in the dark of the cargo hold. Her life had never seemed that valuable, but she'd always done her best to keep breathing. And she still was.

Thanks to Tsi.

Something about that didn't sit right with Enlil. She rounded a corner, heading into the med bay, and came face to face with a snarling demon.

"*Fuck!*" she shouted, pulling back her fist to strike.

"Easy!" Tsi called. "He's on our side!"

Enlil clenched her teeth as she glared at the masked man. Tenlok the Bondsman. She'd never cared for his kind. She noted with some satisfaction that he'd taken almost as bad of a beating as her fighting the Guraggan. His armor was a mess of scratches, dents and pock marks, and one of his arms hung limp. One of his red eyes was shattered. She could see a scar across his face mask where the blade had struck. He let out what sounded like a hiss as she shouldered passed him into the room.

"Gods and spirits! You look like a broken recycler, Tsi," Enlil said.

Tsi was strapped in to the auto-doc, its metal arms working delicately at a wound in her naked stomach. She was even paler than usual, her black hair plastered with sweat across her brow. Enlil realized she'd never seen Tsi out of her gear. Sitting there, half-naked in the auto-doc, Enlil's eyes couldn't help but trace the scars and wounds that dotted Tsi's body. She could see the tell-tale lines of augmentation too, places where the flesh was a little too clean, a little too perfect. She wondered how much Tsi had been born with, and how much had been grown in a vat and grafted to her later. Whatever the percentage, it had been expensive. Incredibly expensive. She had clearly got her money's worth: Enlil counted no less that four scars left from wounds that would have killed an ordinary person instantly.

Tsi gave her a weak grin.

"You look good, Gilded Lily," Tsi said.

"Don't call me that," Enlil grunted. "It's not funny."

"Sorry."

"Forget it. What the hell is he doing here?" she asked, jerking a thumb at the Bondsman, who stood mute in the corner of the room.

"I needed extra muscle to get you out."

"Yeah, but *him*?"

Tsi shrugged.

"He was available."

The Bondsman made a low noise that could have been a chuckle. Or a growl.

"Well, he can get the fuck out of here," Enlil said. "I gotta talk to you alone."

"No," Tenlok said

Enlil rounded on him.

"Wasn't talking to you. The Captain here makes the calls on this ship."

"Not letting her out of my sight," the Bondsman replied. His good hand wrapped around the hilt of a dagger on his belt.

"You really gonna test me right now?" Enlil said.

"Not leaving her with somebody I don't know."

"She's trustworthy, Tenlok," Tsi said. "Besides, she's not even armed."

"Not a lot I'm gonna do with just this," Enlil said, gesturing exasperatedly with her bandaged hand.

The Bondsman didn't move.

"Go clear the ship," Tsi said. "Make sure the Guraggan didn't leave us any surprises."

"I don't take orders from you," Tenlok grunted.

"If you want to stay on my boat," Tsi replied evenly. "You do."

The Bondsman turned his gaze to Tsi and held it for a moment. Then, he rounded on his heel and left the med bay. Enlil made an obscene hand sign at his back as he left.

"Didn't know they stacked waste-packs that high," Enlil muttered.

Tsi laughed.

"I'm serious," Enlil said. "Why is he on board?"

"I told you: I needed help. He helped."

"Yeah, for how much?"

"You could say he owes me his life."

"Well, we gotta get him off at our next port stop. When is that anyway?"

"I gave Strongmind the coordinates for the beacon. We'll pick that up, then make a Slip jump and launch it. Easy as voiding a hull."

"You know, you never explained exactly what in Ten Hells is going on here," Enlil said.

She drew up a collapsible chair, and sat down next to Tsi. She didn't like to admit it, but the gaunt woman was starting to grow on her. She might not have been born Noxian, but she knew the ways of the Poison Suns well enough.

"I'm... not entirely sure," Tsi admitted. "I have some guesses. But nothing concrete."

"Well, some Guraggan just spent the last few hours poking through my insides, so I figure it's got something to do with them?"

Tsi nodded.

"They hit the Inheritor's World," she said. "Not a raid, an invasion. I think they're going to sweep the Frontier, and head for Kios next."

Enlil exhaled.

"Fuck."

"That... was my initial reaction as well."

"So that beacon, it's for the Janissariat?"

"That was my plan, yeah," Tsi said. "They're the only military in a thousand parsecs that could fight what I saw on the Inheritor's World."

"Well," Enlil folded her arms. "There's not a lot left for me on Salvation. I'm not one for trying to salvage a sun-bound ship, but I guess I'm headed the same way as you."

"I don't think it's hopeless," Tsi said. "I think... I think it's what we have to do. What *I* have to do."

"Alright."

The two sat in silence a moment. Enlil started laughing. Tsi looked at her quizzically.

"Kinda stupid, isn't it?" Enlil said. "Trying to take on the Guraggan with you and me, pretty beat up, that psycho Bondsman, a drone that's half-scrap and the cripple—"

"I told you," Tsi said. "Stop calling him 'cripple.'"

"Why do you care?" Enlil asked. "He yours?"

"He's my crew," Tsi said.

"Oh."

Enlil's cheeks burned with shame. Of course. She'd been an idiot not to see it. She looked at the ground as she spoke.

"These things just slip out. A lot of people wouldn't take on someone like him, but I'm sure he pulls his weight," she said.

"You know, a lot of people wouldn't take a drunk with a broken hand in, either," Tsi said.

"Yeah, but you... you said you needed me for a job. With him—"

"I need him. And I need you."

"You told me that back on Salvation. This for a long haul?"

"Yeah," Tsi said. "For a long haul."

"Well... Then I guess I'm your crew, too. For a while, anyway."

Enlil got up, straightening the front of her suit.

"We'll be picking up that beacon soon, right? Guess I better go prep for that," she said. "You just let me know as soon as the 'doc's got time for my hand, alright?"

"Okay."

Enlil paused at the threshold to the med-bay. "Tsi?" she asked.

Tsi looked up at her.

"Thanks," Enlil finished, and headed off into the ship.

Tsi dreamed she was floating again. She was suspended in ether, surrounded by stars. She could feel the void's touch against her skin. The cosmos spread out before her, infinite and beautiful. So very many worlds, so many suns. The dust of civilizations was encrusted to her boots, she had breathed the air and felt the light of so many stars. She looked down and saw a world on fire.

She was falling now, like she always did. Hurtling past clouds, riding downwards on a beam of pure energy. She saw forests bursting into flames, cities disappearing in columns of ash. Oceans curdled with blood. The continents cracked and blistered. Magma rose in currents, rending up from the earth like a razor, cutting the skin of the world.

She could see giants as she fell, gathering the dead in great mounds, merciless automata pulping limbs in their iron hands. As one they turned their faceless helms up towards her—

"You're gonna want to see this."

Tsi awoke in the medical bay, the crackling voice of the

Bondsman over the comms stirring her from sleep. Groggily she rose. Her stomach hurt, but the sutures and grafts were tightly bound in place.

"What's going on?" she asked, thumbing the comm as she tied her messy hair back.

"You've got another passenger," Tenlok said. "Down in one of the holds. I'd hurry if you want to talk to him. He's not going to last long."

Tsi pulled on an old flight jacket and made her way to the cargo holds. There were three, one large, main chamber and two ancillary bays for smaller equipment. Most of the time she kept them empty of everything except basic supplies. She'd done some smuggling, and carried mining equipment around for a while, but mostly they were just extra space. She couldn't for the life of her remember why it had seemed so essential when she built this ship that it had so much storage.

She found the bulkhead door open, the cargo bay lit by a single white light. The Bondsman was in the shadows, his glowing eye the only sign he was even there at all. Tsi barely noticed the mercenary. It was the thing strapped to a surgical table in the center of the room that took all her attention.

A mixture of pity and disgust filled her as she looked at the wretched form. Though he'd suffered the cruelties of a Guraggan physician, there was no mistaking the mangled body of Furner Ketsu.

The old pirate looked up at her, a weak grimace on his leathery face.

"They done my leg," he said, indicating the brutally hacked away stump.

"The rest of you doesn't look great either, Furner," Tsi said.

She walked to his side, taking the man's hand.

"Yeah... I can't see so great right now. What's... what's the damage?"

As she looked him up and down, she saw someone had bandaged his wounds. It was field work, and skillful. The work of someone who knew how to patch a person back together in a hurry. She glanced up at the Bondsman, but the masked man said nothing. She noticed now, too, that Tenlok seemed to have dressed his injured arm.

Tsi swallowed hard.

"Less than a plasma leak, worse than a loose circuit," Tsi said. "We've got an auto-doc, we'll get you into that and it'll all... it'll be fine."

"Got a feeling you're being less that truthful with me," Furner breathed out, his voice barely more than a whisper. "That witch really... heh, she really wanted to know all about you... but I didn't—I didn't say—"

"I know," Tsi said, squeezing his hand. "I... I wish you had told her everything you knew. You stupid old fool, protecting me wasn't worth..."

She trailed off. Weakly, the man reached a heavy hand across and patted Tsi on the shoulder. The Noxian salute, or the best he could do.

"Rode with Captain Black..." he said. "Not a lot of us left. Crew... looks out for crew."

He lay back, and his breathing grew shallow. He slipped into a merciful unconsciousness, Tsi holding his limp hand tight.

"I can finish it," the Bondsman said. "If you want."

"No," Tsi replied, wiping tears from her eyes.

She rose, her shoulders set.

"Help me with him," she said.

"What?"

"Help me with him," she repeated. "We're taking him to the auto-doc. He's not dying today."

"We are nearing our destination," Strongmind said tonelessly into the communicator. "Shall I initiate preparations for retrieval of the pod?"

"Is Enlil up there?" Tsi's voice asked. "I need to handle something in the med bay. She can take the lead on the retrieval."

"No," Hiron chimed in. "We haven't seen her since she went to check on you, I think she's in the main hold. We've all been just sitting here. Listen, Tsi, about our prisoner—"

"I don't have time for that right now, Hiron," Tsi said.

"What requires attention in the medical bay?" Strongmind asked.

Hiron saw the machine's fingers dance across the keypad, and the image on one of the viewing screens changed, revealing the medical bay. Straining his eyes, he could make out an image of Tsi and a man in heavy armor, carrying a badly injured body between them. They set the third figure down on the medical table and began strapping him in to the auto-doc.

"Who's that?" Hiron asked, recognition slowly dawning on him as Strongmind entered another command and the image became a holographic projection, reproducing in miniature what was going on in the medical bay. He'd only known the old Noxian briefly, but he recognized Furner Ketsu on the table.

"It's nothing to worry about, Strongmind," Tsi said. "Someone needs our help, I'm taking care of it."

"I was not aware we had taken on additional crew," the machine said.

"Look, I can't answer questions right now!" Tsi snapped. "Just get the beacon, and we can get out of here and... oh no..."

Hiron could hear a tell-tale ringing over the comms system, and saw in the holo-image warning lights flaring on the auto-doc. Back home they didn't have medical technology half this impressive, but Hiron knew a crash signal when he heard it. Furner Ketsu was dying.

Tsi slammed her fist into a console, loud enough that they could hear it all the way in the cockpit.

"I can help," Wylla said quietly.

Hiron turned to her.

"You can... of course you can. Strongmind, quick, we've got to get her down there!"

Strongmind switched off the image, and muted its connection with Tsi.

"That is not permissible," Strongmind said.

"He's been tortured by a Guraggan physician," Wylla said. "She's probably laced his body with toxins, inserted micro-flensing agents in his blood. If your Captain tries to assist this man conventionally, he *will* die. But if you let me go there now, I might be able to help."

"That is not permissible," Strongmind repeated, turning around to face them. "I have received direct orders. Releasing the prisoner presents a risk to achieving my objectives."

"Strongmind!" Hiron shouted, surprising himself with the anger in his voice. "You know what's going on here! That man is dying!"

"I have my orders."

"Leave it alone," Wylla whispered.

"No!" Hiron said. He staggered up out of his chair, leaning heavily on one crutch while he shook the other at the machine's disfigured face. Something had snapped inside him, and the words came tumbling out.

"You're playing a game with us, aren't you? Aren't you? You do this all the time, you pretend you don't understand what's going on, but you do."

"I have been given an order. I must obey it."

"Tsi didn't order you to spy on her," Hiron said. "She didn't order you to tie up Wylla either! You make decisions all the time without her."

"Initiative is within my programming parameters."

"If that's so, then why is it so important to you that this man dies?"

"He is irrelevant to the objective."

"That's not what I asked!" Hiron said.

"You're making it angry," Wylla pleaded. "It's already over, Hiron, please—"

"Why do you want Furner to die, huh? Why?"

"Release of the prisoner—" the machine began.

"It's not about her!" Hiron roared.

Suddenly, the machine's hand snapped out and yanked the crutch from Hiron's arm. He fell hard, his leg twisting under him. Hiron gasped in pain. The machine tossed the crutch aside casually. It stared down at him, its face half skull and half lifeless flesh.

"You are behaving irrationally," Strongmind said.

Hiron crawled backwards, clutching at one of the chairs. He was trembling, his voice was hoarse, but still he spoke.

"Why do you think you know what Tsi needs better than she does? Or is that part of your programming too?"

The machine was perfectly still. Hiron could hear his own panting breath, and Wylla quietly praying as she had during the firefight. The machine rose and lurched forward suddenly, its arms outstretched.

"Don't"! Hiron cried, raising his arms over his head.

But Strongmind brushed passed him, and efficiently removed

the bindings that held Wylla in place.

"You are on conditional release," the machine said. "Please assist Captain Tsi in her medical procedure."

Wylla got up quickly, a look of bewilderment on her face. She scurried away from Strongmind, making for the door, then stooped to pick up Hiron's crutch. With the poise of a noble, she strode back to Hiron, and gently helped him up. She snapped the crutch into place, and briefly squeezed his shoulder. Then she bowed to Strongmind, before whirling around and running for the medical bay.

"Hiron," Strongmind said. "Please find Enlil and assist her in retrieving the beacon."

Hiron was still breathing heavily, but he nodded, and shuffled away, heading down the stairs into the rest of the ship. He paused to look back at Strongmind, but the machine had returned to the command console and settled down again, as if nothing at all had happened.

Tsi looked sick. That was what Wylla concluded, having finally taken a good look at the woman. She was slim, with straight dark hair and gaunt features, skin that would be considered an unhealthy shade of pale among the Bykon. It wasn't her body that looked ill though. She had a sickness of the soul.

When Wylla had entered the room, Tsi had looked at her with wild and threatening eyes. Gone was the cool reassurance of the woman who had gunned down battle-serfs without pause, stormed this ship and defeated Lady Ornicht almost single-handed. She seemed more like an animal, trapped in the room with Wylla and the man dying in the auto-doc's embrace.

"This device must be deactivated," Wylla said.

"Why?" Tsi asked.

"Look at his life signs. I suspect he's got some sort of reagents in his blood. Subdermal flensers, designed to react to analgesics. It's a favorite of my Mistress's people—"

"I know," Tsi grimaced. "I *know*. They did this all the time during the war, left injured soldiers to be found by their comrades. They'd be taken back for surgery, only to be ripped apart from the insides. That means... that means there's nothing we can do—"

"Not nothing," Wylla corrected. "Is your chemical synthesizer fully stocked?”

"I've had to use up a lot of it in the last week," Tsi said. "People keep getting hurt around me."

The Bondsman grunted, causing Wylla to start. She hadn't even noticed him when she came into the room, but now she saw his war mask glowering at her. She'd seen him through the view screens during the battle, seen him killing serfs with ease, dueling Lady Ornicht herself, and then he'd faced poor Liss...

No, she couldn't think of that now. She'd been surrounded by enemies half her life. Panic and sorrow would not serve her. She could mourn Liss later.

"We need to conduct a cryo-chemical flush," Wylla said. "Stabilize his blood with a cryo-agent, then I can analyze what compound was used and come up with a counter-measure."

Tsi moved to the synthesizer, a compact white unit with a dizzying array of controls and measuring tubes, hooked into a chemical reservoir in the wall. She entered a series of commands, then turned to Wylla and nodded.

"I think we have enough," she said. "Are you sure this will work? It'll take most of our reserves."

"I... cannot be certain," Wylla admitted. "But I believe it is the best course of action."

"Hold it," the Bondsman said. "What about our deal?"

He and Tsi were facing each other. Wylla had assumed this man was her servant, but the way he spoke there was not the clear hierarchy between master and underling that she had come to know so well. The Bondsman was taller than Tsi, broader, and covered in armor. Tsi was still clearly weak from her own injuries, but she faced him without a trace of fear.

"What *about* our deal?" she said.

"You're not wasting my chance on him," the Bondsman said.

"You'll get exactly what you deserve, Tenlok. *When* I say so."

"That wasn't our arrangement."

"I don't think you're in a position to bargain right now," Tsi said.

Her hands had curled into fists and she had drawn one foot back slightly. Wylla could tell she'd be ready to strike in a heartbeat if it came to that.

"You're really going to risk everything on her word," Tenlok said, jerking his head at Wylla. "You remember who she works for, right?"

"She's a Bykon," Tsi said. "She couldn't hurt Furner if she wanted to."

"It's a lot to risk on the word of an enemy," the mercenary said, suddenly turning his gaze to Wylla. To her shame, she flinched.

"She's *not* my enemy," Tsi said. "You'll do more good helping Enlil in the cargo hold. Leave us."

"I told you I don't take orders from you."

"If... if I may," Wylla said quietly. "Time is of the essence. We need to start the procedure now if we are to save this man's life."

"Go," Tsi said.

The mercenary slipped past Wylla without a word. There was a tense silence for a moment, before Tsi let out a sigh and muttered something to herself.

"If it pleases you, Captain, we can begin," Wylla prompted gently.

"Of course," Tsi replied. She pressed a button, and one of the wall panels folded open to reveal an array of medical equipment. "Take whatever you need. I'll follow your lead."

CHAPTER 22

It had taken Enlil a few hours to clear the main hold, mag-strapping everything that couldn't be shoved beyond the bulkhead doors. Tsi's ship could have made a decent light freighter, but from the look of it the woman basically only traveled with guns, explosives and liquor. She really had been a pirate once, Enlil thought.

The kid was shuffling around, even more awkward than usual in his vac-suit. Enlil caught his eye and his face flushed beneath the clear visor of his helmet. He'd have to work on that.

Meanwhile, the Bondsman was leaning against a wall, fidgeting and flexing his right arm. He'd patched himself up somehow in the ensuing hours. Enlil hadn't seen the killer spend any time in the med bay, but she knew he was wired to the gills anyway. All he needed was an arc welder and some spare sprockets to keep running. One of his eyes was still broken though. He'd have a hard time dealing with a strike from his left.

He hadn't helped with clearing the hold at all, just tilted his head at her silently when she'd told him what to do. The kid had been eager to help though, and between the two of them they had got the place cleared and ready to bring the beacon in.

"Okay," Enlil said, signaling for the two to join her at the center of the hold, near the loading winch.

"This isn't gonna be easy, but it's not hard neither. Ship ain't set up for a proper space haul-in, so we're going to have to tether the beacon and bring it on board by hand. Understand?"

Hiron nodded uncertainly. The Bondsman shrugged.

"Kid, I need you working the winch. You just sit tight while me and gruesome take two tether lines out and attach them to the beacon. When I give you the word, all you gotta do is hit that button," she said, pointing at the controls. "We'll be hooked to the lines, so it'll bring both of us in. You make sure your safety line is secure, too. Don't want to have to catch you if you slip out or your magnetics fail. Got me?"

"Got you," Hiron said.

"Why don't we have propulsion gear?" The Bondsman asked. "Make this a lot easier if we weren't on puppet strings the whole time."

Enlil shook her head.

"What Tsi had is fucked," she said. "Looks like the Guraggan were curious about it, took apart some of it, looted some, trashed the rest. Gotta do this old fashioned. What's the matter? Scared of a little space walk?"

"I don't use bad equipment when I don't have to," Tenlok said. He made an adjustment to his helmet. There was a subtle hiss as it clamped tighter around his neck. "Alright, I'm void-hardened. Let's get this over with."

Enlil snapped her own helmet into place and checked her vitals. Everything was green on her HUD. She checked the kid over once, then tapped him on the side of the helmet.

"Keep this thing on," she said.

The boy nodded vigorously. With that done, Enlil entered a command at the winch console, and the cargo hold began to vent. There was a loud rushing noise, then silence as all of the oxygen was filtered out of the room. With slow grace, the outer door opened onto the twinkling darkness.

"Comms check," she said.

"I can hear you," said Hiron.

"You are reading adequately," Strongmind's voice came over, toneless and clear from the cockpit.

The Bondsman's comm unit clicked twice in affirmation.

"Alright. Strongmind, we're opened up. Keep us steady, me and Tenlok are about to make the jump."

"Maintaining course," the machine replied.

She could see the beacon, drifting behind them, perhaps two hundred meters out. Magnifying her visor, she could pick out its details clearly. It was about as tall as Enlil, its shape vaguely recalling an egg drawn by someone who could only think in angles. The beacon's surface was black as the void, lit by tiny green warning lights. Practically invisible to anything but a close visual scan, Tsi had been very careful to make sure no one found and grabbed this thing before they did.

Enlil looked at the boy one last time. He was gripping the console for dear life, staring at naked space beyond. She could see he was magnetized to the deck, but for someone who had never walked on a hull before it must have been little reassurance. She glanced at the Bondsman, who was looking straight ahead. He nodded subtly.

Enlil switched her mag-boots off, and pushed. Then, she was drifting away from the ship, flying towards the beacon. The tether was buckled tight to her waist, but she kept a length of it wrapped around one arm too. It never paid in the void to be careless.

In heartbeats she had left the cargo hold. She'd done this a hundred times, with people she trusted less, but even still she had to fight to keep her focus on the beacon. As the object grew larger in her vision, she suddenly saw something moving beyond it. It was tiny, no more than the size of a fly, and night black too. As it passed the star field she traced its movements, saw the distant flare of engines.

"Strongmind! What's on scans?"

"Vehicle approaching," the Machine said. "Attack vector calculated. Preparing defensive maneuvers."

"The hell you are!" Enlil spat. "You'll kill us if you start bouncing around!"

"Acceptable losses," it replied.

"Wait!" she heard Hiron's voice, shrill with panic cut in. "Give them a minute, they're almost there. I can pull them in—"

"Forty five seconds to first attack pass," Strongmind replied.

"Pull us in! Now!" the Bondsman snarled.

"Belay that!" Enlil said. "We can do this—"

"I'm not dying for that hunk of junk—"

"Thirty five seconds. Preparing countermeasure. Boosting shields."

Enlil stretched her hands out to their limit, willing herself towards the beacon. She could see the craft coming closer. Even at this distance, it was clear that it was an enemy, hunting them. She counted.

One.

The glow of an energy weapon charging.

Two.

Her HUD warning her of a sudden radiation build up.

Three.

The beacon growing larger, swallowing her vision.

Four.

She could hear Hiron's panicked breathing.

Five—

She hit the side of the Beacon and bounced off.

"Fuck!"

She screamed, flailing as she careened into space.

She reached frantically out with her bad hand, caught, claw-like onto one of the beacon's extended antennae. The whip-thin metal cut into her suit like a blade.

The words: *WARNING!—SUIT PUNCTURE* blazed across her vision as she grabbed tight, feeling her hand burn. Blood was leaking past the wound, crystallizing in space. The stars streamed by her, and she grabbed desperately out with her other hand, clutching at the beacon's surface for any kind of handhold.

A beam of light streaked behind her and she felt a wave of heat even through her suit. She turned her head and saw it: blue as a Karenkov Serpent, an energy lance shot towards Tsi's ship. For a moment it seemed like it would blow straight through the little freighter, but then it flickered outwards in a great column of azure fire, glancing off the ship's shields.

RADIATION CRITICAL read one corner of her suit's vision. Another hit like that would fry her gear's counter-rad systems.

"I'm tethered," the Bondsman said. "Reel us in!"

"Enlil! Are you hooked in?" Hiron asked.

"Do it!" Tenlok growled. "She's dead if you don't!"

"Enlil!"

"Do it kid," she grated, holding tight to the beacon wire.

She hadn't had the time to hook the tether in properly. Keeping a tight hold of the base of the antennae and a jutting abutment on the beacon's surface, Enlil slowly twisted her body, bringing her legs down into contact with the beacon. At least now she wasn't flailing the dark like an idiot.

She felt a tug at her hip, and slowly the beacon began pulling in towards the ship. All she had to do now was hold on, and hope they didn't get blown to pieces.

"A direct hit, but enemy shields remain intact."

Skyme's voice was quiet and pleasant, but Lady Ornicht still had to resist the urge to fling something at the little man. She was sitting in the command chair of her bridge, stripped of her armor. The Physician had hooked her to a mobile re-vitalizer, its vascular tubes puncturing her flesh and pumping her full of stabilizing drugs. Her eyes burned with cold malice as she stared at the screens surrounding her, each brimming with data on their target.

They'd flown in quiet and close, waiting until they were practically on top of the enemy to engage. She grudgingly admitted to herself that the little man's quick wits were the only thing that had kept this mission from being a total failure. He had tracked the ship from the moment it blasted its way off Salvation, and kept it on their scans even as her badly mauled retinue was being dragged back on board. So many she had left behind: a dozen serfs, that Noxian who's name she could not recall, and the Breaker.

She still burned with shame at not being able to recover Liss's body. He had been a good servant, as worthy as any Guraggan warrior. She would have to be sure all her memories of him were properly transcribed when the time was right.

"Enemy maintaining course," Skyme said. "They are not taking evasive action."

"What's that mass reading behind them?" she asked.

"Hmm," the little man muttered, keying in commands. "It seems it is... shielded against conventional scanning. At a guess—my lady, this is most interesting. They appear to be trying to bring the object aboard with magnetic tethers."

Ornicht laughed in spite of herself.

"You mean they've tied cables to it?" she asked.

"Yes. It is being drawn in to the ship as we speak. It is outside their shielding range currently, shall I destroy it?"

"No..." she said. She tapped a finger to her temple, the pain briefly leaving her body as she relished the moment. It was the deepest pleasure to find an opponent's weakness, and think on how best to exploit it.

"They must have living crewmen on the object. It's keeping them from taking evasive action. Target their engines with a slow mass round, and prepare an EMP charge as well," she said. She turned to one of her attendants, a hunched technician she'd seized on Aesellion.

"Prepare Theta-90," she said. "I want it in reserve."

The technician kneeled before her.

"Your will is my will," the man intoned.

Ornicht smiled fiercely. She would take this ship whole, and pry its crew apart piece by piece. Breaker Liss would be avenged.

Tsi's front was covered with blood, and her brow was dripping with sweat. She'd worked frantically at Wylla's side for what seemed like hours, learning on the spot all of the intricacies of a Bykon surgeon. Wylla was a remarkably efficient teacher, and together they had finally stabilized Furner. He had more blood outside of him than in, it seemed, but the flensing agents had all been purged.

She looked down at the pirate's leathery face, his eyes closed in deep slumber. She brushed one of the dreadlocks away from his brow. It was funny, he was quite old for a Noxian, but compared to her he was still a young man.

"He'll need a lot of rest," Wylla said. "But all foreign agents in his bloodstream are either purged or at minimal levels."

"He'll live?" Tsi asked.

"He'll live."

Tsi turned and offered the woman her hand.

"Thank you," she said. "I guess we haven't formally met yet. I'm Tsi."

"Wylla Laran-Se," the Bykon replied, bowing to her instead of taking her hand.

"I would insure this man has regular fluid intake for the next seventy-two hours," she continued. "Other than that, he should require no further advanced surgical assistance. Shall I return to the cockpit or do you have a brig?"

"Wylla, you're not my prisoner," Tsi said.

"The machine seemed to think differently."

"Strongmind has his own opinions on a lot of things," Tsi said. "But no, I'll let him know that you've got the freedom of the ship. We'll set you up with quarters once we're in the Slip, and we can see with getting you dropped off somewhere as soon as—"

The lights flickered. Tsi smelled the familiar scent of burning ozone. A sudden power surge.

"Something's hit our shields," Tsi said.

"An asteroid?"

"No. That was definitely an energy weapon," Tsi said.

She dashed from the medical bay, taking the stairs three at a time and sprinting down the corridor to the cockpit. She found Strongmind in his familiar position, monitoring a dozen screens at once while a holo-map traced the movement of their ship. The beacon was behind it, and an unidentified ship was in pursuit.

"I was about to inform you," Strongmind said. "We are under attack."

"By who?" Tsi asked, taking up a position by one of the control consoles.

"Craft unidentified."

"My mistress," Wylla interjected. She had followed Tsi, and was standing in the doorway, watching the screens. "That's a Guraggan ship, called the *Dragon's Tooth*. Lady Ornicht is aboard."

"Prepare for evasive action," Tsi said. "We can't out run her without blowing all our fuel, but we might be able to dodge long enough to turn the tables."

"Negative," Strongmind said. "The beacon is still being retrieved. Two crew members are outside the hull. Evasive action would result in their termination."

"Shit!" Tsi said, striking the console. "Are they pulling in?"

"Yes. We must maintain course."

"Extend the shields," Tsi said, "put the beacon inside, we can't lose it."

"Don't," Wylla said.

Tsi turned her head.

"Why?"

"The beacon is what's making you an easy target. She won't destroy it. Protect your engines, that's going to be her next objective."

Tsi ground her teeth. It would be precious few seconds before the enemy fired again.

"Do as she says," Tsi said quickly.

"I must note for tactical assessment that the prisoner is a Guraggan servant," Strongmind said.

"Just do it. Shift the shields to the engines, and keep us steady. I want evasion plotted the moment we get the beacon in."

"It is unwise to trust intelligence provided by the enemy."

"She's not our enemy. Now do it," Tsi said.

The machine nodded, and entered the command.

Enlil had managed to work the magnetic tether clamp onto the beacon, but was still holding on for her life. Her suit's automatic systems had filled her arm with painkillers, turning it numb. Her bad hand hadn't shattered, so at least it hadn't frozen all the way through yet. With any luck, she'd only lose a few fingers.

"Almost there!" Hiron said. "Doesn't this thing go any faster?"

"You're telling me," Enlil muttered.

The Bondsman was latched to the beacon next to her, totally silent as they were pulled in. There'd be another shot before they got inside, she knew it. All she could hope was that the enemy didn't decide to blast the beacon apart. Or that they missed, by some miracle.

"Incoming projectile," she heard Strongmind say, just as the object crossed her field of vision.

It was an oblong silhouette, traveling with such stately speed that she could track its arc as it moved toward the ship. It was a slow-mass round, a dead shell designed to pass through shields. There was enough time for her brain to register that she was going to die just as the shell struck the ship's hull...

And shattered.

Enlil had seen ships from one end of the Frontier to the other pass through Noxia, and she had never seen one survive a direct hit from a mass round like that. Normally it would have torn through even a Cruiser's hull, turned everyone on board into paste. Instead, she watched as the round struck the hull and shredded itself, shrapnel spraying wildly in every direction. The ship jostled and the beacon swung wildly, but the ship's armor held.

"Gods and Spirits," Enlil whispered.

"Hold on tight," the Bondsman snarled in warning.

A single sliver of the round sliced through one of the tether lines, severing the cable and sending the beacon spinning. Enlil gripped the hull tighter as they spun wildly, her heart pulled up into her throat. Her vision was going black, she knew she'd pass out any moment. All she could do was hope that her mag boots held, but even then her body might be ripped apart by the sudden forces being exerted against it in both directions.

Then she felt a reverberating shock. The beacon came scraping to a halt on the bare surface of the cargo hold. Enlil gasped. They were inside. They'd made it.

"*Close the door! Right now!*" she screamed.

"I'm doing it! I'm doing it!" Hiron shouted back.

She watched, still clutching the side of the beacon, as the cargo doors slowly closed. The enemy craft was coming around for another pass, its weapons glowing bright, but then the door shut, and oxygen started to fill the hold again. Gratefully, Enlil detached herself from the beacon and landed heavily on the deck.

"We're in!" she shouted. "Let's get the fuck out of here!"

"Acknowledged," Strongmind said.

"How quickly can we Slip?" Tsi asked.

Her knuckles were white as she watched the screens, analyzing data as quickly as she could. The beacon was inside, everyone was on board and the hull was sealed. It was a spot of luck that the Guraggan had fired a solid round at them, little knowing that the ship's armor was made of a Kiosan alloy seldom seen outside the Janissariat. Even poor Furner hadn't known exactly what his men were doing as they patched the hull back together for her, just assumed she was being cheap when she insisted that they use stores of her own armor reserve. A lucky thing too, that she still had enough of the metal left to keep the ship together after the beating it'd taken at the Inheritor's World.

"Analysis of Slip Routes not currently possible," Strongmind said. "Excessive mass is present. Error: electronic interference. My scanners are malfunctioning. There has been a radiation spike."

Tsi cursed. They were traveling deeper into the system, away from Salvation, and that meant that Noxia's infamous anomalies were more and more likely to appear. Karenkov Snakes would start frying their un-hardened systems, a sudden pulse of solar energy might knock their shielding out, not to mention rogue asteroids and derelict ships drifting black in the void.

"Strongmind, disconnect yourself from main systems and set us up for maximum EMP shielding. Transfer weapons control to me, and set a course…"

A course where? They could try to arc back around to Salvation, but the Guraggan craft was gaining on them, and their opponent would figure out all her tricks soon enough. They could always turn and fight, but Tsi's firepower wasn't enough to taken on a Guraggan Striker. If she went deep...

If she went deep it would be an insane risk. They'd have to fly for days, contending with the hazards of the Poison Suns. But the Guraggan would have to take those same risks too, and Tsi had something the Guraggan did not.

"Set a course a few days through the system," she said. "Arc us down to the nearest Slip point that's relative to the first asteroid ring. Enlil?"

"What?" the Noxian responded over the comms. She was panting. She had probably only just gotten the beacon secured.

"Get to the cockpit," Tsi said. "I'm going to need one hell of a pilot."

CHAPTER 23

A direct hit, my Lady. No effect."

Skyme was telling her things she could read off the screens for herself, but she could not bring herself to be angry with him. Instead, she felt the first, subtle pangs of joy. The ship had armor, strong armor, like nothing seen on the Frontier. A worthy foe to be sure.

Still, it was troubling. Why had her prey not extended their shields around the beacon? Why had they not tried to evade her fire? Of the paths available to her quarry, these two were the most logical.

"What is its hull composed of?" she asked.

"Unknown," Skyme replied.

"Hmm, have the Bykon—"

Of course. She hadn't known about her prey, because her Hunting Hound was gone. She'd been aboard the ship when the battle had started. Now, seeing how her target behaved, the way they had predicted her attacks, she knew what had happened. The Bykon had been taken prisoner. She was serving Ornicht's enemies now. She let out a snarl of frustration.

"My lady?" Skyme asked.

"Nothing. Continue pursuit. Are we within range for an EM-Pulse?"

"Negative. Something is interfering with our scanners as well. I am doing my best to compensate, but I fear the radiation will negatively affect our ability to target the opponent directly."

"Hmmm... They must be disabled, not destroyed. The pulse would be best..."

Lady Ornicht clicked her tongue in contemplation. She enjoyed pursuit, enjoyed a good challenge, but if she was honest she had only ever been a middling star commander. Flesh and blood and metal she understood. All this guessing at ranges and movement patterns was something better left to machines…

"Is Theta-90 ready?" she asked.

One of her servants, faceless and hooded in silver, stepped forward and bowed his head.

"It is, my lady. It only awaits your command," he said.

"Good. Skyme, prepare a full mass barrage. Maximum thrust, I want us close enough to see them before we fire."

The little man coughed slightly, clearly summoning his courage before he spoke.

"My lady, did you not say the target must be recaptured?"

"Continue the pursuit as I have commanded," Ornicht said, rising from her chair.

She stumbled. Two of her servants moved to brace her, but she swatted them away. Laboriously, she pulled the re-vitalizer's tubing out of the sockets in her flesh. Filmy liquid spilled onto the deck.

"That is unwise, my lady," her Physician muttered, but she was silenced with a glare from Ornicht.

"I will return," she said. "I must make Theta-90's final preparations myself."

Everyone except Furner was crammed into the cockpit. Tsi sat at the command console, occasionally throwing images up from her screen into holo-projections as she traced the pursuit of the Guraggan ship. Strongmind was slumped against one wall like a marionette, put into minimal power mode at her command. Wylla and Hiron had strapped in to their own chairs. Ironically, they were at positions that could double as gunnery control if either of them was so inclined, but Hiron currently had his patched in to the scanning system. At the entrance stood Tenlok, one hand braced against the bulkhead, as if he would fling himself away at any instant to escape the ship's confines.

At the front of the cockpit, every screen hers to command, hands darting across the controls like a musician playing a fevered sonata, sat Enlil. Tsi couldn't see Enlil's face, but she knew the sound of pride in her voice when she spoke.

"This thing can move," Enlil said, following with an appreciative whistle. "Okay, what's going on with her coolant system?"

"Shot," Tsi said. "Strongmind ran a diagnostic, it was damaged in the fighting so we can't push her to full burn for too long."

"Heh, I once made it through Summer's Gap on an old fission drive," Enlil said. "Could fry a Rat-Pak on the controls before the end, but we all made it back in one piece."

"I'll bet."

Tsi grinned.

"They're matching our velocity," Hiron interjected. "Looks like they're still pursuing. Probably lining up their guns for another salvo…"

"I see 'em, kid," Enlil said. "Mag up!"

Enlil suddenly jerked at the controls, and the ship went corkscrewing through the void, the temporary spin playing havoc with Tsi's inner-ear. Despite the ship's a-grav and counter-inertia systems, suddenly producing real spin was rough on even a seasoned spacer's guts. Hiron and Wylla pitched back and forth in their chairs, the Bykon cursing in her mother tongue while the boy let out a nervous laugh. Strongmind's body slumped forward and lolled in place, but everyone else weathered Enlil's maneuvers well enough.

"She's still following," Tsi said. "I'm running possible evasion courses…"

"Don't waste the processor power," Enlil said. "Kid, find me a good mass cluster somewhere nearby."

"Uh, okay," Hiron replied, nervously looking at his console. "I think there's, um, there's something… looks like a group of asteroids, heading one-three-nine, mark eight…"

"Perfect," Enlil said, altering the ship's course. "Lock 'em in."

Tsi had guessed what her pilot was planning, but didn't say it aloud. Enlil needed all of her concentration for the task ahead of her. The ship shot through the void, Tsi warily tracking the progress of their nemesis as it matched them move for move, and gained on them steadily.

Guraggan ships were swift. She had known this her whole life. Speed was something they valued as much as weapons and armor. Better to strike a foe's weak underbelly than plod along, letting them know your every move before you make it.

The Guraggan had examined her ship and not completely destroyed it. That meant it had some value to them. She had the Bykon with her too, a valuable prisoner for the Guraggan to lose. If she were fighting a younger woman, she'd expect her foe to try and cripple the engines and then board her. But her enemy was canny, she had probed

Tsi's ships strengths and weaknesses, not risked everything on a killing blow when the opportunity presented itself.

"They've matched our plane," Tsi said, as the marker for the Guraggan ship on the scanner dropped down behind them, moving so close that they practically occupied the same position on the screen.

"You got the asteroid coordinates locked in?" Enlil asked.

"Uh," Hiron said. "Yeah, yeah, syncing with the main computer. They're locked."

"Hey Tsi, give us all the burn we got on my signal, got me?" Enlil said. "Okay, who here likes betting? I'll give you three to one she fires inside a minute."

The plan was clear: boost to maximum speed and fire at the same time, hoping to strike the asteroid and create a massive backscatter of particulate and radiation that would throw the enemy's sensors off and make their first volley go wide. It'd require precise timing, and a born pilot. Tsi knew she had one of those.

"We're betting? We're betting on this?" Hiron asked incredulously. "Wait, why are you—if you shoot the asteroids, won't some of the fragments hit us?"

"Yup," Enlil said.

"That, I mean, the speed they're going at, they could puncture vital systems! Our shields are barely holding."

"And she's got more than mass rounds in her arsenal," Tsi said. "We won't be able to rely on the ship's armor much longer. But this is the play we've got to make. Keep us steady Enlil."

"I know, I know," Enlil said indignantly. "My plan, isn't it?"

"I'll tell you when they're about to fire," Wylla said.

It was the first time the Bykon woman had spoken in Panglos since she returned to the cockpit with Tsi. All eyes were on her. The Bondsman scoffed.

"I lived with her for years," Wylla said. "I know how my Mistress thinks. I will tell you when she intends to fire."

"No offense, but you got about zero reasons to set our coordinates right and a lot of reasons to want to screw us," Enlil said.

The Bondsman made a hissing noise, that sounded something like agreement. Hiron looked nervously to Tsi, who in turn studied Wylla intently. The Bykon looked back at her, eyes devoid of fear.

Another voice cut through the room. It was even and level, but quieter than Tsi liked, as if the effort of speaking put a great burden upon the speaker.

"Assessment: the prisoner is a valuable intelligence asset," Strongmind said, his voice slow and halting in his powered-down state. "I suggest we act on the information provided."

Tsi nodded.

"Well," she said. "You heard him. Wylla, you give the signal."

Still weak from the day's exertions, Ornicht paused in the drone bay to steady herself. She breathed in through her nostrils and out through her mouth, feeling the pain in her lungs, welcoming it as a sign that she was still alive. Her fist curled. This was the coward's way. Something her Bykon had taught her, a way of controlling pain in the mind. Useless! Why should she care whether she lived or died? That was not her path, to eke out a living, old and crippled.

The pain grew hot, now focused around her curled fist. She tried to conquer it, tried to force it out through her fingertips, clenched her teeth so hard she was sure they would break. She had seen so much, triumphed over so much. Her own failing body would not conquer her.

She fell. Ornicht's knees hit the deck hard, sending another jolt of pain through her body.

Her hands snapped out, catching her fall hard on her wrists and making her cry out in pain. It was a graceless fall, not the way she'd been taught as a child. Rage boiled within her, leaked from her eyes, and she let out a muffled groan.

She was dying. She'd been dying for a long, long while, but now what time she had left was growing short. Her cursed Physician had needled her, begged her to accept nanite treatment. The Bykon had known, too. Known but said nothing. Clever girl, even more clever than Ornicht gave her credit for.

At last, she submitted. Some battles could not be won. She breathed in through her nostrils, out through her mouth, just as Wylla had told her. She let the pain be part of her, analyzed it, detached herself from it. It was no more unnatural to her body than her scars or her hair, or the color of her eyes.

What is broken can be remade.

She rose again, and looked around to be certain none of her

servants had seen her fall. The drone bay was empty save for her and the machines. Each was locked in its pod, watching her with electronic eyes as she walked among them. At the far end of the bay, Theta-90 waited for her, crouched and massive, dwarfing its brethren.

It looked down at her, and she could swear she noted recognition in its many green eyes. She placed a hand on its scarred carapace. Theta-90 had been with her since she was barely more than a girl, the lone survivor of her first drone-phalanx. It had saved her life a dozen times, and she had kept it in top shape, updating its hardware and weapons at every opportunity. She thought of it as often as she thought of her own children.

"It is a great task," she whispered. "Do you understand it?"

"*CONFIRM*," the machine replied, its croaking voice echoing in the empty bay.

"Good. We will launch you soon. I may never see you again, old friend."

Theta-90's many eyes focused on her, but the hulking machine did not speak.

"Skyme," Ornicht said into her communicator. "Charge weapons and calculate attack vector."

"It will be done, my lady," the small man replied from the bridge.

Ornicht reached into a pouch at her waist, dabbing two naked fingers with paint. She inscribed a Guraggan rune upon the machine's chest plate, movements steady as they had been the first time she and Theta-90 went to war. She stepped back, and nodded.

"Victory," it read.

"Launch first salvo," she said.

"I'm getting an energy spike from them," Hiron said. "It looks like they're getting ready to fire."

"Steady…." Wylla said, her eyes fixed on the screens.

"They've locked us," Enlil grunted, hands tight at the controls. "If we don't move now—"

"Steady," Wylla repeated. "Not yet."

The ship was barreling down on the asteroids. The distance between them was vast, but they were close enough that Enlil could trace their subtle rotation on visual scanners. She entered a series of commands, and making minute adjustments to the target lock. She'd flown the deep since she was a child, and knew how to run the complex trajectories in her head with a reasonable amount of accuracy. Enlil just thanked the lucky spirits that Tsi's ship still had a few high yield missiles left.

The Guraggan ship, marked by a small red icon on one of her screens, was steadily closing. They were so tight now she had to increase the magnification.

"They're on top of us!" Enlil shouted.

"Not yet!" Wylla shouted back.

The Guraggan's weapons were hot, they were at a distance where it'd be hard to miss with a full spread of fire. Seconds ticked by, sweat dripped into her eyebrows. This was suicide, it was suicide to trust this Bykon woman, suicide to fly straight on like this. Any moment she expected to see the blinding pulse of their weapons, hear the brief screech of a ripped hull before she was flash-fried into her chair. This was it, this was her last flight. She'd had a decent enough run of it, she supposed, but by the Gods she wished she hadn't gotten killed for finally breaking her rules, for trusting a gaggle of fools like Tsi and the rest.

It was fine, Enlil decided. If she was lucky, she wouldn't feel anything. Just a moment to soil herself, then heat, then nothing. Perhaps she'd see her parents again. Though, come to think of it, she wasn't even certain they were dead. For some reason, that thought hung in her mind, taking her away from the hot confines of the cockpit. It made her a little angry now. Not the steady anger she'd felt for so long, just a kind of subtle bitterness. Of course, one last kick to send her on her way through this shitty life they'd given her. They couldn't even do the decency of letting her know whether they were alive or dead. Typical.

"Now! All the gods, woman, now!"

Enlil realized that Wylla and everyone else in the cockpit was screaming at her. There was a flare on the screen, just as she pressed the fire controls and set the engine to maximum burn. In the span of a few seconds the missile launched, ignited its after burners, and sped ahead of them. It exploded against one of the asteroids, a direct hit, just as they raced passed rocks. The ancient regolith ripped away from the great mass of stone and iron, creating a cloud of dust and fist-sized fragments, hurtling all around them at incredible speeds.

Behind them on the screen she saw countless impact flares. She'd done it. She'd done it. The ship seemed like it was shaking itself apart, their shields were taking a beating, hunks of rock smashed against the hull and bounced off, but near as she could tell, not a single Guraggan round or blast had been on target.

She kept the hard burn going for as long as she thought the engines could take it, then brought the ship down to a steady cruising speed, adjusting their course as they arced deeper into the system. The room was filled with whoops of joy. Hiron was shaking the back of her chair, the kid having gotten up in excitement the moment she'd dropped burn.

"They're breaking pursuit," Enlil said. "Kid, you sure know how to pick 'em. That rock must've been full of something fuzzy!"

"Fuzzy?" Hiron asked, looking nonplussed.

"Naturally occurring radioactive material," Tsi said. "It interferes with sensors. They can't follow us if they're blind."

"It's also worth a lot of money," Enlil said. "Miners'll catch that spike and be hounding for it inside of an hour. Our friends out there are going to have to deal with a dozen claim hoppers trying to fry them now, too. 'Course, it's hit our sensors, so we're gonna fly by dead-reckoning for a bit..."

"I can start working out a course for us," Wylla offered. "I see you have up-to-date charts in your computer."

"Take it easy," Enlil said, spinning in her chair to grin at the Bykon. "You just saved our asses. I think you deserve a drink. Let the kid work on that."

"I—I can definitely help," Hiron said. "Astrogation was one of my studies back home."

"Good," Enlil said. "Hey Captain, crack us some booze would ya?"

Tsi laughed. "I thought the captain gave the orders," she said.

"Not when me an' her just saved the damn ship," Enlil said, winking at Wylla.

Tsi raised her hands in mock surrender.

"Alright, alright. I've got to check on Furner anyway. Hiron, don't have too much fun with them while I'm gone, eh?"

The boy nodded enthusiastically, his ears turning bright red.

Enlil had found that annoying at first, but now she was starting to see why Tsi kept the kid around. Awkward and ugly to be sure, but in an endearing way.

Enlil spun back around to face the console, feeling the familiar joy of escape wash over her. She hadn't especially liked anyone on this boat besides Tsi when she first got on, but shared danger always bred shared camaraderie. Wylla was reliable; the kid too. Even Strongmind seemed less imposing than when she had first met it, though maybe it had more to do with the machine being on minimal power in a corner than anything else. As for the Bondsman...

Enlil realized he had disappeared sometime during the chase. She shrugged. She didn't particularly feel like celebrating with someone like him, anyway.

Ornicht had made her way back to the bridge. She was bracing herself with one arm upon her command throne, not bothering to be seated. She watched with bated breath as every blast in the salvo missed. All save one, fired a moment after the main volley.

"The interference in scanning is getting worse," Skyme said. "I humbly suggest we temporarily break pursuit to re-calibrate, my lady."

"Keep the channel open," Ornicht breathed. "Wait."

The bridge was silent for a long time, until finally, a subtle crackle emanated from one of the speakers. It was an old code, made in bursts of static that could penetrate even the strange cloud of radiation released by the asteroid cluster. Ornicht walked up to the console bank to see the message translated, already knowing what it would say.

"DEPLOYMENT SUCCESSFUL."

She nodded. Theta-90 would never fail her.

"Break pursuit," she said. "Re-calibrate the sensors, and keep track of their estimated trajectory."

There was mutter of affirmation from her servants as she left the bridge. Despite the weakness in her limbs, she felt no pain. By the time she reached her quarters, she could barely stand, but she slumped happily into her bed. It had been a very long few days, but at last it was time to sleep.

Sleep would be good. She always slept so very well after she had won a battle.

CHAPTER 24

urner looked the same, peacefully asleep on the medical bed, strapped down tight against the sudden changes in g-force they had expected. Tsi studied the old man, looking so much like a contented father or a favorite uncle, his leathery brown face serene. A loud, halting snore came from him. Tsi stifled a laugh.

She walked to his bedside and checked the medical readings. He would live. It might take a few days for him to recover, but he would live. She didn't have the resources to make him a new leg, but she just added that to the list of repairs she had to make for her crew. The next port they stopped at, she'd make sure there were good medical facilities. These people had all already endured so much for her. She was shamed that she knew she'd have to ask far more of them soon.

She knelt next to the auto-doc, and opened its maintenance panel. Taking a few tools from her belt she made some adjustments to the machine. Then, she took out a small glass vial and attached it to one of the pumps. She entered a command into the console, and drained one of the chemical reserves into the vial, filling it with crystal-blue fluid. Then she replaced the panel, stood up, and checked Furner again. Gently, she patted one of his hands.

So peaceful. She wondered if he always slept this soundly, or if it was the drugs she had pumped into his system. He'd been a pirate too, after all, just as Tsi had. Did he feel the guilt she did? Did he ever think about the crewmen he'd blasted into the cold void? Or the families that would starve for want of cargo he had stolen?

Then again, Furner had been born here. There was little choice for someone like him. Tsi had been born with so much. She had had so many chances to walk a different path, and she had still wound up living among bandits and assassins.

The hairs on the back of her neck raised. She turned around.

The Bondsman rounded the corner and stepped into the room. He was quiet, but she had heard his boots clicking against the deck a fraction of an instant before here arrived.

"Take it we got away," Tenlok said.

"We did," Tsi said. "Enlil's one hell of a pilot, and Wylla steered us true."

"Trusting your enemies isn't a good idea."

"Who exactly are you talking about?" Tsi asked.

The Bondsman had a habit of staying silent a few moments longer than normal before responding. It wasn't unnerving, but it was certainly odd. She wondered if it was cultural custom, or an attempt to intimidate her. It didn't really matter. She knew how he fought now. If it came to that, she could handle him.

"Your escape pods are set up right," Tenlok said, ignoring her question.

"You thought about jumping ship?" Tsi asked. "I thought Bondsmen were supposed to be fearless."

"I'm not stupid. Our odds against that Guraggan ship aren't great. Better to take our chances in dead space than stay on this thing when it gets vaporized."

"What stopped you?"

"I'd have to take you with me, wouldn't I?" Tenlok said. "The nanomachines you put into me, what's the range on their heart monitor?"

"Ten Kilometers," Tsi said, feeling the weight of the blue vial in her pocket.

"Guess we're staying close together for a little while," Tenlok said. "How much longer's he taking up the auto-doc?"

"I've been meaning to talk to you about that," Tsi said. "My machine isn't rigged to give you a nanite flush. I had to use up most of our chemical reserves taking care of Furner."

"Convenient," Tenlok said.

"Look, it was that or let him die. You know how this works, there's only so much to go around, and Furner needed the resources, so he got them."

"I understand," Tenlok said. "How about the money? You still have that, or does Furner need it too?"

Tsi rolled her eyes.

"I've got your money," she said. "I can even give you a bonus when we get to safe port."

"When is that exactly? From what I can tell, we're limping deeper into the Poison Suns on a ship that's seen better days. You planning to jump into the Slip anytime soon?"

"It's not that simple," Tsi said. "The sun's radiation makes navigation... unpredictable. Add to that the density of mass around here, and we'll be traveling at sublight for at least a few days."

The Bondsman shrugged his heavy shoulders.

"Guess I better get settled in then," he said, turning to leave.

"There's a spare cot off the galley," Tsi called after him. "If you don't mind bunking with Hiron."

"Already got a place picked out," the Bondsman called back.

When she was sure he was gone, she took out the blue vial and studied it for a moment. She'd have to keep it close. It might come in handy. She knew she was playing a dangerous game with the Bondsman, but she didn't have any choice. She patted Furner Ketsu's hand one more time.

No, like always, she didn't have any choice at all.

Hiron was beginning to regret volunteering. Mathematics weren't something he struggled with, but they also didn't come as easily to him as some skills. Even assisted by the computer's calculations, he'd been working at plotting their course for what seemed like hours, sitting in the galley with a data tablet while the women got drunk.

Enlil was sitting on a counter, looking unpleasantly pretty despite her hair still being a tangled mess and her face going flush with alcohol. She repeatedly and loudly assured everyone that the ship was on autopilot and she'd rigged up a basic proximity scanner, but no one seemed to notice besides him. Wylla was quietly holding her mug of clear liquor with two hands, taking a sip occasionally and smiling and laughing politely when one of the others would make a crude joke or a rude comment.

Tsi, on the other hand, was pouring from a silver thermos and drinking with cheerful enthusiasm. She had toasted the crew three times at this point. A little of the sadness that always hung over her seemed to have dissipated.

"Hoo," Enlil drawled. "This is the most I've drunk on a job since

I was ten!"

"I—I haven't had this much to drink in some time as well," Wylla agreed. "I think the last time my lady gave us such large alcohol rations was the anniversary of her second son's blooding."

"They don't let you drink?" Enlil asked, astounded.

"Some Guraggan lords are... less strict," Wylla said. "My mistress is a traditionalist in that sense. We are only permitted to drink on ritual days."

"Fuck her then," Enlil said. "To your freedom!"

She raised her glass, found it was empty, and staggered over to Tsi. She sloppily filled it from the bottle, then raised it again.

"Freedom," Tsi said, raising her thermos.

After a moment Wylla nodded, and raised the mug with one hand.

"Freedom," she agreed.

The trio drank great gulps, then settled in to chattering for a time while Hiron worked. He had just about finished when Enlil leaned over his shoulder, her breath heavy with the scent of liquor.

"Not bad," she muttered, causing Hiron's collar to dampen slightly.

"Oh, well, you know," he said. "I've studied this sort of stuff before, and uh, never done it for real but you know..."

"Get us killed if we go there though," she said, pointing at the screen. "Snake nest. Plot us around it by... thirty eight? That work? Hey Cap, we got fuel for a thirty eight correction at sublight?"

Tsi nodded.

"Should be enough," she slurred.

Hiron marveled at how quickly the two of them had fallen in to talking like old comrades. He'd never found it easy to make friends. A few playmates among the servants as a child, but as he'd grown older his obligations to the clan had meant he had to separate from them, and by the time he had reached young adulthood his deformity had become so obvious that most people regarded him with contempt. It was true that Tsi had been kind to him, but he'd never found an easy rapport with anyone.

"What's a Snake Nest?" Wylla asked.

"Kerenkov Snakes," Enlil supplied. "It's a spot where they tend to show up, form little balls of gas and energy. No one knows why.

Deep-Station clans like to hang out around them, so we'll have to run silent through that spot. Still, according to what the kid's got up here, two days and we're gone."

"It's fascinating," Wylla said. "I've never seen a region of space like this. So many phenomenon, it's a unique convergence of conditions."

"The tri-stars are very beautiful," Hiron added hesitantly. "I can see why people would come here."

"This place is hell, and the people are worse," Enlil grunted, taking a pull from her glass. "Trust me, you only come out here cause you've got nowhere else to go."

Hiron noticed Tsi was staring at the deck, her long, dark hair falling over her shoulders. She wasn't from Noxia, of course, but she seemed to have left and come back as easily as she had gone to Promise.

"Tsi, I never asked you," he said. "Where are you from?"

"All over," Tsi said.

"That's not an answer. We playin' guessing games?" Enlil said, a wicked grin crossing her face. "I think you're Epilotii. Good manners, speak a lotta languages, rich..."

Tsi shook her head.

"I really don't think we should talk about this..." she began.

"No, no," Wylla said. "She can't be from the Mandate. She has a nose!"

"I've met Epilotii with noses," Enlil replied.

"Yes, but high class women always get reconstructed. Everyone knows that!" Wylla insisted.   She stared at Tsi, rubbing her jaw dramatically.

"Goodhome!" she said suddenly, pointing at Tsi. "You're from Goodhome."

"What makes you say that?" Tsi asked.

It was clear to Hiron that she wasn't enjoying the game, but the other two were drunkenly clasping each other about the shoulders, as if steadying their bodies would steady their reeling brains. He wanted to speak up, but Wylla kept going, growing more animated as she spoke.

"You're rich, but you also know how to use a gun and how to fly, so you must be from the Frontier," she said, counting off on her fingers. "This ship has a big cargo hold, and I saw in your logs you travel around a lot, but you don't carry very much, so you have to be trading on the Frontier. And... the whole ship stinks like Gene-Bear. So you *have* to be from Goodhome!"

"I spent some time there once," Tsi said quietly.

"She's too smart to be a homesteader," Enlil said. "You ever met one of those people? Nothing going on behind the eyes. No... you're not from the Frontier at all, are you?"

Tsi shook her head.

"I don't think Tsi's enjoying the game," Hiron said. "Maybe we could talk about something else?"

Enlil ignored him, staring hard at Tsi. She was like Hiron's cats back home, eyes totally focused on her target. There wasn't cruelty in her, no, but there was an intense, merciless focus.

"Lived here a while though," Enlil said. "Know how to fight. Fly a ship. And you got money."

"And you know quite a bit about my Mistress's people," Wylla said, her voice becoming more serious. "You have heavy augmentation, too."

"Tsi, are you a Guraggan?" Enlil asked bluntly.

"No," she shook her head. "Sometimes I think I'm half one, I know them so well."

"Then you're Kiosan," Wylla said. "You're from the Janissariat."

Tsi sighed and closed her eyes. She nodded.

"Nah, really?" Enlil said. "I thought Kiosans were all dust-boned. How long you been out here?"

"A while."

"You fought for the Mad Empress, didn't you?" Wylla asked.

It seemed like more of a statement than a question.

"I didn't fight for the Empress. I fought the Guraggan," Tsi said. "In the first war. Then the Janissaries rose, and there was... there was no place for someone like me. The war ended. So I came here. I tried to find my way, on Noxia and Goodhome and a dozen other places, but I've always had to move on. And now I'm here."

"You've gone a very long way," Wylla said. "Just to go back."

All eyes fixed on Wylla, who seemed to be the soberest person in the room now.

"How do you know that?" Hiron asked.

"Observation is the gift of the Bykon," Wylla said. "We're headed towards Kiosan space, aren't we? You intend to warn them of what my Mistress's people are doing."

Tsi nodded.

"But you don't know everything that you should," Wylla said. "I have something that I must tell all of you. The whole crew should know, before we go any further."

"Crew's all here," Enlil said with a shrug. "Spill."

"No," Wylla repeated. "The Bondsman and the Machine should know too. Their risk is the same as ours."

Tsi nodded. She rose to her full height, seeming to shrug the effects of the alcohol off as easily as Wylla had.

"I've got a spare room down below," she said. "Hiron, take her down there and get her set up. I'll get Strongmind and Tenlok."

Tsi left for the cockpit, leaving Hiron with Wylla smiling expectantly at him.

"Uh, follow me," he said, and shambled down a flight of steps, Wylla stepping elegantly and only a little drunkenly after him.

Wylla had fully sobered by the time the crew was assembled in Tsi's cramped briefing room. The place was musty and small. Chairs folded out of the wall for the crew to sit on around a central holo-display. Wylla had programmed it to show a map of the Frontier, with the Guraggan Hegemony highlighted on one side, and the Janissariat on the other. She had also marked the most common Slip routes.

"We are currently here," she said, marking Noxia. "The fastest route, given optimal conditions would take us to Kiosan space in three weeks. But, there is something you must know. The Guraggan may reach it before us."

"What?" Enlil said. "I thought they were all on the kid's planet. It'd take a good while longer to get all the way to Kios from there."

"Six months, relative, for a fleet the size of the Khagan's forces at Promise," Wylla said. "That is, if they were traveling with an ordinary Slip drive. They are not."

Tsi nodded, a look of recognition in her eyes. Strongmind spoke up, the machine still on a low power mode that kept its body and movements stiff and marionette-like.

"We have hypothesized a new travel method," Strongmind said. "One that negates the necessity of Slip mass-dispersion protocols."

"It's an Entanglement Wave," Wylla said. "A beam of energy faster than the Slip, imperceptible except to those within it. It allows any number of ships to travel instantly between one point and another along the beam. My masters call it the Path of Glory."

Wylla pressed a key, and an image of a Guraggan fleet appeared in the holo-display, taken from the ship's archives. Smaller vessels clustered like parasites around the larger cruisers and warships.

"The Path does have a price, however. Every time a fleet assembles within it, approximately ten percent of its mass is destroyed. This effect seems to be primarily on the outer edges of a mass cluster. Smaller ships owned by low status warriors are kept on the outer edges of the fleet, while the great lords remain in the center, and take the least risk. A certain number of ships are crippled upon leaving the Path, others are utterly destroyed, and some disappear entirely."

"It's a potent technology," Tsi said. "Even with losses like that, the Guraggan could win any war in an instant."

"That's incredible," Hiron said. "How... how did the Guraggan make this kind of thing? I thought they'd been tearing themselves apart in a civil war."

"I do not know," Wylla said. "My own people serve the Guraggan with our scientific skills, yet as far as I am aware no Bykon was involved in the development of this device. All I know is that the Khagan traveled deep and far for many years, and when he returned he had the designs for the Path."

"Wait," Tsi said. "The Khagan died. The Janissaries killed him at the Siege Victorious."

"A new Khagan has risen," Wylla explained. "He's from one of the lesser Houses. When the old Khagan died and the civil wars began, he took his forces and fled towards the Dreaming Stars. My Mistress never spoke his name, but it is said that he was ferocious in the war with the Janissaries. It is said he has never lost a battle."

"There's a first time for everything," Tsi said.

"Sure," Enlil cut in. "But you're saying when we get to Kios, these bastards might already be waiting for us? What's the point, then?"

"We don't have to get to Kios before them," Wylla said. "All that is required is that we get close enough to launch the beacon directly, then it will travel faster than our ship ever could. Noxia is too distant, but I've gone over the trajectory Hiron plotted, and there are a few places that are only a short jump away. It'd be relatively simple to Slip to one of those points, then launch the beacon. If nothing goes wrong, our beacon might arrive before the Guraggan even realize we have escaped them. Lady Ornicht is traveling alone, away from the fleet. She does not have the Path of Glory, and so she is as limited to ordinary Slip travel as we are."

"You notice this ship just got away from her?" Tenlok said from the back of the room. "What's to keep her from going back to them, and telling them to launch the invasion anyway?"

"Shame," Wylla said. "This was supposed to be an easy task. My mistress is old, she believes her days of glory are passed her. If she returns with nothing but failure and speculation, she may be stripped of her rank. She must pursue us, and we, in turn, must escape her."

"That's a lot to risk on pride," Tenlok muttered.

"It's the only option we have," Tsi said. "Hiron, what are our choices for jump points?"

Hiron stood up from where he was sitting, leaning heavily on his crutches. He looked around the room nervously, and Wylla placed a reassuring hand on his shoulder.

"Well, once we break down out of the mass plane, should be by about fourteen hundred tomorrow, we have three options," he said, his voice hoarse. He cleared his throat loudly and pointed at the display, highlighting three stars just on the border of Janissariat space.

"Spuris Minor would be an easy Slip, but, uh, it's totally uninhabited. No habitable planets, no stations, and, well, we need to make some repairs, not to mention some of us need medical care, so, um, I don't, I mean with the Captain's permission, I don't think we should—"

"I understand Hiron," Tsi said gently. "What are our other options?"

"Eridexa is densely populated," he said, highlighting another star. "Opposite, um, opposite problem. Lot of people there means we'll probably be spotted and stopped. The Eridexans are a buffer state for Kios, so they have pretty harsh border controls. Plus side, it's very civilized, so we could get all the repairs and supplies we need..."

"But we might be delayed," Wylla added helpfully. "And they might to try to stop us launching the beacon. Rendering the benefits null."

"And the third option?" Tsi asked.

"Um, well there's a little system on the edge of Kiosan space called 'Chalakhat'," he said. "It's pretty much uninhabited, but there's, um, there's one habitable world and some automated stations with repair services according to the records, so I think... I think this is our best bet."

"Chalakhat," Tsi said after a moment's pause. "I've been there before. It's our best chance. Set a course, I want us to Slip as soon as we clear the plane."

Tsi spent the next day going through preparations for the Slip jump, making sure that the ship was ready for the trip. There were spot repairs she could handle herself, as well as taking stock of the supplies they had. Food and water would last them about a week, if they were careful, but the ship's fuel reserves were by no means impressive. She'd burned through a lot of fuel just to avoid being hit by the Guraggan, and while the Slip drive was well-supplied, her sub-light movement would have to be cautious. They could drift on inertia in-system, only making minor course corrections for some time. If they had to get into another fight anytime soon though, they would be in trouble.

Enlil had taken charge of the cockpit, running their sub-light maneuvers with roguish ease. Sometimes she poked her head in to see Enlil napping at the controls, but the moment a proximity alarm went off she'd snap to and adjust their course on instinct. Really, Enlil's behavior seemed to sum up the whole crew: they were in an uneasy state of calm, ready for things to be thrown into disarray at any moment.

Hiron followed her around like a puppy, always eager to prove his worth. She'd given him plenty to do, but in truth physical maintenance was a waste of his skills. Wylla was busy working with their navigation system, sometimes borrowing Hiron to help her work out certain complex equations. Tsi wished she had more of that kind of work for him. Of the only other people spare for manual labor, Strongmind had to stay in minimal power to keep his sensitive systems from being damaged by random radiation bursts, and Tenlok flatly refused to follow her orders.

So she found herself spending more time with the boy, and, just as she'd sensed back on the Inheritor's World, he proved himself dependable. They were working on correcting a minor circuit fluctuation in one of the secondary engines when he spoke up in a different tone.

"I'm sorry that I couldn't keep the others from, um, bothering you. You know, about where you come from," Hiron said as he passed her a length of repair cord.

"It's alright," Tsi said. "It's not a secret."

"You don't like talking about it though," Hiron said. "I mean, it makes you sad, right?"

Tsi began working the cord over the damaged components, watching as the gel began knitting itself into the fried circuits. In moments it would take the shape of system perfectly, mimicking its function.

"Sometimes," Tsi agreed. "You have a right to know who I am. Where I came from."

"I don't think it matters," Hiron said. "We're all in the same situation, aren't we? We're all running from the Guraggan. I don't think it matters who we were or... or what we did before we got here."

"You saved us," he added. "We owe you. All of us."

"Maybe," Tsi said.

She silently checked that the repair gel was still working, then looked back up at Hiron.

"I'm going to check on Furner," she said. "Think you can handle this?"

Hiron nodded vigorously, and set himself to work. Tsi made her way back to the medical bay, thinking all the time on the boy's words. Somehow, she wasn't so sure that he was right. The last person who had known who she really was had wound up with a knife in his stomach.

Furner was sitting up in the surgical bed. A yellow smile split his face at her approach, and he gestured for her to come in.

"Got me on solid food yet?" he asked.

"Another day of liquids," she said, glancing at his belly. "I think you'll manage."

"Manage? Hell! I'm starvin'! This ain't no way to treat your old crew mate."

"Technically speaking, we were never on the same crew."

"Ah, come on," the old pirate laughed. "You and me were practically bunk-mates."

"In your dreams, Furner."

Furner stuck his fat tongue out at her.

"Well," he said. "I'm minus a leg and some change it seems. When are we heading back to Salvation? I've got a few med-techs who owe me a favor. Get me something brand new, maybe get my eyes to match up right at the same time."

"We're not going back to Salvation," Tsi said.

"Too hot right now?"

"Something like that..."

Furner raised his dark eyebrows at her. It was odd, despite everything that had happened he was chatting with her and prodding her, just as if they were two old mates catching up. She admired that about people like Furner and Enlil: their ability to return to normal as if they'd just thrown some kind of switch. She'd learned to dissociate herself from trauma a long time ago, but it always seemed to creep back in, sooner rather than later.

"Is this a kidnapping? Cause look, I can't work with one leg, and nobody's going to pay for my old carcass," Furner said, cutting the brief silence that had arisen.

"Well, I do have to haul you out of the system for a bit," Tsi admitted.

"Out of the system?"

Furner's smile disappeared.

"How do you mean, out of the system?"

"We need to make a quick Slip jump," Tsi said. "I have to launch a beacon. We'll get some more repairs, patch you up, then bring you back."

"Tsi, this isn't the kind of joke to play on an old timer."

"I wish I had another way around it—"

"I've got things on Salvation," Furner said. "My repair bay, my people. If I'm gone for weeks, that's all going to fall apart—"

"It won't be weeks—"

"Oh, how do you know? You're not exactly the type that everything just falls into place for, are you?!"

Furner spat the words out, genuine anger in his bloodshot eyes.

"We've got a course laid out and a plan. I swear to you, it'll only be a week relative, at best—"

"Save it. You know, I thought you were just doing a quick loop around the belt or one of the outer worlds, now you're saying you're gonna jump stars? The hell is the matter with you?!"

"I'm trying to tell you, you *can't* go back!"

"Why not?" Furner asked. "Why not, huh?"

"Jarawat's dead. The whole Corridor's at war, it might've spread to the rest of the station by now," Tsi sighed. "You know how it is. Once there's a gap in power, everyone has to scramble to try and fill it."

Furner balled his fist and smacked it into his mangled thigh.

"Gods damn it!" He shouted. "I should be there! My crew is caught in the middle of that! We already lost half of 'em protecting your sorry backside!"

"I *know!*" Tsi said. "I know, I brought bad luck to you, and I'm... I'm sorry, Furner. I wish to hell it wasn't like this but it is and all I can do right now is keep you alive. That's the only thing I can give. I'm sorry, but this is all I have."

"Yeah, real generous of you," Furner grunted. "Get my people killed, wreck the station, get my damn leg chopped off, but hey! At least *I'm* still breathing."

Furner's eyes were downcast, his once smiling mouth now taught in a bitter grimace.

"I'd give anything for it not to have happened this way, Furner," Tsi said.

The old pirate slowly nodded, but didn't return her gaze.

"That makes two of us," he said.

CHAPTER 25

It was 'night' on the ship, as far as Wylla could tell. They'd assigned sleeping shifts that mostly overlapped. Most of the crew was asleep right now, only the Machine and her sitting up in the cockpit, monitoring the course that had been set. She knew enough to correct their course if anything started to go wrong, but for now, she had cleared all the holographic displays, and was watching the star fields. She put her feet up on the console in spite of herself, something she would never have done in her old life. A few days out of the services of the Guraggan and it was starting to feel natural already.

She glanced over at Strongmind. It had set itself up in one of the chairs, by a navigation console if she wasn't mistaken. The body was totally slack, like a drunkard. Or a fresh corpse.

Wylla knew she could trust Hiron. The boy was too young and innocent to deceive her. The others though, they existed at an odd half-way point. Enlil had seemed as carefree as one of her friends back home on Bykonus Prime, but Wylla had seen her gun down two of her companions in cold blood. Tsi was obviously an extremely dangerous woman, no less dangerous than Lady Ornicht. Yet she tried so hard to appear compassionate, to *be* compassionate. The Machine though... She could not forget that when it had last lain helpless like this before her, it was secretly plotting to murder her and all of her fellows.

Wylla got up suddenly, and decided it was time to walk the decks. The ship was larger than one might first guess, split into three main levels. She started with the top, above the flight deck. It was little more than a cramped corridor leading to two "attics" where Tsi had stashed supplies of weapons and liquor.

Wylla marveled at how cleverly these two rooms had been hidden. Admittedly, the Serfs had not searched the ship too thoroughly, but they should have spotted such an obvious hiding space. Then again, they'd had to manage a score of prisoners, as well as prepare themselves for a counter attack. They had failed utterly, partly because Wylla had underestimated Strongmind.

She walked past Hiron's cabin on her way downwards, hearing quiet snoring. Then she passed Enlil's, where she heard loud snoring. Wylla paid a brief visit to the medical bay, where Furner Ketsu was sleeping peaceably. She'd grown quite fond of the old pirate during her brief visits with him. He reminded her a little of her father, if he had possessed a much more colorful vocabulary.

Then, she climbed down to the lowest deck, where the three main cargo holds were. She checked the two side holds briefly, and then headed for the main hold. There, the Slip beacon waited for her.

Essentially it was just an engine and a broad-range transmission system, with an outer casing to keep it from being torn apart by high-v dust. She looked at the curious device and slowly walked around it. It was quite an old model, so much so that she wondered where Tsi had gotten it.

"Shouldn't you be flying the ship?"

The voice was harsh, slightly distorted by a helmet vocalizer. She turned, knowing that she would see the Bondsman. He was standing in the shadows, the only indication that he was there at all being the dull red glow from his eye. The demon mask leered at her, its fangs seeming to glisten in the darkness.

Queerly, Wylla felt relieved. At last she had found someone on the ship to truly fear.

"It's on autopilot," she said steadily. "I believed everyone else was asleep."

"Don't sleep much," Tenlok replied, stepping into the light.

He seemed almost a mirror to Lady Ornicht in his appearance and manner, all weapons and armor. He stood with his hands resting on his belt, still as steel. She couldn't help noticing the Nioban Kukri that hung across his chest, or the pistols hanging from his belt and strapped to his thighs. She saw too, the little black dagger that was clasped to one of his vambraces. The weapon he'd used to set Breaker Liss on fire.

"Well, I'd… I'd better get back," Wylla said.

Tenlok didn't move, but something in his gaze held Wylla in place.

"You know how this thing works?" he asked.

"It's a Slip beacon," she said. "They're very common technology. Used in the Hegemony, if that's what you're asking."

"Seemed interested in it."

Wylla looked up at the beacon, its shell studded with tiny winking lights.

"I am," she said. "Tsi told me she's copied all the data she gathered on the Guraggan over forty years onto it, as well as the warning. It's our purpose. Everything we do rests on this strange old thing."

"Suppose your Mistress would want to know all about this. Probably be a big reward."

"I don't know what you mean."

There was something terrible about looking at him, something artificial in his movements. Not the uncanny imitation of Strongmind, more as if there was some odd *absence* of the human spark. She'd seen him in battle, seen how brutally graceful and fluid he had been. Like a fish slicing through water, it was his natural element. Here in the empty hold, he didn't seem out of place, but she felt he had more in common with the beacon and the inert machinery than her.

"I almost died getting this thing in," he said.

"That must have been very frightening," Wylla offered.

As with so many times in her life, she knew she was playing some kind of game with the killer. She did not know the rules, and she knew that if she lost, it would put her in great peril. But she was beginning to understand him, and understand him enough that she could gamble he was not a sadist.

"I don't want anyone messing with it," he grated. "We clear?"

"I wasn't—I'm not—I do not serve the Guraggan anymore," Wylla said, trying to keep her voice even despite the anger that was creeping in.

"Sure. You're free, because Tsi says so. What happens when they overtake the ship and board it? That when I find out you were a captive all along, begging for her to come save you?"

Wylla clenched her teeth.

"I would rather die," she said.

"Might come to that."

"It might," Wylla agreed. "But you don't have to worry about me. I've already made my decision."

The Bondsman looked her up and down, studied her just as she had studied him. Then she saw his body relax, releasing one hand from his belt.

"Alright," Tenlok said.

He nodded to her curtly, and left the hold. Wylla took a moment to catch her breath, then laughed. She was beginning to understand her place here. And the people around her.

Tsi always had a hard time sleeping, but with the ship so suddenly crowded, and the Guraggan still stalking them, she found it doubly difficult. She woke earlier than she'd meant to. With no chance of getting more sleep, she cleaned and dressed herself, then headed to the galley. Hiron was waiting for her, having taken some of the rations and re-condensed them into a stew. She took a bowl and sipped on it gratefully. There weren't any spices on the ship, and so the whole thing tasted more or less like what it was: a protein pack soaked in boiled water. Still, the boy was trying to help and she didn't have the heart to tell him otherwise.

"We should be skirting the Snake Nest later today," Hiron said. "Is there anything we should do about that?"

Tsi pondered as she chewed on a corner of soggy protein square.

"Have you run a diagnostic on the scanners lately?"

"Wylla said something about it. Apparently we're still getting a lot of interference, and the ship's internal scanners keep cropping up errors."

"Probably just some damage from the asteroid debris," Tsi said. "It's not unusual for material to get caught on the ship. It can play havoc for a while, but as we maneuver it should work itself loose."

"She said something about that too. I guess our weight ratio is a little off. Probably just forgot to compensate for the beacon."

"I'll tell her about it when she wakes up," Tsi said. "Or I suppose we could run a calibration ourselves."

"Oh, uh, sure," Hiron said. "You know, I can, uh, I can probably do it by myself if there's anything else you've got to take care of."

Tsi smirked, remembering that Enlil was alone in the cockpit right now. There was no hiding the fact that the poor boy was smitten with her. She knew Enlil was both too old for him and too worldly, but she couldn't see any harm in it. It would free her to work on the beacon and make sure it was in top shape.

"Alright," she said. "You work on the scanner calibration today. Don't let Enlil give you anything to drink though, you hear? She's a bad influence."

Hiron laughed.

"Didn't you take me to a bar first thing on Salvation?" he said.

"I'm a perfect role-model," Tsi replied, feigning indignation. "Enlil is trouble. Completely different!"

"Sure," Hiron said, strapping on his crutches and clambering up the steps to the cockpit.

Tsi was alone in the galley after that, and so she slowly finished her meal, thinking on the day to come. They weren't out of the woods yet, but they had made steady progress. Provided the Guraggan didn't catch them, and the Deep Station Clans weren't on the prowl, they might just make it to Chalakhat in one piece. Then the real trouble would start.

"Switching to manual," Enlil said, taking hold of the controls and slowly angling the ship's thrusters downwards.

She'd slept well the night before. Something about having a whole, uninterrupted sleep-shift to herself in her bunk had done her body wonders. The ship wasn't huge, but everyone had somehow managed to get their own quarters. The last freighter she'd been on had slept three to a room. They'd been hot-bunking it too, so her cot had always smelled like someone else.

The controls in her hands felt smooth and natural. She'd been born to fly the depths, and Tsi's ship seemed almost like it was custom made for her. The control panel was intuitive, she didn't doubt that she could train somebody like the kid to pilot this thing in under a week.

Most of the crew was in the cockpit now, taking up what had become their customary positions. Tsi was in what passed for a captain's chair, Hiron and Wylla sitting to one side of her, the machine lolling in the same place it had strapped itself to when they escaped the Guraggan.

She wasn't sure if Strongmind was dead or alive. It didn't respond to people talking to it most of the time. Tsi had said something about keeping it on minimal power to protect it from radiation spikes.

That was a hazard she'd grown up around. Protecting electronics against it was such a second nature to her that it hadn't occurred to her the drone could be vulnerable. Then again, who ever had designed Strongmind's ridiculous body probably hadn't expected it to go on deep-space missions.

"The Snake Nest is about… twenty k-kliks off," Hiron said.

"Power's good," Tsi said. "Fuel reserve holding at thirty percent. Why don't you show us what you can do, Enlil?"

"That a challenge?"

She pitched the ship downwards, hurtling through the dark. Their port screen had a good view of the Snake Nest: a small ball of white-blue gas, trails of vaporous crystal particulate leaking away from it as they passed. A bolt of bright blue energy suddenly writhed out from it, coiling in their direction before it dissipated. The screen blurred briefly before returning to normal, and she heard Hiron gasp.

"Is that thing alive?" he asked. "It seemed like it was reaching for us…"

"Who the fuck knows?" Enlil said.

Wylla was still bleary-eyed. She'd drawn the short straw and taken a shift while everyone else was sleeping, but now she seemed wide awake, fixated on the Snake Nest.

"I've seen something like that before," Wylla murmured. "This ship doesn't have any probes does it? I'd like to take a closer look…"

"No," Tsi said. "This isn't an exploration vessel. Don't worry, I'm sure some day you'll have a chance to come back here and study to your heart's content."

Enlil almost laughed at the idiocy of that idea. There was no explaining it to outsiders. They saw something like a Kerenkov Serpent or one of the old hulks, and everything terrible about the Poison Suns just faded away. Suddenly they were all curious children again.

"Alright, I've locked our course in," she said. "I'm going to put us on minimal power. If we run silent, it'll take about three more hours before we've cleared the mass plane."

"Good," Tsi said. "I don't want anyone noticing us if we can help it."

"No active scans either," Enlil said. "Don't want the Rock-Drinkers coming down on us."

"Rock-Drinkers?" Wylla asked.

"Deep-Station Clans," Tsi offered. "They're... not kind to outsiders. Their culture is Anthropophagic."

"They *eat* people?" Hiron asked incredulously.

"Sometimes," Enlil said. "They take ships intact as they can. Their stations aren't sophisticated, like Salvation. So, when they take a ship, if there's too many crew to be useful, well... no sense in wasting good meat, right?"

"Makes sense," the Bondsman said from the back of the cockpit.

Enlil cackled at the look on Hiron's face, and noted with some satisfaction that Wylla looked ill as well. Maybe they would think twice about coming back to this system once they'd left, after all.

"Alright," Tsi said. "We'll be practically flying blind for a while. We'll take it in shifts to help Enlil up here, but if everything goes to plan, things should stay quiet. Hiron, you want the first pass?"

"Sure!" the boy said.

Tsi signaled to Wylla, and they left with the Bondsman, leaving just Enlil and Hiron alone with Strongmind's inert frame. The kid had spent the last day shift hanging around with her, messing with the scanner system. Enlil wasn't much of a hand at scanner work beyond the basics, so she had appreciated the help. He was eager to please. She wondered how much work she could fob off on him today.

Enlil put her boots up on the console and leaned back. She had slept well the last night, but she could always sleep more.

"You, uh, need me to do anything?" Hiron asked.

"Yup," she said. "You got your console hooked into the piloting controls?"

"Uh, I can. I think every station is interlinked in this system, you just have to route controls."

"Good. You keep an eye on things. Anything weird comes up on the proximity sensors, you make a course correction. Can you handle that?"

"I... think so."

"Okay, just do that and track our fuel expenditures," Enlil said shutting her eyes. "An' kid?"

"Yeah?"

"Do it quietly."

In her quarters, Lady Ornicht was remembering. The wires had slipped into their familiar places beneath her eyes, electronic tendrils linking with the implants in her brain. The process was painful, but seamless. She had tried other ways of remembering. Some were less discomforting, but there was always a layer of unreality, as if she was watching a screen, not living it again. Besides that, Ornicht liked the pain. It seemed a fair price for going back.

In her memory, she was twenty years old, standing on the deck of a Kiosan Cruiser called *Valiant*. An aspirational name, and one that her crew had lived up to. This was in a time just before the Janissaries had been created, and so Ornicht had slaughtered her way through drones and ordinary men, neither flesh nor metal strong enough to withstand her.

Their bodies were scattered all around. A few survivors cowered in a corner where the Battle Serfs had herded them. She walked among the dead, blood lapping at her boots in the eerie pattern that artificial gravity always produced. She had begun to prefer blades over killing at a distance. The Kiosan's armor and personal shields had improved, and at this time in the war, it had been best and surest to close with the enemy and drive a sword into their throats.

"The bridge is ours," a voice spoke into her ear, the guttural sound of her cousin Intoch.

In the present, Intoch was long dead, but now he was alive, and she longed to see him. They had been sparring partners when she was a child, and she still thought of him fondly. She tried to leave the hangar, wishing to see his face one more time. She could not move though, only observe her old actions. On this day, she had not gone to see Intoch, to congratulate him on his victory.

In fact, as she recalled, she had been quite jealous of him. She and her retinue had fought hard, but he had taken the glory of the victory. Even now, she felt a little twinge of resentment at how the day had been remembered, but she fought it down.

It was good to remember Intoch. This was the last time the two had fought side by side. After the victory, she had spent the rest of the day brooding in her quarters while the other warriors toasted his health and sang songs of his triumph. Within a year, a Janissary had crushed his skull.

Throaty cheers and war whoops sounded from among her comrades in the hangar. Even the Chem-Thralls became briefly excited, before lulling back into their passive, post-combat trance. Ornicht did not join them, then or now. She was too busy searching among the bodies.

"This one!" someone called to her, and she hastily made her way over. It was another Guraggan warrior, Chergis of House Sutaine who had signaled her, and she stopped short of where the woman crouched over a twitching Kiosan.

"Still alive?" Ornicht asked.

Chergis raised her visor, and grinned at Ornicht, before roughly pulling the man's helmet away. He had a handsome face: a strong jaw and a heavy brow. A cut had opened over one glassy eye, and his nose was was broken. He coughed. Thick ropes of crimson dribbled from his lips. *Alive*, Ornicht thought with some satisfaction.

"He's the one that gave you that," Chergis said, pointing to a plasma scar on Ornicht's breastplate. It had been no more than a glancing blow. A full hit would have killed her.

"You brought him down?" Ornicht asked.

"No," Cherghis admitted. "One of my Thralls. He was very fierce, killed three before his weapon ran dry, and they were able to get close enough to crack his armor. Hasn't made a sound all this time."

Cherghis stuck a finger into one of the man's open wounds. He winced, and light suddenly returned to his eyes. Ornicht could see tears forming, but he made no sound besides a sharp intake of breath.

"A good specimen," she admitted.

"Yours, if you want him."

Cherghis was giving her a faintly sinister smile. This was always the way with the Sutaine: their gifts were valuable, but they had some hidden cost. Ornicht had been young then, still with so much to learn, and far too eager to prove herself.

"I do," Ornicht said, staring down coldly at the wounded Kiosan.

She reached down towards him, saw the rage in his one good eye—

"My lady, a signal has been received."

It was Skyme, speaking to her in the present. Reluctantly,

Ornicht removed the cables from beneath her eyes. She blinked hard, willing herself to see the here and now. Her vision was still blurred, but she could make out her chamber, see the trophies on her walls, and the tray of medicines her Physician had left beside her chair. She grabbed a syringe of silvery liquid, closed her eyes, and injected herself with it. The drug hit her bloodstream, and she shuddered. When she opened her eyes again, her vision was crystal clear and focused.

"Speak, Skyme," she said.

"Theta-90 has given us positional data on the target vessel," Skyme continued. "With your permission, I have continued pursuit, though our attempts to correct for local conditions have been... less than successful."

"If you can see them, follow them," she said. "Let me know when we get within weapon range."

"Would you like me to send orders to Theta-90 to disable the vessel?"

"Has it achieved full system-infiltration yet?"

"No, my lady. Per your programming, it has pursued subtle points of egress. It estimates another seventy two hours before full root control."

Theta-90 was a powerful weapon, but even it was not invulnerable. The enemy possessed a sophisticated AI. She was not certain her old friend could defeat it in electronic warfare if it was detected.

"Hmm... we cannot risk it. If Theta-90 is exposed, it might damage our prize unnecessarily and reveal our position too early," Ornicht said. "Keep it on alert."

"There is another item, my lady," Skyme said apologetically. "We have detected three other vessels. They appear to be... shadowing our target. One is keeping its signature lower than the others, I believe it is attempting to get ahead of the target."

"Fascinating," Ornicht said. "Increase speed, and observe very carefully. I want to know the moment one of them attempts to interfere with our prey."

"Your will is my will."

The comms system clicked back into silence. Lady Ornicht rubbed her hands together. Other ships? She knew Noxia was infested with petty pirates, it was practically the system's only export. They added an element of uncertainty to the chase, but she was confident that she could overcome this. No one would take that ship. No one but her.

Disassembled, the Repeater looked completely harmless. It was true of most weapons in this state, just a collection of springs and slides, a charging handle. The metal curve of the trigger was the only thing to an untrained eye that revealed what the weapon might be. Tsi picked it up and began to clean it, delicately and surely with an oiled cloth.

The pistol was a rugged weapon: she'd dragged it through filthy tunnels and exposed it to the void and it still fired straight and true. Still, she cleaned it and tested it whenever she got the chance. She looked down the barrel after drawing a piece of cloth through it. No obstructions, but it had suffered over the years. The metal was worn, weakening. She would need to replace it soon.

Her armory was a small, cramped compartment, lit only by the white glow of her work bench. The printer sat in one corner, long since out of the raw materials she would need to print new weapons and ammunition. She added that to the list of things that needed repair and resupply. The Guraggan had looted most of her stash of weapons, and the wall above the work bench looked strangely bare.

Tsi was no idle collector, every gun and blade she owned had been acquired for a specific purpose, but over the decades the Repeater had become the only weapon she truly relied on. There was a meditative, reassuring aspect to keeping her equipment in top form. She knew consciously that the Repeater would work just as well if she had simply stuck it back in her holster after retaking the ship, but having the certainty of going over every millimeter of the weapon, ensuring each catch and slide still linked together the way it had the day it was made, helped her breath a little easier.

Slowly, she reassembled the pistol, each movement carefully rehearsed through years of practice until she finally locked the slide in place. She raised the gun, sighting an imaginary target on the wall, and pulled the trigger. A dry click was its response.

She began reloading a magazine with spare rounds she had hidden under her bunk. As she pressed each cartridge in, she felt the weight of the blue vial in her pocket. It would be a delicate balancing act, keeping this crew together. If the worst happened, she needed to be absolutely sure she had a working gun.

The cockpit was quiet except for Enlil's snores. Hiron had considered waking her, but she looked surprisingly peaceful, slumped back in the pilot's chair. Even the little string of drool coming out of her mouth reminded him more of his mother's puppy than anything else. Instead he had resolved himself to studying the scanners as intently as possible. They weren't that different from his astronomical equipment back home in principle, and even kept at the absolute minimum, on reception only, they still gave him a good idea of what was going on for thousands of kilometers in every direction.

He'd only had to make one minor course adjustment, when they'd come up on an asteroid about the size of a melon. There had been a moment of raw panic when he noticed it on the scanners, but, almost on instinct he had made the corrections. They had drifted past the little object without incident. Of course, it would have just bounced off the hull if he had done nothing, but Hiron couldn't help imagining a dozen nightmare scenarios where cascading disaster after disaster had overtaken the ship, all because he had failed to dodge one rock.

He flipped the screen to radiation detection. Noxia was a mass of exotic energy fields that made this kind of scanning all but useless, but he had started to find patterns in the gamma waves they received. The presence of the Snake Nest interfered even more, and he was about to switch away when he noticed something off.

There was a pair of repeating waves, all in the same spectrum. With the scanners on minimal power, he couldn't send an active pulse to determine more about them, so he had to rely on his naked eyes and the information they were receiving. Nevertheless, it was clear to him: two radiation sources, sending out steady pulses, almost, but not quite in unison.

Hiron drummed his fingers nervously. Was it his imagination? No, he saw the pattern repeat again. There was no denying that something else in the area was generating radiation, on a steady, regular wavelength. The kind an engine might make.

"Uh, Enlil?" he called softly.

Enlil snored.

"Enlil?" he repeated.

Enlil snored loudly.

"Enlil! Enlil, wake up!"

Enlil snapped forward with a snort, wiping her mouth and rounding on him with a glare.

"Fuck issit?" she said.

He gestured to his screen.

"Come look at this."

She stumbled over to him, yawning dramatically. Enlil leaned over his shoulder, peering at the screen. Then, she breathed a curse.

"Rock-drinkers," she said. "No doubt. Good catch, kid. Get Tsi on comms."

Hiron did as he was told, keying in Tsi's comm frequency. She responded with a curt "On my way" after he explained the situation. Enlil, in the meantime, had taken back the helm, and was easing the ship into a new flight path, using short, minimal bursts of the thrusters to correct their course.

"Should I power up the scanner? I mean, we can only guess at where they are right now," Hiron said.

"Nah, nah, not yet," Enlil replied. "We don't want them to know they've been marked."

Tsi arrived shortly thereafter, strapping her pistol to her waist. She sat down, crisply scanning her own screen as she did so.

"How close do we think they are?"

"Less than a k-klik," Hiron said. "We've got no way of pin-pointing them though."

"Boss, we burning?" Enlil asked.

Tsi rubbed her forehead. Hiron knew their stock of ammunition was low, and Tsi had said they should conserve as much fuel as possible.

"We burn now," Tsi said, "and they'll definitely catch up to us. But with the scanners on minimal they could be on top of us before we know it..."

"I say we burn hard," Enlil stated. "I can out-fly 'em, no question."

"But if we keep running silent they might let their guard down," Tsi countered. "We haven't given ourselves away yet."

"I think... I think I can get us a rough triangulation of their position," Hiron said. "I've got their radiation wavelength, whenever they adjust their engines I should be able to compare that to the length of time it took their last burst to be picked up, maybe get us a rough map."

"Fat chance they give us the time to work all that out," Enlil said.

"She's right," Tsi said grimly. "Even if Wylla was up here helping you, there's no way of guaranteeing we'll have the time to figure out where they are."

Hiron's heart sank. Of course, it was stupid of him to be offering advice. These two had practically lived their whole lives aboard starships. He had only gotten on board one last week.

"Alright, no use waiting around to die. Enlil, your wish is granted. Get us ready for an evasive course, I want us dancing like a drunk Sannatan. I'll prep weapons and lay in a firing solution. Keep an eye on those scanners," Tsi said. "We're going to need you tracking everything once we open ourselves up."

It took Hiron a moment to realize her last comment had been directed at him. He nodded vigorously, splitting the screen in front of him into four sections and preparing for a wide scan. He could track a broad spectrum of information and sort it rapidly this way. A machine like Strongmind would be far better suited to the job, but Hiron felt a small, absurd sense of gratitude that the machine was out of commission. He might get them all killed, but at least he had a chance to prove himself.

"Alright everyone," Tsi said. "Hard burn!"

The Noxian ships seemed to quiver in excitement when the prey fired its engines. Lady Ornicht knew it was only her imagination as she studied the scanner. They were merely making minor adjustments now that they realized their enemy could see them, but there was something about the movement of the craft that reminded her of a bird of prey. Her own totem animal, she had always admired the way the avian species studied their targets before striking swiftly and without remorse. The Noxians were no different. These ones did not waste any time on bravado or even calls for surrender; they instantly rushed to close the distance.

She sat back in her chair, content to watch for now. With any luck, her prey would expend the rest of its resources, and it would be an easy matter to sweep in from above and take them all at once.

They were matching course and velocity steadily, Tsi noticed, as she ran through options for a firing solution. At this distance the best chance would be either wide range explosives, or a directed energy weapon. Unfortunately, Tsi didn't have any beam weapons on her ship, and missiles were in direly short supply. They still had enough ammo left in the mass drivers to put up a fight when the enemy got close, but that would depend on not getting crippled before then.

"Launching one," Tsi said.

She tracked the missile on her scanner as its icon dropped behind them, then flared briefly before disappearing. Unfortunately, the two pursuing ships still pinged back strong.

"N-not reading any effect," Hiron stammered. "Looks like our shot detonated too early."

Fighting in space at this range was never a sure thing, even if they had had the luxury of a weapons-AI. The only solace Tsi could take was that the Rock-Drinkers had to deal with the same hazards she did.

As if on cue, a bright light flared across their screen. A beam weapon, off target by only a few kilometers. She knew the Rock-Drinkers wanted to take the ship intact, but they wouldn't hesitate to breach the hull and let everyone die of vacuum exposure.

"Dammit, they're out for blood," Enlil muttered. "You ever think about flying a less fancy ship? These bastards would have given up a long time ago."

"Keep steady," Tsi said. "We'll clear the mass plane soon enough, then we can Slip."

"But we can't Slip with them chasing us!"

"I know," Tsi said. "That's why we've got to kill some of them first... Take us port, thirty degrees."

"Why?" Enlil shot back.

"Just do it!"

The ship lurched as Enlil obeyed, altering their course. Tsi locked a point in space, and prepped a missile. She calculated the delay, programmed it into the missile, waited a half second longer, then fired.

The missile dropped back behind them, its icon dashing across the screen. One of their pursuers had moved directly into its path, and too late the Rock-Drinker realized Tsi' ploy. The missile exploded, and she saw the enemy ship veer wildly off course.

"Hit!" Hiron shouted. "Looks-looks like you got their motive systems! They're breaking off!"

"Burn hard, Enlil!" Tsi said.

Only one ship wouldn't risk a direct pursuit. The Rock-Drinkers might fire a few more blasts out of pride, but they'd never try to take her on in a fair fight. Tsi was just beginning to relax when something struck their starboard side. A slow mass round had slipped right through their shields and smashed against the hull. The armor held, but only just.

"The hell was that?!" Enlil shouted.

"There's another one!" Hiron said, voice shrill with panic. "A third ship, it's cut us off on the port side!"

"Evasive action!"

Enlil was already rolling the ship, but it was no use. Three beams lanced across the hull, ripping up armor, sending a shock through the internal systems. Tsi quickly entered a series of commands, locking a pair of bulkheads that had just de-pressurized.

"Engine's damaged," Hiron said. "Uh, it looks like that first shot did something to the shields—"

"I'm trying to fly here, kid!" Enlil snapped.

The ship rumbled and shook again, as another mass round struck the hull.

"Cut burn, but keep us dancing," Tsi said. "Let them catch up."

"You blow an airlock?" Enlil shouted. "They're gonna be on top of us any second!"

"I know," Tsi said. "That's our best chance to hit them. Just keep us flying, I'll handle the rest."

Wylla had been sitting with Furner Ketsu when the ship had suddenly jumped to combat speed. She and the aged Noxian had become friends oddly quickly. He had been vividly describing to her how to jury rig a sub-light engine, interspersed with recollections of his past romantic dalliances that could generously be described as "unvarnished."

"You said we just passed a Snake Nest?" Furner asked. "That'll be the Rock-Drinkers."

"Enlil mentioned them. Should we be... concerned??"

"If they get close enough," he said. "They're decent pilots, good shots, but it's when they breach that we should really worry. I'd get into a suit if I was you."

Wylla looked down at her clothes, realizing that her long dress wouldn't be any use if they lost pressure and life support. She'd seen emergency suits near one of the escape pods, but if she moved it would mean leaving Furner alone as the ship pitched and shook. And there was the problem of getting a one-legged man into a suit as well, if she could find one for him.

"Don't wait around," Furner said. "We might not have a lot of time."

"We should secure you first," Wylla said. "If we lose gravity,"

"I've got worse problems than a bump on my head would be," the old man smiled. "Just don't forget about me, huh?"

"I won't," Wylla replied.

She left the room swiftly as she could, making for the nearest escape pod. It was down a narrow ladder she took three rungs at a time. She nearly fell when the ship was hit again, sending shock waves through the rungs. Checking a wall console, she saw there was some sort of damage to the circuits, and a warning light let her know that the top deck had been sealed. Not good. There had already been a breach, and one large enough to trigger the ship's preservation systems. So far nothing had caught fire, at least.

The lights suddenly cut out, replaced by a dim red glow. Whoever was in the cockpit was redirecting power. Fortunately for Wylla, she'd spent years in the dim confines of a Guraggan ship, and so she picked her way down the hall easily until she found the escape pod. She opened an emergency panel to find a pair of 'skin suits': thin, flexible garments with detachable oxygen packs and hard, clear-visored helmets. She unceremoniously stripped down to her undergarments and pulled one of the suits on, one-leg at a time. She had finished zipping it up and checking the oxygen tank was full when she heard the Bondsman's voice.

"Going somewhere?" he said.

She looked up to see him, lit entirely in dim crimson. He looked for all the worlds like a demon, his snarling mask seeming to mock her, its fangs looking as if they glistened with blood. She did not have time to be afraid of him.

She pulled the second suit out of the emergency panel, and tossed it at him. The Bondsman caught it instinctively, then looked back to her, tilting his head slightly in what she was sure was confusion.

"Come on," she said. "We've got get Furner into that in case there's a full hull breach."

She brushed past him while he mutely watched. She paused at the base of the ladder, and looked back at Tenlok expectantly.

"Are you coming or not?" she said.

Tenlok folded the suit under his arm and fell in behind her. The two climbed back to the main deck and made their way silently to the medical bay, where Furner was waiting for them. His eyes went wide at the sight of the Bondsman, but he made no comment.

"Alright, Furner," Wylla said. "Come on, we'll help you. Hold on to his shoulder."

She helped Furner out of the bed. Fortunately he was already in his undergarments, and so they awkwardly wriggled the suit on to him. Wylla noted with some surprise the great care the Bondsman seemed to take in supporting the old man, but as soon as the job was done, he stepped away quickly.

"Get him to one of the escape pods," Tenlok said. "You two'll be safest there."

"Come with us," Wylla said. "You're not going to do much good up here."

"Can't," Tenlok replied. "Have to keep an eye on Tsi. Get down to the pods, there's comms in there. You'll know if you have to launch."

Wylla studied the Bondsman for a moment, but his posture gave away nothing.

"I think he's got the right idea," Furner grimaced. "Come on, I can hobble alright on this leg if you support my other side."

"Alright," Wylla said.

She helped Furner from the room, but when she glanced over her shoulder, she saw the Bondsman was not watching them go. Instead he was leaning over the auto-doc, putting commands into it. From across the room it was impossible to tell, but it looked like he was running a diagnostic.

Furner groaned in pain, and Wylla strengthened her grip on him. She could puzzle out Tenlok's behavior later. For now, she had to keep Furner safe.

"Our shields are steady, but you have to keep us moving," Tsi said.

Enlil didn't reply, only clenched her jaw and input a new series of rapid course corrections and feints. They'd cut fuel expenditures to let the Rock-Drinkers close, but without maximum thrust her movements were sluggish and predictable. They'd taken a pounding, and every time Enlil tried to compensate, it seemed like the Rock-Drinkers had them zeroed in again.

"Flatten us out," Tsi said.

Red warning lights were flaring all across Enlil's screens. Fuel was low, engines damaged, and they'd just detected multiple locks. She wanted to curse Tsi, but following her guidance had gotten her this far. Enlil rolled the ship one last time, and steadied their course. Glancing at her positional data, she could see the enemy was practically on top of them. She only hoped a few bursts of mass-driver fire would be enough to drive them off. It seemed like a lot to bet on one salvo.

"New contact!" Hiron shouted.

He tapped furiously at his console, and Enlil's positional data updated. Another craft was moving in on an attack vector, headed straight towards them.

"Their friend decided to give us another try," Enlil said.

Weapons fire warnings flashed on the screen, and Enlil suddenly saw one of the Rock-Drinkers disappear. The third craft had fired on it and destroyed it in a single salvo.

"No," Tsi said. "That's the Guraggan. They're still pursuing us."

"Nice to be popular, I guess," Enlil said.

"New plan! Burn us hard and fast the second that Rock-Drinker breaks contact. I'm prepping the Slip Drive. Disengaging safeties."

"What?!" Enlil said. "But if we Slip and either of those ships are still close—"

"We might tear ourselves apart," Tsi admitted. "But it's our best shot."

"Remind me never to gamble with you," Enlil said. "I'd make too much money."

"First target crippled," Skyme said, sounding a little too pleased with himself.

A few days as pilot and chief weapons officer had allowed a modicum of smugness to creep into the little man's persona, something which Lady Ornicht did not care for. She was watching a visual simulation of the battle, her own *Dragon's Tooth* soaring high above while the squat, ugly ships of the Noxians pursued Tsi's ship below. This would have been a time when a wing of fighters might have proved useful, but her days of traveling aboard a carrier or any other warship were long behind her. No, this victory had to be hers, and hers alone.

"Lock second target," she said. "Optimum range in ten."

"It will be done."

Ornicht did not have to give the signal. Exactly ten seconds later, Skyme triggered a salvo of energy fire. Blue light shot through the darkness, scoring a direct hit on the second Noxian ship and send it hurtling off course.

"Power surge detected," Skyme said. "They are returning fire."

The whole ship shook suddenly, as a solid round from the Noxian craft slipped through their shields and smashed into the hull. Warning lights flared across all of the consoles. With a gesture, a holograph appeared in front of Ornicht, giving her an instant damage report.

She let out a growl of frustration. The round had damaged a vital circuit-breaker, and was causing a cascade of failures. She had not expected a bunch of primitives to have such potent weaponry. Her technicians were already scrambling to compensate, but there was one system in particular she saw flare out and die. Her Slip Drive.

"Return fire!" she spat. "Now!"

"Firing second salvo," Skyme said. "Direct hit. They are breaking contact."

Ornicht hesitated for a moment, her hunter's instincts longing to pursue the Noxian pirates and make them pay for the audacity of firing on her craft. Suddenly, the prey ship's engines burst into life and the craft shot away from them. It was close to maximum burn for a ship that size, tearing through the darkness at an incredible velocity. Ornicht snarled in frustration.

"Match speed!" she roared, slamming her fist into the arm of her chair. "Ignore the Noxians, keep our primary target in sight!"

The *Dragon's Tooth* plunged after her prey, putting everything they had into pure speed. Her foe was still twisting and maneuvering, fearing her guns. Ornicht smiled. That would slow them down long enough for her to catch them and cripple them too. If she had the time, she might loot the Noxian ships once she was done. Their crews seemed competent, and they might make useful Thralls.

"We are closing," Skyme said. "My lady, our opponent seems to be charging their Slip drive…"

"Impossible. Scan them again."

Ornicht's fingers clenched. If they Slipped now, she'd be too close. Her mass-dispersion field would tear them apart the second they entered the Slip. It was suicide. With her own drive damaged, she could not pursue them, either.

"Scan returned. They have… they have definitely charged their drive, my Lady," Skyme said. "Shall I fire on them?"

Ornicht scowled in concentration. The prize was slipping from her grasp. She had fought so hard, sacrificed so *much*. This was her chance, her moment. If she returned to the fleet empty-handed, she would be scorned, ridiculed as a useless old woman, unable to bring in even one errant ship.

But the Bykon was on that craft. Her Hunting Hound had served her faithfully, guided her through many battles. Ornicht knew she would never find another intellect to match hers. Then there was the prize of the ship itself, armored in an alloy that could turn back even advanced solid rounds, an engine as swift as her own, maneuverable. It was a fierce little craft, and Ornicht would be lauded if she could bring it back in one piece.

Fire suddenly ripped across their hull. Like a fool, she had fallen for their ploy, letting herself get within the reach of their short range guns. Traveling straight and swift, it had been obvious to her prey how to counter her movements and anticipate them. The shots ripped into her hull, piercing it in some places and causing warnings to blare into life all about the command deck.

She was about to snarl the command to return fire, when Skyme spoke.

"Incoming message from Theta-90," Skyme said. "Message reads: Slip coordinates deciphered. How proceed?"

Ornicht smiled. Of course. Theta-90. How faithful, how tireless.

The machine would do what she could not. It would save this entire mission from becoming a disaster. She had been reluctant to unleash it, for like all war-drones it tended towards destruction that could be... *excessive*. Still, under the right circumstances, the right parameters, it could safely bring the ship to her without risking its complete destruction. It might mean sacrificing her precious Bykon, but if it was that or failure...

"Transmit back: No action until post-Slip translation. Then, terminate all hostiles. Cripple transport vehicle but keep intact. Recapture subject Wylla Laran-Se. Await retrieval. Confirm received and understood."

Skyme typed the message in, and pressed the command to send it. There would be a delay of a few moments at the distance they were at, but Ornicht relaxed back into her chair, a confident smile on her face. She had prepared for this.

"They're pulling back!" Hiron shouted. "They're pulling back!"

Tsi breathed a sigh of relief. She'd put everything they had out in a single burst, save one final missile. Short range mass drivers were only really of use against pirates much of the time, but the Guraggan were flying blind in unfamiliar space. She'd bluffed them, let them think she might have something more up her sleeve by filling the space behind them with fire, let the shock of a few hits convince her enemy that it was better to circle back and plot a more cautious attack.

Now they were free.

"How's our mass scan look?" she asked.

"Ten minutes and we're clean," Hiron said, the relief clear in his voice.

"Burn us hard, Enlil," she commanded. "We'll refuel when we get out of the Slip."

"You got it, boss," Enlil said.

There followed ten long minutes of scrutinizing the scanners, but the Guraggan did not pursue them, having elected instead to break off and lick their wounds. By now they would have realized Tsi was preparing to jump into the Slip, but there was no chance they could catch up to her.

She called down to the med bay, and was surprised to hear Tenlok respond to her.

"We're about to Slip," Tsi said. "I thought everyone should know."

"Made it, huh?" Tenlok replied. "I'll tell the other two."

He and Wylla arrived a few minutes later, Furner Ketsu carried on their shoulders between them. The old pirate looked around the cockpit. She knew some bitterness must have lingered in him, but there was an amused look on his face as he noted all the warning lights on the consoles. If there was one thing a Noxian could appreciate, it was a hair's breadth escape.

"Sounded like hell from down there," he said.

"We managed," Tsi replied nonchalantly.

Furner nodded.

"Well, we gonna wait for them to run us down or what?" Enlil asked.

"Alright," Tsi said. "Let's Slip."

She pressed the last few commands, and the ship glided into the Slip, away from the light of the Poison Suns.

Ornicht had sat quietly on the bridge for hours now. The shift had changed, and Skyme had knelt before her and begged her approval that he rest. She granted his request with a flick of her wrist while the second shift took over, made up of servants she was less familiar with. They busied themselves about the bridge, but in truth she was barely aware of them.

Theta-90 had sent one last message before her prey had escaped into the Slip. She read the message one more time, just to assure herself it was real. It simply stated:

"EXTERMINATE HOSTILES. DISABLE AND SECURE TRANSPORT. RECAPTURE SUBJECT: WYLLA LARAN-SE. AWAIT RETRIEVAL. CONFIRMED AND UNDERSTOOD."

Ornicht smiled.

She had won.

PART 3

CHALAKHAT

CHAPTER 26

The darkness of Slip-space surrounded the ship. Light could not pierce this medium. Looking directly into the Slip, it was easy to imagine one was going blind. Hiron had heard stories of people looking at it and seeing all sorts of strange things: ghost ships, dead spacers crawling across the hull, star-demons. Some said you could catch glimpses of your own future, too. Of all the tall-tales, that one had always seemed to have the most truth to him. After all, they were in a place outside of normal time and space. Who was to say there wasn't some forward-echo of themselves just ahead? Maybe if you looked into the darkness long enough, you could see it.

Hiron didn't see anything through the transparent canopy, though. He grew bored of staring at nothing, and closed the blast cover, turning the cockpit dark. There wasn't much need for a pilot right now. He'd mostly come up here just to keep Strongmind company, and because there was precious little he could do on the rest of the ship. The machine had greeted him in its awkward, polite way, but it clearly wasn't interested in talking to him. It had even turned down his offer to run a battle-simulation. He wondered if Strongmind was mad at him, then dismissed the idea as ridiculous. It couldn't get mad. Even if it could, he hadn't done anything to upset it. If anything, Strongmind should apologize for threatening *him*, but Hiron quickly dismissed that thought, too. Secretly, he was thankful for their confrontation. It was important to remember that Strongmind wasn't human.

"I'm, uh, going to take a walk," Hiron said, getting up from his chair and strapping on his braces. "Just call me on the comms if you need anything."

"Acknowledged," Strongmind said.

Hiron left the cockpit behind, and traveled down to the galley. It was an utter mess from the night before, the second of Tsi's "celebrations" that he'd witnessed. He didn't begrudge her having a good time, he knew that different people handled stressful situations differently. For someone who seemed so reserved and competent she didn't seem to care at all that the galley now looked like the aftermath of a battle. He sighed, realizing he had found something useful to do, and began tidying up.

First he collected all the globes, mugs and cups that weren't broken and put them in the cleaner. Then he gathered the ones that had been broken, of which their were many, and tossed them into the recycler. From the look of it, at one point Tsi had had some kind of mug tossing contest with the rest of the crew. Hiron had gone to bed before that happened, though he dimly remembered waking up to raucous shouting and the sounds of something breaking.

Finally, he took a towel soaked in cleaning fluid and began wiping down every surface. He came to the table, and, after clearing it off, pressed a button on the side to slide it back into the wall. As the table did so, it revealed Enlil, snoring softly on the floor. Her jump suit was stained all down the front with spilled beer, and her hair was a knotty mess as usual.

Remembering she was close to impossible to wake, he gently prodded her with one of his crutches, then a little harder when she didn't respond. The third poke woke her up, and she glared sleepily at him and slapped his crutch away.

"What are you doing down there?" he asked.

"Sleepin' it off, fuck's it look like," she grumbled, then rolled onto her side.

"Come on," Hiron said. "Let's get you into your bunk."

It was an awkward task, helping Enlil up to her feet and getting one of her arms around his shoulders, but with a great deal of difficulty and sleepily muttered curses from Enlil, he did manage to do it. Together they shambled down a flight of steps to the quarters Enlil had claimed. The room was cramped, like every other set of quarters on this ship, and it still had a thin layer of dust on some objects. Her cot was out, the blankets in disarray. Hiron helped Enlil lay down, then went back up to the galley and got a glass of water. He returned to find she had already pulled the covers up to her neck, and was groggily staring at the ceiling. He set the water on a stand by her bed, and turned to go, but hesitated for a moment.

"I never thanked you for saving the ship," he said.

"Prefer you didn't."

"Why... why not?"

"Just don't like being thanked, is all," she said.

"Oh. Well, um, I got you some water..."

Enlil rolled over and grabbed the cup, drinking greedily from it before rolling back onto her side. She began breathing shallowly, her chest rising and falling in a slow rhythm beneath the sheets. Soon enough, he was sure she was fast asleep. Hiron shuffled out of the room as quietly as he could, and closed the door behind him.

Tsi had risen early, relative to her own personal clock. She still felt exhausted from the last few days. She'd handled a few of her chores, checked in on Furner, who was still chuckling at the crude prosthetic she had rigged up for him, and Enlil, who's hand was now fully healed. Tsi had never considered a career as a physician, but the rough life she'd led these forty years on the frontier had found her patching herself and others up more often than not. She'd make a decent doctor at some backwater port.

Now, she had Strongmind in the workshop, shifting gears effortlessly from repairing humans to repairing a machine. He lay on a table, his pants rolled up to expose the damage to his legs. Part of his skull was opened up and connected to a tablet so that she could read diagnostic results directly. His new arm seemed to have interfaced with the rest of his systems well, and as near as she could tell there wasn't any left-over radiation damage from flying through Noxia.

"How are the legs?" she asked as she examined his knees. She could see where a solid round had torn through his calf, and on the other leg a laser had fried the joint.

"Internal repair systems are adequate for current function state," Strongmind said.

"Hmmph, you didn't tell me how bad they got your knee," she said. "Honestly, I can't leave you alone for a minute, can I?"

"The duration of our separation was considerably longer than one minute," Strongmind replied.

"I know," she smiled. If the machine understood the gesture, he made no response.

Tsi got out some repair tools, and began to work on the fried joint, clearing away the scoring and reconnecting circuits and synthetic tissue. It was delicate work, almost as delicate as with a human, but at least Strongmind didn't complain. Or require anesthetic. After all, if she screwed it up too badly she could always just hack the limb off and replace it.

"How do you feel about our current destination?" Strongmind asked.

Tsi glanced up at him. Face slack, Strongmind was staring placidly at the ceiling. She turned away to grab another tool as she replied.

"If it's where we have to go, it's where we have to go."

"Chalakhat does not create an intense emotional response in you?"

"Of course it does," Tsi said quietly.

"Do you estimate that may impact our tactical performance?"

"Alright then, go ahead," Tsi said.

She set her tools aside, rolled her chair back and crossed her arms. The machine sat up and looked at her quizzically.

"Come on," she said. "You only ask me about my feelings if you want something, or you're going to lecture me. Which is it going to be?"

"Do you expect your emotional state to impact tactical performance?" Strongmind asked again.

"Doesn't it always?" Tsi said. "Or did you not happen to notice how humans spend a lot of time screaming, shouting and crying whenever we're in danger?"

"You are being deliberately obtuse as a defense mechanism. Would you be more comfortable if you were inebriated? I can acquire alcohol."

Tsi shot Strongmind a dark look, knowing even as she did so that he wouldn't react.

"I don't want to go to Chalakhat, if that's your question," she said. "But we have to. So that's the end of it. If we get into anymore trouble, I'll deal with it."

"I see," Strongmind said. "What is your assessment of the crew? While I was in minimal power mode, my ability to evaluate them was limited."

"Enlil's a good pilot," Tsi said. "She'll be useful for a long time.

Furner's still getting used to only having one leg, but he already knows the ship in and out and he's a hell of an engineer, so he'll keep us flying. I know he'd rather not be here, but until we can take him back to Noxia he'll be helpful. Hiron—"

"I have already evaluated Hiron."

"Okay then," Tsi said. "Well, Wylla's done alright by us so far."

"The prisoner?"

"She's not our prisoner, Strongmind," Tsi said. "You know that."

The machine said nothing in response, only returned her stare with his dead eyes. Tsi realized she'd put off fixing his face for far too long. She didn't find talking to half a grinning skull particularly phasing, but the rest of the crew might object. Particularly since they weren't as familiar with Strongmind's "eccentricities" as she was.

"Anyway, Wylla's been extremely valuable. She's confirmed a lot of intelligence, she knows how to work in a medical bay, and I think she might be a savant. It'll be very helpful having someone who's current on Guraggan House politics on our side."

"She is still a potential liability."

Tsi shrugged.

"Who on this crew isn't?"

"You have not given your evaluation of the Bondsman yet," Strongmind said.

"He's... under control."

"Is he another potential liability?"

Tsi shut her eyes. Just thinking about how she had gotten Tenlok "under control" made her feel ashamed. It wasn't as if she had any other choice. It was the surest method of keeping herself and everyone else safe. She reminded herself that what was at stake here was worth a lot more than her own personal moral code. What a well-rehearsed little mantra that was: evil now for the sake of a greater good later.

"Tenlok is dangerous," Tsi said. "Extremely dangerous. He almost killed me when we first fought. His armor is at least a class four, and I think he's been augmented to the point where he could go toe-to-toe with a Lakhan Drone. So yes, we should watch him. But for now, I've got him completely under control."

"How?"

"Heart-link sensor," Tsi said. "If I die, he dies."

"Efficient," Strongmind said. "An effective and less expensive replacement for chemical bonding. I advise finding a means of expending him as quickly as possible."

"I'm not killing him," Tsi replied. "I couldn't have retaken the ship without him. I owe him. We all do."

"In your own words, he also attempted to murder you," Strongmind pointed out.

"Well, if I held a grudge against everyone who tries to do that... I feel like I'd have to go after half the human race."

"An extremely rational attitude," Strongmind said. Tsi noticed the faintest hint of approval in his voice as he lay back down on the table.

"I have finished my assessment. Please continue with repairs."

"Sure," Tsi said, picking her tools back up and bending over him. "You're the boss."

"I just don't understand it."

Enlil rolled her eyes. The kid was doing that thing again, where he exclaimed aloud, and expected her to respond. He had a lot to learn about crewing a ship. Living in tight confines with someone for weeks, possibly months on end without a station-call meant that all true spacers respected the golden virtues of silence.

"I really don't," Hiron muttered, shaking his head at the screen in front of him.

Enlil sighed, spun her chair around and got up. She sauntered over to him and leaned over to look at his console.

"What don't ya get?" she asked. "Looks standard to me."

"Well, our internal scanners are still acting up. We're registering an excess of mass."

"Maybe you missed the part where we got shot a buncha times and flew through a debris cloud?" Enlil asked sarcastically.

"Yeah, but this, this is almost as much as a cargo pod or something."

"Rocks cling to the hull sometimes. Some of the stuff floating out there's magnetic, radioactive, you name it. I don't know how many times I gotta tell you this, kid."

"Hmmph," Hiron grunted. "It just doesn't look right..."

Enlil had tried her best to be charitable with the kid, but if there was one thing that genuinely irked her, it was outsiders who thought they knew more about spacer's work than her. She didn't let herself get angry though. If the worst she had to deal with was some uppity dirt-foot, this would be one of the easiest trips she'd ever made.

"What about this?" he asked.

He'd pulled up another display on his screen. It was a recording of emanations from the ship. Most of them were standard scanning waves, radiation and heat from the engines. He had isolated and highlighted one though. For the second time, Enlil noted that the kid wasn't a half-bad scanner.

"What do you think that is?" she asked slowly.

"It looks like a transmission," Hiron said. "Coming from us."

"You call anybody?"

"No..." he said. "This was recorded back when we were still in real space."

"Uh huh," Enlil said. "Looks like somebody's been tattling to our friends out there. You see if you can dig up any more signals. I gotta talk to Tsi about this."

The pod drifted slowly through space, twin jets illuminating it in the dark as it drew closer and closer to the *Dragon's Tooth*. Lady Ornicht had spent a long time in a recuperative trance while her subordinates did the negotiating, but at last they had entered her chambers, grovelling apologies before reporting success. The Rock-Drinkers had surrendered.

Ultimately, she'd had to allow two of their badly damaged ships to flee back into the depths, searching for whatever asteroid bolt-hole they called home, but one craft was still in good condition, and so she had claimed it as her due. The pod would link with her ship shortly, and she awaited her 'guests' arrival while her retinue prepared her for face-to-face introductions.

She'd forgone full battle armor, instead electing a form-fitting *bulkchin* suit, concealed beneath a swirling cloak covered in golden patterns. The Physician had injected her with something to giver her face a healthy flush, and another mild stimulant had made her alert, her eyes focused and her mind quick to act. For a weapon she leaned upon a long blade-stave, the stylized lion head on its bottom end concealing a beam weapon. She twirled the stave experimentally, then rested it on her shoulder, striking a suitably casual pose. There was no need to impress these people with her ferocity, the weapons of the *Dragon's Tooth* had already done that. Now it was time to show them the face of their new master.

At last the airlock cycled, and the Rock-Drinkers made their entrance. They had to bow their heads as they crossed the threshold. All of them were incredibly tall, spindly creatures. Their bodies had been rendered selenitic from generations growing up under micro-gravity. Each wore a fully armored survival suit from which they took their names: their faces concealed beneath screens of black glass, war paint and personal insignia daubing their chests and gauntlets. They had come armed, but even towering over Ornicht as they did she could see the subtle signs of fear in their body language. The foremost figure slowly lowered itself to one knee, then leaned forward onto all fours.

"I am called Comet's Tail of the *Golden Heart*," the leader said. His companions all knelt when he spoke, and mirrored his pose. "I give myself and my craft to you, the victor. We breath at your command."

Even distorted through his helmet, the Rock-Drinker's Panglos was painfully stilted. Ornicht had never liked communicating in Panglos. It was an inelegant language, but she understood its benefits. Perhaps if these people served her well, she would learn their native tongue. That was the only way to truly understand one's servants.

"I accept your surrender," Ornicht replied. "Know that you are now the property of House Ornicht, and I am your mistress. Under my guidance, you shall have victories and spoils undreamed of. Your strength shall be added to my strength. You shall be protected by my power, and judged by my will. By the Blue Skies of Old Earth, I swear this."

She paused, the ritual words complete. Now it was time for their specific instruction.

"One third of your crew will serve me directly as Chemical Thralls," she explained. "If they fight bravely, they will be freed into my service. I grant the rest of you vassalage over your star craft. Know that this is a rare honor, and testament to my... estimation of your skills."

Diplomacy had never been Lady Ornicht's greatest skill, but she knew admitting outright that the only reason she was letting Comet's

Tail keep his ship was because she didn't have anyone left to captain it. Better to let him think his valiance had won him into her good graces. She bitterly wished that the Breaker was still with her. He'd have been perfect for this. Instead she had to put her trust in the honor of a carrion-eater.

"Mercy is as precious as water and oxygen," Comet's Tail said. "I thank you."

"Your thanks are unnecessary. I require only your obedience. I will return you to your craft with a compliment of my troops to assist you. Prepare yourself for Slip-jump, we are in pursuit of an enemy."

"The *Golden Heart* cannot make this journey," Comet's Tail said. "We Rock-Drinkers are forbidden to leave the Poison Suns."

"Forbidden," Ornicht said wryly. "Forbidden by whom?"

"It has been our way for generations," Comet's Tail continued haltingly. "The Deep Stations are our home. We only go beyond Salvation for a Great Raid, and one has not been called since the building of Peloken Station."

"You must know something," Ornicht said. "You belong to me now. Nothing that I will is forbidden, not by Gods, or laws, or men. If I will a thing, then you shall make it so."

Comet's Tail raised his helmet to look at her. A reflection stared back at her, eyes cold, lips peeled back slightly in a sneer, twin red locks tied back around her shaved scalp. Ornicht held her own gaze for a long moment, before Comet's Tail lowered his head again.

"I will do what you ask," he said. "But I have no Slip engine."

Ornicht clenched her jaw in frustration.

"You damaged my drive in our battle," she said. "Such skill is part of why I spared you. But repairing my drive will take time... Do you have a Slip-beacon?"

"We have much salvage," Comet's Tail said. "A beacon is among it. It is little use to us, and its engine could not be converted to serve a vessel like yours, or—"

"No matter," she said. "I will send some of my technicians to your craft to retrieve the beacon. We must send a message to the Grand Fleet at once. They will send us a repair vessel, so that we can retrieve my prize. And Comet's Tail?"

The Rock-Drinker looked up at her again.

"If any of my servants come to harm, you and your crew will

be punished."

"Of course," Comet's Tail said. "Their breath is your breath. May I ask, what is to be our prey?"

"The ship you pursued," Ornicht said. "It contains something... valuable to me. I have already sent one of my drones to cripple it. Once I have a Slip engine, we will simply follow them and collect my prize."

Comet's Tail and the other Rock-Drinkers stood up. He bowed low to her, then raised one hand and spread his fingers wide. Ornicht knew little of these savages, but she knew a vow when it was being signed.

"For the survival of the Clan," Comet's Tail said. "We shall return what is yours."

Tsi had called another meeting in the make-shift briefing room, and so Wylla found herself wedged uncomfortably between Enlil, who still smelled ripe from her prior celebrations, and Furner Ketsu, who had the not entirely unpleasant smell of oil and sealing fluid coming from his clothes. The old Noxian had a single metal pole extending from the stump of his leg, to which Tsi had attached the rough approximation of a metal foot. He seemed to be quite proud of his "augmentation", and had taken to making crude jokes about it in the Noxian tongue.

Wylla only caught about one word in three, given the dialect he spoke, but Enlil snickered appreciatively so she had to assume they were funny, if not entirely tasteful. Every once in a while though, Wylla caught Enlil glancing at her, and the laughter left her eyes. Wylla tried to smile at the Noxian woman, but Enlil always looked away quickly. She wondered what she had done to raise her ire. The two hadn't exactly become friends on their short journey together, but she thought she had at least convinced her that she was harmless.

Tsi was standing in the darkness at the far side of the room. Wylla noticed that she was wearing a pistol on her thigh. She'd taken the weapon off while they were in flight for a while, but now it had returned. Her arms were folded across her chest as she studied the room. Once the full crew was inside, she spoke.

"Something's been sending messages to the Guraggan," Tsi said. "One code burst was sent out right after they attacked us by the Serpent's Nest. A second message was sent right before we entered the Slip. We can't be certain of the exact content of the messages, but it's extremely likely it was positional data... and Slip coordinates."

Silence hung over the room for a moment. Furner Ketsu muttered a curse, others shifted in their seats. Wylla noticed that Hiron seemed particularly uncomfortable, while Enlil was perfectly still.

"So we're heading into an ambush," Furner said.

"Quite possibly," Tsi replied. "If the Guraggan have a faster Slip drive than ours, they could jump to Chalakhat before us, and wait for our arrival. There's no way we can alter course without coming out of the Slip, and an emergency halt..."

"Would tear this ship apart," Furner Ketsu said. "We took too bad of a beating in that last scrap. No way she holds together through an emergency translation."

"Exactly," Tsi said.

"Has there been confirmation as to how the message was sent?" Strongmind asked.

The machine was eerily calm as ever, but Wylla was beginning to suspect she was one of the only people in the room who didn't know the answer.

"No," Tsi said. "But both times a message was sent... Wylla was in the cockpit."

She had expected this. Some doubt had gnawed at her mind, even when she thought she had earned these people's trust, even after all she had done.

"Logical," Strongmind said. "She was our prisoner. She would have knowledge of Guraggan codes and transmission frequencies, and stands to gain by the craft being recaptured."

"I didn't say that," Tsi said quickly. "I acknowledge a possibility. That's all."

"Sounds a helluva lot like she's sold us out," Furner growled. "And here I was getting soft on you."

"Why, though?" Hiron asked. "I mean, why would you do it, Wylla? I thought you wanted to be with us."

"We did kinda shoot a bunch of her friends," Enlil said, putting a little too much effort into sounding like she didn't care. "I can see how she'd play that angle."

"If it matters," Wylla said quietly. "I didn't send any messages."

Furner snorted.

"And I never stole anything in my life," he said.

"I posit the most rational action is to terminate her and dispose of the body via airlock at the earliest opportunity," Strongmind said.

"Strongmind!" Tsi barked. "Not helpful!"

"It was merely a suggestion."

"Shit, that's the smartest thing Tin Head's said," Enlil added.

"We can't seriously be talking about this—" Hiron began.

"Drone's right. We gotta cut our losses," Enlil said.

"No one is getting killed on my ship—"

Wylla spoke up, her voice loud and clear enough to cut through the cacophony of voices spilling over each other. She was not accustomed to raising her voice, but it was vital that she be heard.

"Strongmind is right," she said.

Everyone in the room seemed to be staring at her. This time they were in shock, rather than suspicion. Hiron in particular seemed to be on the verge of tears. He silently shook his head, but she kept speaking.

"It's right," Wylla repeated. "I didn't send the message... but from a purely rational point of view, killing me is the right choice. I have no idea if Lady Ornicht has some sort of tracking device hidden inside my body, but I know that I am one of the reasons she is pursuing you so doggedly. I am her property, and she wants me back. Being with me puts you in danger, and for my part... I would rather die than return to her. I only suggest you retain some means of proving that I am dead to her, as it may be useful in warding off her pursuit."

There was a stunned silence after she finished speaking. Wylla looked to Tsi, and saw that one hand was resting on her pistol. She could see tension in the woman's posture, conflict and sorrow in her eyes.

"She didn't do it," the Bondsman said.

He had kept his customary silence until now, but his low, guttural voice filled the room in that moment.

"You people aren't thinking," he continued. "She said it herself, she'd rather die than go back to them. During the fight, she and the old man were down in an escape pod. Why didn't she leave then, if she meant to sell you out?"

"I... I was in it with her," Furner said halfheartedly. "Maybe she thought I'd cause trouble."

"You were dosed to your eyes on painkillers," Tenlok said. "Even a Bykon could have handled you like that. Face it. Doesn't make any sense that she sent the message. You all want to kill her, I'm not going to stop you. But don't pretend it's for selling you out."

His red eye searched the room, but Wylla saw no one could meet the Bondsman's gaze except for Tsi. She nodded subtly to Tenlok.

"He's right," Tsi said. "Wylla didn't do it. They must have… set up a transmitter, maybe when they were in control of the ship."

"That doesn't make any sense," Enlil interjected. "They didn't exactly plan on you getting it back, now did they?"

"What about… what about that mass build-up?" Hiron said. "On the hull. We keep pinging as having excess mass. Enlil said it was probably just dust or a rock, or an issue with our sensors, and I know the sensors are still mixed up, but maybe they attached something to us during the firefight?"

"Of course," Wylla said suddenly. "I—I must humbly apologize, I did not think of this earlier. I believe Lady Ornicht struck us with some sort of transmission drone during the attack near the Snake Nest."

"When?" Enlil asked. "How?"

"It's a relatively simple procedure," she explained. "She would have launched the drone along with a salvo of mass rounds. Intentionally designed to miss, but providing cover for the tracking device. Usually it's only done on larger vessels, but Lady Ornicht was a drone controller when she was younger. She would certainly have the skills for such a gambit."

"That makes sense," Tsi agreed. "Hmm. Well, we can't climb out there and try to scrape it off while we're still in the Slip, it's too risky. We'll peel it off the second we drop."

"That sounds like a plan," Furner said. "I can get to work rigging up some mag-strippers. We can pry that sucker off in less than an hour once we're out."

"It may have defenses," Wylla said. "I would advise caution."

"I am void combat effective," Strongmind said. "With your tactical insight, victory is highly likely."

Tsi breathed out a sigh of relief.

"Alright," she said. "You're all dismissed. We should start prepping for the drop, it's going to be bumpy, but I think we can make it with a day or two to prepare."

Tsi filed out with the others, pausing briefly to make eye-contact with Wylla and nod to her. Whether the gesture was in thanks or in apology, Wylla wasn't sure.

"She touches to her weapons whenever she's worried," Wylla said, watching Tsi as she left the room.

The Bondsman was the only other person left, and he turned his masked face to her mutely.

"You noticed it too, didn't you?"

"Yeah," Tenlok grunted.

"Some people think that weapons are a surrogate for sexual organs. I don't think that's true in her case," Wylla mused. "I think it's more like a child's doll. Part of her knows it won't protect her, but she clings to it anyways. Just knowing that it's there gives her reassurance."

"Haven't put much thought into Tsi's nethers."

"Of course not," Wylla said. "But you have thought about her weapons."

"She's not a bad shot."

Wylla turned towards the mercenary. He was leaning against the wall, arms folded across his chest. It was a habit of his: to stand almost completely still, the weight of his gear keeping him in place. He was like an inverse of Strongmind, whose unnatural body aped human life but betrayed its artificiality in too-precise movements and ill-timed twitches. The Bondsman was a man, or at least had been a man, but he moved like a machine. An object.

"Thank you," she said. "For supporting me."

The Bondsman did not reply. She studied him, unsure of what to say next, until one detail caught her eye again. It hung in a scabbard across his breastplate. She'd seen him draw it during the fight with Liss and Lady Ornicht.

"That's a Nioban blade on your chest. But you're not Nioban," she said.

"They make good knives."

"I knew one, once."

"Yeah. Big guy that tried to bash my head open."

"His name is Liss," she said.

It had been so terrifying, the battle to retake the ship. She'd watched it on the screens, seen Tsi and this man in his demon-mask, cutting through warriors like a storm of gunshots and flashing metal. The Bondsman had fought Liss to a standstill and then...

She had to control her anger. Liss wasn't an evil man. He hadn't deserved what Tenlok had done to him. Yet, Tenlok had also saved her now.

"If you want me to apologize for burning up your boyfriend—" Tenlok started, breaking the silence.

"We were not lovers."

She couldn't read his expression beneath his mask, but he straightened himself and seemed to look right at her now, one eye burning, the other shattered glass. There was a long silence as she returned his gaze.

"You talk a lot," he grated.

"And you don't..." she said, cocking her head to the side. "You shield yourself against the world. Your weapons, they aren't dolls to you... they're part of you. That armor is your skin, isn't it? You wear that mask... but I think for you, it's your face."

"We going to have a problem?" Tenlok asked.

"No," she sighed. "I just... I want to understand you, Tenlok. We're very different. I'm different. This ship is full of killers and machines and, and I'm alone. And I think you might be the only other person here who really knows what that's like. To be surrounded by people you have to trust, who have to trust you, and yet be so totally unlike them that you-that you wish you weren't *you*."

She had taken a step closer to him. Now she was looking up at the mask, and she could see the tiny dappling of shrapnel, the pock marks and laser scars upon its surface. All this, from one battle, one tiny skirmish. It was a miracle he kept this armor working at all.

"You start to wish you were someone else. Someone who could just do what needs doing, and never think, not about herself, not about what will happen next," she said. "A machine, or a monster."

Tenlok shrugged.

"I do alright."

"Then why do you wear that thing?" she said, gesturing to his *mempo*.

"Because getting shot in the face is painful," he said. "And it's easier to take my stimms this way."

"Are you afraid to take it off?"

"I try not to put myself in situations where I can get shot in the face."

"I can't hurt you," she said. "I mean that literally. I am a Bykon. Violence is aberrant to me. I couldn't raise my hand to harm my worst enemy."

"Which you are not," she added quickly.

"Sure," Tenlok replied. "But there are other ways to get what you want. You want me to take this off? Think that would help you understand me?"

"It would be a start," Wylla said.

"I think you already know me well enough," Tenlok replied. "And don't think for a moment that I don't know you."

CHAPTER 27

"You look good in that thing!"

Furner was beaming at Enlil through the thick glass of her helmet. They'd spent an interminable twenty minutes getting her into the repair suit he had jury-rigged. After a good amount of grunting, sweating, and cursing at each other, she finally had the harness on. It was a bulky set of mechanical claws that made her look like some kind of hybrid between a mining drone and a human being. The claws had actually come from a badly damaged mining pod Tsi had handy. Enlil wondered just how much of that woman's life was tucked away in secret corners of this ship.

She took a few awkward steps, turned, and tried to bow to Furner but nearly fell over.

"Feec-Rec!" she spat. "This thing's murder on my back."

Furner laughed as he helped her stand back upright.

"Won't matter much when you're out in the void. Hell, maybe when we get off this ship we can start a mining crew back home."

"As if I'd ever crew with you, old man," Enlil teased.

"You know, my boys never had half the tongue you got."

"Maybe that's cause they were all dead-brains like you."

Furner laughed again.

"Come on, let's get you in the airlock. Tsi said the tin-head's already waiting for you in there."

Enlil followed Furner to the airlock, steadily putting one foot in front of the other as she tried to balance the harness on her shoulders. It felt like she'd added her own body weight and half again onto her back. Her face plate was misty with perspiration by the time she got to the airlock, and was unceremoniously shoved in to the cramped space with Strongmind.

The machine had put on a skin-suit, stretched tight over its massive frame, but it hadn't bothered with a helmet or an oxygen tank.

Instead, it had a missile tube strapped to its back and three spare rounds. Yet another strange item Tsi had hidden away in some secret chamber of the ship. Strongmind looked her up and down before speaking.

"Communication check," it said.

"Yeah, yeah, I hear ya."

The thing was talking to her comms system directly, not bothering to move its mouth. It gave her the eerie sensation that Strongmind was inside her head. She pushed the thought away as she turned to face the airlock exit.

Tsi's voice came crackling over the mic.

"You two hear me okay?"

"Acknowledged."

"Yeah," Enlil said. "What's our status?"

"We're going to drop out of the Slip in five minutes. I'll give you a thirty second countdown. Once we're in real space, I'll cycle the airlocks. You two scramble outside ASAP. Our internal scanners are still acting up, but I should be able to give you the precise location on the hull where our friend is. Clear it off, then get back inside as quick as you can. Furner will be getting the beacon ready for launch at the same time. That all clear?"

"Acknowledged."

"All green," Enlil said.

With five minutes to spare, Enlil did what she always did in cramped, uncomfortable confines: she tried to fall asleep. She'd gotten used to waiting in claustrophobic darkness. Tension used to grip her so tightly, she thought her very bones would shake apart. She was still frightened, of course: only an idiot walks on a starship's hull without some apprehension. She shut her eyes. She didn't fall asleep, not all the way, but she did drift into a pleasant dark warmth for a while before she was brought back to reality by the sound of Tsi counting down.

"Three... Two... One! Airlock cycling!"

The small room had already been drained of oxygen, so the outer door slid open silently. Enlil thrust herself forward, gripping the handles at the edge of the door, and swung herself around. It was always the first, most dangerous step: switching from the artificial gravity of the ship to the void, a place with neither up nor down. Enlil slammed her mag boots onto the hull, locking herself in place as she straightened out. Tsi was already feeding coordinates into her HUD. Enlil tapped the side of her helmet, and an AR overlay appeared, rapidly mapping a path to where Tsi had located the drone.

"It's by the thrusters, port side aft!" Enlil called out.

"Acknowledged," Strongmind said. "Follow me. I will engage defensive systems, if necessary."

Enlil trudged along beside the drone, still marveling at the surreal sight of what looked like a man walking across the hull without a helmet on. Tiny crystals were forming on its skin as it walked, and its hair waved back and forth, almost as if it was being pulled by some unseen current.

They clambered along the hull together, making for the thrusters at the rear of the ship. Enlil was hunched low, but she couldn't resist the urge to look up and out occasionally. She was scanning for other craft with her naked eyes, uselessly. Anything close enough to see would likely mean she was already dead. They'd been insanely lucky on Salvation, and she doubted their enemies would be that merciful twice. Plus, this time there would be no sense in Tsi staying steady long enough for them to get back inside.

A shot streaked passed her head, and Enlil flung herself as low as she could get.

"*Contact!*" she shouted.

"Acknowledged."

Enlil scrambled for whatever cover she could find, finally tucking herself down behind a bulbous sensor pod. She peered out to see Strongmind shouldering its missile tube. Another shot swept passed it, and it returned fire. There was a silent explosion and the missile streaked outwards, a bright blue jet emitting from its tail before it hit the target.

"Shit!" Enlil spat. "That thing's big!"

It was latched to the hull like a massive, grotesque parasite. Four clawed legs burrowed into the hull. The drone's upper torso was vaguely humanoid, but instead of a head it had only a collection of glowing robotic eyes and armored cables. Strongmind's shot had struck the machine directly, but all the missile had managed to do was knock one of the drone's legs loose. Enlil could see the pulse cannon on the drone's left shoulder charging to fire again, and was about to shout a warning when she noticed something else.

A long, tendrilous cable extended from the drone's chest. It had worked some of the hull plating loose, and the cable was slipped underneath, burrowing into the ship below.

"Tsi!" Enlil shouted. "It's a combat drone! Looks like it has access to our systems!"

"I am targeting the connection point," Strongmind said. "Firing."

Strongmind loosed its second missile, but just as the shot sped towards the machine, it suddenly detached its legs and whirled its body about. The combat drone slammed back down into the hull, shielding its cable link with the slabs of armor on its back. No sooner had the missile exploded than the machine spun its head and weapons around, and unleashed a withering salvo at Strongmind.

Strongmind dodged with surprising elegance for a being of its size, but one shot tore through the missile tube in its hands, sending the weapon hurtling into space.

"Fire power reduced," Strongmind said. "Preparing for close quarters combat."

"Negative!" Tsi shouted over the comms. "You two get back inside right now! We've got to launch the beacon."

"I am still capable of engaging the primary target —"

"You heard her Tin-Head!" Enlil shouted as she scrambled past Strongmind, grabbing him by the wrist and pulling him along.

Shots scored the hull all around them as they ran. She only hoped she could make it to the airlock before the thing could blast her apart.

The familiar sound of alarms filled the cockpit. Warning lights flashed in Tsi's vision. Oxygen was compromised. Engines were being interfered with. In a moment, the thing would be able to shut down their primary shielding. Tsi furiously typed in commands, trying to isolate the enemy's line of attack.

There were a dozen system hard points it could have burrowed into, and it had had access to their system for days now. She wondered briefly why it hadn't bothered to murder them all while they were in the Slip, but she realized it probably didn't have any kind of piloting software. It had waited for them to drop out of the Slip, intending to be picked up by its masters once the deed was done.

"Furner," she called out. "How close are you to launching the beacon?"

"I've got those coordinates you wanted programmed," he said. "Just gotta clear the main hold and we can open her up!"

"Hurry," Tsi said. "Let me know when everything's set, then get to the escape pods and lock yourself in."

"We're abandoning ship?" Hiron asked.

Tsi ignored his question, turning to Wylla. She'd still yet to properly apologize to the woman for her earlier accusations. Sometimes trust could be an apology in and of itself.

"Wylla, get yourself and Hiron suited up and get down to the escape pods too. I've got a plan, but it's nothing either of you can help with. I'm locking in coordinates for the pods now."

"I understand," Wylla said. "But, if I may, I might be able to provide insight into what's going on here—"

"You've already done more than enough for me," Tsi said. "Now get going."

"Hold on," Hiron said, even as he was strapping on his crutches. "You're coming too right?"

"There's a third pod. If I make it in time, I'll rendezvous with you on Chalakhat. Once you're in the escape pods, make *absolutely sure* that the inertial shielding is set to maximum, understand? There's a homing beacon in there too, make sure that works, you can use it to rendezvous near the landing zone and—"

"Alright," Hiron said. "Tsi, before I go—"

"Hiron, we really don't have the time—"

"What's the name of this ship?"

He looked at her with such earnestness then, that for a moment she was stunned. Of course. She'd never told him, or anyone, what the ship's real name was. It was like her. It traveled incognito, using whatever names suited it in a given time or place. But it had a real name, a secret name that only she knew. She hadn't spoken it aloud since the day she first boarded.

"*Exile.* She's called *The Exile.* Now please, Hiron. Go."

Wylla took the boy by one arm, and the two left.

Tsi wiped at her brow. She rerouted as much power away from the aft-thrusters as she dared, hoping to cut off the circuit link the machine had, but it was no use. The combat drone was sophisticated, probably a multipurpose weapon, the sort the Guraggan used to send in as scouts to sow terror before a main assault.

She checked her scanners again. Perhaps the drone was interfering with her scans, or perhaps they really had gotten here faster than the Guraggan. There weren't any other ships in the system that she could see, just a single automated station blaring a warning that landing on Chalakhat was forbidden.

Chalakhat. They'd dropped in close, as close as they could possibly get without running the risk of being shredded to pieces. At this distance, it was a pale green orb, wispy white clouds dancing across its upper atmosphere. She took a moment to look at it, to see if even from this distance the black scars on its surface were still visible. Then she went back to work.

"Enlil, Strongmind, are you in yet?"

"All green here," Enlil replied in her snarky Noxian drawl. "Tin-Head took a shot, but what else is new?"

"I remain fully combat effective," Strongmind said.

"Keep your hard suit on," Tsi said. "Get to one of the Escape pods right now. I'm going to try for a hard shot."

"The hell are you talking about?"

"That thing's in our systems. It's already started depleting our oxygen, it'll have full control if I don't do something soon."

"Tsi..."

"Just do it, Enlil," Tsi said. She cut the line, and began strapping on her own skin-suit. Once she was dressed, she put on a helmet too, and secured her life-support pack. Even with the specially adjusted gloves of the suit, it was hard work inputting commands into the control console. Still, she managed to lock a course and speed.

"Hey Captain," Furner's voice came through on the comms. He was huffing, as if he'd just run across half the ship. "Listen, I got some bad news..."

"Talk fast, Furner."

"Beacon's coordinates are good, engine's fine, but the damn thing's mag-lock... Listen I tried my best, but there's some kind of malfunction. It's stuck tight to the deck."

Tsi cursed.

"Get in a pod. You've done all you can. I'll handle the rest from here."

"You, uh, you got it," he said. "And, for the record, I'm sorry. I thought I had the damn thing handled—"

"It happens," Tsi said bitterly.

She had a solution. It wouldn't be easy, but she could still try. She kept an eye on the internal scans, noting that the escape pods were filling up. The third pod remained empty. If she managed to make it there in time, she might just be able to keep her word to Hiron.

With a few commands, she linked the main control console to her helmet display. All she could do was authorize a pre-set order to the computer, but that would be enough. She stood up from her chair, and made for the main cargo hold.

Air was draining from the ship, and the emergency lights had come on once again. As she slung herself down the stairs and through the galley, she thought about how this might be the last time she saw her ship. Either because she was going to die, or...

She shook her head. Attaching yourself to objects was a mistake. It had been a good ship, but ships don't last forever. Nothing does.

"Requesting an update to command protocols."

Strongmind's voice, reassuringly unemotional, broke her meditation.

"Little busy here," she said, as she opened the hatch to the main hold. The hold itself was still sealed, but it had been totally vented of oxygen.

"Command protocol update requested."

She stopped before the beacon. Of course. Strongmind had been pestering her about this since the Inheritor's World.

"If I... if I'm out of contact for a long period of time, or if I die, your primary objective is to keep the crew safe, and your secondary objective is to make sure a warning reaches Kios. Use the homing beacons to rendezvous near the ship's landing site. That enough for you, Strongmind?"

"It is sufficient."

"I'll see you on Chalakhat," she said.

Strongmind didn't reply. Tsi checked the beacon once over, and, good as his word, Furner had left everything in perfect working order, except the magnetic clamps which held it in place. Tsi examined them carefully, guessing that her tug-of-war over the ship's systems with the Guraggan drone had fried their electronic controls. There was nothing else for it.

She ran to the hold controls, and pressed the emergency release. Despite the name, the external cargo doors still opened onto the void very slowly, equalizing the pressure between outside and inside gradually. Tsi's boots magnetized automatically, and she slowly trudged to the beacon. The vacuum had loosened the clamps slightly, but a few hard kicks did little good. She sent the command.

First, the ship accelerated. Not quite at maximum burn, but enough to produce a serious drag. Then the primary and secondary escape pods fired. With the extra momentum from the ship blazing forwards, they'd reach Chalakhat in a day or two, long before their food and oxygen ran out. She would have fired the third pod too, but she had no way of doing that remotely. Everything the ship's computer did now she had already programmed in. She was on a timer before it hit maximum burn. She had also told the ship to kill its inertial compensators. Hopefully, that would be enough to scrape the Guraggan drone off the hull.

Wearily, Tsi drew her pistol. She placed the muzzle to one of the mag-locks and fired. She fired again. The third round broke one of the locks loose. By the time she was on the last clamp, her magazine was almost empty, and precious seconds were ticking away before the ship hit maximum burn. She blasted it, and then gave the beacon a hard shove.

In the void of space, even an object the size of the beacon only needed a little pressure to be set free. It drifted away from her into the darkness. After a few moments, she saw the signature ripple of an object jumping into the Slip. Tsi smiled. She had done it.

Then her world exploded. A solid round tore through the void over her shoulder, peppering her with fragments as it struck the deck. She leaped awkwardly to the side, coming to a stumbling halt as her boots re-magnetized. The Guraggan drone crawled, spider-like along the ceiling of the hold, firing its many weapons at her. It was only Tsi's superhuman reactions that saved her, allowing her to twist and leap out of the way. She scrambled along the deck, firing her Repeater uselessly as the drone closed in. She was scrambling for the door to the cargo hold when a shot exploded in front of her. She felt a dozen fragments punch into her chest, shredding her suit.

INTEGRITY COMPROMISED flashed across her helmet's HUD as she collapsed onto her face. Still running on adrenaline, she clawed a hand outwards, trying to find purchase on the deck, to keep herself moving forwards. Suddenly, something clamped around her wrist and yanked her upwards. She was losing oxygen and on the edge of consciousness, but she found herself pulled out of the hold and being shuffled down a corridor. She recognized the entrance to the last escape pod and was shoved roughly in.

Black was closing in on her from all angles, but she felt someone's hands strapping her into the pod. Tsi rolled her head back, and looked through the blurry glass at a broken crimson eye, and the snarling face of a demon. A smile crept across her lips as she sank into merciful oblivion.

CHAPTER 28

With the exception of Hiron throwing up all over the pod when they broke atmosphere, Enlil had actually enjoyed her trip. She'd been born in cramped corridors and tight confines. For her, spending a few days crammed in tight with Furner and the kid had been almost nostalgic. She remembered a time in her misspent youth when she and one of her wing-mates had wound up stuck in a similar pod, with nothing to do but wait the eight hours it would take a rescue team to come and pick them up. Of course, they'd had a globe of liquor each and their hormones to keep them preoccupied, so by the time a rescue ship had arrived Enlil hadn't exactly wanted to leave.

Not that she was ever going to have as much fun with these two as she had with her old companion, but she and Furner had had a good time telling dirty jokes and she had to grudgingly admit, the kid was teaching her to speak much better Panglos. She'd always been able to get by in trader's argot with the merchants on Salvation, but she was a scavenger and a pirate first. Noxians who slaved away on mining rigs, only to be robbed on their way back to the outer stations had always inspired disdain in her. Sure, the system needed *someone* to do that work, but only idiots went that route if they had the skills to make it on a pirate craft. As a consequence, most of the Panglos phrases she knew were about threatening people and haggling over the price of liquor, stimms, and two-suits.

No, it hadn't been terrible. Now though, reeking in Hiron's sick, the heat was beginning to turn their little pod into an oven. She'd never broken atmosphere before, but she'd taken enough G's in her life to keep her stomach under control when they finally hit the dirt. What she hadn't prepared for, was for the pod's doors to jam.

"Gods and Spirits," she spat, tugging at the handle again. She could see through the view port that they'd landed on their back. A wispy grey mass was somewhere far above them. At a guess, she'd say this was the "sky", something she'd only seen in pictures and simulators. It was strangely disturbing to her, so she tried to keep her mind off it as she fidgeted with the door.

"Pull the emergency lever," Furner wheezed. "Unless you've gotten too comfy in here and want t' stay."

The old man had taken the fall hard. He was breathing heavily, and looked like he was on the verge of passing out, but he still managed to put a twinge of mirth in his words. Enlil found the lever, and gave it a quick yank. A shock went through the pod as micro explosives fired, and the hatch went flying off.

Fresh air filled her lungs. Enlil began choking and sputtering immediately. She staggered up and out of the pod, legs wobbling beneath her. The whole world seemed to shake and spin, she couldn't orient herself. A strange, steady crashing noise was filling her ears, and the ground beneath her feet was soft and yielding. Her nose was filled with a strange scent, like someone had sprayed acid up her nose. She tumbled to the ground.

"Hey! Enlil! You alright?"

The kid patted her on the back as she coughed, sending jolts of pain through her body. She slapped his hand away and spat on the ground. She realized, staring down at her own spittle, that she was kneeling over yellow-gold sand. There were flecks of red in her saliva.

"Fuck," she whispered.

"Uh, do you, um need anything?" Hiron asked.

She waved the kid away and took a few deep breaths. After a moment her head stopped spinning, and she shakily got to her feet. She still felt like she was drunk, and had to blink hard against the harsh light. Slowly, she looked around.

There was the pod, half-buried in the sand. Furner leaned against it, giving her a weary smile. The sand itself stretched out the length of a main deck, and beyond that it turned to rocks, then into a vast green forest. It looked more opulent than even the Jarawat's court: thick trunks of brown and silver were covered in a dizzying array of drooping fronds and snaking vines. She could still hear the crashing noise coming from behind her, and tore her eyes away from that strange and wondrous sight to look on something even more incredible.

Water. Deep, and dark, and blue, waves crashing and tumbling over each other, it stretched out so far that it met with the grey sky. The sound it made as it crashed against the shore was overwhelming, and for a moment, Enlil could do nothing but stare. Finally, she summoned the strength to speak.

"Wow," she said. "Whoever owns this place must be rich."

Trust. That was all Wylla could do. Trust. It seemed to be an endlessly repeated pattern in her life, that she had to rely on people she would rather not. Trust people who threatened her and frightened her. She remembered her father telling her when she was a small child that the path of the Bykon was not an easy one.

"You must walk among the worlds knowing that no one is your enemy," he had said, "And that all are your enemy."

It was one of those nonsense koans they taught to children. And now, traipsing through the forest with Strongmind, she felt her anger boiling over. Why had they not taught her something more useful? All the wise platitudes of her instructors were fine for meditation, but they were worse than useless when she found herself on an unknown world with no one to help her but a disfigured combat drone. Who, she could not forget, had threatened to murder her only days before. A machine that had killed people before her eyes without hesitation. It had manipulated to her, and lied to her, used her as a weak point to exploit—

"Please watch your step," Strongmind said.

"I am!" Wylla shot back, a little too quickly.

She was scrabbling up a rocky path along the edge of a shallow stream. They'd been going uphill since they landed, keeping a rapid pace set by the machine. She hadn't even had a moment to get her bearings before Strongmind was making up her pack and instructing her about what their daily marching orders would be.

Her foot hit a slippery rock and twisted. She let out a yelp as she stumbled, but the machine caught her hand and righted her instantly. She let out a groan of frustration.

"Have you sustained damage?" it asked, still holding her hand.

"I'm fine," Wylla said, pulling her hand away. "Let's keep moving."

"Acknowledged."

As they walked, Wylla tried to calm herself. She summoned up all the old meditative practices she had learned as a child. First, she tried to cast her mind away, think about abstract concepts and puzzles. The thudding footsteps of the machine behind her kept intruding, bringing her back to the present. It had been difficult enough sharing an escape pod with Strongmind for days, but now that she had an open sky above her head and unfiltered air in her lungs, its very presence still forced its way into her mind.

Part of her had wished she'd fought back against its orders when it divided them all up into the pods. It was some obscure calculation based on their relative mass: the two Noxians and the boy, Strongmind with her, Tsi with...

She had no idea what had happened to Tsi or the Bondsman. They had both disappeared in the chaos of the escape from the ship. She could not calculate whether they were likely dead or alive. Somehow both possibilities filled her with apprehension.

She focused on the present moment. One foot went in front of the other. She studied the ground, the leaves, let the babble of the stream fill her ears. Even Strongmind's heavy footsteps became part of the song of the world.

She'd never been to Chalakhat before. She had heard of it in passing. It had been devastated at some point during the last war, well before she was born. She did not know the specifics, but there was something inspiring in its rugged beauty. A world reclaiming itself.

That was a good thing to meditate on, she realized. The land beneath her had been ravaged, but like her it was finding its way, slowly and steadily, to recovering. An insect flitted across her view and came to land on the petals of a blue flower. The creature was tiny and delicate, its chitin a shade of white that was almost translucent. She studied it as she walked past. A fertilizer, carrying seeds or pollen from one flower to the next. Like her, the insect was in danger. Larger animals would prey on it. All it could do was float from one place to the next, hoping there were no predators lurking near the flowers from which it fed.

Like her, all it could do was trust.

Hiron hunched on the beach, drawing in the sand with the end of one of his crutches. It wasn't precise work, but it helped him to try to visualize exactly what was going on. Astro-cartography had been a hobby of his, but terrestrial cartography was something he only picked up in starts and jolts. Looking down the beach, he could see where a sand bar jutted out into the ocean, then the whole shore curved out of view behind the forest, only to emerge again further towards the horizon.

He wasn't spectacular at estimating distances, but he thought perhaps a strong person could walk to the farthest visual point on the beach in about a day. Of course, it would take him at least twice as long. He'd feebly worked his way back and forth to the edge of the forest a few times, testing how he moved in the soft sand. The answer was 'poorly.'

Then again, Furner was still getting used to his own prosthetic. The old Noxian had happily set to work stripping their escape pod of anything that might be useful. He had even torn apart the pod's atmospheric parachute, and made a cloak for himself out of the silvery material. Hiron wasn't sure how much use it would actually be, but Furner seemed to think it made him look dashing. He wasn't about to disabuse the old man of that notion.

It was times like these that Hiron wondered if he was born weak. His body was a challenge, of course, but seeing Furner hobbling enthusiastically around the pod, seemingly oblivious to his injuries, made him wonder if there was something wrong with him on a deeper level. An inferiority of the soul, one might call it. Hiron had known men and women who had been maimed, or ravaged by cancers, or just born small and twisted, like him, but it seemed as if all of them had found a way to persevere. They fell down, but they rose again. Every single time.

Hiron had worked hard, so very hard, to learn to walk with just the support of his cane back home. It had never been enough, though. Not for his parents, not for the clan. Not for himself. Then, he had been injured, and found himself right back where he started: struggling to move on crutches, hopping and shuffling like a mutant quadruped.

He scratched out one of the details on the sand map he was drawing. The mountains stretched much longer, he estimated, and so he drew another little line of them. He sighed, and took the homing beacon out of one of the pouches on his survival suit. He turned it on, and fiddled with a dial on the side of it.

It was a rugged device, designed to survive just about anything. The heavy metal panels on its sides had taken a bad beating some time in the past, but the machine still certainly worked. Unfortunately, with ruggedness came imprecision. It could tell him approximately how far away the *Exile*'s landing site was, but nothing about terrain or exactly where the ship had come to a halt. It could have buried itself halfway underground, or crashed into one of the nearby mountain peaks. For all Hiron knew, the ship could have torn itself apart on hitting the atmosphere, scattering wreckage across the forest canopy, and only its transponder had survived.

Still, with all their long-range communication devices not working, the homer was the only link they had to the rest of the crew. Assuming that they all stuck to the plan, the ship was their rendezvous point. Of course, there were all the possible hazards an unknown world might hold for them to be considered as well.

Enlil trudged up the beach to him, and looked down at his handiwork. She worked her jaw for a minute, as if chewing the idea of it, before casually spitting on the ground.

"The big 'X' is where we're going?" she asked, pointing at Hiron's drawing.

"Mm-hmm," Hiron nodded.

"That line's our route?"

"That's what I was thinking," Hiron said. "There's a stream a little ways away. We'll follow that into the forest, try to find it's source. It'll be like our own little pathway. Plus we'll have fresh drinking water the whole time."

"I don't like the look of those big rocks," Enlil said, looking up past Hiron.

"You mean the mountains?"

"Yeah, 'mountains.' They look like trouble."

"They are," Hiron agreed. "It'll be hard to get through them for Furner and me. I'm hoping as we head inland, maybe there's a valley or a channel that cuts through them somewhere to the other side. Very pretty though. I've never seen cliffs that red color before."

"Might be some kinda iron," Enlil said, clearly disinterested. "Probably good mining here."

"No one's mined on Chalakhat in a long time," Hiron said.

Enlil abruptly patted at her head, then stared at the palm of her hand. She repeated the gesture, growing flustered, then looked up. Hiron could hear the low murmur from the leaves on the trees, slowly growing to match the rushing of the waves against the shore.

"Somethin' sprung a leak," Enlil muttered, looking upwards.

No sooner had she said it, than the rainstorm broke upon them with full force. In seconds, sheets of rain were coming down, soaking Enlil's hair and plastering it down around her face in long yellow strands. She stood there looking upwards, struck dumb. Hiron hadn't seen much rain either, and for a moment, he too was dazzled by the sight.

The drops were fat and cold, and by the time Hiron had gotten to his feet, he was already soaked. He headed for the tree line, the only worthwhile shelter he could see. The life-pod was on its side, hatch open to the sky, and he guessed that it'd be flooded in a few moments. Besides that, he didn't want to spend anymore time packed in there than he had to.

"Hey!" Furner shouted as he came hobbling up the beach after Hiron. "Help me set this up will ya?"

He was waving a silvery tarp as he walked, probably taken out of the survival kit aboard the pod. With some difficulty, Hiron helped Furner stretch the tarp between swaying tree trunks, tying it as taught as they could. Both of them had never spent any time in an environment like this, but Hiron had read something about life on other worlds, and so he fetched a tall stick and thrust it into the soft earth, propping up the center of the tarp.

"Why'd ya do that?" Furner asked as he settled down against one of the trees.

"Makes the rain run off," Hiron said. "Keep it from filling up and collapsing."

"Ah."

Hiron was about to settle himself down, when he realized Enlil wasn't with him. He looked out and saw she hadn't moved from her spot, only sat down with her back to them. Hiron called out to her, and waved one of his crutches in her direction.

"Leave her be," Furner said. "She needs a minute."

"She shouldn't stay out in the rain..." Hiron said.

"First time she's seen anything like this," Furner said. "Hell, I only seen it once before myself. Let her enjoy it."

"Alright…"

Hiron sat down, taking off his crutches and leaning back against a tree opposite Furner. The old man began breathing more slowly, then fell asleep. The earth and tree trunk were wet, but at least he wasn't being rained on directly anymore.

The ocean was roiling, waves crashing against the shore as the storm grew more intense. The tide slowly rose, lapping away hungrily at the beach. There was something both beautiful and terrifying about so much wild, untamed nature. Truth be told, Hiron only half-paid attention to the ocean though. The only thing which truly drew his focus was Enlil.

Wylla washed her face in the lake. Her makeup had long since worn down to a flimsy crust of black and white, the intricate spirals smudged into random streaks. With no one for company but a machine, it hadn't bothered her until she caught sight of her reflection in the lake's still waters. Wylla wasn't a vain woman, but she knew keeping disciplined control of her appearance and her body was the bedrock of keeping control of her situation.

Without ceremony, she settled down on her knees at the shore of the lake, and began splashing its bitterly cold water on her face. She took out a torn rag and dampened it, then scrubbed vigorously, using her shadowy reflection as a mirror. It took her a few minutes to scrub the last bits of paint away, but at last she ran her hands over her face and found that it was smooth and clean.

She glanced over her shoulder. Strongmind had been watching her the whole time. She couldn't help but be disturbed by its twisted visage: the exposed under-skeleton of one half of its face always looked like it was grinning, while the pseudo-skin on the other side remained placid. Strongmind spoke when she looked at it, causing her to flinch slightly.

"Wylla, may I ask you a question?"

Strongmind's voice was pleasant, removing some of the harshness with which it normally spoke. Wylla had no idea what algorithm made the machine decide between trying to disguise itself as a human and throwing its artificial nature in her face. Like everything about Strongmind, she found it jarring.

She rose and dried her hands.

"Yes, what is it?" she asked tiredly.

"Is Tsi dead?"

The question could have come from the mouth of a child. It was so simple and matter of fact, Strongmind's tone belying the weight of its words.

"I don't know," Wylla said. "Come on, let's get moving."

She turned and began walking along the shore of the lake. It wasn't a particularly vast expanse, but she'd charted a vague path that would take them along it and up into the foothills beyond. At a higher vantage point, she hoped to be able to scout a good path through the mountains and on to the ship's landing site.

Strongmind followed close behind her.

"How likely would you estimate the possibility that she has died?" it asked.

"Well," Wylla sighed. "She was in a great deal of danger when I last saw her. Theta-90 is a very sophisticated device—"

"Is Theta-90 the designation of the combat drone we engaged?" Strongmind interrupted.

"Yes," Wylla replied. "It's Lady Ornicht's favorite drone. I caught a glimpse of it through Enlil's helmet-link. Like I said, it's very dangerous, and very smart, and it had the element of surprise on its side."

"I understand. So you would estimate it highly likely that Tsi has been terminated?"

"I didn't say that."

Wylla picked her way over a fallen tree branch. She had noticed something about the trees around the lake. Many of them seemed to be missing limbs in odd places. The wind came whipping down on them just then, and with it came the rain. She had been lucky enough to keep her traveling cloak with her when she crammed herself into the life pod, and now she thanked her ancestors for it as she pulled the long hood up over her head.

The machine, of course, did not need any such protection. It was walking alongside her now, interposing itself between her and the forest. A carbine was slung across its chest, and a heavy pack across its back. She hadn't wanted to trust it with their supplies, but the machine had insisted, and Wylla couldn't very well argue with it.

"We will ascertain whether or not Tsi is still alive when we reach the location of the ship's homing beacon," Strongmind announced, seemingly to itself.

Wylla nodded, but said nothing. She didn't particularly feel the need to engage Strongmind in conversation. She was trying to let herself enjoy the rainfall. It was quite beautiful and relaxing to stroll alongside the lake, hearing the droplets pass through the branches of the trees.

"Have I upset you?" Strongmind asked.

Wylla exhaled through her nostrils. Now, of all times, the machine had decided it wanted to be her friend.

"No, Strongmind."

"You are uneasy in my presence. Is my appearance disturbing, or do you find me difficult to associate with, given that I advised your termination?"

Wylla had to suppress a grim chuckle. It was such a blunt creature. There was none of the intricacies of trying to keep on her old mistress's good side with this one. Still, the machine was honest with her, and so she saw no reason not to be honest with it.

"I've seen you kill, Strongmind. I know it's in your programming, someone designed you and your body to be a warrior. I don't blame you, but... There was a moment on the ship, when Lady Ornicht held it, that I started to... pity you," Wylla said.

"That was the desired outcome," Strongmind replied.

"And you used my pity to give yourself a chance to kill my comrades. You used me as a human shield."

"I would have terminated you as well," Strongmind said. "If that had proven efficient."

"So you understand already, don't you? I can't relax around you, because I know everything you do is false. Even this conversation, right now: how do I know it's not part of some ploy of yours? Maybe you're deciding whether or not it'd be more 'efficient' to strangle me in my sleep. You're not human, Strongmind. You don't make any sense. So yes, I am uneasy around you."

"Thank you for sharing that information," Strongmind replied, not missing a beat. "It will increase my combat effectiveness to have a full understanding of your mental health and any stress factors. Please do not hesitate to share further insights with me, as you feel warranted."

"I surely will."

She stepped over another tree branch, then paused and crouched next to it. Slowly, she picked up the fallen limb and turned it over in her hands, then looked up at the tree line. In a moment she had spotted where it came from. She walked to the tree, and circled it until she found what she was looking for.

"Strongmind?" she called.

"May I be of assistance?"

"This world is uninhabited, isn't it?"

"That is what all official records indicate."

The machine walked up beside her, looking over her shoulder. Wylla ran a finger over the stump of a tree limb. It was partially healed, but the signs were quite clear.

"If this world is uninhabited," Wylla said, "Then who's using an ax to chop off tree limbs?"

CHAPTER 29

Green-gray desert stretched in every direction from where the escape pod had landed. Its silver hull and the shredded remains of the massive parachute that had helped decelerate it in the final moments before landing were the only color that broke the monotony of the desert. Glass crunched beneath Tsi's boots as she took her first few steps from the pod.

It was like walking on the surface of a vast and jagged ocean. Wave-like dunes rose around her, sharp edges sparkling in the light. A chill wind blew just then, causing the glass and sand to shift with an eerie tinkling noise. It reminded Tsi of mourning bells on Goodhome. Despite the cold, she could still almost feel the heat that had formed this place, the vast inferno that had once stretched from horizon to horizon.

Tenlok was a dozen meters ahead of her. He had stopped at the crest of a dune, and gone flat on his belly. Quietly as she could, Tsi padded up beside him. Her chest still hurt from the shrapnel she'd caught escaping the *Exile*, but the Bondsman had patched her up during the two long days it had taken the escape pod to land on Chalakhat.

She peered over the lip of the dune beside him. The glass desert ran for kilometers in every direction. It was hard to spot individual features in this place, everything seemed to meld into a single bizarre kaleidoscope of green and grey and white. On the horizon she could see mountain peaks. If she strained, she could just about spy a small belt of brighter green in the foothills, where the desert gave way and nature slowly struggled to undo the cruel work that had been done here.

Here and there, she could see bits of ruin jutting up from the desert. The rocky remains of sturdy buildings that had somehow managed to not be reduced to ash and powder. They might provide a little shelter on the long trek ahead of them.

"Four days," Tenlok said. "If nothing slows us down."

Tsi nodded. She checked her wrist-link: the planet's magnetic field caused a lot of unusual interference, and the device itself had taken a beating, but she figured she could just about keep their bearing on where the *Exile* had landed.

She rolled on to her back, and checked her pistol, then took off her pack and gave it a once-over. She had water and rations, a bed roll, anti-radiation drugs, some gear for starting a fire. It had been some time since she'd traveled a long distance on foot, but she still remembered spending nights under the moons of Goodhome with nothing for company but a few drones and a herd of hissing Gene-bears.

Tenlok had also turned away from the edge of the dune. He was on his knees, slowly taking off all of his web gear. Tsi watched as he checked each blade, then each gun. The ones he found to be damaged or without ammunition, he simply tossed down the dune without a second glance. By the time he was done he still had a small arsenal strapped to his body, but it was considerably reduced.

"Adding those to expenses," Tenlok said.

"Alright," Tsi replied. "You know, all my money is on the ship."

"Yeah. We better get going."

The two of them stood up together, and began the long trek to the mountains.

Tsi and Tenlok walked for hours in silence. The only sound they heard was the breaking of glass beneath their boots, and the howl of the wind in the distance. Tsi had not bothered trying to engage the mercenary in conversation. The two of them had little enough to say to each other. All that really mattered was getting to the landing site as quickly as possible. She knew it had to be somewhere in the green space on the horizon. The desert would have made a good landing zone, but when she had programmed the ship's route, she hadn't had time to scan for anything other than a set of coordinates that would wind up on dry land and not too far from where the life pods would come down.

It was curiously cold. Tsi regretted having nothing but her survival suit to travel in. She unconsciously checked her front again, seeing the places where the suit had been shredded by shrapnel and crudely stitched back together by the Bondsman. Wind bit through the gaps, chilling her skin. She couldn't exactly complain about Tenlok's help: after all, his medical skills had saved her life. Sewing wounds shut seemed to be something he understood, but mending clothing wasn't his forte.

They walked through the shadow of a ruined building, its upper floors poking above the desert sands. It had been tall and angular once, one of the mighty towers the Chalakhati prided themselves on. Most of them were for huge data repositories. Minimally staffed, they had once held stacks upon stacks of raw hardware devoted solely to maintaining records. They were libraries to rival the Temple of Knowing on Bykonus Prime, or the vast universities of New Kios. All of them had been rendered dust and ruins by orbital fire.

She tried to take some small solace in the knowledge that, at most, only a few hundred people had been in this particular tower when it was blasted apart. Their deaths had been quick.

Millions had lived in the city around them, though. She thought about them burning to cinders as she walked, their last visions being flares of bright light falling upon them from the sky. They had known the Janissaries were coming, the Empress had made certain of that. When their pitiful defensive fleet had been smashed aside, they had little recourse beyond huddling in their homes and praying for mercy. Their fate, burned alive where they crouched and prayed, had been nothing compared to those who had escaped to the hinterlands. They did not know that dying by plasma fire was the Empress's mercy, and that the survivors would feel her true wrath.

They left the ruined tower behind without a word between them. Tsi wondered briefly what the Bondsman was thinking, but she doubted the man had any reaction to this place at all. She'd met a few people like him in her travels: their studied indifference was a way of life. The Frontier could be a harsh place; she couldn't exactly blame someone for choosing to withdraw. Secretly, she was glad to be traveling with him instead of someone like Hiron, who would ask too many questions, or Wylla, who would know too much already. Strongmind would have been best of all, of course, but he was needed to protect the others.

She hoped that the other life pods had landed safely. There'd be no way to tell for certain until they met up at the rendezvous site. Three of the five others had never set foot on a world like this before. In the distance, she could see a rain storm passing across the horizon. She hoped they all knew enough to make shelter for themselves. Hypothermia was a common cause of death among people going on-world for the first time. Spacers who spent their entire lives in controlled environments tended to underestimate how dangerous exposure to the natural elements could be.

It was late in the day when they crested another dune, and Tsi saw something jutting up out of the sand and glass in the wadi below. It was an ovoid object, about as tall as she was and five meters across. A single hatch was set in the side of it. There was no mistaking the entrance to a survival bunker.

"Tenlok," she said, her voice barely a croak from hours of silence. "You keep me covered. I'm going to check that thing out."

"Nobody around," Tenlok said with certainty. "Do what you have to."

Tsi half-slid down the side of the wadi, coming to a halt at its base. They must have been a few kliks outside the edges of the old city. She'd heard that some of the Chalakhati had been able to design and manufacture bunkers like this in preparation for the invasion. With the right resources, under the right conditions someone could live in a bunker complex for years, decades even.

She walked to the hatch and, unable to think of anything else to do, simply knocked on it. There was no response. She circled the bunker's entrance, trying to see if there were any communication devices or access panels. No, aside from the hatch itself, the metal surface was smooth and featureless. She approached the hatch again, and this time tried to pull on its handle, but of course the bunker had been sealed tight. She pulled again and again, each effort growing more frantic until finally she kicked the hatch and stormed off, cursing.

If there was anyone in there, they certainly would have heard her by now. They were staying buttoned up inside, if they were wise. After all, anyone walking around on the surface of this planet probably meant them harm, but if Tsi could just get the bunker open, she could prove to them she was there to help.

She crouched down in the wadi, glaring at the bunker door, puzzling out what to do next. Of course, if anyone was alive in there,

there was another possibility: they'd been hurt. Some kind of accident had left them unable to come to the door, or perhaps they were too old and decrepit to open it by themselves. Tsi ground her teeth. There was no way of knowing. She didn't have a scanner, and the metal the bunker was made of couldn't be penetrated by her augmetic eyes.

She went over her equipment. She had her Repeater, a survival knife, packets of rations, fire starting equipment... despite her proclivities, she hadn't brought any explosives with her. Granted, at the time she'd been bundled in to the life pod she had had more pressing concerns, but now she cursed herself for not stowing a full arsenal on board. Another thought struck her, and she scurried up the edge of the ravine to where Tenlok stood.

"We going?" he asked.

"What've you got on you?" Tsi panted. "Blasting charges? Anything that could break through that?"

Tenlok tilted his head to the side.

"Come on, do you or don't you? This is important!"

The Bondsman looked from Tsi to the bunker and back again. Then, he drew a small black knife out of one of the scabbards on his belt. He depressed a stud on its hilt, and the blade suddenly flared bright orange along its edges. She could feel the heat coming off of it, even standing a few paces away from Tenlok. Tenlok switched the blade off and tossed it to Tsi.

"Sannatans call that an 'ice-pick'. Use it to cut through hard frost," he said. "Don't know how much charge is left on it. Only one I got."

"Thank you," Tsi said, and hurried back down into the wadi.

Her knees were shaking as she approached the bunker door. She took a moment to study it, trying to figure out where its weak points would be. Simply cutting a hole in it was too risky, she might run out of charge halfway through. She settled on finding the spots most likely to hold the hinges to the door. Then, she pressed the blade to metal, depressed the thumb stud, and slowly burnt her way through each hinge in turn.

As the last hinge turned to molten orange metal Tsi stepped quickly to the side, and the hatch fell open. A pall of dusty air rushed forwards from the open arch, and Tsi stood to the side a moment, covering her mouth.

"We're friends!" she called in to the doorway. "Anyone in there?"

Silence greeted her. Carefully, Tsi padded through the doorway and into the bunker. A flight of stairs led down into the darkness. As she took each step, motion activated lights slowly clicked on. Puffs of dust rose around her boots as she walked, until finally she reached the base of the stairs.

She knew what she would find, but still she walked from room to room to be sure, calling out and hearing only her own echo in response. There were four rooms in all: a bedroom, a kitchen, a living space, and a washroom next to the recycler. Someone could have lived down here for forty years, with the amount of rations packed into the kitchen walls. There was even an ancient generator to power a computer or a comm unit. The bedroom was spartan, but comfortable, and the recycler would have meant they could draw condensed moisture from the bedrock below, as well as recycle their own waste for decades, even craft tools out of broken down equipment. A whole generation could have grown up in those four rooms.

But no one had made it there in time. The bunker had lain empty since the time of the invasion. Whoever had made it had probably died during the first wave of strikes, and any survivors had either lacked the equipment, the time, or the inclination to break in. So it had become what it now was: a tomb for someone's foolish dream of survival.

Tsi sat down on one of the beds. It was wide enough for two people. A couple, she decided. Perhaps they were expecting to reproduce, there was basic medical equipment in the living space. Delivering a child in the darkness of the bunker would have been hard, but maybe down here, the child would have given them purpose to keep eking out an existence. To keep surviving.

It was important to have a purpose. She'd sent the Slip beacon away, her job was done. She could stay here, she supposed. A squatter in someone else's grave. It would be a fitting end.

But the crew was still waiting for her somewhere up above. She had to see them through. What happened to her mattered very little. All she needed to do was make sure they made it out of this alive.

Tsi emerged from the shelter to find Tenlok hadn't moved from his spot on the dune. He was sitting cross-legged, hands resting on his knees. She trudged up to the masked man, and handed him back the Sannatan heat blade.

"Anything worth taking down there?" he asked.

Tsi shook her head.

"Let's keep moving," she said quietly, and turned towards the green strip on the horizon.

She set off, and the Bondsman mutely followed.

They walked along the stream, single file. Hiron set the pace in the front, awkwardly picking his way through slick outcroppings of rock and patches of muddy earth. The rain had not let up, and he thought it was foolish to have someone like him at the front, but the other two were having a hard time adjusting to terrestrial life.

They were lucky they'd had gravity treatments. Hiron knew one of the greatest hazards to long term spacers was that their bones could become hollow as a bird's, their lungs unused to breathing natural air. He'd been terrified when Enlil first got out of the life pod that she would die right there, her lungs collapsing in on themselves, bones breaking like twigs.

They had both survived though, and after a night on the beach, the two of them were beginning to adapt to not having a roof over their heads. The uneven terrain was still confusing for them though, so their progress uphill had been slow.

"How long does it take to stop leaking?" Enlil called from behind him.

She still hadn't picked up the word 'rain.'

"I don't know," Hiron replied. "Where I come from, rain is rare most of the time, and pretty brief. I've heard of planets where it almost never stops raining though. Places with a lot of settlements especially."

"Must be rich," Enlil mumbled to herself again. "Clean water just falling down on 'em all the time..."

"I don't think anyone really lives here," Hiron said. "This was the site of an extermination."

"Mad Empress, right?" Furner said. "Place looks pretty for all that."

"It was a while back," Hiron replied. "I don't know much about it. The only things we heard about the war were myths and tall-tales.

Half the people on Promise don't even know there are any other planets, or that people can travel between the stars."

"Sounds like a shitty place," Enlil said.

"It... had its moments."

They traveled on, Hiron explaining to them the cycle of flora and fauna. He was surprised to learn the Noxians knew what trees were. Apparently, one of the greatest symbols of wealth on Salvation was owning private vegetation. Not so different from Promise, in that respect. He'd taken the gardens in his father's fortress for granted, never reflecting on the fact that most people outside the walls only worked with fungi-pens and the tough, radiation-resistant roots that grew in the canyon.

Still, he found the forest more than a little overwhelming. Insects flitted between tall, sinewy trees, and he could sometimes hear high pitched whistling and croaking barks from some native animal. Hiron speculated that this place had been seeded with Earth-life a long time ago. Most healthy colony worlds were like that, a careful mixing of xenoflora and old terrestrial species. He still didn't plan on eating anything here until he had to. Although, the water might contain dangerous microbes, and he had already drank from that twice during their rest stops. One had to take risks, after all.

They continued together until the sun sank in the sky. He helped Furner to make camp, while Enlil went off by herself. When the camp was well set, Hiron hobbled away from it, finding Enlil a few dozen paces away, standing in front of a tree. He heard a slow thud-thud-thud coming from the area.

"What are you doing?" he asked as he watched her.

She pulled a knife from the tree's bark, took ten paces back, then threw the blade into it. She repeated the action two more times before she turned to him.

"Getting used to this gravity," she said, holding the knife up.

"You...throw knives?"

"Yup," she said, striking the tree again with another well-aimed toss.

"But, we have guns for that... sort of thing..." Hiron said hesitantly.

Enlil shrugged as she retrieved her survival knife.

"We do," she agreed. "But ya never know when you're gonna

run out of ammo. Never hurts to be prepared. 'Sides, I'm outta practice. Haven't had a knife on me proper in a while."

"Well, uh, Furner and I are probably going to heat up some rations. You can join us. When you're done, I mean."

"Sure."

She didn't turn from her work, solely focused on pulling the blade back, aiming, and tossing it with expert precision. Hiron watched for a little while, marveling at her skill. Then he went back to where Furner was setting up their heater. He helped the old man finish, making sure there was nothing combustible around the small generator that would serve as their cooking stove.

"Should leave her alone when she's like that," Furner said as he opened a Rat-Pak.

"I just wanted to check on her, that's all."

"Girl like that can handle herself. Patchless, you know?"

"Patchless?" Hiron asked.

Furner pointed to the insignia on his jumpsuit. A beautiful woman with wavy hair, clutching a dagger between her teeth and glaring at him.

"Hasn't got one of these," Furner explained. "No clan. No crew. She hires on with an outfit, but she's never part of it. She doesn't trust anyone, and nobody should trust her. So, ya know, she ain't used to people fussing over her. Might react *badly* if you know what I mean."

"But... we're her crew now, aren't we? I mean, we're all on the same ship. Or, we *were* on the same ship—"

Furner shook his head.

"We're not crew," he said bluntly. "Not Noxian crew. I like you, kid. And I like her alright. But nobody was on that ship because we wanted to be."

"I was."

"That so? Thought I heard your people got dusted and you had to make a run for it?"

"They did... but I wanted to go before that. Tsi gave me a chance to join her crew, and I took it."

"Heh. Good for you. But me, I had people on Salvation. Don't know if any of them made it out, but I gotta go back for 'em. Tsi sent me in the wrong direction. I'm only here cause I gotta be. So's Wylla, so's Enlil, so's that Bondsman. We ain't a crew. We're just a bunch of junk that's been thrown together, drifting away from a bad situation."

Furner paused. He tore a hunk off the Rat-Pak, and tossed it on the stove to sizzle.

"We're flotsam," he said.

"Oh," Hiron said. "Is it bad to be flotsam?"

Furner grinned.

"My momma used to tell me this: son, there's only one thing worse than being flotsam, and that's bein' dead."

Wylla was sitting in a ditch. The machine had dug it using its bare hands with uncomplaining efficiency, ignoring her every time she asked what it was doing. Then it had politely but firmly told her to take cover in it, and proceeded to disguise the ditch with a covering of tree limbs, vines and leaves. It had essentially created what Wylla had heard referred to as a "hunting blind", or an observation post. Now the two of them were huddled together, the muddy earth soaking her legs, while Strongmind watched the lake.

He had picked a low hill overlooking the water. The vegetation was sparse here, giving them a clear view all the way to the desert south of them and the ocean to the east. At least, Wylla assumed they were "South" and "East". She knew they were somewhere towards the planet's magnetic pole, but they had no Geo-positioning system or anything functional to go on besides the homing beacon.

Strongmind had its carbine propped at the edge of the ditch beside it, while it sat, studying the lake.

"Please assist me in observation duties," Strongmind said.

"What are we looking for, exactly?"

"Humans," Strongmind said. "You observed evidence of human activity in this area. The lake is a resource site. Logically, it is highly likely that some element of the human population will return here on a regular basis."

"I still think we should keep heading for the landing zone," Wylla replied.

"That is a tertiary priority," Strongmind said. "My current objective is to ensure the safety of the crew. With communications systems limited, local resources must be employed. I intend to observe the human population, and ascertain whether they or their resources could be useful in locating the rest of the crew."

"And we are hiding in a ditch because of that?"

"Yes," Strongmind said. "They may be hostile. It is best that we have all tactical advantages upon our first encounter. I would also request that you keep your voice down, as sound carries in this environment."

Wylla pondered for a moment. Its logic was sound, but then logic was seldom a problem for a machine. She peered out from the edge of the ditch at the lake below, looking for movement, studying the ripples in the water.

"I don't think we'll notice them," Wylla said.

"Elaborate."

"Well," she continued. "The local culture obviously emphasizes stealth. Consider those severed tree limbs we found: rather than harvesting an entire trunk, the people here only take a few branches at a time. While this might be a conservation effort, I noticed that the limbs seemed to be carefully chosen, but only taken a few at a time from any given tree. They put effort in to taking only from trees that had lost limbs recently, as well. In short, they tried to disguise their harvest as a natural phenomenon."

"Why use tools?" Strongmind asked. "A sufficiently strong human could simply break off limbs."

"True," Wylla said. "I considered that. I think they use tools for speed. This forest canopy provides a natural cover for them. Being out near the lake is probably seen as a risky behavior, they only go there if it's absolutely necessary. I'm not sure what's special about the trees near the lake though, perhaps the abundance of fresh water enhances them in some way. It could also have cultural value. An adulthood ritual, for example."

"A valuable speculation. Thank you."

Wylla frowned. She still wasn't used to Strongmind trying to be polite to her. Guraggan drones were seldom programmed with much in the way of a personality, and now she understood why. It was hard not to hear Strongmind's artificial tone as mocking, even though it was attempting to be sincere. Or at least, as sincere as it could be.

Hours passed. With little else to do, Wylla meditated. A leaking roof of leaves and tree branches was not the most conducive to her mental practice. "One can meditate, even upon the surface of a star," was another saying that came to her. It was true, she had found time to meditate even when she was surrounded by chaos, but for some reason the rain dripping through the canopy above disturbed and irritated her.

She couldn't help but compare herself to Strongmind, who sat practically inert a few feet away. It was in a state of both total relaxation and total observation at the same time. That was one of the benefits of being made, and not born.

Settling herself in again, Wylla tried to steady her breathing. She let the irregular fall of rain on her head become just a part of the background noise. The cold water leaking down her back was no different than the sound of her breathing, or her thoughts, the tiny insects crawling over her heels, or the calls of animals in the distance.

Wylla was finally starting to relax when she heard a loud chirping noise nearby. The third time she heard the noise, her eyes opened, and she turned to Strongmind. It was chirping like a bird.

"Why are you doing that?" she hissed.

Strongmind stopped and looked at her.

"Targets have been observed," Strongmind said matter-of-factly. "I am attempting to lure them closer by imitating a prey species."

Wylla looked out at the lake. At first she could see nothing with her naked eyes, but as she relaxed into the old patterns of observation she had been trained with, the details began to fill in. She saw movement beneath the canopy of trees. Occasionally, a thin human outline would approach the edge of the woods, then dart away. At this distance she could tell nothing about them, other than that there were at least two, and they moved through the forest with the stealth and grace of woodland creatures.

Interestingly, Strongmind's tactic seemed to be working. The forest people were steadily making their way along the lake, heading for their little blind. As they drew closer, Strongmind spaced out its calls. Wylla had wandered the jungles of Bykonus Prime enough to realize this imitation was more sophisticated than she had originally given it credit for. Like any animal that was hunted, Strongmind was exercising caution, only calling out once every few minutes, but loudly enough that anyone looking for them could find them.

Of course, she hadn't discussed with him at all what exactly they were going to do when the other people got within reach. She eyed Strongmind's weapon nervously. She was about to speak when Strongmind's own low voice cut through the air.

"Please remain stationary," Strongmind said. "Our targets are now within range."

"Wait!" Wylla hissed. "Let me try talking to them first..."

"I will consider this."

Two figures crested the hill, moving low to the ground. They covered each other in turn: one would pad forward softly through the scrub, pause, then signal for the other to move ahead. As they drew closer, Wylla realized they were no more than boys. Short and skinny, carrying hatchets and atlatls made of black wood, they could easily have emerged from humankind's ancient past. They wore little clothing, and their bodies were daubed in camouflage paint to match the background. The foremost one, with bright green eyes, stopped and crouched. He sniffed the air.

Strongmind burst up from the ditch, its carbine in hand.

"*Halt!*" it blared.

The boys froze in terror. One shrieked. Strongmind fired its weapon over their heads, and both of them turned and sprinted back into the underbrush.

"What's the matter with you!" Wylla shouted at the machine. Without waiting for its response, she took off into the forest after the two boys.

She ran more on instinct than planning. She had no idea if they would even be able to understand the language she spoke, but for some reason, she felt it was vitally important that she catch up to them. They had to know she wasn't their enemy. They had to know she wasn't a threat.

She couldn't stop thinking about their thin frames. Something was wrong here. These people were starving. Were there only the two of them? She couldn't imagine two boys surviving alone in the woods, and even as she tore through the forest after the sound of their shrieks and fleeing footsteps, she worried for their safety.

She was calling after them, trying to shout that she meant no harm, when suddenly something caught her foot and she hit the ground face first. Then she was floating in mid air, upside down, her limbs flailing, mouth full of dirt. Rough hands grabbed her and spun her around. She had been caught in a snare trap.

She looked into the face of a scowling man, his thick black beard flecked with white.

"Call off your machine. Now," he hissed in Panglos.

"Strongmind!" She shouted. "Strongmind! Stand down! Stand down!"

The machine came clunking through the brush, and stopped to regard the scene before it. As Wylla bobbed, suspended by a vine lasso from her ankles, she too took in her surroundings. The two boys had turned, their expressions stony, holding atlatls with sharp metal arrows in them, ready to strike. The bearded man was not alone, a half dozen other people were visible in the woods, each with an expert firing position. Some carried rifles, others aged pulse weapons. A few raised bows and arrows. Like the boys, they all had their skin smeared with camouflage paint, though some of them were wearing body suits or clothing gone to rags.

The bearded man spun her around again, and raised a cold metal knife to her throat. Wylla breathed in as she looked at Strongmind. She could tell the drone was calculating its chances.

"Give it up, machine," the bearded man said. "Or I'll open your master's throat right now."

Wylla almost laughed. He was a fool if he thought her life, any life mattered to Strongmind. Long seconds ticked by as the machine stared at them.

Then, slowly, it lowered its weapon, and raised its mismatched arms.

"I surrender," Strongmind said.

CHAPTER 30

Enlil decided she did not like night time. On ships and stations, there was always a cycling of shifts. "Night" was an old concept, something left over from when most Noxians were born beneath blue skies. Generations living and dying in the light of the Poison Suns had changed the culture over time, and people had gotten used to the idea that while some slept, others worked. Lights stayed on, unless something was wrong.

On this planet the sky just got darker and darker, and then it went out entirely. They'd made a shelter, barely halfway towards the hill Hiron said would give them a good look at the surroundings. It was little more than a tarp stretched between a few trees. No walls, nothing to close them in and protect them.

She hated the feel of unfiltered air on her skin. She wished she had kept her EVA helmet handy. She could maybe sleep in that, protecting her from all this strange wind. Furner and the kid had fallen asleep easy enough, as soon as the rain let up, but Enlil sat there for hours, staring at the darkness.

The stream was nearby and loud, and she heard strange creatures calling to each other. Sometimes they sounded very close by. She particularly hated the ones with high pitched voices that sounded like alarms to her. Hiron had called them 'birds'. That was something she knew of, but had only seen once directly. They were actually pretty popular as symbols. Captain Black had decorated his armor with screaming falcons, and she'd crewed on more than one ship called "Star Hawk" or "Raptor."

The only time she'd seen one though, was in the possession of an Epilotii merchant who had come to Salvation not long after she'd been sold. The Epilotii woman had carried a little creature with a sharp beak and bright green wings on her shoulder. The bird had shrieked and repeated nonsense words, and glowered at Enlil with dead black eyes. When the merchant asked Enlil if she wanted to touch it, she had declined, too afraid of the strange creature. Now, she cursed her younger self for a coward. Something that small couldn't do her any harm.

She'd been afraid of just about everything back then. She had learned over time, and many harsh lessons, that fear could be useful if it didn't overpower you. It was like a drug: a quick kick of stimm before you breach, and you'll fight like a war god. Dose too much and you're useless.

Furner was muttering in his sleep. Like a lot of old hull-breakers she knew, he had nightmares. Bad nightmares. He twitched and fumbled, rolling from side to side, sometimes shouting. The kid was quiet.

Enlil got up and walked to the stream. Her legs were still shaky. It was strange how rough the ground was. She couldn't fathom how dirt-foots handled this without tripping over themselves all the time. Then again, she'd seen how badly new spacers handled EVA suits. Even Tsi didn't have the fluidity of someone born in the void when she moved around.

Tsi. She was probably dead, Enlil decided. She had been alone, on a damaged ship, against a combat drone with enough ordinance to fry a whole boarding party. Which made their journey to the ship's landing site utterly pointless, but Enlil didn't exactly have a better idea of what to do.

Hiron had said this place was uninhabited, and she trusted the kid, despite how dumb he could be. They were stuck on this rock. Their only hope of getting off was that the ship was still in good enough shape they could boost her back through the atmosphere and find some way to call out for a pick up. Enlil knew for a fact the ship didn't have enough fuel to break the atmosphere. She was well and truly stuck.

Enlil had reached the stream by the sound of it, and she sat down in the darkness. Slowly, she pulled her boots off, and dangled her feet down. She gasped as the water ran over them, cold and crisp, washing away days of dirt and grit. The cold started to numb her, but she kept her feet under, staring down at the stream as it did its work. It was so clear and shiny, even in the darkness. She realized it was reflecting the sky above. A great river of twinkling stars passed over her feet and she looked up.

The sky was clear, a deep black studded with white stars. Another thing about dirt-foots she couldn't understand: why did they want to go into the void so much? She'd been born out there, lived there, and she had been certain she would die there. It was only luck that she'd been given treatments when she was younger to make surviving on the ground possible. As much as she hated the night and trees and the noise, and the way the ground was uneven and trying to trip her up, she was still certain of one thing. She would rather be here than home.

Dawn rose, and Tsi rose with it. As far she could tell, Tenlok didn't sleep. The Bondsman was sitting cross legged a few feet away from her as she got up off of her bedroll, looking out at the dawn breaking across the desert of shattered glass. She regarded him for a moment. He was statue-still, more like the ruins of the desert than a man. A lifeless silhouette.

Then he ruined the illusion by turning to look at her. He didn't say anything, only stood and watched as she packed away her things. Once she had everything she needed stowed and on her pack, they set off towards the forest to the north.

The cloud cover had cleared, the wind had died, and Tsi was starting to sweat. She could keep going for hours and hours, but this kind of heat was not something she enjoyed. Clear days were beautiful, but they impeded her progress.

Nervously, she looked at her communicator. Chalakhat had enough radiation in its atmosphere that a standard comm unit was only worth anything out to a few hundred yards, and yet there was still some paranoid part of her that was terrified another member of the crew had called out to her, and she had been too busy to respond.

No, the comms were as inert as ever. She had no one for companionship on this journey but the crunching desert beneath her feet, and the silent Bondsman.

They walked and walked, only stopping every few hours so that Tsi could drink water, or make herself a meal. The rations were tasteless, almost texture-less. There had been a time when she couldn't care a wit about what she ate, and a time, earlier than that, when she was a true connoisseur. She remembered the first time

Marta Olon made her Gene-Bear steaks. She had chewed her first piece at least fifty times before she swallowed, the meat was so tough. Tough but flavorful, and the woman had surely known her way around spices.

Tsi allowed herself a smile as she sipped her late afternoon tea. It would still be an hour or two before the sun slipped behind the sky. They could keep going a few hours into nightfall. In all honesty, her own desire for sleep could be suppressed, she could travel as far and as hard as the Bondsman.

"So," Tenlok said. "You wanna talk about that bounty on you from Goodhome?"

Tsi slurped her tea for a moment and didn't respond. She had been waiting for this for a long time. She'd wondered what the Bondsman had recognized in her when they first met, pondered why his eyes had locked on her when she was in the court of Gyje the Third Son.

"You probably know a fair amount about me, don't you Tenlok?" she asked.

"Twenty thousand credits," he said. "Most people on Goodhome never see that kind of money. Posting specified 'alive', too. Get nothing for your corpse."

"Guess I'm popular."

"Not the word I would use," Tenlok said. "Done a stretch as a bounty killer. People only post warrants 'alive' for two reasons: either they want to cut on you before they kill you, or they want you back."

Tsi finished her drink, and began packing her meal away. She had nothing to fear from the Bondsman. He would die before she did.

"I wouldn't know anything about that," Tsi said.

"Yes, you would," Tenlok said. "We're gonna be out here a while. Need to know who I'm dealing with. Someone's willing to pay a lot for you. I'm wondering why."

"I'm paying you," Tsi retorted as she stood up and began to walk. "And if you cross me, you die. That's the only thing you should concern yourself with."

"Can't keep you alive if you don't tell me who we're up against."

"The Guraggan," Tsi snapped. "Isn't that enough?"

Tenlok had fallen into line behind her. The two of them were walking through the desert as if nothing had happened, despite Tsi's balled fists and the pulsing veins on her forehead. Something about the masked mercenary, something painfully familiar, irked her in the way he talked.

"The Guraggan and a bunch of farmers from Goodhome," Tenlok said. "What happened? You steal somebody's prize stud? Make off with the temple donation box?"

"I killed a man called Vylk Preston," Tsi said.

Tenlok was quiet for a moment. She could tell he wasn't the type to be shocked by murder. Still, the wind chimed over the broken glass of the desert as they walked for what seemed a long time.

"You aren't the first murderer I've traveled with," Tenlok said.

"I said killed," Tsi replied. "Not murdered."

"So it was justified."

"He came at me with his carapace cutting knife."

"Why?"

He'd cut to the heart of the issue there. Most people Tsi had known had heard this story in a moment of weakness. Either when she was drunk or so filled with sorrow that she couldn't contain the truth anymore. She had confessed to it a few times. Her listeners hadn't bothered to ask her that question. There were few enough of them, and they had all assumed that any madman who came at her with a knife must surely have been in the wrong.

Not Tenlok though. Not a Bondsman. Murder was something he specialized in. He knew all the reasons that could drive someone to try to take another's life. Gutting someone like Tsi wasn't aberrant behavior for him, it was a calculus. Unlike poor Vylk, Tenlok only had to figure out whether Tsi's carcass was worth anything before he decided to end her.

"He and I had a disagreement," Tsi said. "He thought I'd cheated him, I thought I'd been honest."

"Lover? Or was it money?"

"Why does that matter to you?"

"Need to know who I'm traveling with," Tenlok repeated. "My life is bound to yours."

"I wish to hell it wasn't," Tsi shot back. "I'd have left you on Salvation if I could have."

"You needed me," Tenlok replied. "I got you out of

there alive."

"I *saved* you!" Tsi said, whirling around on him. "I could have left you in that hangar, but it was my choice, *mine*, to go back and get you. You would be mounted on the Guraggan's wall right this minute if it wasn't for me."

"I was only there because of you," Tenlok said. "Or do you expect all your slaves to be grateful?"

Tsi's anger boiled over.

"You are *not* my slave!" She shouted. "For all I care, you could walk into the desert and… and…"

"And die?"

There was something utterly infuriating about his ghoul-mask. It mocked her with its twisted, sneering features. She wanted to punch it, but instead she kept her curled fist at her side.

"For all I care, Bondsman, go die in the desert," she said, voice cold as ice.

"Normal contract, I'd take you up on that offer," he replied. "Except the dying part."

"You're so righteous, aren't you? The wise killer, thinking he knows everything about everyone. You're the one who sells himself to the highest bidder, not me, alright? It wasn't me that made you what you are, it's not my fault that your life—"

"You infected me," Tenlok said. For the first time she heard genuine emotion in the Bondsman's voice. Genuine hatred.

"You infected me," he repeated. "It wasn't my choice to stay with you. There was no contract, no negotiation. I'm only here because I'll die if I leave."

"And you're so very terrified of death," she hissed.

"Death is with me everywhere I go," Tenlok replied. "I choose who I'm bound to. You enslaved me. Don't pretend you didn't know what you were doing."

"I did what I had to! You tried to kill me! You murdered the Jarawat!"

"She was a threat. So were you."

"It must be so easy," she said. "Going through life like that. Someone's either a threat or they aren't. The whole universe reduced to binary. Tell me, Tenlok, have you ever taken a side on anything besides your own?"

"I take the side that pays me. So far, I haven't seen anything from you. And I need to know..."

To Tsi's surprise, Tenlok sighed. The sound came rushing out of his mask, like a leak of air, and she saw his armored shoulders sag. She had been so angry with him, she had heard the hate in his voice, but looking at Tenlok now all she saw was exhaustion.

"I need to know if you're as good as your word," Tenlok said.

His voice was still the sound of metal against metal, but Tsi couldn't help but notice the trace of sorrow, of desperation in his words. How many men had she known like this? All armor and weapons and throaty growls? And underneath it all... sorrow. And tiredness. Just like her.

She took a deep breath.

"I killed Vylk Preston because he was my friend, and he found out who I really was, and he decided that I had to die for that," Tsi said. "So I put a knife in his stomach."

She waited, but the Bondsman said nothing.

"Don't... don't you want to know who I really am?" she asked.

"Why?" Tenlok said. "Got my suspicions, but it doesn't matter. Just needed to know why those farmers on Goodhome want you back so bad. Now I know."

Tsi looked at the Bondsman's mempo, trying, hoping to see something more there, but there was still only that pitiless ghoul face, and those foul eyes staring back at her. It was worse than speaking to a drone. She knew there was a human being under that mask, there had to be. Yet he, like so many people she had known, went through life dead-eyed and without care. Then he spoke again, his voice still that same throaty growl.

"They want you because they don't know who you really are," Tenlok said. "But I know. That's good enough. Just be sure you've got the money together when we get off this rock."

"I will," Tsi said bitterly. "You'll get your payment. And you're not my slave. I'll make sure you get the treatment you need."

Tenlok only nodded in response.

"Let's get going," she said.

Once again, the two of them headed off across the desert of broken glass. As Tsi walked, she saw her shadow keeping pace with the two of them. No matter how fast she moved, it seemed always to be on her left, just as the Bondsman walked steadily along on her right. Unconsciously, she felt at a pouch on her thigh. The vial of blue liquid was still there. She thought about taking it out and giving it to him.

No, she decided. It was too late for that. For both of them.

CHAPTER 31

Wylla had almost forgotten how good a simple cot could feel. After a night or two of sleeping in the open, not to mention days stuffed in a life-pod, she had relished laying down on the canvas bed, pulling a rough cover over herself, and falling into a deep sleep. When she had been just a little girl, she had spent some time with the Order of the Open Palm. At first she had hated the stern nuns and the scratchy bedding she was given, but slowly she had begun to understand, and even enjoy a life of privation. The Open Palm had given her spiritual and mental instruction, but the greatest gift they had given her was training to endure hardship.

Thinking back on it now, the nuns were the first people in Wylla's life to make her feel powerless. Perversely, she appreciated that harsh lesson. So many people she had met in her life were desperately trying to maintain control, none more than her erstwhile Mistress. Lady Ornicht's rages and her threats were dangerous, but even as Wylla had knelt in supplication, she had felt a twinge of pity of the Guraggan. She had never learned to accept that some things were beyond her power.

She was woken with the intoxicating scent of hot broth. A woman with silver hair and a lined face had come into her room while she was sleeping, carrying two bowls. She handed one to Wylla, and sat down on a little stool opposite the bed. The room was small, with walls of corrugated metal and an earthen floor, but Wylla had begun to find it oddly pleasant. As far as captors went, these people were not the worst she had ever had.

"I'm Narri," the older woman said.

Wylla bowed her head in gratitude.

"I am called Wylla Laran-Se," she said, before taking an experimental sip from her bowl.

The hot liquid was undeniably delicious. She could see chopped roots floating in it, and it had a pleasant, spicy aroma. She took another greedy sip before letting the bowl sit and cool for a moment. Rat-Paks were all that sustained her during her time in the life pod, and she hadn't known which of the local berries were safe for human beings to eat, so she was thankful for an opportunity to taste real food prepared by human hands.

"Very nice to meet you, Wylla," Narri said with a smile. "I've got a few questions for you. Did you come here in one of those escape pods? We saw three of them fall from the sky a few days ago."

"Yes," Wylla replied, seeing no reason to lie. "Our craft was badly damaged. The captain ordered us to abandon ship, so we did."

Subtly, she studied Narri as she spoke. At a guess the woman had entered old age some time ago. She was hale and well-built. Her hands and fingernails were dirty, showing she obviously did manual work. The slight paunch to her stomach showed that she got enough to eat. Wylla concluded that Narri was these people's leader.

"Interesting. What went wrong?"

"A drone attack," Wylla said. "We were fleeing an enemy. One of their drones managed to get aboard our ship. It would have killed us all, if our Captain hadn't intervened."

Narri sat back, clicking her tongue.

"Lot of trouble," she said quietly. "Lot of trouble, indeed. How many of you were there?"

"I'm not sure how many survived," Wylla replied. "The machine and I were the only ones in our pod. You said you saw three pods land?"

"Mm-hmm," Narri said. "One a little south of here, the other out towards the sea. Third one went into the Glass Desert though. Unlucky."

"Why?"

Narri arched her eyebrow.

"Do you know where you are, Wylla?"

"Chalakhat," Wylla replied nonchalantly.

"You know what happened here?"

"I have... heard stories," Wylla admitted.

It was hard, in the Guraggan Hegemony, to sift fact from myth. The Guraggan were not expert propagandists, but all the information about the last war had been colored with their legendry and philosophy. History was one of the many subjects her people considered a valuable study, but ever since their conquest, it had been hard to find out about events not directly witnessed and recorded by a Bykon. Even then, scholars had to be careful with what they wrote, lest they insult some young warrior's honor or a House's name. The slaughter on Chalakhat had attracted little attention in the Hegemony. They had been too busy trying not to lose the war to pay attention to their enemy's barbarity.

"They tried to burn us from the skies," Narri said. "The Glass Deserts are what's left of our great cities. Air was poison for a long time, but slowly, we've come back. New trees are growing. A thousand years from now, Chalakhat might be covered in green again."

"I am sorry," Wylla said simply.

"Mmm," Narri murmured. "You're wondering how I came to be here, aren't you? That's the story they tell, isn't it? That we all died at the Janissaries hands? But someone always survives. No matter how hard they try to stamp us out, someone always survives."

"Your resilience is very admirable," Wylla said. "My people are called the Bykon. We, too, know what it is to live at the mercy of Empire."

Narri scowled.

"A Bykon, eh?" she said, the warmth dropping from her voice. "I thought you gave up a little too easily. That killing machine you've got out there, that part of an invasion or something? Has the war started again? Your masters coming down here to finish what the Janissaries started, is that it?"

"I am a free woman," Wylla said. "I have no masters any longer. I came here, just as I said, because we were fleeing an enemy. The woman who used to own me was hunting us, but we eluded her."

"That's dung!" Narri growled. "No one escapes the Guraggan."

"We did."

Narri looked at her hard, but Wylla returned her gaze unflinchingly. She could see the fear in the older woman's eyes. How many years had she spent hiding, Wylla wondered. A whole culture had grown up among the survivors on Chalakhat, living in terror for generations, doubt gnawing at the back of their minds that some day, their enemies might come back. Despite her harsh words, Wylla couldn't feel anything but sympathy for the silver haired woman.

"I know what it's like to live in fear," Wylla said. "I understand why you might fear me, or my companions. But you must believe me when I tell you, we mean you no harm. We're just like you. All we want is to escape our enemies. To survive."

"Is that why you brought your combat drone down here?"

"Strongmind isn't mine," Wylla said. "It belonged to the captain. It... hasn't hurt anyone, has it?"

Narri shook her head, her features softening.

"No, it hasn't hurt anyone. It seems very worried about you though. It keeps asking us to check on you and make sure you're alright."

"It takes its job very seriously," Wylla said. "Have... have you seen any of my other companions?"

Narri leaned back for a moment and sipped her broth. She was clearly giving herself time to think, which was answer enough for Wylla. The old woman spoke at last.

"Scouts are tracking three people, wandering through the forest near the beach," she said. "Other side of the mountains. Two men and a woman. They're moving very slowly, the men look like they need prosthetics."

"If Strongmind and I could be taken to them, I would appreciate that," Wylla said. "We do not intend to stay on your world. Once the crew is assembled, we'll make our way to where our ship landed, and try to repair it and leave as soon as possible."

"I know about your ship," Narri said. "A salvage party is headed there right now. We'll bring your friends here soon, too. But Wylla, you must understand: you can't leave."

"I told you, you can't stay out in the rain," the kid said.

Enlil wiped her nose on the back of her cuff and then stuck her tongue out at Hiron. She'd been sneezing all the way up the hill. It was probably the worst chill she'd gotten since she was a little girl. Cold wasn't generally something she'd worried about. Even on Salvation, parts of the station that were cool were rare and precious.

"You the captain now?" Enlil asked sarcastically.

Hiron gave her a hurt glance, so she slapped him on the back playfully.

"Come on, ease up kid. Just—"

She sneezed.

"Just havin' some fun with you."

"I know, I know," Hiron grumbled. "We don't have very much medicine though. If one of us gets seriously sick…"

"We'll vent that hold when it needs venting," Furner chimed in.

He was huffing and puffing harder than the kid was, but he still gamely kept up with the two of them. Enlil had decided Furner wasn't so bad. A little annoying, like most old men, but not bad.

Her only worry was the pace they were setting. The kid seemed to be able to make his way through the undergrowth well enough, but she knew she'd travel a lot faster alone. The thought of leaving the two of them behind had crossed her mind more than once. She had a direction to go in, after all, but she couldn't guess at what kind of hazards were ahead. Almost falling in the stream twice had made her cautious around slippery stones, for example, and now, her mucus-filled nose was a warning against her little night time sojourns.

At long last, they made it to the top of the hill Hiron had spotted the day before. It was a little rump of bald land, treeless and decorated only with a few rocks and scrub-grass. The rain had cleared, and now the day was bright and clear. Enlil sat down on one of the rocks and looked up at the clear sky.

It was a deep, clean blue, unlike the murky grey of the ocean. The sun shone high, its light making the little beads of moisture on the grass sparkle like precious gems. Enlil pulled up a tuft on the grass, sniffed it, felt the wetness in her hands. She half-considered taking a bite of it. She knew some animals fed on grass. Why not humans? In the end though, she tossed it away.

Hiron had opened up his pack and was fiddling with a pair of binoculars. The kid finally managed to set the binocs up the way he liked, and began sweeping the area around them. Meanwhile, Furner settled down on a rock near her.

The old Noxian rolled up a pant leg, revealing the metal rod and crude prosthetic foot that had replaced it from the knee down. He rubbed his stubbly chin as he considered it in the light. Enlil took out a Rat-Pak and cut herself a hunk of protein chew.

"Fashionable," she called to him in Noxian, between bites.

"Yup," Furner said. "Soon as we get back to Salvation everyone's gonna want one."

Furner rubbed the metal pole. He repeated the gesture, looking confused.

"Huh, damnedest thing," he muttered.

"What's that?"

"It itches," he said.

Enlil cocked an eyebrow.

"Like at the join? Oughtta be careful about that, could start an infection."

"No, no," Furner said. "My calf itches."

"Your calf?"

"Yeah," he said. "The one that's not there anymore."

"You're losin' it, pal," Enlil snorted.

"Maybe."

Furner shook his head, staring at the rod. Then he rolled his pant leg back down and tied it tight. He looked back up at her and smiled, switching back to Panglos.

"Hey, Hiron!" he called to the kid. "Ya see anything good? Gilded Lily an' me are getting bored."

Enlil tensed.

"Stop calling me that," she said.

"Oh, come on!"Furner laughed. "You're really embarrassed about your nickname?"

"She doesn't like people calling her that name," Hiron said.

He lowered his binocs and hobbled over to where the two of them sat. Enlil could tell he was trying to sound serious, but there was something inherently comical about his twisted little body. She didn't laugh though. The kid had earned that much.

"It's fine, kid," she said. "Furner's just trying to get a rise out of me."

"Short fuses mean blown circuits," Furner said piously. "How'd ya get that name, anyway? I never heard the whole story."

Enlil sighed. Hiron was looking at her with curiosity as well. She decided it was better to just tell them, rather than have Furner speculating loudly for the rest of their trek.

"First big haul I ever did," Enlil began.. "Woulda been... maybe a little older than the kid here. Anyway, we took out a Nioban Ore-Hauler, trying to make a cut past Rotten Glass."

"Stupid of them," Furner said. "Rotten's one of the first places people look for someone tryin' to slip by unnoticed."

"Yeah. They had a full hold. Probably just bought it all too. So we took it, dragged our prize back to Salvation, stripped it for parts and sold the metal right off to their competition. Like I said, big haul, even someone as young as I was got a pretty good cut."

"Not a bad start to an illustrious career," Furner said.

"Well, I was young, never seen that much money before in my life so, naturally I started spending it. End of the week, I'd blown my whole share on booze, tattoos, and two-suits. I was tossing around money like a noble lady, and since people had a hard time saying my name and had been calling me 'Lily' instead..."

"Gilded Lily," Furner said. "I get it. That's not the worst. They used to call me 'Blocker' because I got stuck in a sewage tank once. Took a while to live that one down. And get the smell out of my clothes."

"What's a 'two-suit'?" Hiron asked.

Enlil laughed. Furner turned to the kid, grinning.

"They don't got two-suits where you're from?"

"His kind don't travel a lot," Enlil said.

"Ah," Furner nodded. "Well, waaay back, before anyone had anything like A-Grav, when the first people started heading out into the dark, they ran into a problem. Lotta people, living real close together, only a matter of time before people start doin' what people do right?"

The kid nodded, but Enlil noticed a faint trace of red around his cheeks.

"So," Furner continued. "Trick is, even if you could get your engines going, which was hard back then, problem with zero-G is that when you bump into something, it just drifts away from you. So people realized if they wanted to get anything done, they needed to be able to strap themselves down, and strap themselves to each other. So, some genius invents a space suit that you can hook in to another, and nine months later the first babies are born on a ship!"

"So it's, I mean, do you actually still... uh, *use* one of those?" Hiron asked haltingly.

"Fuck no!" Enlil snorted.

Furner raised a finger in protest.

"Rock-Drinkers do."

"That's feec-rec," Enlil said, rolling her eyes at Furner. "Those creeps just jab each other with a tube and be done with it."

"I got a cousin who was captured by them once. He said that one of their Engineers took a fancy to him, and…"

Enlil was about to interject with some choice words when she realized that the kid was staring at something away from them. She turned to get a glimpse of what he was looking at, and realized there was a figure standing at the edge of the woods. Enlil rose, drawing the rifle from her pack cautiously. She switched the safety off, but the figure waved to her and she recognized it at last.

"Wylla?" Hiron called out. "Wylla you made it!"

The Bykon walked over to the three of them at a stately pace. Enlil could tell something was wrong, and began scanning the trees.

"Enlil," Wylla said. "Please put your weapon down."

"Fuck's going on here, Wylla?" Enlil said.

"We'll all be safer if you put the weapon down. Please."

"Why?" Enlil shot back.

Wylla took a deep breath, glanced downwards, then back at Enlil.

"Because if you don't, the Chalakhati will kill you."

"Chalakhati?" Hiron asked. "What are you talking about?"

"Think she means them," Enlil said, nodding her head at the tree line.

There were a dozen figures now where none had stood before. All armed. All grim faced.

"Well, shit," Enlil said, dropping her rifle. "I guess we're coming with you."

Tsi stood at the place where the desert ended. That morning, she had seen the first few scrub bushes. As they walked, the bushes became more regular, springing up here and there, until at last the came to the top of a dune and could see the forest and the mountains beyond as plain as the day around them.

It had taken all of Tsi's resolve not to break into a run the moment she saw that green expanse, but she had not given in to her childish impulses. Instead, she and Tenlok had walked down through the last few hundred paces of the desert together, the sound of rustling glass slowly replaced by loose sand and the trampling of dry roots beneath their feet.

At last, they stood here, looking in to a forest of thick-trunked trees and foliage so dense the sun only passed through in faint beams of golden light. She had to stop at the sight of it. For some reason, despite having gone from one end of the Frontier to the other, having been through hardship and seen wonders, Tsi knew that nothing would compare to leaving the desert of glass for this green land.

She could hear birdsong. The calls of wild animals. Somewhere not far away, she was sure she could also hear the sound of a waterfall. She thought of those beautiful diamond-clear rivers for which Chalakhat had been so famous. Her legs seemed leaden. She couldn't move, only stare in wonder at the forest.

Tenlok cleared his throat but didn't say anything. Slowly, Tsi walked to the edge of the forest. She knelt down, and put a bare hand on one of the gnarled roots of a tree. Running her hand up and down the rough surface, she had to reassure herself that it was real. Then, she plucked a blade of grass and tucked it away in her pocket.

She signaled Tenlok with her hand, and the two of them walked into the forest. They took turns leading, swapping a short bush-blade Tsi carried back and forth to cut a path. Soon, Tsi's arms were stained green with chlorophyll. She was tired, her limbs ached, but she was smiling. All that mattered was going forward.

They stopped to rest by a river. The current was swift, creating a furious roar as it tumbled over great stones and slapped against the banks. Tsi could see fish twisting and coiling in the water, strange creatures with rudimentary eyes and long feeding tendrils. They were strong little swimmers though, fighting through the current with a determination that Tsi admired.

She looked upstream, and there she saw it. Without a word, she broke into a run, leaving the Bondsman to clatter after her. She sprinted across wet rocks and vaulted fallen tree limbs, feeling like a little girl again. The wind whipped through her hair as she ran, until finally she rounded a curve on the river bank and came to a halt.

There it stood: a waterfall. Sheets of shimmering water slid down the craggy crimson rock face, looking exactly as Tsi had remembered it. She sat down on the bank, watching the constant motion, hearing its roar as it plunged and thundered into the lake below. Gently, she stretched out one of her hands and dipped her finger into the lake's water. She felt it play over her, cold and clean.

Sorrow still pulled at her, being here on Chalakhat. A sorrow so deep it threatened to drag her down completely, but for a moment she was at peace. Only for a moment.

"What's with you?" Tenlok said from over her shoulder.

His armor was dripping, and Tsi realized he had probably fallen into the river trying to catch up with her at least once. She laughed, and the Bondsman cocked his head to the side.

"It's fine," she said. "I just... really wanted to get here, that's all."

Tenlok looked around and shifted his weight, obviously unsure of what to do.

"That tracker of yours still working?"

"It is," Tsi said, pulling it out of her pack. She checked the rugged device over one more time, just to be certain.

"Landing site's about a day away, give or take. I think she landed just beyond that mountain," Tsi said, pointing upwards at the red peak beyond.

"Looks like rough going," Tenlok said.

"I agree. I think we should make camp here. I'll see if I can't work us out some kind of course based on the tracker's readings."

The Bondsman didn't say another word. He simply walked into the woods and began clearing out a space for her to set up her bedroll and a shelter. Tsi watched the waterfall a little while longer, then she too got to work preparing their camp.

The work was done in less than an hour. She'd set up her bedroll and a little heating unit, a tarp above them in case it rained. The two of them made a quick circuit of the lake as the sun began to set, making sure there weren't any hazards in the area. Tsi knew a few large carnivores were indigenous to Chalakhat, but their population had likely died off during the purge. She debated whether or not to make their camp as visible as possible, but decided against it. They would either run into the others along the way, or meet them at the landing site. There was no need to attract anymore attention, and truth be told, a part of her desperately wanted to leave the lake and the waterfall as undisturbed as possible.

As the sun finally set and the night began to creep back in, she sat along the shore, watching the light slowly leave the lake's shimmering surface. Tenlok was leaning against a tree nearby, practicing his habit of absolute stillness. It was odd, seeing his thoroughly artificial form juxtaposed with the natural world. There he was, a figure wrought in blue metal, and yet as the night swallowed them, he seemed to be as much a part of the forest as the stones and the lake and the trees.

Then again, Tsi was almost as augmented as he was. Her muscles, her eyes, parts of her brain. She could just barely remember the face she had been born with. It didn't look too different from the one she now wore, she thought. But she never wanted to see that face again. She wasn't that person anymore.

She knew it was finally time to tell the crew the truth. When they all met up again, she would explain everything to them, consequences be damned. She almost wanted to tell Tenlok right now, but she knew the mercenary would either shrug or cock his head, and say nothing at all. It didn't matter. He would hear it with the rest of them, when the time came.

She looked up at the shadowy outline of the mountain beyond, and something caught her eye. Blinking hard, she switched vision modes several times, just to make sure she was seeing what she thought she was.

"You see that?" Tenlok asked.

"I do," Tsi replied.

On the mountainside, not far from them, someone had lit a bonfire. The red light flared in the darkness, and she was sure she could see figures standing by it, looking out into the night, just as she looked up at them.

Someone was out there in the darkness.

Waiting for them.

CHAPTER 32

They woke Enlil up just before dawn and made her come and sit at the campfire. These people, with their faces painted green, weren't so bad. They hadn't even roughed her or the kid up when they'd been taken, just marched her a little too fast to a cave in the side of the mountain.

Being in the cave had felt more natural to her. Having a real roof over her head was reassuring, and the small room they had put her in felt remarkably like the quarters on a ship. After her interrogation by an old man with a bushy beard, they left her alone. She had slept very well.

Now, the whole crew was made to sit around a campfire. One of the Chalakhati put out a pot filled with some kind of broth, and the five of them breakfasted together in an odd sort of calm while their captors waited in the woods nearby. They were sitting at the edge of a rocky cliff, cleared of trees and overlooking the forest below. Enlil could see what looked like a small trail cut through the bush coming up to them. Not far away was the entrance to the cave where they had been kept, and further down below she could see a waterfall and a lake. This whole place seemed to be veined with lakes and rivers, and she still couldn't shake the notion that someone incredibly rich owned it.

"I do not advise attempting escape at this time," Strongmind said, to no one in particular.

"Yeah, I saw a couple of them have pulse guns," Enlil said as she sipped broth. She'd had worse. "They'd fry half of us before we got into the bush."

Their reunion with Wylla and Strongmind had been brief the night before, but now, no one seemed to be able to find anything to say. Furner and Hiron sipped their broth quietly, while Wylla stared into the fire. Enlil had never quite been able to figure the Bykon woman out. She was practically a different species. Enlil couldn't imagine going through life not even able to think about knifing someone.

"So," Enlil said. "You two run into Tsi?"

"I think that's who we are waiting for," Wylla said. "The Chalakhati saw a third pod land. They said it was in the Glass Desert, a dangerous place..."

"But if anyone's going to survive that, it's Tsi," Enlil said. "So we're, what? Bait?"

"That seems likely," Wylla said. "These people are afraid of us."

"Why?" Hiron asked. "We don't even have weapons anymore."

"We got tin-head here," Enlil said. "I think he could count for half of them, bare-handed."

"Direct combat would result in unacceptable losses," Strongmind said blandly.

"They live here in secret," Wylla explained. "They've been hiding out for a generation, and they're terrified of being discovered."

"So what?" Furner asked. "They gonna cook us just for crashing on their planet?"

"I don't think so," Wylla said, looking as if she was mulling over the idea herself. "If they had intended on murdering us, I believe they would have done so by now. I think they're still... gathering information while they decide what to do with us. They certainly don't want us to leave."

"So we're bait then," Enlil said.

"It's the only logical solution," Wylla said. "They've been lighting this bonfire, trying to make it as visible as possible. If Tsi survived, she'd have to investigate."

"Well, if she plays it cool we might all just walk away from this one," Furner said. "Or in me and the kid's case, hobble."

Hiron gave an appreciative chuckle.

"There is another possibility," Wylla pointed out. "Tenlok is the only other person unaccounted for. If he is with her..."

"We might still be screwed," Enlil said.

A misty fog had rolled in less than an hour after dawn. Despite this, Tsi could still see the bonfire burning in the distance. She was drawn to it like a moth. So much that had happened on this world already had an eerie, dream-like quality: she felt as though even if she wanted to turn away or seek a different path, she couldn't.

Tenlok had spotted a game trail, and the two of them walked along it, her in front, the Bondsman behind. Always, Tsi kept the fire in sight, watching it through the trees and rushing around the next bend in the trail when the foliage became too dense. The sounds of the animals had grown more quiet in the dawn and the fog, and Tsi kept one hand on her Repeater as she stalked through the forest.

She was cautious, but she made no attempt at stealth. Whoever had lit that fire wanted her to find them. She hoped it was the other members of the crew, but if it was, why hadn't they gone ahead to the landing site like she'd planned? Perhaps one of them was hurt and needed help, or for some reason they had decided it was best to wait on that bald knob of earth rather than press on alone. There was a lot that could go wrong in an emergency landing, and Tsi reminded herself again that half the crew had never set foot on a planet like this before.

"Look at this," Tenlok said.

Tsi back-tracked to where the mercenary was crouched at the side of the trail. He pointed to a spot a few yards away, where the trail split off in two and another track wound deeper into the forest. Disguised against the color of the forest, but clearly visible to Tsi's practiced eyes, there was a trip-wire laid out across the trail.

"Strange," Tsi said. "A little obvious, isn't it?"

"Yeah," Tenlok said. "It's a warning. Someone wants us staying on this trail."

Carefully, Tsi approached the trip wire and crouched down to study it. It was a simple construction, but the wire itself was made of old cabling, of the kind one could strip out of an advanced piece of equipment. Examining the cable, she saw there were signs of wear on it. It had been used repeatedly, possibly for years. Whoever made this knew what they were doing. Tenlok was right. The trap wasn't made to catch them, it was to tell them where to go next.

"None of the others could have set this, and there isn't supposed to be anyone else here," Tsi said. "The Chalakhati were exterminated. Resettlement was forbidden."

"Big planet," Tenlok said. "I can think of worse places to hole up."

"Whoever they are, they're waiting for us at the end of this trail."

"So?" Tenlok said as he drew a carbine from his back and extended its stock. It was a short-barreled, ugly little weapon, but handy in the tight confines of a forest. She'd carried something similar for a while when she lived with the Noxians.

"We take it slow," she said. "No shooting unless I say so."

Tenlok rose, but said nothing. She wasn't sure if she should take his silence as agreement or not. She'd have to play this by ear.

"Alright," Tsi said. "Let's go meet our new friends."

Wylla wished she had one of her instruments with her. The spike-fiddle she missed in particular. Liss had always been extremely fond of it, though she played for herself more than any audience. It was another meditation technique, to let the moving of the bow and the sound of the strings become her whole world, empty her mind and let the music flow through her rather than trusting to any strict instructions or formal compositions.

It had been almost an hour since they were gathered at the bonfire, and there had been no motion or change since then. She hadn't seen her captors since they were brought out and given their breakfast, but she was certain they weren't far away. It was a strange sensation, to be unbound and unguarded, yet still held in another's power. She knew it quite well.

Enlil was clearly agitated. The Noxian woman got up and paced around, stretching her scrawny legs, but ultimately that was all she did.

Wylla looked at the Machine, but as ever, there was nothing to read on its emotionless face. It did not even turn its gaze away from the fire. She wondered if it was still powered on, or if it slept in its own strange way.

The fog had grown thick. She tried to close her eyes and go away inside her mind, but it was fruitless. Then she heard the snapping of twigs, and the wet slap of boots against mud.

Like a strange vision, Tsi emerged from the fog. She was walking up a trail along the side of the hill. She stopped at the edge of the clearing, relief briefly flashing across her face when she saw the five of them. Over her shoulder, Wylla could see the red eye of the Bondsman.

Boldly, Tsi walked out into the open.

"You alright?" she called out to them. "Anyone hurt?"

"We're good, Tsi," Enlil called back. "Might want to check with our hosts, though. Think they want to talk to you."

"I guessed that much," Tsi said, her voice loud.

She walked further out, now standing at the edge of the cliff face that overlooked the rest of the forest. She stood there, silhouetted against the grey fog, and called out again.

"I'm right here! You wanted to talk with me, right? My name's Tsi. These people are under my protection. I was captain of their vessel."

There was a rustling in the trees, and Wylla saw Narri step out. She was dressed like the other Chalakhati now, her face daubed in green and black camouflage, flecked with crimson here and there. She wore a breastplate of the kind a modern soldier would wear, but it was a spear tipped with jagged metal that she carried, not a gun. She looked at Tsi with a scowl on her lined face.

"I'm Narri," the old woman said. "I took your people captive. Why did you come here, Tsi?"

"Our ship was damaged. We needed to abandon it, and—"

"No," Narri said. "I know the story your people told. Why did you come to Chalakhat? No one comes here. No one even passes through here for years at a time. This place is cursed, don't you know?"

"I... know what happened here," Tsi replied. "I didn't think there was anyone left on this world. Please, I thought this would be a safe place for my crew, I had no idea—"

"No idea there was anyone left here but ghosts," Narri growled. "That's what we want everyone to think. We're ghosts."

"Let my crew go, and we'll be on our way," Tsi said. Wylla could see that Tsi's hand was on her pistol, but her tone was still even.

"So what? You can tell the Janissaries to come and finish the job they started?"

"I would never do that."

"You came here dressed for war. How do we know you aren't part of a scouting mission? Or some trick?"

"I told you, I didn't even know you were here!" Tsi said. "I never would have even come through this system if I knew you were! This is all a mistake."

"Careful with that tongue of yours, off-worlder," Narri said. "I've got you outnumbered. I could wipe you out with a word if I wanted."

"There's twelve of you."

It was the Bondsman who spoke, his throaty growl carrying through the fog. He was still at the end of the trail, but now he had gone down into a crouch, his carbine braced against his shoulder.

"Tenlok!" Tsi barked.

"Two pulse guns and a bunch of spears and bows," Tenlok continued, ignoring her. "Odds aren't in your favor."

Anger flashed in Narri's eyes, and she gripped her spear tight.

"You don't know what we're capable of. How many of us do you think you can kill before we get to them?" she said, pointing at Wylla and the others.

"Doesn't matter," Tenlok replied. "I've got enough phosphorous rounds for you and all your friends. Burn right through those trees you're hiding behind. And you."

Wylla's breathing was coming in short and sharp now. Hiron looked at her worriedly, Furner's face was plastered with sweat. Enlil was in a low crouch, looking like she was ready to run at any moment, and Strongmind had focused its vision on Tsi.

Wylla saw the Bondsman's finger tightening around the trigger, turned to see Narri's spear trembling in her grip. The trees were rustling, the Chalakhati were whispering to each other in panic. She caught a glimpse of one of the boys she'd seen earlier, small and trembling as he peered out from the foliage. With nothing else to do, Wylla decided to pray.

"Gods and Ancestors," she whispered, "Grant me wisdom that this, I ask of you, be right and just. Calm their hearts, sooth the fire of hate in their breasts. Let them see the path, let them find peace, for it is their way as it is our way. Gods and ancestors, give me wisdom, that this, I ask of you, be right and just."

She chanted the prayer, quietly, hurriedly. It was the span of three recitations before she heard a loud click, and opened her eyes. Tsi had stepped in front of Tenlok. She had removed her gun belt, and was holding her arms apart wide. With a thump, she let the belt fall to the ground.

"Stand down, Tenlok," Tsi said.

"You're making a mistake," he growled back.

"Trust me. This is the only way forwards."

She turned, unarmed, and walked towards Narri. Narri stepped backwards warily, looking between, Tsi, the Bondsman, and her warriors in the trees. Tsi kept her hands raised the whole time. When she got to within a few strides of Narri, she stopped, and let her hands drop back to her sides.

"I'm in range of all of you now," Tsi said. "You want to kill me, now's your chance. We can all die together... or we can live. You know I came here because my people matter to me. I'm guessing it's the same for you. I can see you've got children with you, and you and I both know they don't belong here. Don't make them pay the price for our mistakes."

Narri looked at Tsi long and hard, then at the edge of the forest. At last she sighed, and released her grip on her spear. She signaled with one hand, and, warily, the Chalakhati emerged from their hiding places. They walked slowly into the open, all twelve of them, in makeshift armor and paint. The older ones still had a hardness in their eyes, but the children looked nothing but relieved.

"There will be no fighting today, Captain Tsi," Narri said. "I release your people, and welcome you now, not as prisoners, but as our guests."

Tsi spent a tense day in negotiations with the Chalakhati. They welcomed her and the others back to their home. It was a network of small rooms carved into the mountain caves. The tunnels themselves were a natural formation, burrowing deep into the mountains, but the Chalakhati only occupied a few of the outer caves dotted around the mountain. From what Tsi gathered as she spoke with Narri and her husband, a bush-bearded man called Harken, the little tribe circulated from cave to cave seasonally, and even dispersed among them time to time.

They hid their whole lives, Tsi learned. They watched the skies warily, tried to stay under the canopy's cover as much as possible, and seldom lit fires outside. Narri was the oldest. She had been a young woman when Chalakhat fell, but her memories seemed fragmented and she was reluctant to speak of it with Tsi.

Tsi was glad for that. She had no need to relive the slaughter that had happened here. There had been enough signs of it out in the Glass Desert, seeped into the sands themselves.

They were sitting on the floor of Narri's room, a low table made of old plastic containers between them. Harken had made them more of the broth these people subsisted on, and now the two of them sat across from each other, still circling the same issues over and over.

"Our scouts should return from where your ship landed by tomorrow at the latest," Narri said. "We sometimes seek out crash sites and jettisoned pods for salvage. My people will know if your craft is still workable. But... I expect a price to be paid. For letting you leave here."

"Go on," Tsi said. She was too tired to argue any longer, and it had taken much of the day to convince Narri her crew leaving was even an option.

"I want my choice of whatever's on your ship. We need medicine and weapons, and metal for making tools. There's a smuggler, Saldevar, who comes here from time to time, but we haven't seen him in years now. We survive well enough, but there are things from off world we can't make that would be useful."

"My stocks are almost bare," Tsi said. "But I'll give you what we can."

"Good. Medicine especially. There used to be more of us, but last winter... there was a bad fever. Most of the children didn't make it."

"That's terrible," Tsi said.

"Two of my granddaughters," Narri said. "I buried them in the forest myself."

Narri trailed off for a moment, looking in to her cup.

"So," she said. "Medicine. That's what we need the most of. As much of that as you can give us, and we will let you fly free."

"I don't have much, like I said. But what I have is yours. The crew has mostly healed from their injuries and, well, you need it more than we do."

"Thank you," said Narri.

Enlil had left the caves and gone back out to the cliff side. The bonfire had long since been extinguished. The sun was setting again, turning the sky pink and purple. She still wasn't used to that. She'd seen sunsets in recordings, heard them described before, but there was something bizarre about watching the light itself go away.

Spending her life in space, she'd become used to the idea of light as a constant. It was either there or it wasn't. This half-way between point shocked her. She wasn't sure exactly how she felt about seeing something so strange, so overwhelming, and learning that it happened every day.

The Bondsman was leaning against a tree nearby, watching the same sight she was. For a moment, Enlil debated ignoring him. She didn't care of his kind. But that seemed strangely wrong, somehow, and so at last she opened her mouth.

"Didn't take you for the sunsets type, Tenlok," she said.

Tenlok turned his head to look at her.

"Caves are cramped. Those people aren't exactly fond of me."

"Pretty normal reaction," Enlil said. "You did threaten to set them on fire."

The Bondsman didn't respond. Enlil sat down at the edge of the cliff face, letting her legs dangle over. She looked down at the canopy below. Part of her wondered what it would be like to jump. She could feel the pull of gravity in a way she never had before. She had to remind herself she wasn't taking a hull walk. There were no safety cables here, no jets to bring her back home. She looked up, and Tenlok was still there, watching the sunset with her.

"Some maneuver the Captain pulled today," she said.

"Stupid move," he grumbled. "Could have got herself killed."

"It worked, though."

"In all your time, how often did giving up your weapons improve a situation?" Tenlok asked.

Enlil had to think on that for a moment. Her fighting knife was still tucked into one of her boots. 'Hers' she thought of it as, but of course it was nothing but a standard survival blade she had taken from the life pod. She wouldn't see her own fighting knife again, as far as she knew. It was still back on Salvation.

"Maybe once," Enlil said. "I was on a royal bender down at the Ninth Cycle, and one of my old mates told me I probably shouldn't be carrying a Repeater, so I gave it to him for safe keeping. Later I wound up getting into a fight with the barkeep. She was my favorite, but I was gone enough I'd've probably vented her if I could've. Hmm... never did see that Repeater again though. Sly bastard... so once. Yeah."

"Once," Tenlok echoed. "And not when someone had a gun trained on you."

"True."

"She takes stupid risks," Tenlok said.

"Yup," Enlil replied. "You're looking at one of 'em."

Tenlok said nothing, so Enlil continued.

"When I met her, I was on my last legs. She could have done me right there, but instead she gave me a second chance. I don't... usually go in for that kind of crap, but Tsi's different from most of the people I've met. There's something about her, like she's not crazy but it's... it's like everything's one way, and she's trying to make it different. Make it *better*. You know? And she knows it's crazy, and I know it's crazy, but she tries anyway. I don't know. I've just... I've never seen someone like that before."

Tenlok was silent. Enlil didn't know why she bothered talking to him. He was almost as dead inside as the drone. Finally, he spoke again.

"Yeah. Like I said: Stupid risks."

Hiron woke to a commotion outside his room. He'd been sleeping on the dirt floor, wrapped up in his bedroll, not far from the loudly snoring Furner. While the room was almost as cramped as the life pod had been, he appreciated having a place to sleep that was dry and warm. His whole body ached, though. He hadn't realized how much he'd been exerting himself until he sat up from his bedroll and felt pain in his twisted legs.

Someone was moaning, their cries of anguish echoing through the cave. He could hear padding footsteps and hushed voices. A brisk command attempted to quiet the injured person, but they only groaned loudly in response.

Quickly, Hiron crawled over to where he had left his braces and began to fumble them on. His legs and forearms were cramping, but soon his adrenaline kicked in and dulled the pain. Unfortunately, it also made his hands shake, and so he had to repeatedly bind and re-bind the straps before he had the crutches securely strapped around his arms. Furner had woken by this point, grumbling a curse in Noxian, but Hiron paid him no mind. He poked his head through the woven cords that served as their door, and looked towards the mouth of the cave.

The hideout was unlit, but a grey light was coming from the mouth of the cave. Hiron could see it was overcast outside, and raining. Four figures struggled around a third, who was twisting and moaning on the ground.

Hiron looked across what he'd been thinking of as the 'main road' of the hideout: a narrow path that cut through the dozen or so small, box-shaped rooms that made up the cave's living quarters. The place was large enough that what could be called a small town was contained within, with a central path through the box-rooms and several other routes carved into the floor between the Chalakhati's simple homes. Tsi was standing at the entrance to her own room, warily strapping her pistol around her waist. She caught his eye, and signaled for him to wait. Then she briskly walked towards the group of people at the entrance.

Quietly, Hiron followed her, his curiosity getting the better of him even as he realized it was a mistake. Three of the Chalakhati, including their leader, Narri, were gathered around a young woman whose hair was full of twigs and leaves. Her skin had the same camouflage paint that the others wore, but it was smeared and had been rubbed off in places. Her clothes were even more torn than the others, and her feet were calloused and black-soled. She clutched a filthy satchel desperately in one hand. From the dark red stains on her clothing and her incessant moaning, Hiron could tell she had been badly hurt.

"Where are the others?" Narri asked, as two of her companions held the young woman down and began stripping the clothing away around her wound. Hiron recognized an injury from a solid round: it was a tiny, puckered red hole just above the woman's hip. She'd apparently tried to bandage it at some point, judging by the filthy brown cloth that fell away from the wound, but for some reason the injury hadn't healed at all.

"Dead," the woman gasped. "I was... I was... only one got out..."

"Who attacked you? How many? Was it the Janissaries?"

"No," Tsi said. "The drone. It's still active."

"Drone?" Narri asked. "What drone?"

"The one that boarded my ship," Tsi said. "You said your people went to salvage it, right? That Guraggan drone was the reason we had to abandon ship in the first place. I locked my ship in for a crash landing, reduced inertial compensation and killed the atmospheric shields. I was hoping the drone would get scraped out of our hold on the way down. I was wrong."

"You didn't say anything about it still being alive!" Narri roared.

"It wouldn't matter if I had," Tsi replied. "Your people were already on their way before we even met. What matters now is—"

The wounded woman let out a terrible moan. One of the Chalakhati stroked her hair, muttering soothing, useless phrases, while another tried to dress the wound. Blood was still leaking from it. Hiron realized she must have been traveling with that injury for a long time, perhaps more than a day over rough country. It was odd that someone so badly hurt had managed to escape...

Hiron looked up to see that Tsi was staring at the wound as well. She had trailed off, and seeming to see the injury for the first time. Suddenly, she grabbed the woman's satchel and pried it from her death-grip.

"What are you doing?!" Narri demanded. "That's ours!"

Tsi ignored her and rummaged through the bag.

"Do all of you carry equipment like this?" she asked the wounded woman. "Quickly! Quickly, tools like this, did everyone on the team have a set?"

"Yes..." the scavenger croaked back. "Velle was the first one to the ship... she took out her welding kit... then it blew her apart..."

"It thinks you were a repair team," Tsi said. "That's why it shot you with a tracking bug. It thinks you're part of my crew."

"What are you saying?" Narri asked, horror in her eyes.

"It followed her here," Tsi said. "We have to leave. Now!"

No sooner had the words escaped Tsi's lips than Hiron could see something moving in the trees beyond the cave's mouth. He heard the sound of branches breaking, of soft rain on hard metal, and the familiar electronic buzz of a pulse weapon being charged.

There was a deafening roar as the first salvo was fired. Trees burned and the rock of the cave walls shattered, sending splinters raining down as Hiron flung himself to the ground, desperately trying to cover his neck with his hands even as his crutches clattered into each other. Two of the Chalakhati were torn apart in an instant, one hurling himself in front of Narri and being turned to paste by a single shot, while other tried to run and was cut down with a swift burst of solid rounds.

Hiron looked around frantically for Tsi, but couldn't find her. People were screaming, guns were sounding. Blood had flecked across his face. He wasn't sure whose. Teeth chattering, he crawled across the cave floor towards the wounded scavenger. She'd been abandoned the moment the firing started, and for no real reason Hiron could think of, it was suddenly vital that he went to her.

Hiron crawled up alongside the young woman, but as soon as he was there he realized it was no use. What was he going to do? He wasn't strong enough to pick her up, he couldn't drag her to safety either. He could do nothing for her.

Beyond the cave entrance, he could see a massive, lumbering shape slowly walk through the shattered trees. Arachnid-like, it stalked forwards on four legs. Its armored carapace was ravaged with heat scars, but its weapons still bellowed, loud enough that Hiron felt his eardrums would burst. His whole body shook as the machine advanced. Its many eyes held neither rage nor pity as it poured fire relentlessly into the cave, the sounds of its guns answered with cries of agony and fear.

Hiron grabbed the wounded woman's hand. It was the only thing he could do.

CHAPTER 33

Screaming filled Wylla's ears. It was an odd sound: the Chalakhati had spent so much of their life in silence, that the sudden, primal cries of fear that ripped forth quickly left them croaking and hoarse. They sounded like adolescents. It was funny how often in moments of sheer terror like this, Wylla still found herself observing and drawing conclusions as she had been taught.

She was hidden behind a rocky protrusion from the cave's floor, keeping herself as low as she could while fire lanced through the air above her. She saw one of the Chalakhati break cover, firing a rusted pulse gun from his hip. A round tore through his thigh, sending the leg spiraling away from his body as a second shot blasted apart his chest. Wylla had seen the work of Guraggan drones before, but she had never been on the receiving end of their violence. Now, she understood the visceral shock these weapons inspired.

"Back! Back!" someone was screaming.

Wylla looked and saw Narri herding people towards the rear of the cave. She was pointing frantically to a tunnel, so low to the ground that one would have to crawl on hands and knees to get through. Even as she was about to make a run for the tunnel, a shot struck the wall above and sent a shower of rock cascading down, covering the entrance.

Theta-90 stood now at the cave mouth, its brutal form silhouetted against the gray light and the green trees beyond. There was no way out. No way, except past that thing.

She saw Tsi taking cover behind one of the domiciles, her pistol in hand. Strongmind was with her. The two would occasionally pop out and snap shots off at Theta-90, but they were accomplishing little.

Summoning all her courage, Wylla rose and sprinted across the open to their position. Bullets whipped past her, but miraculously, she made it to Tsi without so much as a graze. Panting from the brief exertion, she crouched between Tsi and the machine, bracing her back against the wall. On a low rise above them, she caught sight of Enlil, firing off a burst from her own survival rifle before she ducked back into cover, cursing at full volume as a spray of shots chipped away at her cover. Opposite Enlil, Wylla spied the Bondsman. Tenlok was behind a pile of metal scrap the Chalakhati had collected, but he was not firing at Theta-90. He seemed to be working on something out of sight, concealed by his body. He glanced over his shoulder at Tsi, then returned to his frantic work.

"Tactical Assessment: enemy force consists of one heavily armored assault drone. Explosives reserves: negative. Survival odds: low," Strongmind said with the same tone of voice as someone remarking on the weather of the day.

"Thank you, Strongmind, we gathered!" Tsi barked as she reloaded her weapon. "Wylla! Does that thing have any weaknesses?"

"Get close enough with any kind of conventional weapon, you might be able to damage its joints," Wylla said, shouting to be heard over the din.

"We'll be cut to shreds if we break cover. Other options?"

Wylla pondered. She had never been a military adviser, her skills had been analytical. Still, she had learned much in her years of service to Lady Ornicht. There had to be something she could recall, some crack in its armor. She risked a glance out, and saw Theta-90 still firing away, the barrel of its rotary-cannon turning molten red.

"Heat!" Wylla said. "If we can damage its coolant systems, we might be able overheat it. Cook it from the inside out!"

"Sounds like a plan! How do we get to its coolant systems?"

"There's some piping on its rear chassis, I think!"

"Hell," Tsi said. "It's got us boxed in here. We've got to draw it away from the cave. In the open, we've got a shot!"

"I might be able to distract it," Wylla offered. "Ornicht might have given it orders to retrieve me!"

"No chance," Tsi retorted. "That thing was tracking you the same way it is everyone else. It'll blow you apart if you step into the open."

"Ancestors protect us," Wylla said. "Well, how do we get by it?"

"We've got to lure it deeper into the cave, then get someone to rush behind it. Tenlok! Got anything in your bag of tricks?"

"One smoke, one incendiary! That's it!" the Bondsman shouted back.

"How about your phosphorous rounds?"

"Full mag!" Tenlok said, his back still turned to Tsi.

"We can work with that," Tsi said. "Strongmind! Tenlok! When I give the signal, smoke the drone. Enlil and I will cover you. Get Hiron into cover, then try to get by that thing! I'll be right behind you as soon as it leaves the cave! Understood?"

"Acknowledged," Strongmind said.

"You got it boss!" Enlil shouted as she reloaded her weapon.

"Need someone to take over for me here!" Tenlok called back. He rolled over slightly, and Wylla finally got a good look at what he had been working on.

It was one of the boys from the forest. A pulse blast had burned a hole in his stomach, and the Bondsman had been field dressing him, for all the good it would do.

"I'll handle it!" Wylla shouted. "Cover me!"

On her signal, Tsi, Enlil, and Strongmind all let loose a torrent of fire. Wylla sprinted across the open ground, vaulting over a fallen Chalakhati and scrambling up the rise to where Tenlok was concealed. She dove to the ground and wedged herself in alongside him, her elbows scraping against the rough stone of the rise. Tenlok wordlessly handed her his medical kit as she looked over the boy.

He was fading in and out of consciousness, his lips quivering. His hair was woven in tight braids, matted with dirt and blood. Wylla stroked his brow as she tried to figure out the best way to treat him. Even if she had a full surgical suite, her chances were slim.

"I gave him half of this," Tenlok said, handing her a syringe of painkiller. "Give him the rest, if you have to."

Wylla took the syringe in her hands and examined it for a moment.

"But this would—"

She looked up at the snarling ghoul mask, and recognition dawned on her.

"If you have to," Tenlok repeated.

"I understand. I'll do my best for him."

Tenlok nodded to her.

"Ready!" he shouted, detaching the smoke grenade from his belt.

"Now!" Tsi roared.

Even as the world erupted into further chaos, all Wylla could do was look down at the dying boy, and stroke his hair. She set the syringe aside, and looked over the medical kit. The Bondsman had done his best to save the child's life, but he wasn't a healer. Wylla was.

It was the duty of the killers to face the drone. It was her duty to help this child. She would save him, she vowed.

She had to.

Hiron felt shock wave after shock wave as the drone's cannons fired above him. It stood only a few meters away, lighting up the whole cave with the blasts of its weapons. Walls shattered and crumbled. Most of the Chalakhati had found cover of some kind, but an unlucky few would get caught by shrapnel. One particularly brave soul had rushed forwards and hurled a spear at the drone, but the weapon had simply bounced off its armored hide. The man who had thrown it had been reduced to nothing but chunks of meat.

The drone took a single thunderous step forwards, the thud of its mighty, pistoned leg striking the earth sending a shiver down Hiron's spine. He had no idea why it hadn't killed him yet. Perhaps it thought he was dead. He looked up, and realized his luck had run out as the machine's many eyes contracted and focused on him.

A bullet sparked off its carapace. Another struck the side of its armored head, and it turned away from Hiron.

"Leave him alone, you damned hunk of scrap!"

Furner Ketsu was raising a rusted Chalakhati rifle to his shoulder, a primitive, bolt-action weapon. He fired it, worked the bolt, fired it again. For an instant, the drone seemed to not know what to make of this attack. Furner was screaming at the top of his lungs, making no effort to hide himself as he trudged forwards on his one good leg.

"Yeah! Get a good look! How do ya like someone who shoots back!" Furner roared.

The drone finally decided it was time to kill Furner. It raised the arm that ended in a pulse-gun, but then the world exploded in white mist. Hiron could see bullets and pulse shot sparking off the machine's hulking outline through the thick cloud as it fired back, temporarily blinded. Footsteps sounded behind him, and a gloved hand grabbed his shoulder and yanked him to his feet. He found himself looking at Tenlok's mask, and let out an involuntary squeak of fright.

"Get moving! Now!" the Bondsman roared, dragging Hiron along with him.

"Wait!" Hiron stammered. "What about her?"

"Who?"

"The scout! She-she—"

Tenlok shoved him down roughly, and Hiron found himself in the ruins of one of the hovels. Furner was laying alongside him, a gash along the old Noxian's brow, but a wolfish grin upon his face. He jabbed Hiron in the ribs as Tenlok disappeared back into the mist, the sounds of battle erupting from its depths.

"You see that? I haven't done that since I was twenty!" Furner laughed.

Hiron could barely hear him. He was peering into the mist. The sounds of the fight were moving away from the cave entrance, but the fog from the smoke grenade was still thick. He could just about make out a limp form on the ground, and started to crawl out to it.

Furner's hand caught his.

"Kid, where are you going?" Furner asked.

"That woman that got hurt," Hiron said. "She's still out there. Maybe we can—"

"Kid..." Furner said, pulling Hiron back and settling him against the wall. "There's nothing you can do for her no more."

"She's in trouble—"

"We'll get to her when this is over, alright?" Furner said quickly. "Okay? But ya can't do anything for her right now. Alright?"

"Alright," Hiron whispered. "Alright."

It was working, Tsi thought with a thrill as her legs pounded underneath her. It was working. The smoke cloud had confused the drone long enough for Strongmind and Tenlok to get passed it, and now it had retreated out of the cave. The moment she had seen its outline recede beyond the cave mouth, she had shouted for Enlil and launched into a sprint, reloading her pistol along the way.

She burst out of the cave entrance, hurling herself to cover behind a fallen tree nearby. Fresh air, rich with the smell of burning ozone and propellant powder filled her lungs. Rain drops beat down on her. A rainstorm had blown in during the course of the fight, soaking the trees and turning the ground into a morass of mud.

Theta-90's upper torso was spinning left and right as it fired, trying to track Strongmind and Tenlok simultaneously. The two warriors were circling it, staying mobile, darting from cover to cover as they fired. They had never trained together before, so their movements were unsynchronized, but both fought with a mechanical precision matched only by their opponent.

"Left! *Left!*" Tenlok shouted.

Strongmind moved to the machine's left, shooting from the hip as he did so. Tsi and Enlil added their own shots, and the machine spun to face them, its haphazard fire slicing through the trees, sending splinters and trunks flying to and fro. The pulse gun was already near the point of overheating, its long barrel blazing like the embers of a fire.

Tenlok's carbine fell from his hands, and he drew his Nioban Kukri. Tsi saw him sprint forwards, the twin stimulant tubes in his mask writhing like serpents. He launched himself into the air, landed on the drone's back, and grabbed one of its coolant cables. The Kukri flashed in the rain as he brought it down once. Then, suddenly Theta-90 spun its torso, sending Tenlok hurtling to the ground with a slap of one of its mechanical arms.

One of its four legs shot out, smashing into Tenlok's side and rolling him a dozen paces through the mud. Tenlok let out a pained gurgle as the drone advanced on his prostrate form. It fired a few rounds from its rotary cannon, but Tenlok's point defense shield still worked, and the hail of bullets turned to white hot mist and spattered against his armor.

"Enlil! Cover me! Strongmind! Target the coolant tube!"

She did not wait to hear a response from her companions, but sprinted out from behind cover. The drone had pinned Tenlok beneath one of its legs, and brought its rotary cannon to bear for a contact-shot against the mercenary's chest. The cannon had fired so many rounds the length of it was the color of magma. Rain sizzled and turned to smoke where it struck the barrel. Tsi's boots tore through the mud and she hurled herself the last few paces.

Her shoulder collided with the cannon just as it fired. Throwing her whole body weight and all her enhanced strength into the charge, she pushed the cannon away, bullets exploding into the muddy ground. The drone reared back on its hind legs, all of its eyes now focused on Tsi. It swung the cannon around, bludgeoning her with its burning surface. Tsi rolled with the blow, though it drove the wind from her lungs and sent pain lancing through her whole body. She wound up flat on her back in the mud, Theta-90 looming over her. It aimed the cannon squarely in her face, but only the screech of the spinning barrels greeted her.

"AMMUNITION DEPLETED," Theta-90 intoned.

It raised the cannon to bludgeon her again, but Tsi rolled out of the way, scrambling to her feet. She caught a glimpse of Strongmind as he jumped onto the drone's back. His mismatched bronze arm flashed outwards, the blade shooting out from his wrist. With a single slash, he severed the damaged coolant tube. White fog and blue fluid sprayed like arterial blood from the injury, and Theta-90 recoiled. It knocked Strongmind away with a swipe of its arms.

Theta-90's back now faced Tsi. She sighted another coolant tube and fired on it with her pistol. Her hands were shaking from exhaustion, but the second shot struck a plate holding the tube in place, and it spilled outwards, loose as viscera.

"Enlil!" Tsi shouted. "Knife!"

Enlil drew her survival knife. With the loudest curse Tsi had ever heard, she hurtled the Noxian blade with all her might at the exposed cable. The blade ripped through the thick cabling, and yet more coolant sprayed.

"WARNING! HEAT CRITICAL!" Theta-90's voice blared out an alarm as it spun wildly, trying to track one of them to fire at.

"Back," Tenlok growled from where he lay.

He pulled the pin on his incendiary grenade, and hurled it at the drone. Instantly, the war machine was covered in blazing liquid. Flames engulfed its armored hide, the rain hissing as it struck the burning machine.

It staggered and stumbled like a drunkard, writhing back and forth and lashing out at them with its burning limbs as they scrambled away. Suddenly, the machine thrust its forelegs down, causing a wave of mud to erupt up from the ground. It furiously began slapping mud against itself, dampening the fire.

"Fuck," Tsi breathed. The drone was smarter than she thought.

She ran forwards, and scooped up the carbine that Tenlok had abandoned. Still half a mag left, she turned, carbine in one hand, her Repeater in the other. She wasn't fast enough though: Theta-90's smoking arm struck her hard in the chest, sending her tumbling through the mud once again. She lay on her back as the machine trudged forwards, staring at her with eyes of shattered glass, its automated voice still blaring out heat warnings. It raised its forelegs high to crush her. Tsi waited for the inevitable blow.

It did not come.

"Request supporting fire. Immediate."

Strongmind's calm words rose above the din of the rain and Theta-90's endlessly repeating warnings. He had thrown himself between Tsi and Theta-90, and now, every muscle of his synthetic body straining, he held its two massive forelegs in his metal grip, keeping them from crashing down on Tsi. Strongmind turned his head, and Tsi locked eyes with him. She smiled.

In a flash, she had recovered her weapons. "Request granted," she said.

Both guns blazed in her hands. The phosphorous rounds cooked off against Theta-90's armored hide, pushing its internal cooling system past the breaking point. The molten metal burst apart as the rounds from Tsi's Repeater tore into it in turn. Its internal systems exposed to the naked air, Tsi emptied her pistol into Theta-90, each round blasting through its fragile circuitry.

The drone recoiled again, tearing itself away from Strongmind's grip. It took a faltering step, then another, retreating from them like a wounded animal. At last, it collapsed against a tree, and its shattered eyes winked out and turned black.

Tsi looked at the dead hulk of the drone, almost daring it to come back to life. No, she realized. Her fire had torn through its very heart. There was nothing left of that machine now, but smoking metal.

Strongmind stood beside her in silence. She turned to see Enlil help the Bondsman to his feet, and support the wounded mercenary on her scrawny shoulders. Her eyes met Enlil's. Enlil gave a thumbs-up.

After a moment, Tsi returned the gesture.

CHAPTER 34

When the time came, Tsi went with the burial party. They split into groups of two, each carrying a body between them, wrapped in a plastic sheet. The Chalakhati all wore long machetes on their belts, and before they set off into the bush, each took out their blade and sharpened it under Narri's careful guidance.

Of her crew, only Hiron had wanted to go. She had forbidden it. Strongmind would have come, if she had ordered him, but she thought it might be an insult. A burial was a sacred thing, a time for the living to let out their last emotions for the dead. Strongmind's stoicism would have disrupted that.

Tsi walked with Narri, carrying the body of the scout between them. She was the one that Hiron had wanted to accompany. During the fighting he had been trapped with her, and hadn't realized until it was long over that a piece of shrapnel had punctured the woman's skull. Tsi had tried to comfort him by telling him she had felt nothing, but that always did little good.

Narri traveled silently, hiking up old game trails and through watery mud uncomplainingly. The rainstorm had died down, leaving behind a steady, grey drizzle. The plastic sheet grew slick with rain water, but Tsi kept a tight hold of it. At last they came to a spot that seemed like any other, and Narri signed for her to stop.

They set the body down gently between them, and uncovered it. The shrapnel wound was still in the woman's forehead, but otherwise she had been quickly and efficiently cleaned, and her body stripped of anything useful. Narri crouched at the young woman's head, Tsi at her feet.

"Her name was Chamelle," Narri said. "A good one. Lost her parents to lung rot when she was little, so we all raised her together."

"She was very brave," Tsi said. She could think of nothing else to add.

Narri nodded.

"Well, we'd better get started. Have you ever done this before?" Narri asked as she unsheathed her machete.

"I'm familiar with this kind of burial," Tsi said.

She took out her own blade. It was Enlil's knife. It seemed appropriate to use this weapon. After all, it had helped save all of their lives.

Together, Narri and Tsi set to work butchering the body. They did not speak as they went about their task. There was no reverence in the movement of their blades, nor was there false gaiety. It was simple one more task to take care of.

At last, Narri used a rock to break the bones, and then what was left was unrecognizable as having ever been a human. She cleaned the plastic sheet and folded it, then hoisted it onto her shoulder.

"We'd better get back to the camp," Narri said. "The animals will come soon to get rid of all this."

Tsi nodded. As she fell in behind Narri, something gnawed at the pit of her stomach. She felt she should say something, but the words wouldn't come to her. What was she to do, she wondered. Should she apologize, for bringing suffering here? The Chalakhati had already been through so much. Narri had said herself that they had lost people to disease, to accident, not to mention the difficulty of simply surviving. Still, Tsi had added yet another burden to their already troubled lives.

Just like she always did.

Wylla rose early and packed her things. It was odd how soundly she slept after Theta-90's attack. The Chalakhati had been up all night, stripping the drone's body for parts and burying what they could not use, or tending to their injured. She had spent much of the day prior helping with the wounded, but there was only so much that could be done, and once she was satisfied with her work she had collapsed gratefully into her cot and drifted off to sleep.

Now she stood at the mouth of the cave, watching the rain fall. The ground around the entrance was still a mess of mud and fallen trees. She could see the places where Theta-90's clawed legs had torn up the earth. It wouldn't be long, though, before the land began to reclaim this place too. The trees would decompose, and new life would take root. Soon there would be nothing left to show that this battle had ever taken place at all.

Tenlok and Hiron were with her. The boy sipped a mug of tea. The Bondsman had been injured in the fighting, but had refused to let her treat him. He insisted he didn't need any help, but she had noted that he walked slower than he used to, and leaned heavily against the wall whenever he could.

"The child will live," Wylla said, catching Tenlok's eye. "I thought you might want to know."

"Still got my kit?" Tenlok asked.

Wylla took the medical kit out of her pack and handed it to Tenlok. He took it wordlessly and stowed it within his own gear. Wylla sighed. She'd have more luck talking to a stone than the Bondsman.

At last, the Chalakhati and Tsi returned from their burial party. She was surprised to see that some of them were laughing and joking with each other, though Tsi and Narri remained sullen eyed and quiet. People dealt with grief in many different ways, Wylla knew. On Bykonus, a burial was a time of ecstatic celebration as well as weeping. Liss had found that confusing, though he had always been a somber man.

Liss. He had been her one companion in Ornicht's retinue, the only person she truly trusted. Despite his flaws, he had been a good man. She glanced at Tenlok, remembering how the Bondsman had shot him and left him to burn without a backwards glance.

Tsi stood in front of them, Narri and her husband Harken beside her.

"They've agreed to take us to our ship," Tsi said. "We've got no guarantee it'll fly again, but at least we can take a look. The path's already been scouted, so we should get there in a day or two."

"We're ready," Hiron said, as Strongmind and Furner filed up from within the cave, their packs secured for the trip.

"Alright," Tsi nodded. "Harken, you lead the way."

It only took a few days to get to the landing site, following trail markers left behind by the first scouts to go out. Hiron's legs and forearms ached at the end of each day, but he had actually begun to enjoy watching the Chalakhati's field-craft. There had been Dath Clan scavengers who could do similar things outside the canyons of Promise: leaving hidden markers in the wasteland, subtle messages that only they and their close companions would notice, let alone read. Oddly stacked stones, scratches in the bark of trees, all these things told Harken and his two companions they were headed in the right direction.

Of course, they still had the homing beacon, but all that gave them was a general direction and distance for the ship. Without the black-bearded Harken, Hiron was sure it would have taken them three times as long just to clear their way through the forest. The only thing he truly disliked, besides the exhaustion at the end of each day, was the fact that Harken insisted they light no fires and remain quiet at night. Laying in his bedroll in the dark, with no sound but the calls of animals and the patter of rain, it had been easy for Hiron's mind to wander back to the day of the drone attack.

He played the events in his head over and over, trying to think of a way that it could have turned out differently. Perhaps he could have dragged the injured woman to cover. Or if he had a rifle, a lucky shot might have distracted the Guraggan drone long enough for someone to come and save her.

He felt like a fool, fantasizing about that. There was nothing he could have done, which was the problem. He was useless.

These thoughts played through his head every night until the dawn came. Sleep had crept up on him without him realizing it, but he started each new day on the trail even more exhausted than the one before. Finally, they came to a resting spot on a hill, overlooking a valley below.

"There," Harken said, pointing down into the valley.

Sure enough, there was a long trail of blackened and shattered trees, and at the end of it, in a clearing of its own making, was the ship. It hadn't struck the planet at full velocity: there would have been a massive crater, and little left of the craft. No, Tsi must have programmed it to make an emergency landing, slowly decelerating itself as it broke through the atmosphere, until it finally came to a crashing halt here.

The Exile, Tsi had called it. Looking at the ship, damaged but whole, Hiron felt the troubles of the last night begin to fade. It had been a long journey, but once again they had come out the other side.

There had lost much, he knew that well, but they had still made it all the way here.

As a group, they began the slow descent towards the ship.

They were moving single file through the forest, Harken at the front, Tsi just behind him, and the others trailing along behind her. They walked slowly and cautiously, but Tsi could barely contain her excitement. She was so close to her home. She felt she could practically kiss the *Exile*'s hull.

Just then, she thought she saw something move at the corner of her eye. Harken's eyes widened. The others were quietly chatting to each other, unable to contain their excitement, just like her. None of them sensed what she and the Chalakhati did.

The animals had stopped calling. The only sound above the chatter was the rain. Rain against trees, against the ground, against the hull... against metal. A lot of metal.

There was a sudden commotion, and Tsi leaped backwards, the Noxian Repeater instantly in her hands. A dozen figures seemed to materialize in the woods around them, each moving as swift and silent as a shadow. Someone fired a weapon, but their attackers were in among them in an instant.

Tsi saw Tenlok draw his pistol, but a gauntlet wrapped around his wrist and he was thrown to the ground in an instant, one boot upon his chest and a rifle barrel pressed against his neck. Enlil let out a curse before someone grabbed her, seizing her tightly in a headlock as she struggled futilely. Wylla stood mutely, but that was not enough to save her. She was staring at the dark figure that had Enlil pinned down, when another burst from the underbrush and tackled her.

One by one, the entire party was subdued, the only ones to escape being Tsi herself and Strongmind. They had managed to dodge their black armored attackers, and sprinted full tilt through the forest. Bursting out into the clearing, Tsi darted for cover behind one of the *Exile*'s landing struts.

Strongmind's gun was in his hands, but he did not fire. It would do them no good. Peering out from behind the strut, Tsi got a good look at their attackers. Silently, more armored figures emerged from the darkness.

Active camo-cloaks hung from their shoulders, each slowly

shifting colors from the background pattern of the forest to a dull white as the enemy stood in the open. They wore armor the color of brass and ebony, overlapping plates and joints so thick it would be easy to assume they were machines. Metal crests swept backwards from their helms, giving their heads an elongated, inhuman look. Cold blue sensors glowed from their visors, wrought to look like the empty eye-sockets of a human skull.

Janissaries. There was no mistaking them. Though it had been a long time since she had last set eyes on one, their equipment had changed little, and their brutal efficiency had changed not at all. She had probably walked right past them while they waited, invisible to all but the most trained eye. They had used her ship as bait, and she had fallen for it.

"Disarm yourselves and step away from the craft," one of the Janissaries ordered.

"We have insufficient firepower to offer meaningful resistance," Strongmind said, his voice low.

"I know," Tsi replied.

Slowly, she holstered her pistol and stepped out into the open, her hands raised. The Janissaries aimed their weapons at her and Strongmind, but there was an odd uncertainty in their movements. None of them approached her.

"You are in violation of Kiosan Law," the Janissary said, clearly their commander. "It is forbidden to land on this world."

"I know," Tsi said. "I wouldn't have come here if I had a choice."

"You are the owner of this craft?" the Janissary asked, pointing a metal finger at the *Exile*.

Tsi nodded.

"You are also the one who sent a messenger beacon from this system?"

"I am," Tsi replied.

The Janissary jerked his head back towards the forest.

"And the people traveling with you are its crew?"

Tsi hesitated for a moment.

"Two are not. An old man with a black beard, and a young man in rags who carried a spear," she said.

The Janissary commander signaled to one of his men, who

darted back into the forest. She did not hear any gunfire, and so she prayed that the two Chalakhati had been released.

"You are now prisoners of the Janissariat of Kios. You will be taken aboard the *Sun Blade* to await judgment, along with your crew."

A dozen Janissaries advanced out of the tree line. The barrels of their weapons shook as they advanced, as if they could not quite bring them to bare on Tsi. The commander slung his rifle, and walked towards her cautiously. He stopped when he was in arm's reach of her, and peered at her curiously.

"Who are you?" he asked finally. It was somewhere between a threat and a genuine question. Tsi could sense the genuine confusion in the Janissary's voice, all his old programming coming back in her presence.

It was time. At long last, it was time. The truth would set her free.

"You already know who I am, Janissary," Tsi said. "I am the Empress of Kios."

CHAPTER 35

I've never dealt with this much feec-rec in my whole damn life," Enlil said.

She paced the prison cell like a caged animal, glaring at the transparent door that held them in. The room was small enough that she could cross it in five long strides. She knew that, because she had counted it, more than once, as she went back and forth.

The others were jammed in with her, sitting shoulder to shoulder on the benches along each wall. Strongmind and Tenlok seemed to be having a competition as to who could express the least emotion and concern for their situation. Neither had said a word since they were separated from Tsi, quick marched into a transport ship and flown up here.

Hiron was staring glumly at the floor. He had taken their capture the hardest. Unlike her, the kid had never seen the inside of a *real* brig before. Furner had fallen asleep, like the old hand he was, and despite her pacing and cursing, nothing seemed to rouse the man. Wylla had sat on a bench away from everyone else, tucked her legs up under herself, and closed her eyes. Her breathing was steady and calm, and she mouthed words, but did not speak. Meditating.

Something about that irked Enlil. She sat down next to the kid, looking across the room at the Bykon.

"You know," she said aloud. "The least they could have done is tell us what they did with Tsi."

"Could've tossed us out the airlock," Tenlok replied laconically.

"You don't think that's what they've done with Tsi, do you?" Hiron asked, looking up from his scrutiny of the floor.

"No, she's alive," the Bondsman said. "For now."

"Hate these people," Enlil said. "If we were dealin' with a decent crew, they'd've sent someone to work us over by now."

"Kiosans are particular," Tenlok said.

"You dealt with these people before?" Enlil asked.

The Bondsman shrugged his shoulders.

"Once or twice."

"Shit, I never even seen one until today," Enlil continued. She was rocking back and forth, unable to contain her nervous energy. "I heard about 'em before, of course. Hell, when I was on the *Jenny* we used to fantasize about making a big haul off one of the border worlds, like Lotus or Johakim. Never expected to actually deal with 'em though."

"I mean, Tsi's Kiosan," Hiron pointed out. "We've all been dealing with her."

"Yeah," Enlil said.

The room went quiet again. Her feet tapped against the deck, and she realized she hadn't had anything to eat or drink in a long time. She'd have killed for a hit of Red Ether right now, or a suck-globe of good quality brandy.

Enlil's stomach growled. She searched the pockets of her coverall, hoping she had stashed a sliver of a Rat-Pak in one of them. There was nothing though, except for lint and a few tiny metal bolts. She took one of the bolts out.

She turned it over in her hand. It was very light, its surface silver with a slightly oily sheen. It was the kind of thing only really useful for minor repair jobs, patching inner panels and securing circuit boards.

With nothing better to do, she flicked it at Wylla. Her first toss missed, but made an audible metal clang against the wall. The Bykon did not react. Enlil's second shot struck her square in the forehead.

Wylla's eyes snapped open and she jumped up from the bench, grimacing in rage.

"What did you do that for?!"

Enlil laughed.

"I didn't know you people could get angry," she said.

"Oh, I can get angry. Believe me."

Enlil stood up, squaring off with Wylla. She walked close enough to the other woman that she could feel her breath.

"Yeah, I can see that," Enlil said. "Real shame you can't do anything about it."

She shoved Wylla in the shoulder with just enough force to

make her take a step backwards.

"I—I don't think this is helpful," Hiron said.

"What ya gonna do?" Enlil asked, ignoring the kid and shoving Wylla again. "Oh, that's right! Nothing. You can't do anything. I can slap you silly, and you'll just stand there and take it, won't you? Just like ya did down there. They came at us hard, and you just stood there."

Wylla glared at her in response. Enlil shoved her again, hard this time, causing Wylla to stagger back. She was getting close to the bench. Wylla shoved her again.

"Come on, Enlil," Furner said groggily, having been roused from his sleep. "What's the point of this?"

"What's it take to make you snap?" Enlil asked, Wylla her sole focus. "I start beatin' your head against the wall, you finally gonna try and protect yourself?"

"You do what you have to, Enlil," Wylla replied. "I know what this is: you're frightened. We've fought so hard, come so far, just to wind up in another jail cell. Now you're powerless, and the only way you can respect yourself is if you prove you're stronger than someone else. Well, you're stronger than me, Enlil. So go ahead. Do what you have to do."

Enlil's fist cracked into Wylla's jaw. She fell into the bench, but steadied herself and got back up. Enlil cocked her fist again, but suddenly Furner's bulky form was between them. He put a pair of meaty hands on her shoulders, moving her away from Wylla.

"Alright! Alright!" he shouted. "The hell's the matter with you, Enlil?"

Enlil broke his grip on her and stalked away. Furner had switched to speaking Noxian, which had jarred her for a moment, but she still felt the undeniable pull of rage. She wheeled to glare past his shoulder at Wylla.

"I'm sick of having to deal with that holier-than-thou coward," she said in her native tongue. "Maybe if we start treating her like what she is, she'll learn to pull her own damn weight. She didn't do a Gods-damned thing when they came for us! Not one thing!"

"You've got a plate loose," Furner said. "This isn't the time or the place to be going at each other!"

Wylla wiped blood away from her lip, returning Enlil's gaze. The anger seemed to have faded from her eyes, now Enlil saw only pity there. She grit her teeth and her cheeks flushed.

"Just sick of that damn bitch, is all!" she said, throwing her hands up and turning away from the others to hide the sudden tears of shame she knew were welling up in her eyes. She cursed herself. What a fine time to lose control.

The cell door slid open, unannounced. A security drone stood framed in the doorway, its polished silver carapace shining in the harsh light of the brig.

"Prisoners are required to attend current inquiry," the machine said tonelessly.

"All are ready for transfer," Strongmind replied, its voice equally bland as it rose to its feet. "Warning: the psychological condition of my human cohabitants is deteriorating. There has been a physical altercation."

The security drone's faceless head swung to look at Wylla.

"Is medical treatment required?" it asked.

"I'm fine," Wylla said.

"Suggest relaxation of security standards to reduce chance of repeat altercations and improve prisoner psychological condition," Strongmind said.

"Data irrelevant," the drone replied. "Follow me, please."

"Where are you taking us?" Hiron asked as they filed out of the cell, the air still thick with tension. "I, uh, didn't quite catch all that."

"Per standard Janissary Capture Protocols, the crew is in the process of evaluating whether or not to execute your leader," the security drone said. "Your testimony will aid in the making of that decision."

The inquiry chamber was simple and spartan. Tsi stood on a raised cylinder at the center of the room, harsh footlights illuminating her while the rest of the area was in near pitch darkness. She could see light glinting against the Janissaries' armor, and glowing blue eyes watching her from the darkness. She counted twenty sets. Most of the command staff of a ship this size.

There were humans in the room, too. The judicial auxiliaries would be the ones to actually pass judgment and carry out the sentence. The Janissaries were only there as mute witnesses.

She had expected no less. Her children wanted vengeance

upon her, a vengeance she had long denied them. This score would serve as surrogates for the countless legions she had created. No, not *created*, she corrected herself mentally. The legions she had damned.

"You are Daketya Anat, once called Empress of Kios," one of the judges said from the darkness. Her voice was high and refined, one of the rare examples of a Kiosan noblewoman joining the auxiliary service. A scholar, Tsi guessed, due to her slightly old-fashioned dialect.

"I go by 'Tsi' now," she replied.

"You are ashamed of your old name?" another judge asked. His voice was deep and resonant. She could see none of her audience clearly, but the light glanced off armored shoulder guards and medallions, and she could just make out the outline of a large, broad-shouldered man.

"I'm not that person anymore."

"You have altered your physical appearance, and been in hiding since the time of the Great Rising. Tell us, as a matter of record, how it was that you survived the attack on your palace on Kios Prime?"

This third judge had taken some kind of wound to her throat. Her voice was harsh and grating, coming through an artificial larynx, and she paused briefly for air between each sentence. She was a veteran, of the kind too proud to have a proper replacement grown and grafted to her body. Even though her job no longer required her to run through hails of pulse fire, this woman wanted everyone to know she had been a soldier once, and paid the price for it.

"I think there are people in this room who know it well enough already," Tsi said. "Ask them."

"We are asking you," the second judge intoned, voice echoing through the chamber.

"Fine," Tsi said. "I escaped... because they... the Jannisar—"

She began to stumble over her words. Her throat felt tight. She had rehearsed this moment so many times before, had practiced it in her mind. Now she was here, and those twenty sets of eyes were burning into her. She swallowed hard. She had to see this through. She owed it to them.

"The Janissaries could not harm me. I coded it into their minds, their conditioning. From the moment they took their first steps, a force as primal to them as breathing, was to never hurt me."

"Impossible!" the first judge scoffed. "Our Protectors rose

against you! You underestimated their dedication to honor, to the people of Kios."

"Protectors?" Tsi asked. "That's what you call them? Even now, we speak of them as if they are not in the room with us. I suppose it's only natural. I didn't make them to be human beings, I made them to win the war."

"That does not explain—" the second judge began.

"How they deposed me? I was getting to that. As I said, I made them to win the war. They decided that I... was interfering with that goal."

Tsi could still see it in her mind's eye: the golden towers of Kios Prime falling in great columns of flame. Fire in the streets. She could hear the ancient glass murals of her palace being shattered by gunfire, smell the scent of cooking flesh. How bravely her personal guard had fought, she reflected. How uselessly.

"They stormed the palace," Tsi said. "One of my advisers bought me time. My Shadow Guard, a woman called Rynela, took my place. At the time she was my exact physical double. She was the one who was killed, by ordinary humans, not Janissaries. While they were displaying her severed head on the steps of the palace, I disguised myself and fled. The Janissaries who saw me flee thought I was a civilian. They dismissed the fact that they could not fire on me as mercy, not realizing it was programmed into them. Then I simply made my way off world."

"How?" the third judge, the soldier, asked. She was the oldest, the only one who had lived through this. Tsi felt a strange kinship with that brutal mechanical voice in the darkness. Perhaps she had even commanded this woman once.

"An advanced starship that I had specially designed. It had been intended as an escape craft in case the Guraggan ever approached the capital. I had no idea I would need it to escape my own people."

"The craft you traveled to Chalakhat in," the second judge stated, more than asked. "A fascinating vehicle. We are repairing it now. It is remarkable that you never thought to share such an advanced design with your own forces."

"The *Exile* was a secret," Tsi said. "And... I designer her myself. She was mine. I had no desire to share her with anyone else."

"What a primitive impulse," the first judge said piously. "Still, it fits your psychological profile. You are an atavistic individual. Perhaps we should be grateful to you: only someone with your brutal mind could have created our Protectors, and we have all reaped the benefits of the Janissariat."

"Spare me," Tsi said. "We're wasting time. You've already decided whether or not to execute me, haven't you?"

"We have," growled the third judge. "We are not debating your execution. That decision has already been made. The purpose of this inquiry is to verify the information you sent us on that Slip-beacon."

"Everything that was on that beacon is true," Tsi said. "The Guraggan may already be moving against you, but if you prepare yourselves now, mobilize at least ten Legions around every major world, then you might have a chance—"

"You do not advise the Janissariat in matters of strategy," the second judge retorted. "You are an enemy, and anything you say will be treated as disinformation until it is proven otherwise."

"That's idiotic!" Tsi snapped. "Why would I risk everything to come here? What possible purpose could that serve?"

"We have discussed several possibilities," the first judge said. "When we have finished interrogating your crew, we will come to our decision."

"My crew..." Tsi said. "Please, you must let me speak to them. I have to... I have to explain—"

"You do not have that privilege," the third judge said. "We have learned enough from you for now. Take her away."

Two Janissaries rose from the darkness to stand at either side of Tsi. Lights came on along a flight of steps down from the platform. Tsi walked down the steps and onto a lighted path that led through the darkness into the bright, white corridor beyond. Flanked by the Janissaries, Tsi slowly made her way back to her cell. They could not hurt her, as she had said. But if the Tribunal was anything to go on, there were plenty of people on this ship who would.

They were split into groups of two, and each put in dull grey interrogation chambers. Similar to the brig he'd been in, the interrogation cell was totally barren save for a bench, a desk, and a chair. Hiron sat down gratefully. He had no idea what the sorting process had been, but he had wound up paired with Tenlok.

The mercenary stayed standing for a few moments after the door was closed behind them and they were left alone together. Then he kicked one foot up on the bench and leaned against the wall, folding his arms across his chest.

"How long do you think we'll have to wait?" Hiron asked, more to fill the silence than anything else.

"A while," Tenlok replied. "They want to listen to us. See if we talk about anything interesting."

"Oh," Hiron said. "Um... *do* we have anything interesting to talk about?"

Tenlok shook his head.

"Nothing they can't ask us in person."

Hiron stretched out his twisted legs and rubbed his knees. He'd had a good amount of time to sit still in the brig, but days of rough travel across the surface of Chalakhat had not done him any favors. He hadn't really spoken to anyone since they'd been loaded onto the transports and taken to this ship. Indeed, now that he thought about it, he didn't even know the name of the ship they were on. It had all seemed so sudden, but then there had also been a great deal of time spent simply sitting and waiting.

The doors finally opened and the interrogator entered. She was a fit woman in a high collared uniform with red hair, coiled tightly around her scalp. A piercing in her septum was connected to her ears by twin chains of polished silver, and one of her eyes had been replaced by a cybernetic, its flat orange color giving her an unearthly appearance. She sat down without a word, took out a recording device and switched it on.

"State your names and any relevant titles aloud for the record," she said in clear, unaccented Panglos. "I am interrogator Jehyle, presiding."

"Hiron Dath, First son of Brem Dath, Inheritor of the Black Canyon," Hiron said quickly. "Uh, Slaughterer of Legions."

To his surprise, the interrogator snorted.

"Relevant titles," she repeated, trying to keep her composure.

"Tenlok," Tenlok said. "Bondsman."

"Ah," Jehyle said. "Well, our business here is brief. I just need to know how long you've been traveling with the subject, any relevant activities, and your general estimation of her."

"I'm invoking article three of the Bondsman's Guild-Kiosan Exclusion Treaty. Came here under duress, I need my equipment returned to me and to be transported to the nearest neutral world after receiving emergency medical treatment," Tenlok said.

Hiron looked at him in astonishment. He'd never heard Tenlok speak more than a few sentences at a time, and never in legal gibberish.

"What kind of medical treatment do you need?" Jehyle asked.

"Ocular repairs and a full bloodstream flush," Tenlok said. "Tsi injected me with a nanite weapon. I'm heart-linked with her. She dies, I die."

The interrogator drummed her fingers against the desk.

"We'll see what we can do about your medical condition. You're prepared to swear this status was... involuntary?"

"She stabbed me with a nano-knife."

"You must understand, people in your profession make similar... arrangements frequently, of their own accord. We need to be sure this 'heart-link' wasn't just part of your professional operations."

"This wasn't a Bonding," Tenlok said, and Hiron realized he heard genuine anger in his voice. He hadn't known about this, why Tenlok was with them. In his naivete, he'd assumed that Tenlok was hired by Tsi, or perhaps even a friend of hers.

"Of course," Jehyle said. "Your medical condition will be taken into account when we decide what to do with you. As for the treaty, I am sure you're aware that the Bondsman's Guild no longer exists, aren't you?"

"I'd heard," Tenlok said.

"Therefore, you have no legal basis to request extradition."

Tenlok shrugged.

"Worth a shot," Tenlok said. "Alright, I've been with Tsi a few weeks, relative. Killed some people for her, fought the Guraggan. Helped her shoot that beacon off. That's about it."

"So you are prepared to swear you have engaged Guraggan troops?"

"I am too," Hiron piped in. "They've been hunting us since Tsi and I met on Promise."

"Ah," Jehyle said. "You have been traveling with her how long?"

"About three weeks," Hiron said. "All voluntary. She hasn't abused or mistreated me in any way, and... She saved my life, ma'am. More than once."

Hiron looked nervously at the Bondsman.

"His too," he added. "I don't know anything about the heart-link, but on Salvation, he was separated from us, under attack. She went into fire to rescue him. I don't know who she was before I met her, I don't know what she's done, but she's had chance after chance to leave us behind and save herself and... she always comes back, ma'am."

Jehyle glanced questioningly at Tenlok. He nodded.

"What the kid says is true."

"So, it would be accurate to describe her as loyal?"

"Yes," Hiron said without hesitation.

Tenlok nodded again.

"But she can also be ruthless, clearly," Jehyle said. "Well, I have a few more questions—"

"She's also—that is, if I may," Hiron interrupted. Jehyle arched an eyebrow.

"Begging your pardon," he said. "But there's something else about her too. She's, well..."

Hiron paused, searching for the right word.

"She seems like something haunts her," he said finally. "It's as if something terrible happened a long time ago, and she feels like it's her fault. And... And she wants to make up for it."

"Repentant?" Jehyle asked.

"Yeah," Hiron said. "Repentant."

"Ain't tellin' ya shit," Furner said.

He crossed his arms over his gut, and leaned back, kicking his feet up on the interrogator's desk. The interrogator, who was a young man with hair turned prematurely grey, massaged his temples. Enlil could see a vein standing out on his forehead. She didn't bother to hide her laughter. The poor kid had spent the first hour just trying to convince them to speak to him in Panglos.

"You are not on trial," the young interrogator repeated. "No criminal culpability—"

"We don't really care," Enlil explained. "We don't talk to people like you. Not about crew."

"So... she's your... 'captain', maybe?" the interrogator asked hopefully.

Enlil exchanged a glance with Furner. Furner shrugged.

"Yeah, you can call her that," Enlil said.

"And," the interrogator continued with an exasperated sigh. "Would you call her a good captain, or a bad one?"

"Neither," Enlil replied.

"Maybe you didn't understand the question," the interrogator said, speaking very slowly. "Is she good... or bad?"

"She's neither," Enlil said. "She's the best."

"... I've told you everything that I can," Wylla said.

Her conversation had begun pleasantly enough. The officer's name was Soret, a slim, small man whose facial jewelry she envied slightly. But after an hour or two of discussing her opinions and evaluation of Tsi, he had begun to ask her about the Guraggan.

"You must be more specific about this... transportation device. What principle does it function on? What is its energy source?"

"I don't know," Wylla said. "I've only seen it used a few times. It's a beam of some kind. The effect is comparable to an entangled particle, as I understand it, but somehow my masters—"

Wylla stumbled over the phrase for the third time in this conversation. Something about Soret reminded her of life with Lady Ornicht. He seemed to turn his head and narrow his eyes in exactly the same way the Physician had.

"My *former* masters," she corrected, "Have found a means of using the beam to transfer matter instantaneously while minimizing the effects of mass disruption."

"It sounds preposterous," Soret said. His tongue flicked across his lower lip in an oddly reptilian fashion.

"I would have thought so as well," Wylla said. "But I tell you I *have* traveled on it. None of your systems are safe so long as they have this weapon. The Khagan's plans are not a secret—"

"Khagan?" Soret interrupted. "You must take this interrogation seriously. There hasn't been a Khagan in decades, since the last one was killed at the Siege Victorious."

"A new Khagan has risen," Wylla said simply. "He bound the Houses together once again. The Path of Glory was his greatest weapon, but that is not what unites them. He promised them you: he said that the Hegemony would return, and turn all of Kios to ash."

Soret sat back in his chair, studying Wylla carefully.

"She is not lying," Strongmind said. The machine had been present for the interrogation as well, but Soret had barely asked it any questions. Wylla knew uncomfortably well that the best way to interrogate a drone was to simply crack open its skull and dig around inside its circuits. Of course, Strongmind had turned that on her. And she had wound up here. Once again surrounded by those she was unsure she could trust, once again considered an enemy by all, a friend to none.

"Thank you, drone. Your input is not necessary," Soret said.

"Auditory evidence contradicts that assessment."

Soret shot the machine a nasty look.

"In any case," Soret continued, "We have only your word and the beacon as evidence of this supposed device. I assure you it is being treated seriously, but you must understand how incredible this is."

"Of course. Kiosans don't keep gods, do they?" Wylla asked.

"No," Soret said. "It is not forbidden, but superstition is unpopular here. Why do you ask?"

"I think we are finding ourselves at the heart of a strange miracle," Wylla said. "A great danger has arisen, and the only warning that you have comes from those who you consider your enemies. A circumstance so unlikely, you find it incredible. But perhaps the better term for such a circumstance is 'miraculous'."

"You do understand then. We must examine all the possibilities, and determine which is the most likely. Whether this is part of some plot, or..."

"Or Tsi is telling the truth," Wylla said. "And you are in danger."

"It is unlikely, but possible," Soret conceded.

"As I said: a strange miracle. I only hope you have the strength to recognize it."

Tsi had too much time to think. She was left alone for hours while the tribunal deliberated, no companion save the blank walls of her prison. It was oddly fitting: she'd once been infamous for using a form of neurological oubliette on her enemies. They would be put in a room not unlike this, then hooked up to an AR device. Signals would be fed into their brain that made it seem as if the walls were slowly closing in. Then the jailers would simply leave them until they died of thirst or starvation. Perhaps the Janissaries intended that to be her final punishment.

No, she decided. It was too creative. They always wanted things done brutally and quickly, much like Strongmind. She wondered about his fate. Had he been dismantled? Were they probing his memory banks? There were still secrets he held, things even he did not know that she had locked inside his electronic brain. She wished she could have had a chance to apologize to him, to everyone, but the Janissaries had separated her as quickly as possible after their capture.

The door to her cell slid open unannounced, and a Janissary stepped in. They were difficult to tell apart, as she had used a limited pool of genotypes in their creation, but the decorations on this one's armor marked him as a *Bolesht*, the third highest ranking commander aboard the ship. His chest plate had a designation code across one pectoral, and the name *Sun Blade* on the other.

The Janissary bowed to her politely.

"Empress," he said. "I am Bolesht Ares-9881. I have been selected to inform you of the Tribunal's decision."

"What's happened to my crew?" Tsi asked, ignoring his words. "Whatever you do to me, you should know they had no part in anything that happened during my reign. Most of them weren't even born yet, they—"

"The sentence is death. To be carried out at the beginning of the next day shift," the Janissary said bluntly. "Your companions will be released."

"I see," Tsi said.

She felt light. The wait was over. Perversely, she almost looked forward to it. Just eighteen more hours, and then it would all finally be settled.

"The 90th Orta wished to express its gratitude for the information you have provided," the Janissary continued.

He was stiff in his motion and speech, even for one of them.

Something was going on behind his visor. It was customary for the Janissaries to remain masked in the presence of others. The reason was two-fold: most found their physical appearance disturbing, and distancing themselves from the common soldiery reinforced their status as an elite. There was another purpose to the custom though, one Tsi had been keenly aware of when she had instituted it. If they were faceless, they were disposable.

"You're going to heed my warnings then," Tsi said. "If you can get just ten legions mobilized at each of the major contact points, you might be able to stop the invasion before it starts."

"There are only forty legions left in the Janissariat, Empress."

"What?" Tsi asked incredulously. "*Forty*? That's barely enough to protect the capital systems. What happened? Why are there so few of you?"

"Insurrections. Pirate raids. Border skirmishes," Ares replied. "Nothing compared to the first Guraggan War, but we have still suffered losses."

"Losses without replacement? What happened to the cloning banks?"

"We destroyed them."

The words hung in the air. Tsi was struck dumb for an instant, though as realization dawned on her, it seemed blindingly obvious.

"Tell me, Empress," Ares continued, "Why do you think we would ever want there to be *more* of us?"

"I..."

Tsi tried to speak, but she could form no words. He was right. It was a painful thing to be a Janissary, and she had never considered that they might know that, too.

"Forty legions isn't enough to win this war," Tsi said.

"Even with human auxiliaries."

"You have warned us. A message has already been sent to the High Commanders. We will prepare."

"You will lose," Tsi said quietly. "Everything I did to get here... it's all for nothing. You'll still lose."

"It was not completely futile," Ares said. "Your return means that you can finally pay for what you have done."

"I suppose you're right," Tsi said, smiling bitterly. "That's not nothing, is it?"

CHAPTER 36

The airlock opened with a hiss, and Lady Ornicht stepped aboard. With Liss and Wylla gone, her retinue had been reduced to just the Physician and herself, so she had brought two of her new acquisitions with her. The Rock-Drinkers had to lower their elongated heads as they crossed the threshold. Their spindly frames and ribbed survival suits gave them an exotic flair that Ornicht took some small pride in. They might not be the most formidable creatures she had ever brought into her service, but they were at least... unusual.

Serfs bowed and scraped before her, making all the usual noises necessary to appease her honor. It was custom when boarding the vessel of another Guraggan that one be welcomed by the serfs first, so that the host did not have to debase themselves in ritual greeting. One of the serfs prostrated himself before her, and, with great ceremony and artful gestures, splashed scented water on her boots. When he was done, Ornicht strode past him without a word, heading for the audience chamber where her host awaited. One of the Rock-Drinkers paused and knelt down, placing the tips of his gloved fingers in the puddle of water. Miniature tubes hidden in the gauntlet began to suck up the fluid.

"Come," Ornicht said, and the Rock-Drinker reluctantly rose and fell in behind her.

She would have to break them of that habit.

At last they made their way through the dimly lit corridors of the starship, its twisting halls and spiraling stairs designed to deliberately confuse and misdirect a boarding party. Her host was waiting for her, draped casually across a couch carved of bone-white minerals. Chem-Thralls and Battle Serfs waited in the wings, watching Ornicht with hawkish eyes.

The host had eschewed armor for this meeting with Ornicht, wearing instead a simple, tight fitting garment of the kind used in melee training. Her arms and legs were sinewy and vascular, proudly displaying a long, jagged scar that ran from the outside of her right thigh down past her knee. The injury had only healed recently, and was still red and puckered in some places.

Ornicht smiled. There was something childish in the display, especially compared to the wounds mapped across her own flesh.

"Mother," the woman on couch said. "Welcome to the *Crimson Alaunt*."

"It is an impressive ship, Morhodil," Lady Ornicht said. "You must be proud."

"You like it?" Morhodil asked, springing up from the couch. "It was a gift from the Khagan himself. A reward for my victory over House Batule. I slew Lord Batule himself, you know. I kept some of him as a prize; I may even make a Warborn from him."

"I take it he gave you that little scratch, too?" Ornicht asked, indicating the scar.

"One of his Thralls," Morhodil said dismissively. "It capitalized on a mistake of mine."

"You always were poor at guarding your right," Ornicht said. "But enough chatter. What did the Khagan say to my message?"

Ornicht tried to keep her voice cool and level, but her body was tense. It had been days since she sent her own beacon to the Inheritor's World to update the fleet on the progress of her mission. She had waited here, silently, on the edge of Noxian space for a reply. At last, it was not a repair ship that had returned, but the *Crimson Alaunt*.

"The Khagan has sent me to collect you, dear mother. He was... concerned at your inability to retake this one ship, but it is of no matter. I will assist you from here on."

"I do not need *help*," Ornicht said. "Everything is under control. I just need repairs—"

"Oh, the Khagan is quite aware of how 'under control' things are," Morhodil smiled, her bright white teeth hiding the venom of her words. "He was, in fact, grateful for your reconnaissance work. You said the ship was headed for Chalakhat?"

"Yes," Ornicht replied irritably. "It was all in my message."

"Good. That is where you and I shall head next, under the Khagan's orders. We will pick over the bones and see if we can't find that little ship of yours."

"Pick over the bones? Speak plainly, girl."

Morhodil smiled again, a serpentine expression she had picked up since reaching maturity that Ornicht did not care for at all.

"The ship has already reached Chalakhat. By the time we arrive, her message will have reached the Kiosans anyway."

"Theta-90 was on board. It's more than capable of crippling them before they—"

"Theta-90 is an obsolete piece of scrap metal you kept out of nostalgia, mother. If it had succeeded, it would have sent the beacon back to you. Face the truth: you've gone soft. You refused to destroy that ship when you had the chance because you wanted your pet Bykon back."

"How dare you!" Ornicht snarled. She twitched her hands reflexively, causing the twin mono-blades to slide out of their sheathes on her forearms. There was a scraping of metal against metal as every one of Morhodil's servants drew their weapons, training them all on Ornicht. The smile didn't leave Morhodil's face as she waved a hand dismissively, and her troops relaxed.

"I apologize mother," Morhodil said. "I spoke out of turn."

Ornicht only growled in response as she sheathed her own blades. It was humiliating, being manipulated by her own daughter like this. Morhodil had always been too clever. Too clever, and too cruel.

"By the Skies of Earth!" Ornicht snapped. "You are not the Lady of Ornicht yet, Morhodil. Do not forget that. Our House is strong because of its unity. It does not do for you to challenge me and insult me. Not before the Khagan, not before your siblings, not even on your own ship!"

"House Ornicht is strong because we win, mother. We do not falter. Ever."

Ornicht seethed at her daughter's words, but remained silent. The girl was right. She had made mistake after mistake in the pursuit of this one ship. She had lost her two most favored servants, countless thralls and serfs. She was ashamed. Then she remembered the ancient words of her people: *What Is Broken Can Be Remade.* There was some solace in that, at least.

"What I've been trying to tell you is that your failure doesn't matter. The Khagan has decided that the time has come."

"He means to strike Kios, then?"

"Dear mother," Morhodil said sweetly. "The invasion has already begun."

Enlil sat awake, staring at the ceiling. The others were all either dozing or sitting quietly in their communal cell. None of them had felt much like talking after their interrogation, and Hiron's half-hearted suggestion that they try to find a means of escape had been met with disinterest. Where was there to escape to? She'd found out that the ship they were on was called the *Sun Blade*, and that it was a cruiser. It was far too large to just stumble around, hoping to find an unguarded hangar. Not to mention none of them had any tools or weapons. Strongmind still had that knife up its arm, she supposed, but the machine wasn't feeling very communicative. Tenlok had his armor too, but he'd been searched so thoroughly she doubted he'd managed to hide anything.

Enlil glanced over at Wylla. The Bykon woman was asleep, her head fallen forward onto her chest. She felt a twinge of guilt as she looked at the cut on her lip. There had been no call for what she'd done. She'd been through danger with this woman, but the moment things really turned against them, she decided to vent all her frustration on someone who couldn't fight back.

What exactly did that say about her, Enlil wondered. Traveling with Tsi, having a mission, it had all seemed like a chance to *be* something, but now... Now Enlil wasn't sure she'd ever be anything but what she was: a scavenger. An oxygen-rat. Just scraping by to survive, ready to lash out at anyone and anything at the slightest provocation.

Enlil's was resting her head against the wall of the cell when she noticed it. Starships were always filled with millions of hums and murmurs and buzzing sounds, so many that it became white noise after a while. There was one sound though, that Enlil always recognized: the low rumble of a shield generator.

"Our shields are out," she said aloud.

A few of the others stirred groggily.

"Our shields are out!" she repeated. "Something's gone wrong."

"What? How can you tell?" Hiron asked, rubbing sleep from

his eyes.

Wylla had snapped into alertness instantly. She cocked her head slightly and listened for a moment.

"She's right," Wylla said. "There's something wrong. The generator isn't making any noise."

"Three people are approaching the cell," Strongmind announced.

Enlil could hear the sound of shuffling feet. Without a word, she, Strongmind, and Tenlok stood up, their fists clenched and ready for a fight. They positioned themselves around the cell door, Strongmind standing in front of it, Enlil and Tenlok to either side.

"Wait, what are you do—" Hiron started, but Enlil silenced him with a look.

The door slid open.

"Oh!"

Enlil recognized the voice. When she peered around the corner, she saw the young man who had interrogated Furner and her standing in the hall, looking confused. Two other people in matching uniforms were in the hall with him. One of them, a short, slim man with those funny golden chains decorating his face that Kiosans seemed to like, was carrying a satchel full of equipment.

"We, uh," the young man started, before the third interrogator, a woman with red hair stepped forward.

"You have to get out of here now," she said. "We're under attack. We've brought you everything we took off of you when you were captured, take it and we'll get you to your ship."

"Guraggan?" Enlil asked.

"Yes," the woman said. "Lots of them. They came out of nowhere. We've taken some bad hits, they took out our engine in the first exchange. Looks like they want to board us."

"Let's move," Tenlok growled, roughly grabbing the satchel. He ripped it open and began strapping weapons to himself, stopping only to toss guns to Strongmind, Furner and Enlil. She checked her magazine, and found it was fully loaded.

"Awful trusting of you," Enlil said. "Why're you letting us out?"

"Because," the short man spoke up. "We compared our findings and realized you should be released. You're decent people, in your own way."

Enlil snorted.

"Regardless," he continued. "None of you deserve to die here."

"Where is Tsi?" Wylla asked.

"Tsi?" the young man asked, seeming at first to be unfamiliar with the name. "Oh, um, she's... she's still in her holding cell. Three levels above us. But you have to go now, they'll be breaching any moment, and we can't guarantee your safety in a firefight."

"We're not leaving without her," Wylla said firmly.

"Damn right," Enlil said.

All of them stood together, no more words passing between them. They would leave the ship with Tsi or not at all.

"She's not a woman worthy of this kind of loyalty," the red haired interrogator said.

"Worth is irrelevant," Strongmind replied. "Please direct us to her."

"I'll do it," the younger interrogator said. "You two get somewhere safe."

Enlil watched as the trio exchanged a brief salute. Then each of the other two took it in turn to grab the kid's hand, while striking their own chests with a balled fist.

"The Janissariat will remember you," the woman said. "I'll see your name written with the names of the Protectors."

"You have to survive to do that," he replied with an impish smile.

She nodded, and then she and the short man sped down the hall, away from them.

"Alright," the young man said. "Follow me."

Tsi could feel the gunfire reverberating through the hull. She'd actually heard the first few impacts of enemy fire, then the alarms had sounded. After that there had been a long silence, then the familiar warning klaxons announcing a hull breach. Boarding skiffs had already hit the ship, and now the enemy was fighting their way bulkhead to bulkhead through the ship.

For the second time that day, Tsi contemplated her death. It seemed it was going to come a few hours ahead of schedule. She didn't mind. She only regretted that she would not have the chance to say her goodbyes.

"Please stay away from the door," she heard Strongmind's voice clearly say from outside her cell.

For a moment, Tsi thought she had finally lost her mind. Then the cell door was forcefully kicked inwards. Standing in the hall, armed to the teeth, was her entire crew. Strongmind stood in the doorway, face placid as ever, but Tsi felt she could shout for joy.

"Strongmind!" she said. "You—how did you all—"

"We were assisted by this interrogator," Strongmind said, pointing towards a nervous looking young man in an ill-fitting uniform. "His name is Plett."

"Plett," Tsi said, as she leaped from the bench and headed into the corridor. "I cannot possibly repay you for letting my people out."

"What's done is done," Plett replied. He cast his eyes downwards briefly, and Tsi realized he was not just nervous, but ashamed too.

"Letting me go wasn't your idea, was it?" she asked.

He nodded.

"Thank you all the same," she said.

"Here," Plett said, not looking her in the eye as he handed her a pass-card. "This will get you through all the main doors. Your ship is in Hangar Nine. It should be space-worthy."

"Thank you," Tsi said. "I won't forget this."

"I wish you would. If it was up to me, you'd stay here," he said simply. "I'm going to try to find a life-pod."

He turned to the rest of the crew.

"Good luck to you all," he said. He nodded to Tsi curtly, then walked briskly away.

Tsi watched him go for a moment. It had been so long since she was reminded what ordinary people thought of her and her legacy. The boy wasn't old enough to have been born during her reign, but he had been raised to despise her. If he survived, he would never live down the shame of releasing the Mad Empress.

"This is yours," Tenlok said, tossing Tsi her Noxian Repeater. "Fully loaded."

Tsi checked it to be safe. She didn't have her holster, but that mattered little. She guessed she would be needing it drawn all the way back to the *Exile*.

"Okay, everyone," Tsi said. "We don't have much time. Strongmind, you and Tenlok take point. Enlil, you and I are second wave. Furner, protect the rear. Everyone, double time."

They fell in quickly, following Tsi's clipped instructions as they pounded down the corridors of the *Sun Blade*. She kept the pace going as fast as they could, but Hiron and Furner could barely keep up. It wasn't long before they were exiting a lift though, and were standing before one of the massive loading doors that opened onto a hangar bay. A nine was written above it in classical Kiosan script.

Beyond was a row of starships: transports and fighter craft that hadn't managed to launch before the attack started. She spotted the *Exile*, its hull thoroughly patched, engine coolant gathered in shallow pools around its landing struts where it had spilled as the repair crew had abandoned their positions.

The hangar bay doors had been opened, leaving only a thin force field between them and the void beyond. She could see the flare of weapons in the distance, crimson hulled Guraggan starships so close she could pick them out against the stars. There had only been three Kiosan ships in the fleet sent to investigate her message, and, though she could tell they fighting fearlessly, they were hopelessly outnumbered.

She could not study the battle for long however. The hangar itself was a war zone. Chem-Thralls sprinted across the deck, screeching and half-naked, their bodies so pumped full of stimulants that they did not notice as pulse rounds blasted their limbs from their bodies. A Guraggan boarding skiff had ripped its way into the hangar, and disciplined Battle-Serfs were laying down covering fire from behind a group of shield drones. The bulky quadrupeds were slowly trudging forwards, angling their thin metal shields to absorb their enemy's fire.

The Janissaries, for their part, had taken up positions all over the hangar. Aided by human auxiliaries, they were holding their own against the waves of Thralls. They scythed foes down with bursts of fire, expertly covering each other as they re-positioned and hurled slow-grenades with deadly precision.

"The ship! Cover to cover! Go!" Tsi shouted.

Tenlok took the point, sprinting to a half-dismantled landing craft. He took a knee there, and fired on the Guraggan while the others took it in turn to run across the open, crouching down in the shelter of the craft behind him. They leapfrogged their way across the deck, one shooter taking up a position and covering as the next one ran to the nearest place of refuge. The Janissaries seemed not to take notice of them, their attention focused entirely on the dozens of Guraggan troops pouring fire on them.

They were behind a stack of supply crates now, just one quick sprint to the extended boarding ramp of the *Exile*.

"Tenlok and Wylla," Tsi said. "You're on point. Wylla, you get the ship's door open, Tenlok you keep the covering fire up once you get there. We'll send everyone across once you're in position. Clear?"

"I understand," Wylla said. "I'll get the ship prepped for launch the moment I get inside."

"Stay close," Tenlok said to her. "Alright, your mark, Tsi."

Tsi peered out from behind cover. Bodies littered the deck, but the battle was still raging. A hole had been blown in one of the walls of the bay, and more Guraggan troops were streaming through.

"Go!" Tsi shouted.

She aimed her pistol and fired, the others adding their own shots to the volley. Wylla grabbed Tenlok's hand, and together the two of them sprinted across the open stretch of deck. She saw solid rounds spark and dissipate, caught by Tenlok's point defense shield as they ran. Miraculously, they both made it up the boarding ramp unscathed. Cool as ice, Wylla entered the access code into the door panel. She glanced back at Tsi, then disappeared into the ship.

Tenlok had taken a position on the boarding ramp, and was firing at the oncoming Guraggan. It was working, Tsi told herself. They just needed to keep this up a little longer.

"Furner! Enlil! You two are next! Enlil, get in the cockpit the moment you're in!"

"You got it, captain!" Enlil replied, a fierce grin on her face.

The two Noxians ran across the deck, shots sparking all around them. Despite his crude prosthetic and the fact that he'd clearly seen better days, Furner kept pace with the long-legged Enlil, screaming obscenities at the top of his lungs the whole time. He stumbled and fell on the boarding ramp, but Enlil dropped her carbine and grabbed his arm, helping the old pirate up into the ship.

"Strongmind, Hiron, your turn!" Tsi roared.

"I can't! I can't!" Hiron shouted at her. His lips were trembling, his arms shaking in the straps of his braces. "I'm too slow, I'm too slow, we'll be killed—"

"Focus!" Tsi said, grabbing him by the shoulder. "Strongmind's going to help you, alright? You can do this!"

"I can't..." he whispered, tears in his eyes. "I can't."

"Yes, you can. You've faced worse than this!"

The boy only looked at her, wordless terror in his damp eyes. Tsi took one of his hands in hers.

"Please," she said. "I need you to do this for me. Please."

Unable to summon the words, Hiron finally nodded. He braced himself and made ready to run. Tsi took up her position, Strongmind between them, one massive hand on the boy's shoulder.

It was then that Tsi realized something. She had seen thralls and serfs and drones, but she had not seen a single true Guraggan warrior. This was a vital target, it was unusual for none of them to be present for such fierce fighting. She peeked out from behind cover, and immediately regretted it. As if summoned by her thoughts, two figures emerged from the breach in the far wall.

Nomic Shi, jackal-faced and wielding his mono-glaive, snarled orders and gestured at his troops as he advanced. His metal body shone in the reflected glare of weapons fire, making him look like some bizarre demon out of ancient myths. Beside him, inhumanly serene, was the armored form of Turon Chryte. His many colored cloak seemed almost surreal in these surroundings, its beauty utterly incongruous with the blood and fire all around them. The mono-wire hung coiled and sparkling in one of his hands. The twin green orbs of his augmetic eyes met hers, and he flung back his cloak, raising his arms high, fists clenched.

"You!" he cried, his voice carrying above the din of the battle. It was not a cry of rage, but of pure joy.

Turon sprinted towards them, vaulting over the debris of the battlefield, armored boots crushing the fallen heedlessly. The mono-wire spun around him, deflecting stray shots that came his way. The cloak, still showing the tears that Tsi had made in it when they had last met, flared in the air behind him as he ran.

"*Go! Now!*" Tsi screamed, firing her pistol at the charging Guraggan.

Strongmind grabbed Hiron by the arm, and the two of them dashed out into the open. Tsi fired and fired again at Turon, nervously glancing between him and her two friends as the seconds ticked by. Hiron was only a dozen paces from the ship when a laser beam struck one of his crutches. He tumbled to the ground.

"No!" Tsi screamed.

Strongmind instantly knelt beside the boy, shielding him with his body. His pulse carbine snapped to his shoulder and he began firing quick bursts one-armed, while he grabbed at Hiron with his free hand. Shots ripped into the drone as he tried to get Hiron back on his feet, but the boy couldn't get up fast enough. Tsi, Strongmind, and Tenlok all fired on Turon Chryte as the Guraggan closed on them. Tsi broke from cover, rushing towards the Guraggan, a wordless battle cry erupting from her throat.

She was too late. The mono-wire flashed out, ripping through Strongmind's weapon and sending it flying across the hangar. A bullet ripped into Strongmind's side, causing him to stumble. Tsi's feet were pounding against the deck as the Guraggan stood above her two companions, spinning the mono-wire high. Just as he was about to bring it down, something smashed into him. A figure in armor the color of brass and ebony, moving at a dead sprint, had tackled Turon and sent him sprawling. He rolled backwards, regaining his feet in an instant, and let out another ecstatic shout.

"Janissary!" Turon cried as his opponent rushed towards him, aiming a blow for his eyes with a night-black blade.

Tsi fired at the Guraggan, seeing out of the corner of her eye Tenlok moving to cover Strongmind and Hiron. The drone and the boy were stumbling up the ramp as she closed on Turon. The Guraggan flitted and dodged away from bullets and blows with equal ease. He whipped the mono-wire outwards, and it sliced through the Janissary's shoulder, sending the limb flying in a spray of sparks and blood.

Pain was nothing to a Janissary, though. The black armored warrior saw Tsi approaching, and did exactly as she had expected. Exactly what she had designed him to do. He sacrificed himself for a chance at victory.

The Janissary flung himself forwards. Turon took a step back, whipping the mono-wire across the Janissary's stomach. The wire sliced effortlessly through armor and flesh alike, but Turon did not realize his mistake. Still and perfectly framed for an instant, his mono-wire no longer dancing about him as he made the killing stroke, Tsi aimed her pistol. She emptied what was left of her magazine into Turon.

Each bullet sent him staggering backwards. One sparked off his eye, another punched through his chest. He fell to the ground. Dead or not, he wouldn't be rising any time soon.

"Tsi! We have to go! Now!" Tenlok roared from the boarding ramp.

Tsi knew he was right, but she couldn't help herself. She grabbed the dying Janissary under the shoulder, and dragged him bodily with her across the deck to the *Exile*. When she reached the bottom of the boarding ramp, Tenlok stopped firing and dashed over to help her. Together, the two of them hauled his bleeding form up the ramp and into the ship.

Once they were inside, the door slammed shut behind them.

"We're on!" Tenlok shouted. "Get us out of here!"

"Brace yourselves!" she heard Enlil shout back from the cockpit.

There was the roar of the engine, and the ship lifted off the deck and blasted into space.

Up in the cockpit, Enlil had strapped herself in and taken to the controls instantly. She took them in a downwards spiral the moment they left the hangar. There were dozens of contacts flaring all across her screen, some she could see with her naked eye. Ships burst apart in flares of plasma fire, pulse beams and missiles streaked through the darkness. She wasn't here for pyrotechnics though. She just needed to get the hell out of this place.

Strongmind had set itself up in weapons control.

"All systems nominal," it said. "Four contacts approaching."

Enlil saw them. Guraggan fighters, on their way back from a sortie against the Kiosan ship. All fighters flew in erratic, swarming patterns to fool sentry drones, but she could match them turn for turn.

"Hold on everyone!" Enlil shouted. She pulled a hard turn, upping the g-forces they were experiencing briefly, then kicked the ship forwards in a straight, flat trajectory. She had presented the fighters with an irresistible target, and they sped towards her, angling for the perfect shot.

"You got this tin-head?" Enlil asked.

"I do," Strongmind replied.

There was a sudden burst of light as the ship fired three missiles. Having perfectly predicted the fighter's flight path, each missile found its mark without flaw. Enlil smiled as each contact winked out of existence, one by one.

"Good shooting, tin-head," Enlil said.

"Your piloting is also effective," Strongmind replied.

Enlil laughed. She burned them hard for a few more minutes, but the Guraggan were totally focused on the Kiosan ships. Soon they were drifting through the dark, and the battle was far, far behind them.

Tsi crouched in front of the Janissary. She hadn't bothered to take him to the medical bay. There was nothing that could be done. More of his blood was smeared over here arms and chest than was in his body, she was sure.

She studied his chest plate, and wasn't surprised to see it read Ares-9881.

"You've done well, Bolesht," Tsi said.

Ares only exhaled in response. His breathing was becoming slower and slower. Gently, Tsi reached for the sides of his helmet. The Janissary weakly tried to pull his head away from her.

"Not... for you..." Ares whispered. "My face... not... for you..."

"I understand," Tsi said. "I... I want you to know. I am sorry. I am so sorry, for everything I've done to you. You were my children and I... I wish I could go back and change it. You have to know I am going to find a way to fix this. I'm going to find a way to stop the Guraggan. Kios will not fall, I'll make sure of it."

"You... cannot," Ares said weakly.

"I'll find a way," Tsi promised.

The Janissary shook his head again in frustration. He was in his last few moments. Blood was no longer leaking from his wounds. He raised his remaining hand to point feebly at her.

"You... cannot... be forgiven."

Tsi said nothing, only nodded. She watched as the Janissary's chest rose and fell for the last time, and then he lay still.

Strongmind was in the cockpit with Tsi. They had been close to the edge of the system when the Guraggan had attacked, and in only a few hours, they'd be able to jump into the Slip. The rest of the crew had gone down to the galley, captivity and danger having inspired in most of them a serious appetite.

"Please select coordinates," Strongmind said.

Where to? Tsi wondered. The Web of Eden was still safe, a good place to hide out and plan. Sannat was still a free world too, and close enough for only a week's journey. Hell, there was always Noxia again.

"It doesn't matter," she sighed.

"I cannot calculate a Slip route if you do not select coordinates."

"I know," Tsi replied. "I just... don't know where to go."

"You require time to process," Strongmind said. "I understand. I will await your instructions."

The two of them sat in the cockpit together silently, as they so often had before.

"Perhaps," Strongmind finally said, "There is another task you need to attend to. This may help you in deciding our next destination."

"There is," Tsi said. "But I don't know if I'm capable of doing it."

Strongmind turned in his chair. He looked her straight in the eye and said simply:

"You are."

Tsi smiled. She reached out and patted the machine's hand.

"Will you come with me?" she asked.

"That is within my capabilities."

The two of them got up and walked down to the galley together. The others were lounging and eating. Enlil was sitting on the table, passing a bottle back and forth between herself and Furner, while Furner spoke animatedly to Wylla, who laughed uproariously at his jokes. Tenlok was cleaning one of his guns, something Tsi realized he could easily do somewhere else. Hiron sat in one corner, eating from a bowl of food and occasionally calling out questions to Furner.

Tsi took a breath.

"Everyone," she said. "I'd like to speak to you all."

The conversation died down. All eyes turned to her. Enlil took another swig from her bottle.

"Sure boss," she said. "What about?"

"The truth," Tsi said. "All of it."

Tsi did not know where her journey would end, nor if she was on the right path or the wrong one. Yet, standing here with these people, she realized something as she spoke. She had only one direction left to go.

Forwards.